TEAL SWAN

HUNGER OF THE PINE

WATKINS

Sharing Wisdom Since 1893

This edition first published in the UK and USA in 2020 by
Watkins, an imprint of Watkins Media Limited
Unit 11, Shepperton House
89–93 Shepperton Road
London
N1 3DF

enquiries@watkinspublishing.com

1 3 5 7 9 10 8 6 4 2

Designed and typeset by JCS Publishing Services Ltd

Printed and bound in the UK by TJ International

A CIP record for this book is available from the British Library

ISBN: 978-1-78678-414-8

www.watkinspublishing.com

HUNGER OF THE PINE

We are initiated.

We are apprenticed by pain.

Our beauty … Our purpose … Our growth

Is forged in the fire of our difficulties.

Like a blacksmith, our suffering relieves us of our
rough and tattered edges

Painfully at first

Until we are broken open.

And our soul pours like water through our every
thought and word and action.

It extinguishes the fire of our pain.

It weathers our curses to such a degree that they
become blessings.

And then, we are free.

PART ONE

MONODY

CHAPTER 1

The muffled tapping of the soles of her favorite high-top sneakers sounded against the floor of the endless hallway. From high above her, the windows, which were no larger than jail cell windows, cast an array of silken light shards on the floor below her. The hallways of the school were empty. She was late again. She could smell the all-too-familiar smell of cafeteria lunch being prepared. Like a tedious symphony, her breath and heartbeat played their anxious notes and she tried to time her footsteps to them. She hated being late. She hated the heavy feeling of people's stares. She hated the texture of shame.

When she reached the classroom, she extended her hand and felt the chill of the metal handle against her fingertips. A paralysis came over her. She couldn't afford another tardy, but she couldn't force herself to go in. She couldn't face them all. It was better to actually be alone than to feel, like the proverbial exile, alone in a crowded room; the feeling of being the outcast. But that she was. "Tomorrow," she thought as she pulled her hand back from the door and, with a pivot, ran down the hallway to the nearest bathroom.

She leaned against the pink tile wall to catch her breath. She could feel the heavy husk of childhood at times like this. She could feel the prison of it, the burden of not being able to choose what to do with the hours in the day. She couldn't hide in the bathroom forever. She knew that, but right now she almost wished she could. The row of mirrors on the opposite wall reflected the emptiness she felt inside. She shifted toward them until she was standing before her own image looking back at her. The honesty of the image of herself made her uncomfortable. But she did not look away.

Aria Abbott was 17 years old to the day. There was a warmth to the paleness of her skin. It honored the sharp angles and curves of her face. Her cheekbones sat high below a pair of rather feline eyes. Almond-shaped and olive green, they stared back at her, unmoving. There was a depth to her eyes, an ancient knowing that both beckoned and warned. The reflective surface of them felt like a membrane preventing her from falling into a foreign world. Like two albatross wings, her eyebrows reached toward her hairline. Her hair fell in disorderly waves and cascades to greet her shoulders, picking up light along the way. The color of it reminded her of the chestnut seeds she used to collect as a child. Her nose was aquiline, only a small shadowed indentation between it and a pair of sultry button-shaped lips the color of pink champagne.

Aria reached up to touch her chin and neck, and her fingers slid across the softness of her skin. Like most teenage girls, Aria was never satisfied with her reflection in the mirror. Fine-boned, she stood just over 5ft 4in tall. Her youth had only just begun to peel back, exposing the hint of curves. Curves that belonged to the woman, which had been dormant throughout her childhood. As she stared at her own reflection, Aria could feel the fierce intent of puberty pulling her immaturity away. She wouldn't miss it. Aria had grown lonely in the prepubescent world of playthings and penny candy. Her childhood had been frosted with despair. It had felt more like a prison than a privilege; a prison sentence that was not yet fully served.

She had been sitting in the bathroom, listening to the relentless flow of the water in the pipes behind the wall, bored for what felt like ages, when the bell finally rang. Aria sprang to her feet, knowing that the bathroom would soon be inundated with other girls. Gathering up her backpack, she pushed past the heavy doors and out into the hallway. A rush of noise assaulted her, the deafening chaos of hundreds of students making their way to their next class. She joined them reluctantly. A wave of insignificance consumed her as she was swept up in the flux of students. Walking in the two-way traffic of the school hallways between classes always made her feel like a tiny blood cell in a crowded artery.

Aria reached her class and sat in her desk in the fourth row, watching the other students settle into their places. She had perfected the art of acting aloof and collected when the truth was that inside, the buzz of anxiety ricocheted incessantly inside her chest and made her breath shallow. This class was like all the others. She would listen to the squeak of the marker against the whiteboard. She would watch the contained gestures of her teachers. She would learn and regurgitate the material taught to her, not because she was interested in it, but because she was afraid. She was afraid of the consequences of not doing so. Aria could not conform and she did not fit in, but she went to great lengths to avoid drawing negative attention to herself.

For Aria, school was yet another part of the prison sentence of childhood. Unlike so many of her fellow students, she had no plans to go to college. She swore to herself that after her time was up she would not sit in another classroom for as long as she lived.

Aria had no friends to speak of. Loneliness graced the corridors of her life. So when the final school bell rang, she put one of her headphone earbuds in her right ear, chose a song to play and pulled her hoodie over the top of her head so that it hid her profile. Ignoring any others, she made her way to the city bus stop, where she waited with a loose collection of vagrants, students and businessmen. The bus swayed this way and that, starting and stopping to let people on and off. She glanced at their faces, trying to feel the people beneath them, but averted her eyes if they tried to make eye contact. The very connection that she wanted so desperately to make frightened her.

The bus pulled up to a stop in a suburban neighborhood on the south end of the city. Aria inched her way sideways past the other passengers' knees and briefcases. The air outside was unfriendly, a frigid grayness known only to cities. She walked the six blocks to her house with her face turned toward the cement sidewalk, careful not to step on the cracks. Aria didn't like to think of herself as superstitious, but when all was said and done, she was. She made the turn toward her house reluctantly. Went up the stairs and stood before the pastel plaque on the door that read "Bless O Lord, this thy house, and all who enter in." Turning off her music, she opened the door. The air inside carried the fake scent of cheap cinnamon potpourri.

Inside, the sound of clanking in the kitchen was suppressed by a voice that called to her, "Aria, is that you?"

"Yeah."

Her mother stepped around the corner, wearing a patchwork apron. The bangs of her bobbed, sandy hair were perfectly curled. She was wearing a scowl on her face. "I got a call today from your school," she said in an exasperated tone. "You can't keep doing this."

She paused and then continued, "I called your new case worker. She said we should take you to see one of the counselors. Is that what you want?"

Aria stared at the carpet and said nothing. Irritated by the silence, her mother went on. "Your father and I have told you again and again that you have to set a good example for the littler ones."

Aria looked up from the carpet. She wanted to yell. She wanted to scream but nothing came out. Despite the fury that burned its way through her veins, all she could say was, "Sorry."

Her mother fidgeted, a pair of plastic tongs still in her hands. "Don't do it again," she said. "If you keep sloughing school you're not gonna graduate." Aria granted her nothing but more silence. So her mother ended the one-sided conversation with, "Your father will decide what to do about this later. Do your homework before you watch TV."

Aria sprang out from beneath the tension like a racehorse out of the gate. She ran upstairs and closed the door to her room. She could still hear the sound of her younger siblings in the background. She reached below her bed and felt around until her fingers found the texture of her journal. Pulling it up onto her bed, she grabbed a pen from her backpack and began to write her frustrations down between the lines on the paper. *She is not my mother. He is not my father. Who the hell does she think she is? I hate her.* She underlined the word *hate* with three straight lines for emphasis.

The woman who was downstairs cooking was not her mother. The man who would be coming home soon was not her father. The children whose noises she could hear beyond the door were not her siblings. The omnipresent dust of the past covered Aria's world with grief. There is something about the shock and groundlessness that comes with grief that makes the world around you stand still. Aria's world had been standing still for quite some time now.

Aria didn't know where her real mother was. She had been taken by the state at seven years old. From what Aria had been able to piece together, her mother had dropped out of high school when she was 16 years old after finding out that she was pregnant. Her name was Lucy. She was named after the Beatles song "Lucy in the Sky with Diamonds." She used to play that song for Aria on repeat when Aria was young. The lyrics were etched into Aria's memory for all time. Her mother loved music. She had always wanted to play the guitar but because Aria came along, she hadn't had the time or resources to learn. When Aria was born, Lucy stared down at her perfect little face and felt that this baby was her great creation, this baby was her song … her aria. And so Lucy named her as such.

After Aria was born, Lucy had struggled to afford day care. She worked at a fast-food restaurant to afford a low-income apartment. Aria could only just remember the contours of her face. Most of all, she remembered the look of desperation and she remembered the bruises. When Aria was four, her mother had met a man named Travis. He was in his 20s when he got a job washing dishes at the fast-food joint that Lucy worked in. Travis became enamored with Lucy. They began flirting at work and he eventually asked her out on a date. Desperate for love and support, she was relieved to find someone to share her burdens. Travis moved in shortly after they met. Aria could still remember the sound of his blue Camaro.

Two weeks after he moved in with them, Lucy walked to work on a bitter cold morning only to find a note on the door of the building that said "Closed out of business." The owner of the chain had known the business was going under for quite some time, but could only bring himself to tell the managers. And the managers did not bother to tell the staff. With no warning, just like that, Lucy was out of a job.

For the next two weeks, she tried desperately to find work, but each time she went in for an interview they would tell her something to the tune of, "We'll call you back within two weeks to tell you if you have the job." Despite her embarrassment, sheer desperation drove Lucy to apply for food stamps. But when she walked up to the desk with her paperwork filled out, the woman behind the social services desk informed her that it would take up to 30 days to receive her benefits in the mail. She went to a local food bank but the doors were closed for the night. That evening, Lucy stole a can of soup and an apple from a local supermarket because she didn't know what else to do.

Aria recalled the arguments that began between Travis and Lucy. She remembered the numb paralysis that would devour her when she heard their voices gashing through the air in the apartment. Sometimes she could hear her mother being hit or held against a wall. She would hide in her mother's closet and close her eyes and ears until Travis slammed the door and she could hear the sound of her mother weeping. It became a common scene. Aria would venture out to find Lucy bruised or bleeding, staring out the window as Travis drove away, muttering "please don't leave, please don't leave, please don't leave" between panicked tears.

When the rent came due later that same month and neither Lucy nor Travis could pay it, an eviction notice came in the mail. At that time, Aria did not understand what was going on when she watched her mother crawl underneath the secondhand linoleum table in the kitchen and cry. All she knew was that they were in trouble. They were facing homelessness. Lucy had to pull Aria out of daycare. The television became her babysitter at that point.

But then one day Travis burst through the door of their apartment with a smile on his face. He walked straight up to Lucy and slapped what he was holding in his hand on the table. It was three $50 bills. "Where did you get it?" Lucy gasped, exhaling in relief but also suspicion. Travis pulled her into the bedroom to explain. He had an acquaintance that made his money selling crystal meth and prescription pain pills. When Travis had lost his job, he couldn't believe his luck when he was offered some money in exchange for doing a hand-off to a local nightclub. It was Lucy's poverty that forced her to consent.

Travis soon stopped looking for other jobs. What was the point? He could make enough money to afford the apartment and his car, and best of all he didn't have to answer to anyone. After realizing how much money he could make as a supplier instead of a runner, he began to cook meth himself in the utility closet of their apartment. Lucy was so naive that she didn't know how toxic the process of cooking meth really was. So when Aria developed a cough and dizzy spells, Lucy didn't know it was because of exposure; all she could think was she couldn't afford to take her to the doctor. When Aria's symptoms worsened and lethargy began to set in, Lucy was so desperate that she asked Travis for some money. He smiled and said, "Yeah, I'll give you the money but you got to deliver something for me." She nodded in acceptance and later that night Lucy ran drugs for Travis for the very first time.

For a few months, Aria's life began to settle. She started kindergarten at a nearby public school and Lucy didn't seem afraid about money anymore. She even took Aria to get an ice-cream cone after school every Friday. It was a luxury they could never have afforded before. But then Lucy came home one day in January to find all of Travis's things gone.

His absence sent her deep into the torment of a depression. She could not function on her own. For a couple of weeks, she would walk Aria to the school bus and then go back to bed and stay there. Aria would make her way back from the bus stop in the afternoon, drag a chair to the counter and climb up on it to find whatever food was left in the cupboards. She tried to cheer her mother up with little pictures she scribbled with marker on the backs of food wrappers. She would watch hour upon hour of shows on Nickelodeon. She wanted to play outside but Lucy always said no. Lucy had withdrawn from Aria's life. She couldn't face her own life any more than she could face her daughter.

One day when Aria returned from school, she tried to open the door to the apartment only to find it locked. She sat down on the steps and tried to distract herself from worry by finishing her homework in the stairway. Having nothing solid to write on, she wrote the answers to her worksheet against the cement of the stairs. The imperfections in the cement made the pencil lines look scribbled. After hours of sitting there, just as it was getting too dark to see her paper, Aria heard the sound of footsteps and laughter coming her way. It was her mother's laugh. With excitement but also fear, she froze to wait for her mother to turn the corner. Lucy tripped up the stairs with Travis in tow. They were both drunk. When Lucy spotted Aria, she smiled and reached down to grab her chin and plant a kiss on her face. She missed and fell forward, catching herself with her hands, and began hysterically laughing. Aria wanted to get out of there as fast as she could but her legs wouldn't move. She was confused. She was afraid of Travis and didn't understand what he was doing back there, much less with her mother.

Travis carried Lucy into the house and placed her on the bed. She grabbed at him when he tried to leave, but he left her anyway. She was so out of it that she soon passed out. Aria stayed silent and let Travis pass by her. On his way back to the door, he handed her the uneaten half of his Snickers candy bar.

"You be good now," he said and closed the door behind him. Once the door was shut, she ate the candy bar as fast as she could. Like most nights, she went without dinner.

The next morning, Lucy was still passed out. When Aria couldn't rouse her from her sleep, she walked to the school bus alone. When the time came for lunch, she lined up her orange lunch tray and, shy as she was, scooted it down the length of the counter while the cafeteria lunch ladies placed various foods upon it. She carried her tray as carefully as she could to a place in the far corner of the cafeteria. She sat down on the bench of the long table, trying to find sanctuary from the violent noise of the room. Aria picked up her Sloppy Joe sandwich and placed it to the side of her tray. She couldn't stand the thought or taste or texture of meat. But she was too shy to tell the lunch ladies not to put it on her tray. It was easy enough to find someone who wanted a second helping. She ate everything else on her plate, saving the best for last; the vanilla pudding, which tasted vaguely artificial, was nonetheless a comfort to her. The thickness of it made her feel like life might be OK after all. She closed her eyes after each bite to extend the pleasure of it. School lunch was just about the only opportunity she had to eat at that point in her life.

That day when she got home, the door was unlocked, but her mother wasn't there. Aria turned on the TV and waited for hours until Lucy finally did come home. But when the door swung open, she saw Lucy had deteriorated. Her hair was messy and had lost its shine. Mascara stained the bottoms of her eyelids. She could barely keep them open to walk across the living room. "Mom!" Aria called out to her. But Lucy did not respond. She just stumbled toward the bedroom, shedding her purse and coat on the floor behind her in her wake.

Some time earlier, Travis had returned one of Lucy's frantic calls in which she was begging him to return. He had agreed to meet her in the parking lot of a nearby mall. When Lucy confessed to the misery she felt after he'd left, he told her that he knew what would make her feel better. In the back seat of his blue Camaro, Travis pulled out an old licence plate and a bag from under the seat of his car. He pulled some crystalline shards from the bag and crushed them into a fine powder against the metal plate. He then showed Lucy how to snort the powder through the hollow shaft of a ballpoint pen. Lucy was nervous when she snorted the powder for the first time. But four minutes later, her heartbeat began to race. She felt the pressure in her body rise. She could feel herself lifting out of the despair. Euphoria took over her body and blunted the edge of her emotions. She started to feel good about herself. She started to laugh and the implosion of her misery turned into an explosion of aggressive confidence.

Lucy was high. She had left her worries behind. She felt like she could take on anything.

Desperate to stay feeling better and desperate for his affection, Lucy was willing to do anything to remain close to Travis. When Aria was at school, Travis would pick Lucy up in front of the apartment and they would deliver crystal meth to different locations and people around the city and neighboring towns. After they were done, they would get high together.

Lucy had become a tweaker.

Travis eventually disappeared from their lives. Aria and her mother saw him from a distance in the parking lot of a movie theater some time after he disappeared. He was opening the passenger door of his car for a woman dressed in high boots and a miniskirt. It caused Lucy to go on another binge.

When Aria was six, they lost their apartment. Lucy had pawned off everything just to afford her addiction. They moved from apartment to apartment, staying with random people that Aria didn't know for days or weeks at a time before moving again. For the next eight months, Aria watched her mother go through seemingly endless cycles. She would come home from school to find her mother manic, high with a kind of synthetic empowerment. On days like that, Lucy would drag Aria around the town, determined to show her a good time. But Lucy was delusional. All too often her enthusiasm would turn into aggression and she would find herself in altercations. These would push Lucy into a state of energized paranoia. Several hours later, when the high would wear off, Lucy would isolate herself and succumb to hallucinations. Disconnected from reality and losing a sense of herself, she would lie under the covers of the bed or on the floor of the bathroom, itching and clawing at her skin.

For the few days following these episodes, Lucy would crash. As if she had lost the will to live, she slept away the hours. When she came back to life, she appeared starved, emaciated even. Her skin was beginning to turn gray. The exhaustion would not lift. She would exist in this state of living death for a week or so before deciding that the only way to alleviate the pain was to use again. And so she would. Giving in to the craving, Lucy began not only snorting meth but also slamming it.

The week before the state took her away, Aria could remember lying by her mother, who was passed out on the couch, staring at the track marks on her arm.

A few weeks after Aria's seventh birthday, a school secretary came to escort Aria to the office in the middle of class. Even at that age, she knew as she walked to the office that life as she knew it was over. She was scared they were going to tell her that her mother was dead. Everything began to feel surreal. She could feel everything begin to move in slow motion. The world went silent. All she could hear was the sound of her own breath.

Inside the office, the school principal sat at a desk in front of two police officers, whose backs were turned toward her as she entered the room. They sat her down in a third chair and explained to her that her mother was very sick and in the hospital. Having contracted hepatitis B, she had developed jaundice. Upon seeing her writhing in pain, her skin and eyes yellowed, one of the people at the house they were staying in had become so worried about her that he had driven her to the hospital. The principal assured Aria that as soon as her mother was better, she could go back to living with her, but until then, she would be living in a group home.

He lied.

Aria left with the police that day and met with a social worker who placed her in an overcrowded group home. Since Aria had no address, she could not go back to collect her things. She went to the home with only the clothes on her back.

In one day, she had lost everything. Nothing was familiar anymore. It was the last time she saw her mother. The following years were a blur of group homes and foster homes. She switched schools sometimes more than twice each year. Aria didn't belong anywhere. The pain of those years was reasonably suppressed in her memory.

When Aria was 14, a group of members from a Christian church brought a truckload of donations to the group home she was staying in, so that the children could receive stockings for Christmas. The children had been prepared by the staff to thank them by singing Christmas carols. Aria took her place in line and was singing Rudolph the Red-Nosed Reindeer when she noticed a couple watching her rather intently with a look of pity in their eyes. A few weeks later, she was informed that there was a foster family who wanted to take her in and consider adopting her.

Aria was filled with mixed emotions. She would have done anything to get out of state homes. But she was also afraid. "What if they don't like me?" she thought to herself when she rounded the corner with the social worker to meet them for the first time. She dared not get her hopes up; after all, she had been in and out of so many foster homes that she knew the chances of finding a family who wanted to keep her at this age were slim. Aria was surprised to see that the couple who were to be her new foster parents were the very same couple who had been eyeing her at the Christmas celebration only weeks before.

Robert and Nancy Johnson had met in college. Two months after they were married, Nancy was pregnant with their first child and she dropped out of school to become a homemaker. This, she felt, was her true calling. Mrs Johnson was a God-fearing woman, determined to walk the path of righteousness no matter the cost. Aria couldn't help but feel that under her carefully perfected exterior, there was someone inside of her screaming. She strived toward goodness and toward making everyone around her good too, with a verve that was downright exhausting. It was especially exhausting for Mr Johnson.

Mr Johnson was a shell of a man. Even though he had grown up Christian too, the veracity of his wife's faith kept him imprisoned beneath a wardrobe of cardigans and khaki dress pants. Purity was such a heavy expectation from the society that he found himself in that all of his deeper, carnal urges had to be suppressed and denied. But, as Aria soon found out, suppressed urges cannot be suppressed forever. If they are, they tend to be indulged in secret. Mr Johnson was the head of the household in title alone.

Mrs Johnson had given birth to two children before her last pregnancy, when she developed placenta accreta. The doctors had to perform a full hysterectomy to save her life. The event rocked their marriage and shook their faith. Mrs Johnson felt like God was punishing her by taking away her God-given gift to bear children. She was inconsolable for months. But when she saw the children at the group home, she spied a kind of hope. She suddenly grasped a greater vision. Her prayers were answered. She could see clearly that God had not taken her ability to bear children away to punish her. God had taken her ability to bear children away so that she could see her greater purpose, as a mother to those who have no mothers. The Johnsons had adopted a little three-year-old girl the summer before, bringing their collection of children to four before they set their sights on Aria.

The day they came to meet Aria for the first time, they brought a plate of homemade chocolate-chip cookies. Aria sat in a chair and reluctantly took one from the stack, watching

the couple with an enthusiasm that was watered down by
an equal amount of suspicion. A caseworker listened with a
quizzical smile on her face while Mrs Johnson spoke: "The
Lord has trusted us with the care of his children. We believe
that by providing an example of God's love, we are giving these
children, who have had a rough start, the opportunity to know
him personally.

"Through the witness of our family and the hearing of the
gospel message, these children can say yes to the Lord, and
because of that they have a real chance at a good life."

Sentimental tears welled up in her eyes as she finished her
message. And she stared at Aria longingly. It was arranged for
Aria to move in with them the following week. That was three
years ago. Aria had been living with them ever since.

CHAPTER 2

"Dinner time!" Mrs Johnson called from the bottom of the stairs.

Aria ran her fingers through the silky black fur of the cat napping on her bed. Clifford, who was the only family pet, preferred to sleep his days away in Aria's room. Her younger siblings had named the cat after the famous cartoon *Clifford the Big Red Dog*, in the innocent hope that the cat would soon grow large enough to ride. Aria loved Clifford. She buried her face in his side and breathed him in, letting the inhale and exhale of his purr console her. She felt a trace of belonging with Clifford that she felt with no one else.

She walked into the little dining room adjoining the kitchen. The table was set with white plastic plates and paper napkins. To one side, a sheet cake with unlit candles took up a good portion of the table. On its surface, "Happy Birthday Aria" was piped in red gel that almost ran into Mrs Johnson's haphazard attempt to create buttercream flowers. Aria took her usual place and watched the pans and serving bowls make their way divisively through the hyperactive movements of the other children to be placed in the center of the table. Aria loved food. It was the only thing in her life without ulterior motives. She could trust food.

Once everyone was seated, her younger sister was prompted to say grace. They all folded their arms and bowed their heads for the length of the speech. There was a palpable relief when grace was through. To Aria, grace felt like a spiritual tollbooth you had to pass through to get to where you wanted to go.

"Mom," Aria said, "can you pass the soup?" Mrs Johnson had insisted the week after Aria moved in that she begin to call her Mom. This bothered Aria. Regardless of the fact that Lucy had abandoned her, it still felt like a betrayal to call any other woman Mother. It felt fake and contrived every time she said it.

Mrs Johnson hefted the heavy pot in Aria's direction so she could ladle the soup into her bowl. Delicate steam wove its way through the air just above the bowl. A few dots of amber oil hovered on the surface of the broth. Aria found a bay leaf in the bowl and picked it up between her index finger and thumb. She placed it in her mouth and held it there. The sound of the room faded and gave way to the experience of it. If wisdom and perspective had a taste, she thought, it would be bay leaf. It reminded her of a candid black and white image of an old hand-hewn log cabin with its occupants, in 1800s clothing, smiling at one another. She could taste the image of a wood-burning oven at the end of summer, right before summer slowed down into fall. It tasted like a nostalgic antique.

Everyone had settled into the rhythm and quiet of consuming the meal when Mrs Johnson's voice cut through the scene. "Aria cut first class again today." She was aiming her statement in her husband's direction.

He looked up from his plate. "Is that so," he said, rolling the bite of food he had in his mouth around to make way for the words while he talked. "I'll have a talk with her later," he said, eyeing Aria with a disciplining stare.

The stare was like a veil concealing an intimacy that shouldn't exist between father and daughter. Aria felt a chill go through her. She had hoped that the fact that today was her birthday would allow her more than the usual leniency for her errors. She had underestimated Mr and Mrs Johnson's tendency to make birthdays feel like every other day of the year.

For the rest of the dinner, she was replete with unease, watching the rest of her family converse, anticipating what was to come. Oblivious to her discomfort, they laughed and talked and ate and sang her the happy birthday song as if rejoicing more in the sound of their own voices than in the celebration of Aria's existence.

When dinner was done, the youngest kids went up to their rooms to play. Mr Johnson walked over to the television and sat down in the recliner. He pressed the buttons on the remote control until he found a golfing tournament and settled in to watch it in a fixated silence. Aria got up to help her two oldest siblings do the dishes while their mother sponged off the table. Mrs Johnson was wearing a look of self-satisfaction as she cleaned.

It was at times like this that Aria felt her lack of belonging the most. This after-dinner routine was standard procedure. Everyone seemed unbothered by the unconscious, mundane repetition. That is, everyone but her. She felt like a fish trying to make its home with a nest of birds. She couldn't breathe in the emotional atmosphere of this house. It wasn't the presence of emotions that bothered her. It was the lack of them. It was the vacuum of those moments where the surface veneer of a happy family sat like a film over the truth. The truth was, it was all just one giant act.

Aria retreated to her room, holding a bowl of vanilla ice cream. The house was quietening for the night. Clifford, who was smoothing the white patch of fur on his chest with his tongue, looked up at her when she entered the room. She sat down by him, stroked his head and began to eat her ice cream. Vanilla tasted stable and cozy to Aria. It was like the parts of childhood that one might actually miss, like warm towels fresh out of the dryer. She spent nearly an hour staring out the little window in her room at the rows of identical houses on the block. She watched cars come and go. She watched people take out the trash. She watched dogs zigzag in disorganized patterns on the end of their leashes until twilight turned into night.

She was lying awake with her covers pulled over her head when she heard a soft rapping on the door of her bedroom. The familiar sound of Mr Johnson's gait became louder as he approached the bed. She stayed frozen, pretending to be asleep. The covers were pulled up on one side, letting a rush of cold air flood her spine. His weight as he crawled into bed jostled her and tilted the mattress.

Suppressed urges are exercised in secret. It had been like this for two years now. On some nights, when Mr Johnson could find an excuse to be absent from his wife, he would slip into bed with Aria. This time, her school absence was the perfect excuse. Mrs Johnson trusted that he was going to set her straight, but setting her straight was not what her husband had in mind at all.

She could feel his hands against her back. Her tear-blinded eyes turned up toward heaven. She was no longer a child. He was no longer a man. This was their little secret, the secret that devoured Aria's life with confusion. She did not know if it felt wrong or right. He was the only father she had known and she was terrified of him, but she wanted his affection so much that she would lie silent to let his hands slide across her naked body.

The warm desperation of his breath gripped at the skin on her neck when he spoke. "You're such a bad girl," he said as he rolled her toward him. Aria's arms fiercely folded over the top of her breasts in self-preservation, her closed hands pressed together, covering her lips. It only encouraged him further.

"Why do you want to seduce me?" he asked. "Are you lookin' for a spanking?"

He lifted his body on top of hers, unaware of the crushing strain of his weight. She squirmed and fought to breathe. She struggled out from underneath him, which made him laugh. "Don't you tease me now," he said. He caught her hair and smelled it. His hand traced the length of the inside of her thigh. He began to jerk off with his other hand, his breath sucking in and out in sporadic spurts of exertion.

Aria was incapacitated by the bankruptcy of his heart. She surrendered to the simultaneous feeling of pain and pleasure as his fingers crept between her legs. She was only half there. Drowning in his perverted domination, she took the only exit that was available to her.

She looked over at the snow globe that was sitting on the desk adjacent to the bed. She was inside it, the silence and refuge of the secluded world it contained, the fake snow and sparkles falling on her face all she could feel, all she could *let* herself feel. Aria might be unable to escape the moment with her body, but she could leave her body behind and escape with her mind. It took her a moment after he had cum before she could let herself drift back, waiting for him to leave before grabbing tissues to clean herself with and drifting into a haunted sleep.

The next day, Aria rifled around in the various toolboxes of the garage, leaving lids open and tools scattered until she found the blade of an X-Acto knife, a deranged craving pulsing in the marrow of her bones. Like poison, despair trickled through her veins. She needed to be relieved of it. In a focused frenzy, she found a roll of duct tape and paper towels and carried them to the upstairs bathroom, and closed the door. Stripping down to her jeans and bra, she climbed into the bathtub, where she crouched and proceeded to let the blade speak against her skin. She shook as she drew the blade across both forearms, repetitively making diagonal cuts in both directions. Her skin yielded to the blade. Blood welled up out of the cuts and dripped over the side of her arms to splatter against the floor of the bathtub.

This wasn't the first time Aria had intentionally cut herself. It was a habit that she had successfully concealed for months before her younger brother caught her doing it. When Mrs Johnson first became aware that she was cutting herself, she removed all the locks from the internal doors of the house and proceeded to shame Aria for it. She sat across from Aria at the kitchen table and read her a collection of Bible verses that pertained to the way God expected the human body to be treated. It was the way she dealt with anything. Any and all of Aria's emotions were invalidated. Mrs Johnson had a habit of turning Aria's feelings back on her by telling her that the way she felt meant that there must be something wrong with her, because in Mrs Johnson's mind, there was no other valid reason for her to feel the way she felt. Of course this only served to exacerbate the problem. Aria hated Mrs

Johnson. But Aria's feelings were internalized. She became
hypercritical of herself and that hatred, now internalized, was
focused on herself.

Aria turned on the water faucet to a trickle. She felt the
soothing relief eat away at the static of her anxiety. Her
breathing slowed. She felt alive in this moment, mesmerized
by the blood making its way, in streams that looked like
watercolour, down the drain. Relief was all she wanted.

But the relief was short-lived. Having heard Aria hurry
from the garage to the bathroom, Mrs Johnson gave in to her
curiosity. She opened the door slowly. Aria was startled by the
noise and tried to hide her arms. But it was too late. "Aria!" she
gasped, rushing over to the bathtub.

She pulled at Aria's arms so she could see them clearly. Once
she was confident that none of the cuts were deep enough
to need stitches, her panic turned to exasperation. She stood
with her hands on her hips, shaking her head back and forth,
and paced the length of the bathroom, muttering to herself.
"What do you think you're doing?" she asked in an angry tone,
looking at Aria out of the corner of her eye. "What have I
done? What have I done to deserve this?"

Aria flushed with shame as she went on. "I'm taking you
to see someone, this has got to stop!" she barked. She turned
her back to Aria for a minute and then turned back to face
her. "Do you think this is the right place for you? 'Cause I just
don't know anymore."

"Yes," piped Aria, suddenly overtaken by the very real threat
of being abandoned again. She began to sob.

At the sight of her tears, Mrs Johnson began to cry too. She
shook her head, trying to conceal the contortion of her face.
She turned to leave the room and through the sounds of her
cries she called behind her, "You clean it all up and for God's
sake don't show anyone." Her footsteps and sobs sounded
down the hallway to her room.

Aria's world was spinning. As if a perfect mirrored reflection
of Mrs Johnson's sobbing, she cried into the container of the

lonely bathroom. She knew she was on thin ice and had been for quite some time.

The Johnsons had been planning to adopt her shortly after fostering her, just as they had done with her younger sister. But Aria's frequent behavior problems had caused them to delay, and now, Aria was facing the possibility of being given up entirely. Her deep fear of being forsaken bubbled up with each sob.

She sat in the bathtub, crying, until she was shivering and the blood had stopped running from her forearms. She turned on the warm water. It stung as she cupped it over her arms, washing them clean of congealed blood. She dried them off and wrapped them sloppily in paper towel, anchoring it to her arms with uneven strips of duct tape. When she was done, aside from the warmth of it having been used, the bathroom looked as if nothing had taken place. She dumped the bloodstained towel down the laundry chute and walked to her room to find a long-sleeved hoodie to wear.

That week, Aria found herself contained within the astringent walls of a psychiatrist's office. She flexed her feet. The leather couch squeaked under her weight. She filled out the patient intake form as the man sitting across from her studied her. When she handed him the completed form, he set it on his desk and proceeded to talk. "Do you know why you're here?" he asked.

"Yes," Aria said. "I've been hurting myself."

"It says here that you're in foster care, is that true?"

The psychiatrist shifted in his chair, adjusting the glasses on his nose as he awaited her answer. Aria nodded.

"Why are you hurting yourself?" he asked.

"It feels better. Everything just gets really quiet," Aria said, pausing to put her elbows on her knees and resting her temples on her palms. "I don't see why this is such a big deal to everyone."

"It's a big deal to everyone because we can't have you being a danger to yourself, or to anyone else for that matter," the man answered. He looked down at his hands in his lap and Aria could see that he was balding.

Sensing that this man was accustomed to extreme emotional displays, she seized the opportunity to release the pressure. "I fucking hate this place," she said. "Who the fuck would want to live here?"

The psychiatrist received the words and stayed silent, welcoming more expression. Aria glanced around the room. "Life is like an air-filled syringe to the veins," she said, playing with the end of her sleeve. "I wish that love could make this world good, instead of sugar-coat it."

"Are you saying that you feel like love is fake?"

"Yes, love is fake!" Aria shouted.

The psychiatrist scribbled notes on the pad of paper in his hands. It made her feel like a lab rat there to be studied. As if to cut him off from his writing, Aria said, "You people don't care about me, you don't care about me at all. You just want me to die so you can be rid of me."

"We don't want you to die – that's precisely why you're here," he said, not looking up from his paper.

A marked silence fell over the room. Eventually he looked up from his notes and steered the conversation in another direction. "You've experienced a pretty big loss; how do you feel about losing your mother?"

Aria looked at him in obstinate defiance. "I don't think anything about it," she answered.

He scribbled again in his notes. It went on like this for over an hour, the psychiatrist trying to extract information from her, Aria evading his questions. Inside she was dying. Inside, she heard the truthful answer to his questions arise within her chest; she knew that she was not OK. But she couldn't let him know that.

When the appointment was over, the man stood up and put his hands in his pockets. "I'd be glad to keep seeing you if you want to come," he said. Aria nodded and said OK. But she did not intend to return.

Aria made her way to a chair in the waiting room next to Mrs Johnson, who had been anxiously awaiting her return. The psychiatrist waved her mother into the room. The door closed behind them but they didn't realize that Aria could still make out the conversation.

"I'm fairly certain that Aria has manic depression," the psychiatrist explained. "The file I received from the agency said that she was treated for methamphetamine toxicity. I have to tell you that mood disorders are fairly common in children who have been exposed to meth."

Aria could imagine Mrs Johnson looking at the floor rather than at the man telling her the news. "Yes, they said it was a possibility. But I just couldn't imagine that with the right upbringing, she wouldn't get better." After a brief pause, she went on, "I have four other children at home. She can't keep doing this. She's a bad influence on them and I'm at the end of my rope."

"I'll write you a prescription for Lexapro," Aria heard him say. "You can try her on 10mg a day. It may take up to six weeks to notice an improvement."

"Thank you," Mrs Johnson said, before coming out and making another appointment with the secretary at the front of the office.

The atmosphere between Aria and Mrs Johnson was icy on the drive back home. Neither of them said a single word. The city seemed to move in slow motion compared to the speed of the car. The world outside the car was like a movie Aria was watching rather than a world that she was a part of.

That night, before she went to bed, Mrs Johnson entered the room with a glass of water and a tiny white pill. She held them out to Aria and smiled as if hopeful that the pill would take all of their worries away. Aria swallowed the pill and handed the empty glass back to her. "Did you finish your homework?" Mrs Johnson asked.

"Yeah," Aria said.

"Good," Mrs Johnson said and left the room in a state of satisfaction.

Aria pulled out her journal and made her sentiments known. *This is hell*, she wrote. *I wish I knew what sins could be forgiven and that love could feed the world instead of sugar-coat it. I wish I wasn't left wanting a time when I still believed an ocean existed inside every spiral shell, and the sound there was waves instead of a change in the goddamn air pressure. They gave me pills today. I'm six feet under and a thousand feet deep; they have forgotten the shadow I creep between. I'm alone. I always have been and I always will be.* She ended her entry with a scribbled zigzag that took up the remainder of the page.

That night, Aria tossed and turned with stomach pain. She couldn't sleep. She felt nauseous but couldn't throw up. She stayed home from school the next day. After two days, Mrs Johnson suspected that it was a side effect of the new medication. She called the psychiatrist's office and described the symptoms. The doctor told her: "Lexapro has been known to cause nausea and stomach pain but the benefits outweigh the risks so keep her on it for another week. The side effect should go away."

Aria agreed to take the pill for two more days. She writhed in agony on the floor of her room until she couldn't take it anymore. She resolved to stop taking the pills. From then on, when Mrs Johnson brought the pill in to her before bedtime, Aria only pretended to take it. As soon as she left the room, Aria would spit it in the wastebasket in the corner of her room. Mrs Johnson was satisfied in her ignorance. When her daughter started feeling better, she felt confident that the side effect had worn off and that Aria was getting better.

That is, until she found the stash of unswallowed pills, on the very same day that Aria's school called to tell her that her daughter had been suspended for being caught with a packet of cigarettes in her locker.

Aria sat outside the door in the hallway, listening to Mr and Mrs Johnson's voices float back and forth. They had one thing in common: an air of defeat. Mrs Johnson had not bothered to take the issue up with Aria that day. She was past that point.

"She can't stay here, Robert," she said. "We have other children to think of and it's not getting better. God give me the strength for this."

She paced the room as her husband sat on the bed. To Aria's amazement, he said, "I agree. She's better off where she can get placed with a family that's equipped to handle a girl with these struggles."

Mr Johnson felt a foreign sense of reprieve at the prospect of Aria going away. The guilt that had preoccupied him for so long as a result of the indiscretions between himself and Aria might just come to an end. Somewhere inside of him, he felt a glimmer of hope that if Aria left, she wouldn't tempt him anymore. He could live with himself. He could return to normal.

Aria could not believe her ears. She was sure that the secret they shared would at least bind him to come to her defense. She was sure that it would compel him to want her to stay here. But clearly she was wrong. She was worth nothing to either of them. Abandoned by one mother and hated by a second, and with a father who used her for his own idle pleasure without giving a damn, she stood up and retreated to her room. She shut herself in the closet and sat beneath her hanging clothes, confined in a sphere of sorrow.

She didn't hear the surprise in Mrs Johnson's voice at her husband's words. "You really think so?" she asked.

"I think Aria needs more help than we can give her. I've got to work and you've got your hands full here at the house, and I just can't stand seeing you like this every day."

"But she's my daughter ..." Mrs Johnson started to weep. "She's got to know that God loves her. No, I won't give up on her, Robert. I can't do that."

In the closet, memories nagged at Aria. In the dark, she could see the sorrel-colored brick of the Eccles Children's Home like it was yesterday. She had been there longer than at any other group home. She remembered the way the bleak linoleum hallway shone. The air of tragedy that hung in the place, only slightly more pungent than the smell of industrial cleaner. A dormitory of rooms with bunk beds, four children per room. The new ones crying at night, but no one there to comfort them. The emotional deprivation so thick you could breathe it in. There was nowhere for all the torment to go, so the children aimed it at each other. You couldn't get attached to anyone, because there was no knowing when they were going to be placed in a foster home and leave you. It was anything but a "home," it was just a place where she was forced to fall asleep at night.

She couldn't go back to that place.

The torment of the idea of being returned to the group home compelled her to move from her place in the closet. She walked from one end of the room to the other in a frightened daze. She was breathing heavily. She decided to confront the Johnsons about their decision but when she walked down the hallway to their room, she could see through the crack below the door that the light in their room was out. They had already gone to sleep.

Time stood still again, just as it had that day 10 years ago when they had walked her to the school office to tell her that her mother was in the hospital. Again, as she walked down the hallway of the house she had thought would be her home, it felt like she was walking in slow motion. Aria went back to her room and lay under the covers of her bed. Her tears had given way to an unnerved numbness. It was not a conscious decision. The decision came from the deep recesses of her soul, a soul that could not bear the idea of being abandoned again. The decision was clear. She had to leave this place. She had to run away.

Aria rode the first wave of adrenaline across the room to fetch her school backpack. She emptied out the books onto her bed and proceeded to fill her backpack with all the things she could not leave behind: her journal, a change of clothes, her toothbrush and toothpaste, a hairbrush, the blankie she had slept with for eight years and the snow globe beside her bed. The abrasive rip of the zipper jolted her into feeling again. She was terrified. Glancing around the room one last time, to make sure she had not left anything she could not live without, her eyes settled on Clifford. He was patiently sitting on the desk in her room, watching her intently as if he could sense what she had planned. Aria was leveled by the surge of grief she felt when she noticed him. For a minute, she entertained the notion that she would be leaving him and, with him, the only real sense of connection she had ever had. But when she thought of taking him with her, the gush of relief she felt was enough to convince her to do it. She would make it work, no matter what. She picked up her coat that was heaped on the floor and zipped it halfway while she walked toward the cat. Lifting him into her coat, she kissed his head and made cooing sounds. As docile as he was, he made no protest. She felt guilty, realizing that her siblings would wake to find the family pet missing, but she zipped up her coat anyway, concealing Clifford inside.

Aria bent down to swing her backpack onto her back. She turned off the light in the room she was about to abandon. It felt empty already, even though everything was still in its proper place. She walked down the stairs, trying to make as little noise as possible, and crossed the floor to the doorway. She did not look back when she reached the door. As far as she was concerned, she did not have the option to second-guess herself. She unlocked the door and cracked it open with delicate movements, maneuvering her body past it. In the heat of the moment, she could not feel the cold of the air when it received her. She turned around to close the door as quietly as she could. The familiar wooden plaque on the door rattled a bit when she closed it.

She looked briefly at the house she was leaving forever. Surprisingly, she felt a fondness that she could not recall feeling before. But this was no time to turn back, so she spun around and tiptoed down the steps. When she reached the sidewalk, she began to walk swiftly, looking back over her shoulder only once to make sure that she hadn't woken anyone in the house. When she saw that the lights were still off, she held Clifford tight to her chest and began running.

Aria had run away from home.

CHAPTER 3

The air outside was biting. Aria was caught up in the rush of having made the decision to leave them before they abandoned her. It made her feel like she was finally part of the outside world. She was out in it, instead of looking at it through a pane of glass. The darkness swallowed her up and she welcomed it. She felt a stronger sense of belonging in the shadowy spaces, between where the light from the street lamps could reach, than she had ever felt in the façade of that cinnamon-smelling shitshow called a home.

She let the fury of her rejection of that life fuel her movements forward. It seemed to allow her to run further and faster than normal. It was empowering. But beneath the fever of that empowerment, Aria was terrified. She was terrified of the feeling of arriving wherever it was that she was going. She knew that once she got there, there would be nothing but silence and nothing but stillness. There would be nothing but space to second-guess herself.

A few times Aria stopped to check on Clifford, whose still demeanor beneath her coat owed more to his state of confusion than it did to pleasure. She felt guilty that he was along for the ride to suit her best interests rather than to suit his own. "It's OK," she said down to him, cradling him closer in an attempt to soothe away the anxiety, which was so obviously telegraphed by the agitated swivel of his ears.

Aria had run away without a specific destination in mind and that no longer made sense. No matter how hard she tried to search for a great idea, the corridors of her mind would only offer up a slideshow of familiar places. She decided on the one she felt most suited the current situation: the bleachers flanking her high school football field. She had spent time there on several occasions while skipping school, feeling exactly like she did now, like

31

a fugitive. A fugitive intent on biding as much time as possible before making the next move.

The school looked menacing at nighttime, like a sophisticated modern megalith that seemed to be sleeping. As she walked to the edge of its grounds, Aria felt as if the building itself might wake, like a guard dog. Though it was spring, the grass under her feet had not been graced by the impulse of the season. It seemed dead, or dormant at least, and colorless. Making sure to draw no attention to herself, she found her familiar place underneath the bleachers. She was used to them during the daytime, when the sun had warmed them so deeply that they were soothing to the touch. This was different. At nighttime, the metal was like silver ice. She felt judged by them. And just as she'd been afraid of, a few minutes after she crouched down, the stillness and silence set in. The unfamiliar nature of this well-known place made her begin to doubt herself.

Clifford was unsettled by the stillness too. As soon as her body settled, the cat began squirming. He tried to jump up and out of the collar of her coat. "No," she said, "stay here." Trying to keep his movements hushed but to no avail, eventually she resorted to using one hand to untie the worn laces of one of her high-top sneakers and pull it out. She tied the shoelace to Clifford's collar, like a leash, and watched, saying nothing, as he contended with it for a few minutes before lying down in the dust in a state of defeat. His tail was swishing. His ears were half pinned back. He had a look on his face of so much chagrin; Aria thought to herself that he almost looked human. She felt guilty but, in her own state of distress, could conjure nothing within herself to remedy it.

Aria's mind tried to distract her by running frantically through every possible scenario for how things could play out. She thought about going back home. She thought about being captured by the police. She thought about hitchhiking to another part of the country. She thought about running into the wilderness and creating a life for herself in nature.

For a second, she decided to go back home, but then, as if snapping out of a daze, she remembered the conversation she had overheard between Mr and Mrs Johnson. They had already made up their mind to hand her back over to the state. If she went back home, she wouldn't get there until dawn had already broken. Having them find out that she'd spent the night out of the house was like putting the signature on her eviction notice from their lives. It wasn't an option.

That realization no longer was just a mental one. Her expendability hit her chest and stomach with the force of a semi truck. She unzipped her backpack to find her blankie. Holding it, she pulled Clifford close to her, as if the closer she held them both, the higher the chance was that the agony would go away. But it didn't. Instead, that despair eventually lulled her into a cold, restless, dreamless sleep.

Panic woke her after just a few hours, panic that robbed the peaceful transition between sleeping and awake; panic that reminded her of the reality of her life in that moment before her eyes had even opened. The light that was slowly brightening before the sun had risen issued a warning. A warning of being found out.

Aria collected Clifford under her coat again, pulled her backpack over her shoulders and snuck away from the school grounds. Walking away, she turned back and realized that she was leaving her life behind in layers. First, the place she was supposed to belong with a family, called home. Second, the place she was supposed to learn to belong in society, called school. She was conscious that this meant she was dropping out. As much pain as there was in making the choice to leave it all behind, it was scary how easy it was. It took no effort. The fact that she could just slip away like this meant that there was nothing holding her there in the first place. That anything she thought was there to hold her wasn't real. Grieving the loss of the illusion of that external security, she boarded a city bus.

Sitting in the very back of the bus, she kept her eye on the driver. Careful to conceal Clifford, she moved her body as much as was necessary to keep him placid and to not look suspicious. When she'd stayed on the bus for so long that her continued presence there began to create a palpable tension, she got off. She was in a part of town near the museum. To Aria, it felt like she had stepped away from one flavor of sadness straight into another. The path of devastation seemed to have led her in a circle against her will.

As she watched a conflux of school children gather in factions on the concrete steps of the museum, Aria remembered her real mother bringing her here during one of her manic episodes all those years ago. She could almost see herself, like a hallucination overlaying the current scene, walking up those steps, small enough at that age that she had to focus on climbing them. She remembered knowing that her mother's drug-induced enthusiasm and her desire to both connect and be a mother would be short-lived. But Aria didn't care. She had decided to soak up those up-days for as long as they lasted so they could carry her through the desolation of all the other days.

She recalled them almost running from exhibit to exhibit. On that day, even though she asked for nothing more than to be with her mother, there was nothing Lucy wouldn't give her. Lucy bought the tickets to the museum and ice-cream cones and toys from the gift shop as if there was no limit to abundance in their world. She thrust them into Aria's little arms as if to say that the world could be her oyster. Aria had laughed because it was an experience she had always wanted to have.

She'd wondered for a second if her mother knew something that she didn't. Maybe something wonderful had happened and they didn't have to struggle anymore. But she knew deep inside that underneath that laughter and that hope, they couldn't afford any of it. That feeling reminded her that her mother was not fully there. Lucy was interacting with the world as if through the veil of some alternate reality that was better than this one. Still, Aria tried to keep up with that unattuned alternate reality, and, for the day, she had managed to feel closer to her mother than she had in years.

It was one of those times in her life where she came closest to the vision in her head of what it might be like to really have a mother who loved her and who showed her the wonders of the world. Aria felt nostalgic about that day, as tainted as it may have been. It was a good day.

But then, standing there, staring at the museum, Aria thought to herself, *I had two mothers – one who took me to the museum and bought me everything I could ever want. And another who woke up the next day and panicked about the new toys she saw in my room and then returned them.* It just so happened that these two mothers Aria remembered were both Lucy.

Aria spent the day in a state of shock. She figured that hanging around a public place like this would keep the people looking for her (assuming there were any) off of her trail. Her hope was that people would mistake her for a high school student on a field trip. And to her surprise, no one ever did suspect a thing.

On a few occasions, she let Clifford out onto the sidewalk. People would come by to pet him and remark at the cuteness of such a docile cat, which was behaving more like a dog on the end of her makeshift leash. She was able to sneak Clifford into a public restroom in the subway station adjacent to the museum, where she created a puddle for him to drink from in an indentation in the tile floor. Aria waited for the brief seconds in between people coming and going to stop pretending to wash her hands and instead drink from the faucet. They both went without food that day. And as the night set in, Aria realized, not having thought of it before leaving, that she had no idea how she was going to get food for either of them.

When the sun went down, she snuck into the public bathroom one last time. She pulled out her toothbrush and toothpaste and hairbrush and brushed her teeth just like she would have if she were home. She watched herself in the dirty mirror, pulling the bristles of her hairbrush through her hair. The way she felt had changed throughout the day. Now, she wasn't feeling empowered anymore. She wasn't feeling sadness anymore. Instead she was feeling lost in a world that she now realized she was completely unprepared for. She found herself staring at a leak of orange soap fluid on the sink, in a daze, when the automatic lights switched off. "Come here, sweetie pea," she said to Clifford, scooping him up again.

That night Aria found an open entryway to an office building on a side street, a few blocks away from the museum. All the lights inside the building were off, so she felt reasonably sure that she wouldn't be detected there. The russet of the bricks made it feel warmer inside than it really was. Once she was out of the elements, her skin relished the lull of the air there. She sat down and pulled her blankie out of her backpack. She let Clifford wander in the tiny area. He sniffed around for a time before relieving himself on the floor. Aria initially jerked up to try to stop him, but realized it was no use. She erupted into tears. Tears because she had no way to clean it up. Tears for fear of getting in trouble. Tears at the tragedy of the situation she had found herself in. Even though she didn't have the luxury of wondering why she, specifically, was the unlucky one who had wound up with this life, she cried tears as if she was attending her own funeral.

Aria stayed in the entryway that she had planned to sleep in for less than an hour until the fear of being found out, and the desire to distance herself from the potential trouble of the mess that Clifford had made, got the better of her. She decided to find another place to stay for the night. But the city was too cold. The universe seemed to watch her with an ocean of indifferent stars. Cars passed her, their engines babbling of destinations unwilling to wait. Any place she tried to settle into quickly became unbearable. Her body would not let her sleep. So instead, she spent the night walking and stopping, walking and stopping. It was hard to walk with one shoe missing its laces. It was hard to walk with the foggy, weak discomfort of hunger. But it was harder not to walk.

— * —

At first, the Johnsons thought they owed Aria's absence to her characteristic delinquency. They assumed that she would eventually come home with some excuse for her absence and that she would deliver that excuse so as to imply they were "in the wrong" for even asking where she was. But by dinnertime, Mrs Johnson gave in to the nagging uneasiness in the background of their routine. After checking Aria's room and finding no clues to her whereabouts, she called the police just after sundown. Now, two nights had come and gone.

"When did you last see her?"

"Did you have any worries about the state of her mental health or any other cause for concern when you saw her last?"

"Has she ever run away like this before?"

The questions the officer asked seemed to float impersonally across the room. For reasons beyond her understanding, Mrs Johnson was less focused on the questions themselves than she was on how wrong it felt that he could ask them in such a detached way. Her arms were unconsciously hugging her sides as if trying to hold her together. She watched the officer scribble in a notepad every time she or her husband gave an answer. She had been so consumed by Aria's disappearance that she did not even notice that their family cat was also gone.

Upstairs, the occasional squeak of a floorboard or scuffing of a drawer being opened was audible from a second officer who was examining Aria's room. Given Aria's past as a ward of the state, they did not have to wait to file a missing person's report. But as much of a blessing as that was, the police seemed unmoved by her absence, as if it were a let-down to be expected from a "child like her."

When the police had collected all the information that they could, Mr Johnson saw them out. Instead of comforting his wife, he stood there looking at her as if to say, "I don't know what to do." And he didn't know what to do. About Aria missing. About his wife's distress. He was just standing there, waiting for direction.

It was at times like this that Mrs Johnson's picture-perfect family image began to burn at the edges, like filmstrip caught in the projector. She got up and found herself watching her other children – sent into the backyard during the police visit – through the window over the kitchen sink. This was her way of coping, to busy herself with petty tasks. The warmth of the water offered itself to her in ways that her husband would not. She found a certain security of control in the way the soap predictably cleared the filth from the dishes. Watching the children play outside, witnessing them explore the limits of gravity with smiles on their faces, she couldn't help but be struck by their innocence. Mrs Johnson could not figure out why God would let things happen to corrupt that innocence.

At times like this, she would speak to God in her own mind. Today, her invisible prayer was to understand why one child is born into a home like theirs, with loving parents and all the advantages in life, and why another child is not. She could feel her husband standing behind her. It bothered her that he did not seem vexed by these kinds of questions. Perhaps it was because he was a man. She envied his capacity to simply accept whatever life threw at them. She also hated him for it.

They had already driven to every place across the city where they thought Aria could be. Necessity meant the other children were sustained with takeout food. Even though they reveled in it, it challenged Mrs Johnson's delicate self-concept as a mother.

Now they were playing a waiting game. A waiting game heavily tainted by guilt and notions of all the possible things that might have happened to Aria.

CHAPTER 4

"*You have not mothered me life, you have not fathered me life.*"

The sentence repeated like poisonous poetry in Aria's mind. She had been hiding behind a Pizza Hut for what felt like hours, waiting for the store to close. Beneath the delirium of her hunger, she felt humiliated. Before leaving, she had not considered what her life might be reduced to, nor what she might be reduced to doing after she ran away.

In a trickle as slow as molasses, all the employees had gone home for the day, except one. She could see him through the window, appearing and disappearing while puttering around the store. He bore his heavy weight like a cross that had been nailed to him long ago. She felt infuriated with how satisfied he seemed with his meager sense of power and the blatant underachievement that, tonight at least, he seemed oblivious to.

"Can you just be done already, goddamn, what the fuck is there to do?" She said the words out loud even though, with both distance and glass between them, he would never hear them. The projection of her irritation did not hurry him at all. How could she expect it to? This man was oblivious and she was hidden to the point that he would never know that she was there. Eventually, her irritation was disrupted by the assault of the sound of grating metal. The back door had opened. She watched the man carry four pizza boxes out to the dumpster and throw them in.

Aria waited despite her nerves, like a predator knowing that it cannot act on its prey just yet without losing the chance altogether. She suffered a few more minutes of watching him resume his puttering before all but a row of dim fluorescent lights went out. Still she waited just those few moments longer to ensure that he was gone before rushing to the dumpster to tie the loose end of the shoelace that was affixed to Clifford's collar to the dumpster wheel.

The weight of the lid was uneven against her palms. When she lifted it, to throw it back, a warm waft of sickly plastic rot came rushing out to greet her face. She turned away too late to avoid it. She found it funny that no matter where a dumpster was, or what went inside it, they all smelled the same. Grabbing two of the pizza boxes that she had just seen the man throw away, she closed the lid again and sat down on the pavement to eat as fast as she could. The white cheese had already hardened and the tomato sauce had turned to a paste. When she bit into it, the crust smelled like flour, having lost its succulence without the heat. But her starvation elevated both its status and flavor. It was the best pizza she had ever eaten.

Aria pulled the cheese off two slices, and placed it in front of Clifford. Her voracious chewing was making her view of him jiggle as she watched him. In the stress of the last few days, Clifford had failed to groom himself. His coat, which was usually shiny, was beginning to look dull.

Clifford sniffed at the cheese apprehensively. He seemed to be put off by it. *Maybe it's the tomato*, she thought to herself. For the last two days, Aria had been suppressing the awareness that she did not have the wherewithal to take care of Clifford out here on the streets. She felt selfish for bringing him. And yet, until this moment, she had been able to lie to herself about his wellbeing enough to overlook the fact that he was beginning to decline. He had not eaten anything. She had tried on multiple occasions to find him something. But each time, he had protested. She wondered whether his pickiness genuinely owed itself to his tastes or whether it was a form of emotional protest taken out on the food. She knew the answer.

Aria felt sick to her stomach. Again, she found herself almost amused by one of the painful aspects of her current state. The body can be starving, but when it is too starving and you feed it, it rejects the food. One more of life's little design flaws.

Nausea had a way of capturing all of her attention. So much so that she did not notice the man that she had been watching in the store just minutes before, rounding the corner and catching sight of her.

"Hey! You there!"

The words cut through her like a skewer. Suddenly, she was in a race. He was hurrying toward her, with the intention of shooing her off. Would he reach her before she could untie Clifford? Her fingers fumbled to loosen the knot.

It was anyone's game. Like a gift from somewhere beyond her, the idea occurred to unclip the latch to Clifford's collar.

Aria grabbed him and ran as fast as she could. She knew there would be no way for the man to catch up to her, given his weight. But she felt his words again skewer into her back. "You stay the hell out of here!" And then, more faintly, "If you come back here, next time I'm calling the cops."

She rounded the corner into the alley of a nearby building. She was out of breath and the shoe that was missing its laces was only halfway holding on to her foot. Her heavy breaths quickly became the doorway for suppressed tears. She was crying. Smothering Clifford's bulk with her arms, she could feel nothing but his resistance to her. Having ended up in this touch-and-go hostage situation, he looked as aghast as a cat could ever look.

The close call with the Pizza Hut manager was what it took to corrode Aria's denial of the situation at hand. She could not keep Clifford with her. In that moment, she felt herself splitting in two, torn between her need to keep him with her, and her need to know he was both safe and happy. After she had been taken away from Lucy, he was the only living thing she had felt true belonging with. She held him there against his will, letting the gravity of the awareness sink in until it broke her heart. By the time it was successfully broken, she knew what she had to do.

— * —

The public park was bleak this time of year. Still it was an oasis of calm, fenced in from the bustle of the rest of the city. She had returned to the familiarity of the public subway station bathroom by the museum and had spent most of the night there. Having locked herself into a stall, trapping the now collarless Clifford in her lap, she had successfully managed to go unnoticed. Upon waking, she was so tired; she began to wonder if she could still consider herself sane. As if on autopilot, she joined the citizens of the city, making their way by foot on their morning commutes. She stopped with them at stoplights and moved with them when they became fluid again. She spent the day at the public park, sitting and walking through the dappled, swaying light, worrying about the greasiness of her hair and letting Clifford sun himself while watching out for dogs, who frequently showed both shock and hysteria at his being there.

Nature, she thought, must possess some secret to living that people were not privy to. It seemed to Aria that the little yellow flowers, which were leading the way for the arrival of spring, were God's way of laughing at her. In truth, Aria did not believe in God, certainly not in the way that Mrs Johnson did. But she could feel *something* bigger than herself, and bigger than everything, at work in the world. She just didn't know what that was. She didn't know so many things. She was unsure of her body, yet she was stuck in it. She seemed to be navigating her way through life with a lighthouse that remained unlit. Aria often followed these mental pathways of existential thinking to escape the world instead of to venture deeper into it. Today, she followed these mental pathways to avoid the reality of the decision she had made.

Aria had been waiting to take Clifford home until she knew that the Johnsons would be home, having finished work and picked up the younger kids from their school. She felt disheartened to realize that now when she thought of them, they felt less and less like a mother and father to her. The possibility of that ever feeling real to her was gone. Mere days had passed and already the life she had lived with them for the last three years felt like it belonged to someone else. The life she had been living on the street felt more real to her. There was more continuity in it. It felt more like where her life began and therefore, more true to who she really was. Whether she wanted that to be the case or not, there was some dark relief to be found in that belonging as opposed to always feeling like a fish in a nest of birds.

When it was time, Aria pushed through the friction of the part of herself that needed Clifford with her, the part that could not face what she was about to do. She left the sanctuary of the park and boarded the last city bus she would ever take with him. Clifford was motionless. Perhaps he has sensed what was about to happen. Perhaps the weight of Aria's heartache had subdued him. She was saying goodbye, long before she ever actually said it. When she reached her neighborhood, she felt nostalgic. It was already a lost life. It was one more place she had never belonged, only tried to. Each house boasted only marginal differences from the others that surrounded it, as if they had all been fashioned with a cookie cutter. More so than ever before, she could feel the fakeness of this neighborhood. Like a perfectly groomed tree, it had been crafted out of someone's vision of the great American dream. A dream where all the family problems were to be kept closed tightly behind those idyllic front doors.

Walking closer, she spotted the house that she had tried to consider a home. She was not afraid of being seen. At this point in her life, Aria had perfected the art of going unnoticed. She was far enough away that she could watch them like the ghost of someone who was one of them once. This time, when she kissed Clifford on the forehead and held him one last time, the tears did not come. "I love you, Bobbins," she said in a whisper, using the nickname that he frequently went by in the house. "I'm gonna miss you." She let a succession of kisses repeat this sentiment to him before she released her grasp on him. "Go on, run home," she whispered louder, as an instruction. With no reservation, Clifford fled toward the home as if it were his salvation.

Aria watched him run up the front steps onto the porch and survey the door, only to find it closed. He did not meow to be let in. He was a quiet cat in general. Instead, he sat down on his haunches and began licking himself passionately, restarting the grooming he had ceased during his time with her. She felt her heart break a little bit more, seeing him so relieved and at home in this place that she could not belong to no matter how hard she had tried.

She moved so as not to be noticed by any of the neighbors returning home. Half an hour passed. Clifford was still grooming himself when the front door opened. Mr Johnson almost tripped over Clifford, not having seen him until the last second because his view had been obscured by the black trash bag that he was carrying in front of him. Clifford darted past him and disappeared into the house. Mr Johnson poked his head back in the door to follow his trail or maybe to yell something that Aria could not hear. He then closed the door behind him and walked the trash bag he was carrying out to the black garbage bin by the side of the garage. Aria tracked his movements. She had memorized them. They were the same ones he always made … his part of the Johnson family routine. Today, that routine made her queasy. It was obvious to her, sitting there, that dreams pull apart before they ever manifest. Her dream of mattering to this family, or any family, would obviously never come true. Had she hoped to arrive and find a squadron of cop cars with flashing lights? Had she hoped to see Mrs Johnson reduced to tears, begging them to find her daughter? Had she hoped to find Mr Johnson gone, turning over every stone to find her? She became conscious of these desires only now, once she could see that the reality was quite the opposite. Instead, Aria observed that she had already been forgotten. Had they even realized she was gone? "Of course they did," she muttered under her breath in response to the thought. She imagined what they were doing inside. She imagined the smell and sounds of Mrs Johnson cooking. She imagined watching cartoons with her other adoptive siblings. She used to find the weight of them leaning against her on the couch obnoxious. Now, she missed that weight. She could see it now as a gift, rather than an imposition. A gift she had thrown away by running away.

For the briefest of moments, Aria entertained the thought of walking back through the door, but then she reminded herself of their plans to return her to the group home. Having said goodbye to Clifford, who did not seem upset to leave her, and having seen how forgettable she really was, she let her anger rescue her from the despair. It lifted her up and out of her state of drowning. Because of that anger, she could not access the feelings of grief underneath. They existed like watery depths inside her somewhere, beyond her awareness. And she was glad of that.

Aria took her shoes off, holding them in her hands, and ran. She ran as if by running away from those watery depths within her, she would not carry them with her. She ran until she couldn't.

Several neighborhoods away, there stood a vacated house. The real estate sign in front of it had been there for so long that it now projected crooked from the earth. It was obvious from the wear of the siding and the untended landscaping that no one had lived there or visited for a long time, and most likely wouldn't.

Aria spotted a doghouse through the chain-link fence. The heavy chain affixed to the metal post beside it meant it was most likely built for a guard dog. The red paint had faded so badly that most of it had given way to gray, weathered wood. The once-black shingles had turned the color of ash and were lifting and corroding at the edges. Despite the dilapidation of the little shelter, she felt it calling to her, a promise of being able to let go of the tension of living like a fugitive for so long. She slipped her shoes back on, leaving the one that still had laces untied, and walked toward it.

Most people would have felt demeaned by crawling on their hands and knees into a doghouse. But Aria had always felt much closer to animals than she had ever felt to people. Though the dust that covered the floor made her cough, she felt soothed by the thought of the dog that once lived there. She curled herself up in a fetal position, not caring whether her head was in the dust. Not caring how much of it she breathed in. She imagined herself curled up with the dog that once lived there. The image of him was so strong she could feel him guarding her and soothing her to sleep.

There are times when the pain that someone faces is so great that the mind cannot wrap itself around it. The mind cannot dissect it to find meaning and it cannot analyze it to figure out how to avoid it in the future. Instead, the mind simply submits to the dizziness of it. This was one such time for Aria. That dizziness came upon her like a sandstorm. And in the process of submitting to it, she fell asleep.

CHAPTER 5

A week had passed since Aria had spent the night in the abandoned doghouse, a slipshod week of learning the ins and outs of life on the streets of Chicago. She had found a mission that allowed vagrants to stay for three nights per month. Having lied to the staff about her age, she was shown to a room that looked roughly like a refugee camp. It was a large gymnasium, converted into a human-scale rat cage. The flooring had been peeled up, exposing the cement floor underneath. It was easier to clean this way. Pipes of different sizes platted the ceiling like a maze overhead. The entire room was covered in bunk beds, with no sheets to cushion the thinness of the mattresses. Standing in the crowd of other women and children who had been ushered in with her, Aria suddenly regretted being there. But being too shy to draw attention to herself by rescinding her decision, she stood still and contained her feelings, listening to two directors who were in charge that night, reading out the rules of the shelter.

One woman read them in English, then the other repeated them in Spanish. They were made to strip to their underwear and hand over their shoes and then clothing. Aria watched one of the mission volunteers take her clothes and backpack over to a metal locker, among a row of hundreds, and lock them in. They were to sleep in underwear. It was a way of ensuring that violence was kept to a minimum. If one of the women tried to kill another one in this place, she could not make a getaway, because her clothes and shoes would be locked up. Each woman was then given a pile of threadbare sheets, which she was expected to make her bed with.

The mission volunteers made Aria nervous. Most of them were homeless themselves. They simply viewed volunteering as a way to better manipulate their way into getting their own needs met. Many of the women staying there made a quick thirty bucks in the daytime by going to a blood plasma donation center nearby. Aria followed a group of them the first day, but did not go inside. The entire experience at the mission had made her feel like an animal at a slaughterhouse. She squirmed at the thought of giving in to that likeness one step further by willingly letting them drain her blood. The other women kept the money they had made there in the pockets of their clothing. On more than one occasion, Aria witnessed one of the volunteers stealing this money out of the pockets when she took the clothes to the lockers before it was time for the lights to go out. Having your possessions stolen, no matter how few possessions you had, seemed to be part of life on the street.

"Lights out" was not really lights out in the mission. In fact, half of the lights stayed on all night long. Long, fluorescent bulbs that hissed as if cursing the women that lay directly underneath them. Every so often, in a muddled chorus, a child started crying in the middle of the night, and then another and another. Their cries usually subsided, but only so the children could avoid further scolding, not because they were being soothed. Aria had come to the mission thinking that she would sleep better there than she did out in the frigid night air. Being there, however, she realized that sleeplessness was another part of life on the streets that simply had to be accepted. On multiple occasions, she lay in her bottom bunk completely bewildered by the fact that so many women seemed to have no problem whatsoever sleeping in those conditions. Again, this made Aria feel like she did not belong.

In the morning, at about 5.30am, the other lights went on in the large room. A woman shouted for everyone to wake up and then they were ordered not to leave their beds until a volunteer had collected their clothing and handed it to them personally. In exchange, the women turned in the bed sheets they had used for the night, which were placed in an industrial waste bin to be taken to launder.

With clothing in hand, they then formed a line outside the bathroom. The lines in the mission seemed to last forever. Every so often Aria's attempt to dissociate while standing in them was interrupted by the bark of someone trying to get the women already inside the bathroom to hurry up. Inside the bathroom, there was a row of toilets with no doors, and opposite each toilet, a sink with no mirror above it. Adjacent to this was a room completely covered by stained and aging off-white tiles: the community shower area. The walls were studded with silver nozzles, only one of which worked properly. During her stay there, Aria witnessed more than one tussle over which woman got to use that nozzle. But, as dilapidated as it was, there was hot water. This was what made Aria come back the next night and the next. Aria became conscious that she always took hot water for granted until she had no access to it anymore. The swelter of it whittled down the sharpness of the fear she felt constantly now. As much as her circumstances did not seem to improve from day to day, at least the water could fool her into hoping that they would. Even if it was illusion, she could feel like it might be a fresh new start.

Despite the mandatory showers, the mission smelled rancid. It smelled rancid because people's clothes were rancid. The women were prohibited from washing them in the sinks. When they had used their ration of soap for bathing, they were handed a towel, which they were made to deposit in a large bin before putting their polluted clothes back on. It was just as well. The industrial soap at the mission smelled like tallow. It made Aria sick to her stomach.

As usual, Aria said next to nothing during her time at the mission. Some of the other women, who, like Aria, stayed for successive nights, began to wonder if she could speak at all. In her silence, Aria simply observed. She listened to conversations to extract advice that the other women were unaware they were even giving. Advice about where to get food and water, places where the police didn't hassle you during the day, places to go undetected at night, places that gave away things like clothes and toiletries for free, places to get temporary labor jobs for the day, places to loiter and, perhaps most importantly, places to procure street drugs. It took Aria a few minutes of confusion to figure out what they were really talking about, seeing as how none of the women overtly used the word drugs, nor did they use any of the names she had heard commonly used for them. Instead, they spoke of things like Smoke, Bo-Bo, C-Game, Chicken Feed, Base, Brown Sugar, Dirt and Seccy.

If she wanted to stay at the mission, she had to be there by 5pm. Each person trying to get a bed for the night had to fill out the required paperwork about who they were and where they were going. Each night Aria lied on nearly every question. She felt the tension of the potential of getting caught in that lie, but she soon came to find that no one really cared. The actual mission of the mission was to proselytize.

After check-in, it was mandatory for the women and children to listen to a preacher for at least an hour. The first time Aria was subjected to this routine, she was struck by the sheer effort put into the man's seemingly effortlessly dressed-down attire. As with a politician, it struck her as contrived. His dress was chosen to evoke a sense of commonality with the vagrants who stood before him every night. She could feel the self-gratification oozing through his philanthropy. As a result, the words, which made a pretense of the words of Christ, were contaminated. They were contaminated by the overwhelming feeling that, as if life had not been cruel enough to these people already, they were now all being used as pawns to guarantee someone else's admittance into heaven. It reminded her of Mrs Johnson's faith … A mediocre veil drawn over the reality of things to make them look better than they truly were.

At the end of the sermon, they were encouraged to gather in a circle and hold hands while the priest led them in prayer. "God, our father, let us see the kingdom come today. Forgive us of our trespasses. We know that we are sinners and cannot therefore save ourselves, but instead rely upon the mercy of your salvation. Use our problems not to cast us out, but to draw us closer to you so that we might have a saving relationship with you through your son's redemptive work at

Calvary. Give us hope in this life and the life to come that is found only in Jesus Christ. Thank you, Lord Jesus, for coming to earth. We know you to be the Son of God who died on the cross for our sins. Thank you for bearing those sins and giving us, who accept you into our hearts, eternal life. Many of your children standing here today have lost everything, but Lord God, offer them the gift of everlasting life. Where they may inherit all things. For that, and for the glory of the name I pray in, Jesus Christ amen."

He spoke as if he was putting words in her mouth and speaking them to some presiding spirit who was either pleased and therefore merciful, or displeased and therefore vengeful. Aria felt humiliated by his words. She could not find in herself a sinner. Instead this "God" they spoke of had stood by and watched year upon year of trespasses against her. It was they that had sinned. It was they that should be asking for forgiveness. And it always struck her as odd that anyone with a life as bad as she had experienced would be asking for life to be eternal. *Why not pray for life to be over?* she thought to herself, waiting for the spectacle to end. She could see beyond the pretenses. She could see that the person who was most insecure in his relationship to God was the very man trying to secure everyone else's.

After the sermon, anyone who felt ready to put their trust in Christ was welcome to step to one side of the room for their salvation. A galvanized metal utility tub that looked vaguely like a watering trough was filled daily with freshly blessed tap water. The priest would instruct any woman who was ready to commit to Christ to sit in the water, holding her left forearm with her right hand and using her left hand to pinch her nostrils closed. The baptisms were short, faith placed on a conveyor belt. The same ritualized words were yelled to the woman being baptized, as if yelling them made them more effectual.

The whole display made Aria despondent. What upset her most was that night after night, women stepped into the water with the hope that their problems might be solved. She could see it in their eyes when they sat down in the water and waited for the immanence of their baptism. The innocence would return to their faces as if they were children, suddenly brittle in their vulnerability. But Aria knew this promise, like every other, was only the promise of inevitable disappointment. A step backward instead of forward … A step that only those who had not yet accepted their ill fate would be dumb enough to take.

The women were not allowed to be at the mission during the day. This gave the volunteers time to launder and organize and clean the floors in preparation for that night's wave of arrivals. In truth, even if it were an option, Aria would not have exercised it. She was eager to escape the tension of the impossible position that they were all placed in. So much of life being homeless, including life at the mission, was like drinking poisoned water. The impossible position of relying on someone for charity, knowing that there were conditions for that charity. It gave a whole new meaning to selling your soul.

The various religious organizations that offered help throughout the city engaged in a covert kind of parasitism with the people who needed them the most. On the one hand, like everyone else, Aria was too desperate to turn down the help. On the other hand, by accepting it, like a man who is so poor that he has no choice but to enlist in the army, she would have to consent to enlisting in God's army. Or at least act as if she would. Of the people she encountered who had made it their mission to help people who lived on the streets, only a handful actually cared about them. For the majority of them, it was obvious that their preoccupation with the homeless was in fact a preoccupation with using them. Using them to bolster their self-concepts as good people. Using them to bedazzle their résumés. Using them as write-offs for their companies; using them to increase the head counts of their congregations. And most of all, using them to secure their own place in heaven. Aria hated it. Being a naturally prideful person, she hated to be so desperate that she was forced to give them the satisfaction. Because of this, when the women and children at the mission were sent out for the day, she followed some of that inadvertent advice that she had been given and she went to wait outside the library until it opened its doors at 8am.

There was a book at the library called *A Dictionary of Angels*. No one had opened it in what must have been 20 years. It wasn't that Aria believed in angels. She opened its inelastic pages simply to give herself the feeling of them. She imagined them sitting in the rafters of that voiceless place, being carried to where they wanted to go not by wings, but by the shafts of sunlight coming through the windows. She imagined the room to be heavy with them, watching and championing the people who had buried themselves in the whispers of the books on the shelves.

Being at the library afforded Aria the opportunity to feel like she was a normal person in society again, less like a castaway. She spent most of her time there thumbing through books that looked like they had been forgotten. There was something virginal about them. Perhaps she felt compelled to give them company because they were forsaken, much like herself.

With the remainder of her time, Aria reviewed the cookbooks and looked up on the public computers some local resources catering to people in her position. Each cookbook offered an artistic pilgrimage into the world of the chef who had created it. And, like the thorough recipes they contained, each one presented a different flavor. So far, her computer searches had proven to be time well spent. She was able to locate a sober living home and ask the manager there if they had any shoes left over from the clothing donations they received, which the residents might not want. Once the manager had sized her up and established that she didn't present any threat, she was left there to look through the pile. She pretended to try on a few pairs before pulling the shoelace on a pair of tennis shoes clean of its eyelets. She stuffed it in her jacket pocket before telling the manager that there was nothing that fit her in the pile. She tuned him out when he proceeded to give her a list of alternative suggestions for where she might find some shoes.

Aria was attached to her All Star sneakers. She felt down to earth and classic in them. When she looked at them, she could sometimes hear the song Cecilia by Simon and Garfunkel playing somewhere in the recesses of her mind. It seemed to her that this new way of living was demanding that she give away every principle she possessed for the sake of basic survival, most especially her principles of good taste. Those high-top sneakers were a form of self-preservation. The one standard she could keep, when all others had to be surrendered.

When she had walked a safe distance from the sober living home, she sat down to thread the shoelace she had taken into the holes that trimmed the quarter of her shoe. She was now walking around with shoes that boasted two different-colored laces, one white, one neon orange. Despite the noticeable clash, she was glad to feel the balance of the even pressure hugging her feet when she walked. But threading them made her think about Clifford. She imagined his empty collar still hanging from the shoelace, still affixed to the wheel of the Pizza Hut dumpster. To say she missed him was to distort sentiment. So many times in her life, the only words available to describe the way she felt fell short. She did not miss him. The absence of him was a torture.

CHAPTER 6

"Let your roots grow down into him and let your lives be built on him."

Col. 2:7

Nina Heng, Aria's foster care case manager, stared at the stenciled words across the wall. *Some partnership*, she thought to herself. She was armed that day with a stack of papers in a manila folder, more for her own sense of security than because she needed them. Being in her position meant being an equal partner and team member to the foster parents as much as it did advocating for the children under her supervision. Sometimes she was gladder of that part of the job description than others. This was not one of those times.

Having grown up in poverty as a first-generation immigrant in Chinatown, Nina had witnessed firsthand just how little say children have in the course of their lives. She had defied her family's hopes of her becoming a doctor, lawyer or accountant, all careers that they imagined would garner her more esteem. Instead she decided to work in the child welfare system, determined to give a voice to the voiceless.

On this day, neither Mr nor Mrs Johnson could ever have guessed at her indigent beginnings. She sat in the overwhelmingly neutral-colored living room with both the poise and the costume of a woman who had grown up with a silver spoon in her mouth. She knew they would mistake her stiffness for manners rather than seeing that it was simply a byproduct of the fact that the Christian overtones of the house made her uneasy.

"The missing persons report was filed over a week ago; we've provided them with a photo and Aria's medical records," she explained. "We've made several attempts to notify Aria's mother but haven't been able to contact her yet. We've listed Aria as missing with the National Center for Missing and Exploited Children and we've notified the court. As you're probably aware, this kind of thing is not unusual to see with kids in the system. Do you have any questions for us at this point?"

Mrs Johnson looked to her husband to respond. She could not believe the lack of surprise on the caseworker's face. The interactions that had taken place between them in the past had seemed so much less mechanical than this. She found herself wondering if this coldness meant that they were being blamed for Aria's disappearance or if the truth was that Aria was always just part of the protocol of the job.

"What do you mean it isn't unusual to see kids just run away like this?" Mr Johnson said forcefully. "I'm sorry, but it can't be usual for a child to disappear for almost two weeks into thin air." Mr Johnson tried not to express his disdain for incompetence in his question, which was really a statement. Unfortunately he didn't succeed.

"Many of these children have a long history of running away," Nina replied. "Aria is one. As you know, she ran away on several occasions from multiple group homes that she was placed in before being placed with you.

"Some of the kids run away because they miss their families. Aria is one of those kids who, unfortunately, was separated from her mother at a later age and so there may be a desire to find her mother and force the process of reconnection. Others run away because they can't abide by the rules of the houses they are placed in. Others run away because they are in bad foster homes where abuse is taking place."

Mr Johnson recoiled. "Are you trying to imply that we should have been more lenient or that we didn't provide enough love for her here?"

He could feel the discrepancy inside himself when he said it. He was terrified that the real truth of Aria's disappearance had more to do with him than with anything else. But he would not admit this guilt to anyone but himself. Instead he covered it over with defensive bluster.

He need not have worried. Nina guessed at nothing anyway. Instead, she said "not at all" and proceeded to sit with Mr and Mrs Johnson for just over an hour, suppressing her nerves while calming theirs. She explained the facts and the realities of the situation at hand until the color had all but drained from their faces. There was something in her that liked to shock such obviously idealistic and therefore optimistically delusional people. Although she appreciated their interest in these forgotten children, she also felt that people like this were one reason why the children had been forgotten in the first place.

Despite her fear about Aria's wellbeing, wherever she was, Nina walked to her car feeling almost at ease with Aria's decision to run away. She hated foster parents like this. People who simply did not get that if a child didn't have a problem before being separated from their parents, they had one the minute they were. People who expected that putting a roof over a child's head or a warm plate of food on the table or a Bible verse on the wall would somehow whitewash over the pain and make it not exist anymore. Nina found it as abusive to deny and erase the emotional truth of a child as it was to physically abuse them. Call it her personal pet peeve. Driving away, she knew deep down that Aria, with her perpetual feeling that no one cared about her, was just as likely to disappear completely as she was to pop up again as if nothing had happened.

When all was said and done, Mrs Johnson was once again grappling with her faith. Unable to accept that it was actually as hard as they said it was for authorities to find a child. Unable to accept that, with all her efforts to make Aria feel loved, she hadn't succeeded. Unable to accept that God had a good plan for creating the suffering behind the statistics she had just been given.

The other children in the house, having heard the door close, had flooded into the living room to watch cartoons.

She sat by the youngest of them, petting her bangs as if this child were the last surviving emblem of her identity as a good mother. She didn't look to her husband to comfort her or to do anything else useful this time. They would deal with reality in their own way.

To her surprise, he sat down beside her and stared at the television set. She knew that he wasn't really watching the TV. She knew he was grappling with the very same reality as she was. The fact that everyone had done everything that could have been done. Now they had to wait, but not wait. Their lives could not be put on hold forever, especially in light of the statistics they had just been given. The only thing they could do was to keep an open door in their hearts if Aria ever did come back.

Mrs Johnson was wrong. Her husband wasn't grappling to swallow the same reality as she was. Instead, aside from feeling the increased seriousness of the situation, Robert Johnson was feeling much the same as he had felt when Aria had first disappeared. He was trying to stitch together the two sides of himself that hoped to rip him apart. One part of him felt the guilt and doom of knowing that he was the real reason she'd left. He feared his fate because of it. He hated himself for it. Aria had been more accessible to him and more open to his affections than Mrs Johnson had ever been. He knew it was wrong, but it also felt so right and *special* that the wrongness failed to prevent it.

He knew that self-blame was selfish. But it drowned out even the grief at her loss and the worry that he had for her wellbeing.

The other part of him felt immeasurable relief that Aria had run away. He did not trust himself when she was around. When she was there, something about her seduced him into a state of possession. It both excited and terrified him. He could not control himself. The fevered pleasure of their secret time together was always followed by the feeling that he had sold his soul to the devil. He hated walking through the doors of church, knowing that God wasn't fooled by him and might never forgive him for what he had done. He felt hypocritical singing the hymns. Even though every person in the pews was facing forward, he could feel their fingers pointed straight at him. He hated crawling into bed with his wife like a dog with his tail between his legs, knowing that if she ever found out what he had done, what he had caused Aria to suffer, their life together would be reduced to shredded paper on the floor. He would lose everything.

And so the two of them sat there on the couch with the dance of the cartoons in pixels on the screen, their children fixated on it, Clifford in his new monogrammed collar, asleep on the arm of the couch. Two separate lives under one roof. A living arrangement called a marriage. It was a sham, a game of pretense. They could feel that sham peeking through the visage of their lives. It did not compel them to action. Instead, it froze them both where they were seated. Waiting without waiting.

CHAPTER 7

A string of boutique shops lined both sides of the street. Any time one of their doors was opened, the unique scent of the store boiled out. One of these shops was a restaurant that was open for both breakfast and dinner. During lunch, they would prop open their door and welcome anyone who wanted to eat there for free.

Aria had found this place in one of her searches on the library computers the week before. She had become accustomed to eating only one meal a day, if she were lucky. For the last two days, that one meal a day had been the soup and breadsticks offered here. She felt shy to go there, guilty even to be accepting charity. But this place was such a comfort. There was nothing fancy about it. The linoleum flooring was the same that had been put there in the 1950s. It was turning yellow and the extent of its pomp was a floral design that looked like it could have been copied from the draperies at an old age home. Plastic folding tables were covered with large sheets of paper that had been clumsily ripped. And plastic chairs, like the ones that had been ordered in bulk for her school cafeteria, were arranged around them.

A long line usually formed out the door and down the street, a line that boasted all kinds of people. Some who had not seen a shower in months, whose clothes were torn and fetid. Others who looked like they had simply walked off a job site to take opportunistic advantage of a meal they didn't have to pay for. When Aria reached the front of the line, she could see a collection of giant stainless steel vats, three flavors of soup to choose from each day. Their fragrances mixed into one, like a complex curry. Next to the soups were plastic tubs full of breadsticks left over from the day before. Aria reveled in their toasted and yeasty aroma.

Each person in line grabbed one of the brightly colored, plastic cafeteria trays, and told whichever staff member who happened to step forward from the disarray of multitasking which soup they wanted. They were handed a generous ladle of that soup in a large styrofoam cup, a plastic spoon with a napkin, three breadsticks and two handfuls of salted peanuts. On the way to the seating area, a row of self-service water jugs and paper cups lined the counter. Some days, Aria was lucky enough to find a table. Other days, she had to find a place on the sidewalk.

Today, Aria arrived early enough to find a place at a table. She planned on keeping to herself, and was fully involved in her relationship with the food alone when she was assaulted by the energy of unattuned enthusiasm belonging to a man who had decided to place himself in the chair directly beside her. There were plenty of tables open, she noticed. She was puzzled by his oblivious nature already. Common social protocol dictated that people would sit as far away from each other as possible, until there were literally no seats left and you had to sit next to one another, whether you liked it or not. The defiance of this social norm made her feel violated and distrust his motives. Though her body language reflected the sentiment, she tried not to overtly react to him so as to give those feelings away.

He was tall and effeminate with cadet-blue eyes, high cheekbones and an overhanging brow. At 19 years old, his lips were full and wide, just hiding a gap in his upper front teeth that was more fashionably quirky than it was unsightly. His hair was buzzed on the back and sides, leaving a quiff of bleached pompadour-style hair on the top of his head, which he had swept to one side as if frustrated with the way it wanted his attention. Aria did not pay attention to his pants. But she noticed that he was wearing a powder-blue shirt with cap sleeves, whose neckline dived almost far enough to expose his sternum. On the front, in white letters, were two words with boxes beside them, the first "Single" and the second

"Taken." The box next to the word single was run through with a check mark.

Not even half a minute passed before, growing uncomfortable in the tension between them, he decided to crack it. He put out his right hand, dissecting the space between Aria's face and her plate, and said, "I'm Taylor."

As if on involuntary autopilot, but still keeping turned to a distrustful angle relative to him, Aria put her right hand in his and accepted the handshake. "I'm Aria," she said.

She had planned to resign herself to an even more awkward silence sitting next to him after that, but he would not let it happen. "What's your deal?" he asked. "I mean, why are you here? I've never seen you here before."

Aria shrugged her shoulders, partially because she didn't know how to answer and partially because she did not want to give herself away. Seeing the shrug, Taylor turned away slightly to take the pressure of his focus off of her. "Oh, I see, you're not a talker. That's all I need today."

He took a sip from his water cup and began to whisper to himself in exasperation that he obviously wanted her to see. Though she could not fully hear what he was saying, it seemed he was having a dialogue with himself about the downward spiral caused by his bad luck. It was obvious the ulterior motive for sitting next to her was his need for connection, or at the very least, some mental stimulation.

Feeling guilty for the wall she had erected against him, Aria dialed down her coldness and said, "No I can talk, it's fine."

Instantly, his monologue stopped and his enthusiasm returned.

"Do you come here a lot?" she asked.

"Depends," he said. "Sometimes I'm here every day and sometimes not for a while. But I guess you could call me a regular." He winked at the staff behind the counter, who took no notice of him.

It was clear to Aria that this Taylor was lonely and that his method of coping with it was to invent an idea of closeness with people, where it didn't actually exist.

"Shouldn't you be in school or somethin'?" he asked in his blunt manner, which Aria had already ascertained was not rudeness, but rather the vein of his personality.

"I dropped out," she said, bracing herself for some kind of judgment that never came.

"Me too," he exclaimed through a mouthful of breadstick. He shouted it as if delighted to have something in common with someone … anyone at all. Immediately, he opened the door to his world for her. "I got jumped at a group home because I really didn't follow the rules and really they were just trying to get rid of me."

Aria felt a surge of contradictory feelings toward Taylor the minute that he said that. On one hand, she felt an immediate commonality and rapport because they had been in the same position. But just as immediately came the familiar ingrained feelings of competition. At the group homes, attention was scarce. For Aria, and most other children who grew up there, the feeling of hearing that someone grew up in group homes was similar to the feeling of opening a restaurant that your life was dependent on and having someone open a restaurant right next door to you on the same street.

But she consciously curtailed the feeling. Aria could read between the lines of what he was saying. She knew how bad it was for LGBT youth in group homes. But she let him continue to avoid telling her the real reason he had been jumped.

"My mom got breast cancer when me and my sister were really young," Taylor continued. "She went in for chemotherapy and when she came back, she wasn't the same mom anymore. She would beat us and scream at us and my dad left her 'cause of it. She'd put us in the crisis stabilization center for thirty days here and there, but pretty soon, they took us away for good because of it and then she died."

Although it was a story that would have been difficult to tell for most people, growing up in group homes and foster homes made it so that telling the story of the tragedy of your life became something routine. Something you could do with almost no emotion, as if it were just a matter of fact. Something the advocates would add tragic emphasis to when trying to get someone, like a foster parent or a judge or a teacher, to cooperate with their prerogatives.

"I was in over fifteen foster placements. Most of 'em just fostered us so they could get the government checks. They'd kick me out of the house in the morning and tell me not to come back until curfew, so I didn't get picked up by the cops."

Taylor continued to eat in a way that suggested he expected someone to take his food away before he was finished. While he ate, he bled himself clean of so many details of his life story that Aria was having trouble processing it all. Eventually, he turned the stage over to Aria, who reluctantly did the same in return, but with less zeal and decorative detail. He prompted it out of her with impolite but endearing questions.

By the time they had finished their food, Taylor had decided they were friends. Just like that, their paths through life were affixed together. When two people don't have a place to live or a set life to speak of, it doesn't work the same way it does for everyone else. You don't pop around for get-togethers and common interests on occasion and *gradually* get to know one another. Instead, you walk in the same direction rather than going your separate ways. You form a symbiosis until that symbiosis ends, which you have already learned could come at any minute.

Aria was glad of it, despite her reservations. Even though she was intimidated by Taylor's overly familiar nature, which felt foreign to her, she also felt sheltered by him. She felt softened by his casual way of implying that they had known each other for their whole lives.

— * —

Taylor and Aria returned their trays before leaving the shop. They walked north up the street, stopping to look in the windows any time Taylor noticed something exciting inside. Having stayed at the mission for three nights, Aria had exhausted her monthly admittance there, so that night, she followed Taylor to the back exit of a nightclub, where he had been sleeping and keeping his things in a friend's 1996 Buick LeSabre.

It was almost impossible to fall asleep. The sound of the bass from the club pounded like impending footsteps against her exhaustion. Taylor was unfazed by it. Having found a companion, he felt replete. They were cuddled under two flannel sleeping bags that had been unzipped to function as blankets, each leaning against opposite sides of the back seat, when Taylor made a confession. "I want to be an actor," he said. "I've been saving up for a year and a half now to go to LA."

He reached into the front pocket of one of the bags below his feet and pulled out a piece of paper that was now soft with wear, handing it to her. It was an advertisement he had printed off of craigslist.

WORK/STUDY POSITION AT LA'S PREMIERE SITCOM ACTING & WRITING SCHOOL

We are currently looking for creative people for our Work/ Study Program. Excellent attitude and willingness to learn a must. Social media skills are a plus. These are work/study positions – ongoing weekly acting class in exchange for a four-hour work shift each week. That means you come to our studio twice a week – once for your class time and once for your work/study shift. All terms and conditions for attending class apply.

This is an amazing opportunity to grow as an actor/ creator/writer by staying in an environment where you'll be guided into a career. Make one of LA's top acting schools your home base and surround yourself with dedicated, career-oriented actors and writers at a dramatically reduced price. Our studio has the best reviews of any acting studio in the city. Check out our incredible five-star reviews on Google and the testimonials on our site. Minimum six-month commitment. We look forward to hearing from you!

Aria handed it back to him when she had read it. She could feel the way he cherished it. "Isn't it awesome?" he said. "If I can get there, these people will teach me to be an actor. I'm gonna go next week."

"What do you like about acting?" she asked.

"I guess I like becoming someone else for a while," Taylor admitted. "One of the schools I went to used to put on plays sometimes. I loved being on the stage and just forgetting myself. I'd pretend I was the character I was playing and I'd try to feel what it was like to have their past instead of mine. I guess it feels good to just not be me for a little while.

"Plus I wanna be rich and I love to be the center of attention." He giggled as he owned up to it, then went on. "Plus I've got a friend there who said I could work at the restaurant she works at until I get accepted at the acting studio or land an acting gig, whichever comes first."

He was silent for a few seconds and then, as if hit by a stroke of insight, peeled back the corner of his side of the blanket and said, "You should come with me if you can. The bus costs two hundred bucks. I bet you could even work with me at the restaurant when we get there."

He looked at her like he expected an answer from her right then and there. She smiled at him and raised her eyebrows as if to say she'd consider it. Satisfied with the response, Taylor pulled the blanket back to buffer his face from the cold of the window, closed his eyes and leaned his cheek against it.

That night, after Taylor had fallen asleep, but before she could, Aria imagined herself as a waitress. She reached for the inviolable feeling of self-sufficiency.

She imagined waiting tables. She imagined what she would wear. Though it felt out of reach, she loved the idea.

She imagined LA to be a land of promises, a place where no one could hold you back from personal advancement. She could feel the sun on her face, she could imagine palm trees, which she had only seen in pictures but never in real life.

Just before she fell asleep, she found herself wondering what the leaves of palm trees really felt like, whether they were hard or soft. It didn't matter whether this vision of her future was given to her by someone else. What mattered was that suddenly she had one.

CHAPTER 8

On Sundays, at the community Christian church, the preacher stood in front of the pews, using a lectern to buffer himself from the onlooking crowd. Behind him, white organza fabric had been fashioned, like a curtain, to hide the bare wall behind it. Affixed to the center of the scene was a giant wooden cross, illuminated by cream-colored Christmas lights.

Aria was sitting in the pews. The sound of the lecture was drowned out in the churn of her thoughts. Aria had found hope in the idea of going with Taylor to Los Angeles. It was hope she had no intention of relinquishing. There was just one problem. She didn't have any money. Having exhausted every potential for making the money that she needed, she had finally resolved to steal it. It was now a matter of where to steal it from. Before settling upon church as the best place to go unnoticed while getting ahold of someone's wallet, it seemed she had spent the entire day running through different scenarios in her head. She eyed the purses sitting on the floor or beside women in the pews. She tried to profile people for how much of an impact the loss would have on them and for who might have the total amount she needed, instead of only part of it.

Halfway through the service, three musicians stepped up in front of the room. Their imperfect tones were loud on the notes they felt confident playing and soft on ones that they didn't. Aria was embarrassed for them. She couldn't figure out what the congregation was doing during this time, which seemed to be like a disorganized intermission. But when the woman sitting next to her handed her a giant basket full of bills, she realized that she was expected to make a tithing and pass it on to the next person. For a split second, she thought about making a run for it with the money. She passed it on, though, unable to face the implications of doing so.

But she could not stop thinking about that money. She watched the priest thank the crowd and hand it to a dutiful member of the congregation, who then disappeared with it into the hallway adjacent to the curtain. Aria waited for ten more minutes before pretending to excuse herself to the bathroom. She even asked a few people where it was. They pointed her in the opposite direction to where the man had gone.

Acting as if she was going to the bathroom, she sauntered into the outlying hallways of the building and wandered frantically through the maze of corridors, trying to ascertain where the money in that basket might have been taken. Soon, she spotted a door with a door mount that read "Pastor Ferguson." It was a long shot to think that it would be open. It was also a long shot to think that the money would be there. But Aria reached for the doorknob anyway. To her surprise, the door was open. She looked both ways to ensure that no one had seen her before slipping inside.

Sitting on the desk, as if part of a cosmic joke being set up in her favor, was the basket, still filled with money. Waiting for the pastor to allocate it to its proper place, it was just sitting there. Aria ran toward it and grabbed money out of it by the handful. She stuffed all but a few of the bills into her backpack as fast as she could, not bothering to count it, terror-stricken that someone might catch her in the act.

She waited a few seconds for the right moment to exit, and while she was waiting she caught sight of a picture of the pastor's family, neatly displayed in a frame on the bookshelf by his desk. In the picture, his wife and two kids were all wearing white T-shirts. It was a close-up taken at a park. They were smiling and posed as if to suggest that it was placed there to set an example to the other members of the church. As contrived as it was, before Aria exited, she felt that all-too-familiar punch of envy, the bait of a belonging that would never be hers.

Aria left the building in a collected manner that would have suggested to no one what she had done. She made her way into the waiting room of a hospital – Taylor had given her the idea that it was the perfect place for someone underage to go unnoticed by the police. Placing her backpack on her lap, she was able to disguise her actions in smoothing out and counting the money that she had just stolen. From what she could tell, it amounted to $519.

She felt torn. On the one hand, she felt guilty to have unintentionally taken so much more than she thought she had taken. On the other hand, it provided unfathomable relief. She entertained the idea of all of the things she could do with it, replacing the basic luxuries she had gone without. But then she remembered that she could not afford to just spend it. She didn't know what the future held and liked the security of knowing that she could use it as a kind of secret safety net.

Taylor had gone off to find food for both of them. When he arrived at the hospital, he was carrying a container of Chinese takeout, full to the brim with white rice. Rice was dead cheap. You could fill your belly with it to offset the hunger and buy yourself some time to find better food. Aria didn't tell him that she had stolen money. She hadn't even told him that she didn't have any in the first place. No matter how close they were to each other, they both knew that in a state of desperation, relational ties meant next to nothing.

For the first time in weeks, while Taylor napped in his chair, Aria took out her journal and wrote. She wrote about everything that had happened to her in the last few weeks. She cried as she wrote. It was as if her pen had uncorked everything she had been suppressing and the grief could finally get out. Like every day in the hospital, in those hygienic halls looking over the city, the windows kept grief in and held life out.

With a kind of cold devotion, the machines that kept lungs breathing in and out told of people's inability to see death clearly enough not to fear it or resist it.

Aria could see despair in the minds and movements of the people there, holding each other's grief tightly. Trying to survive the unknown together. Every trivial thing erased by the emptiness of loss ... By the earthquake of a moment of change. She felt at home there, with people who, due to the tragedies that required them to sit in that hospital waiting room, shared her despair.

— * —

A few mornings later, they approached the counter to purchase their tickets to Los Angeles.

"Hello, I'm Taylor and this is my sister. We're going home to see our father in Los Angeles. He's really sick and in the hospital, our mother is already there with him. We thought he was gonna get better, but he isn't so the whole family has to be there with him."

Taylor handed the receptionist a forged minor travel consent form and both of their drivers' licenses. There was an awkward moment. The woman behind the desk took the paper and the IDs and stared at them for a while, looking up at the two teenagers as if wary of making a mistake that would put her own job on the line.

Aria and Taylor felt the tension build and the insecurity start to pull their perfect plan apart at the seams. Aria was terrified that the police might have given her name to the bus station and that at any moment, she would have to make a run for it.

"At least one parent or guardian is supposed to be here at the counter to sign for an unaccompanied child," the woman eventually said. "But your sister is seventeen. Children seventeen years of age and older can travel unaccompanied with no restrictions, so she doesn't need this."

She placed the unnecessary document to the side of her desk and began to type on the computer in front of her. Her words let them off the hook. Taylor gave Aria a quick smile that expected acknowledgment back for his incredible talent at getting away with things – even if they hadn't needed the documents.

"I hope your father gets better," the woman said, as the printer beside her elbow spat out documents. "You two have a good trip. The bus departs at 6.30pm and it boards twenty minutes before departure, right out those doors," she said. She slipped two tickets and the IDs under the tiny opening in the bulletproof glass.

Taylor took them, saying, "Thank you, ma'am … come on, sis," and strolled away in a manner that would give the impression they were in fact brother and sister.

Guarding the tickets like treasure, Aria and Taylor spent the day waiting in the area near the Greyhound bus station to board the bus that would take them from Chicago to LA. They had entertained the idea of spending the day seeing the places in the city that they might miss and perhaps would never see again, but decided against it. They couldn't afford to miss the bus, even if that meant waiting the entire day for it to come.

First, they walked to the shade of a bridge by a river four streets away from the bus station. Motivated by their triumph, they took two rocks and laughed as they tediously scratched a message into the bridge's surface. The powder-white words "Goodbye Cruel World" began to emerge from the now-blemished grunge cement. They were conscious that if anyone saw the message, they would think that someone had committed suicide. They found it funny. But the words' true meaning was a goodbye to the life they had lived there in that city. They were bound for an entirely different life. A life that was no longer a dead end, but one full of possibility and promise.

They spent the rest of the day sitting outside a gas station, under the overhang of the roof, trying to nap and escape the bite of the sun. Aria surprised Taylor with a jug of peanut butter and crackers purchased with some of the extra $314 that remained from the money she'd stolen. They ate it together like it was a celebration meal.

By the time Taylor's twelfth check-in on what time it was with the gas station attendant resulted in the answer of "six o'clock," Taylor had worn out the man's patience. They lined up early with their tickets to board the bus. When the driver stepped down from the open door, wearing a fluorescent yellow vest, they felt the same tension that they had experienced earlier that day begin to revisit them. But all he did was check their tickets and motion them inside.

CHAPTER 9

The valleys and plains they passed along Highway 40, though dry, gave more of a lonely impression of open ocean than of land. The sun seemed to be fixed on life, sucking the water from everything. The main streets of the old western towns were littered now with impermanent chain stores. Absent of a building code, it looked as if the businesses that came there had all snagged themselves on the destitution, unprepared for the kind of customers who leave their Christmas lights on all year long. Since the beginning people had been coming to the West, mistaking the impression of endlessness for opportunity.

In her naivety, Aria had expected to see cowboys herding cattle on the plains, but the people who would be driving those cattle, growing gardens or canning their own food seemed to have been swallowed up by the wave of modern society and left behind by it. Now the cowboy, who once conquered the Native American, found himself conquered, his life made obsolete. To Aria's dismay, they lived in trailer parks or houses that were falling apart on the outskirts of what could hardly be called cities, living on cigarettes and chew and easy-access television. Instead of working the land, they worked on oil rigs or metal shops or corporate dairy farms because it was all they could afford to do.

The West was conquered barely over a hundred years ago and still, Aria could see it was already full of a hard-won, gunshot, broken history and the kind of wounds that never heal. But beyond the hot crackle of the grasshoppers, she found there to be a slow, heartbreaking beauty; a vastness that could never be possessed.

They traversed an unpeopled wilderness where the night sky was so dark, the stars were a bright, white dust instead of interspersed lights, not just those which could outshine the nebulous glow of the city. There were sunsets and wildflowers.

Animals outside cages, people outside metal and glass. A violent dance of nature, where life itself was distilled to its raw, original self.

The bus had driven through the night. Aria was staring at a man in an army uniform sitting three rows up from her. She caught herself wondering about his life, creating possible scenarios about where he was going and why. Scanning the rest of the occupants of the bus, she felt out of place amidst the rows and rows of blacks and Mexicans in front of her. Not that the bus felt like a safe place to be in the first place, but when the racial coin was flipped, she always felt as if one wrong move would bring centuries' worth of resentment for what her forefathers had done crashing down on her head. She felt outnumbered. Even so, Aria loved the way that so many people with so many different stories, most of whom would never cross paths in a lifetime, could all end up as if by fate in one place and on a temporary odyssey together.

Aria felt the bus slow and diverge from the highway when it pulled in for a morning meal stop on the day they were due to arrive in LA. It was one of 19 stops they made along the way. The turbulence it created woke up most of the passengers, including Taylor, who had been sleeping for nearly the entire two-day ride. His eyes opened, as if he were coming out of a daze. He sat straight up and looked around with a childlike movement that said "are we there yet?"

They had pulled over at a gas station that was conjoined to a Burger King. The driver announced that they would have 30 minutes before they were expected to be back on the bus. Promising Taylor to meet him back on the bus when she was done in the bathroom, Aria rounded the corner into one of the aisles, hoping to be hidden from view by the conflux of passengers perusing the shelves. She picked up items, assessing them one by one, hoping to appear normal, like every other customer. When she was sure that the people manning the counter were sufficiently overwhelmed with customer purchases and she was out of view of all of the security cameras in the room, she disguised her action as best as she could and picked up two honey-flavored granola bars, concealing them in her jacket pocket.

She felt disgusting. Disgusting for stealing and disgusting because she had not found a way to shower in too many days to count. At first she wandered into the bathroom to see if there was any way to wash herself there, but the constant influx of passengers made her decide against it. She stood in the hallway where the bathrooms were located, trying the few different doors that were there in the short spaces of solitude between customers entering the bathrooms. The first door turned up nothing but a storeroom full of boxes of unopened products. But the second turned out to be a utility closet. In the brief moment it took to glance inside, she saw that there was a sink there. Aria closed the door to pretend again that she was up to nothing long enough for a man who was headed for the bathroom to disappear inside. Then she opened the door again, snuck inside and locked the door behind her.

The cement floor was stained brown from years of heavy use. All around her, in some form of organized chaos, were cleaning products and tools, a collection of brooms, two ladders, a rolled-up hose and empty buckets thrown on top of one another. The yellow handle of a mop projected from the deep porcelain washbasin affixed to the wall. Rust stains had tainted its original color. Aria had collected three empty water bottles in her time since running away from the Johnsons. She had been using them for everything from gathering water in drinking fountains to filling them with hot tap water to keep her warm at night, to placing them on the ledges of windowsills to catch the light in a way that comforted her. She found it almost farcical that something she'd never thought twice about would be one of the things she now treasured the most.

Looking down to confirm that there was a drain in the center of the floor, she pulled the bottles from her backpack and began to fill each with water from the faucet. Still afraid to be discovered, she rushed to strip naked and place her clothes up on a high shelf, out of reach of any potential water spray. The water, not intended for the human skin, was freezing. As fast as she could, refilling the bottles again and again, she soaked herself with it. Tiny goosebumps began to rise up to meet the water.

Aria briefly looked for soap with which to clean herself, but only discovered a jug of solvent cleaner, intended for cleaning floors. She considered whether or not it would be dangerous for her skin, but decided to take the risk. She soaped herself vigorously, including the length of her hair, which she stuck under the faucet of the sink. She hoped that the force of the water would do a better job of washing the suds out than the trickle from the water bottles would.

When she was done, she patted herself off as fast as she could with sheets of paper towels she found on a roll sitting on the shelf beside her and squeezed the water from the ends of her hair with them. After pulling her clothes and shoes back on, she put the damp bottles back into her backpack. Aria stood there, holding on to the straps of her backpack and listening to what was happening on the other side of the door for a time, before deciding to exit. When she did, no one noticed. Aria didn't know whether that was a relief or whether she wanted them to notice. On the one hand, she did not want to get in trouble. She hadn't wanted them to catch her there. On the other hand, the ease with which she was going unnoticed made her nervous. She was beginning to feel invisible, as if she were a ghost. She was beginning to slip through the cracks in between people's caring.

Aria went outside to sit in the sun. Her wet hair made parts of the fabric of her coat look darker. Even though the air was cold that morning, the luxury of the sunlight wasn't lost on her. She let it caress the contours of her face. She opened the top of her coat to let it touch the edges of the ever-present ache in her heart, but was interrupted after a brief time by the sound of the bus driver giving everyone a five-minute warning.

She was the first person back on the bus. Taylor was
the last. He had made a nuisance of himself during their
meal break, failing to establish a rapport with any of the
passengers, with whom he had tried to establish several
connections. They seemed irritated by his chummy
demeanor. As he walked down the aisle, the few people with
an empty seat beside them seemed to tense up for fear that he
would sit down next to them. "Hey," he said, all but crawling
over Aria to claim the seat next to the window. "That felt
great to stretch my legs for a while."

Aria afforded him a customary smile. She extracted from her
pocket the granola bars that she had stolen and handed one
to him. For a half a second, he seemed taken aback, then said
"Ah, thanks" and immediately ripped open the packaging. The
homey oat-and-honey flavor mollified the both of them. As
the bus made its way back onto the highway, they ate without
talking, feeling lucky for the snack, which for both of them felt
like pure indulgence.

— * —

Taylor was in heaven. Out on the open road, he felt like life
was finally moving forward. When he was getting what he
really wanted, his body had a way of responding by letting go
of the pain of years of not getting it. It did so with memories
and it did so with tears. Instead of sleeping, he listened to Aria
begin to write in her journal and stared out the window at
the blur of sagebrush and other cars passing by. His eyes were
burning, having welled up in response to memories that his
body was exhaling up and into his awareness.

He remembered when he was five years old and had wanted
a bike so badly. He wanted it so that he could feel just the
way he felt now. He had woken up on his birthday to see a
bike poorly wrapped in wrapping paper in the center of the
living room, waiting for him. Later that day, he and his older
brother had gotten into a fight over it and, as a punishment,
his mother had forced all of the kids into the car. She drove to

the Salvation Army store where she had purchased the bike and then proceeded to force him to re-donate it. He remembered the divine weight of the bike when the man at the store took it from him. He had gained his freedom and, in the same day, had lost it.

He remembered the incarceration of the group homes. When he was 12 years old, two other boys at his group home had placed two of their CDs inside his room and then reported them missing. When the staff had resorted to a room check and had found the "missing" CDs in his room, they immediately called the police. If Taylor had been a kid in a normal family home, the consequence for stealing would be a scolding or losing TV time or being grounded. In the group home, the consequences were the cops being called. No matter what he said, they would not believe that he hadn't taken them. And so, he became hysterical. Eventually, in response to the escalation, the staff made the decision to drug him with antipsychotic medication. He was arrested and taken to the juvenile detention center. He remembered thinking that except for the fact that he was completely alone in the detention room, jail was not much different than the group home.

He remembered sitting in front of the judge, who scowled at him with displeasure, passing judgment for something he had never done. Judgment from an ignorant position of never having lived through any of the conditions that he had been forced to live through. Taylor wished the judge would suffer the same way that he had suffered, but knew that day would never come.

When Taylor had tried to explain himself, the judge had barked, "I'm not buying it today," and had sentenced him to both probation and counseling. When he was released from the detention center, he was driven to an entirely different group home. He had been transferred. This was what it had felt like when he was young, an endless routine of hopping, of never belonging to one place, of never staying long enough to grow roots.

As he watched the country passing by, Taylor felt like he was leaving the prison of it all behind. He felt defiant and victorious. He saw his father's face in his mind. Taylor couldn't decide if his father had been sad to lose him or if he was glad to see him go. He wondered why he was not enough. Not enough to value, not enough to want. Not enough to make his father stay, instead of leaving them all behind when he did. The cool of his father's indifference could not calm Taylor's fury at not being loved enough. He felt the agonized sea of parting ways crack and heave against his heart. The sound of his heartbreak rang like a bell underwater. But he did not break under the blow of it. The hope he held for the life he was headed toward wouldn't let it happen. He was done wanting, done waiting for a life he would never have there. He was done wanting things from people who would never give those things to him. As they were driven across that open country, the promise he made himself – not to return to where he had come from, unless he came home a big success – amounted to little more than a whisper. But that whisper was still a vow.

The austerity of the desert eventually converted itself to palm trees and freshly watered lawns. They had arrived in Los Angeles before dinnertime. It felt strange to Aria to watch the people she had spent the last couple of days with scatter and disappear, knowing she would most likely never see any of them again.

The quality of the air was completely different. The city buzzed with enterprise and it excited her. She could tell immediately that the law of that land of opportunity was "every man for himself," but there seemed absolutely no one to try to get in your way. Every person they passed walking out of the bus station seemed to be striving for something and to be so busy in the striving for it that they had no time for anything or anyone. They were observing that fast current toward success, knowing that soon, they too would be in it … but not today.

It was so crowded at the station that Taylor took her hand to lead her through the crowd toward a row of silver and black pay phones. He shuffled around in various pockets to produce a phone number written on a piece of napkin. Holding the phone between his shoulder and face, he dialed the number. He was still, listening to the dial tone for what seemed like forever. Despite the crowd, Aria could hear him leave a message. "Hey, it's Taylor. I'm in LA! I brought a friend with me. I'm gonna call you back in a little bit because you didn't pick up. We could really use some help around the city. Do you know anywhere that we could stay the night? OK, call you back soon."

Taylor repositioned the telephone receiver in its holster and looked at her with a slightly embarrassed look, as if disappointed with himself that she was now in the position of waiting with him and not knowing exactly what to do. Aria pretended to just barely come up with enough money to go half in with Taylor on a packet of corn nuts and strawberry Pop Tarts from the vending machine. They sat down to eat in the waiting area of the station and exchanged observations about the other people and their initial impressions of the city.

Taylor tried six more times over the next five hours to reach his friend. He left upbeat, eager messages each time. Aria began to wonder whether this friend of his was truly a friend or whether, like everyone else in his life, she was just someone with whom he had conjured an imaginary sense of closeness. The sun had now set on the infant hours of their time in this new life, so, having resolved to try calling again in the morning, they set out walking.

Both of them felt daunted by the newness of this place. The more familiar you are with a place, the easier it is to navigate yourself through it. They were learning the hard way just what parts of familiarity they had taken for granted. Not wanting Aria to be targeted for the curfew violation they had heard applied in LA to any unaccompanied minor, they spent only short times in plain view of the cars passing by.

Eventually, out of options and exhausted, they decided to spend the night under a freeway overpass they had noticed during their walk, which already had a few tents under it. Taylor and Aria both imagined that the permanent-looking nature of the camps were a good indication that the people living there had already established it as a safe place to be. The chances of being singled out and harassed by cops among the other vagrants were smaller. Being careful not to impose on preciously guarded territory, they sat down a short distance from one of the tents. The people there, heavily layered in tattered clothing, seemed to exist in their own little worlds. None of them even acknowledged a change when the two sat down to claim a portion of the territory.

The static hiss of the cars passing by overhead inflicted itself on their attempts to fall asleep. That night, they did not give each other space. Instead, they were braided together, hoping that body warmth would quell their angst. The ground was cold and unforgiving, as was the incline that promised to keep them dry should any rain fall. It was a strange, distorted form of safety. They both slept fitfully, never quite dropping into the dark tranquility of sleep. Instead, they spent the night engaged in the gnarled and fragmented images of the shallow dreams that exist just above it.

When morning came, the sun did not get a chance to wake them; discomfort did. Their bodies throbbed and did not move with their usual quickness. They said nothing to each other, but tried to rouse themselves from the hangover of exhaustion. The sun had not risen yet. Instead the light had converted itself into purple.

It took a few moments for the slowness to be pierced through by panic. Aria had wrapped her backpack around the bottom of her leg, sure she would react should anyone try to take it. But now she reached out to find it gone. "God damnit!" she yelled, causing Taylor to jump too. "Someone stole my fucking backpack. I can't believe it. Someone stole my fucking backpack."

She jumped to her feet, her eyes scanning the area around them frantically. She was furious at herself. She was furious at the stupidity of not holding it between them, or at the very least using part of it as a pillow, like Taylor had done. She was uneasy with herself that she hadn't woken up at the sound of it being taken.

Aria knew the likelihood of finding the backpack again was slim. But against all odds, she saw something vaguely the color of it just over a hundred meters away. She left Taylor to run over to take a look. As she got closer, she could tell it was indeed her backpack. Now all she felt was the fear of what inside it might be missing. The crunch of broken glass broke through her leery focus. It called her attention to the ground. Sparkles had spilled out across the gravel. A short distance away, the globeless base to the snow globe she had brought with her was lying there on its side. She rushed forward and searched desperately through her discarded backpack.

The money was gone, all of it. Whoever had taken it had thrown and scattered whatever contents of the backpack that they didn't have a use for before abandoning the scene.

Aria gathered her clothes and her journal and the plastic bottles, zipping the body of her backpack around them. She lifted it onto one shoulder and stared down at the base of the snow globe. The bright yellow cartoon-like half moon and the tiny figure of the girl sleeping on top of its bottom curve were now chipped and exposed to the dirt of the floor. She remembered how she used to play in the dirt as a child. Back then the dirt seemed to make this world whole. She remembered how as a child, she used to pretend. Or maybe she didn't pretend at all and that was what made it all so much more perfect than this. She remembered how many times she had escaped the torture of her world by imagining herself to be cradled inside the safe confines of that snow globe. She had imagined she was the girl that the moon held, come to life. She had imagined the benevolent cradle of that moon underneath her. She imagined the sparkles falling against her face.

That was a game for a child. In just one night, Los Angeles had stripped that innocence and safety from her. Even though it was difficult, Aria left the snow globe behind, an emblem of the life she had walked away from. She left behind not only the comfort it had given her, but also every circumstance that caused her to require that comfort in the first place. It was almost poetic. She walked back toward Taylor before he could reach her. It was a poem that belonged to her alone.

PART TWO

FUGUE CONCERTO

CHAPTER 10

Aria felt the all-too-familiar cinching, the slippery, warm feeling of newly sloughed blood. Having been so preoccupied with surviving day to day, she had forgotten that it had been over a month already since her last period. She looked around for some kind of quick solution, but there wasn't one.

"I think I just got my period," she said in an abashed tone. She rushed down an alleyway between buildings and rustled with her shoes, trying to remove them before she bled through the inseam of her camo pants. Being careful not to step on the floor with them, she removed her socks and wadded them into a makeshift pad, and motioned to Taylor who was staring at her, looking concerned. "Can you come stand over here and shield me?" she asked him.

"Do you want me to look away?" he asked.

"It doesn't matter," Aria replied.

Taylor leaned against the wall of the building, using the bulk of his shape to conceal her, while trying to act like he was just hanging out there in the alleyway. Aria tried to flatten herself against the wall of the building. She unbuttoned and unzipped her pants just far enough to be able to slip the socks between her legs. She felt like a slave to her own body, which had now put more pressure on her, as if everything else was not pressure enough. This was not an aspect of life on the street that she had even considered before today.

They'd decided to abandon their attempts to call Taylor's friend who had promised to help him if he ever came to LA. She had not picked up a single one of his phone calls. Instead, they took three hours to reach a public park and Aria went straight into the public bathroom. She washed her socks out at one of the sinks as fast as she could, to cover up what she was doing. Her blood blushed deep crimson against the steel shine of the sink.

Aria filled up one of her empty water bottles and squirted a stream of orange hand soap from the dispenser into her hand. Using her elbow to try to latch the door of the bathroom stall closed, she straddled the toilet and used the soap and water from her bottle to wash herself off. Knowing she would bleed through toilet paper, she used it temporarily while trying to dry off her socks under the hand drier. It soon became obvious that she wasn't going to be able to get them any drier without it taking too much time, seeing as how she had to stop for the other women who needed to dry their hands. So she folded her socks together and put them back in place. She would have to stay there near the bathroom for the rest of the day. Perhaps for the next five days.

While she was cleaning herself up, Taylor resolved to make them some money so Aria could get a packet of sanitary pads. He told her he had a soft spot for women because he'd had a lot of sisters over the years and he'd seen what they had to go through every month. So she spent the majority of the day moving from place to place in the park, watching Taylor passively panhandle next to a crosswalk just outside the park fence with a sign that said "Hungry, Anything Helps." Aria didn't know what to do with the kindness. She felt dissected by it. One part of her wanted to soak up the solace of that care and trust it. Another part of her wanted to stop him from doing it. She feared that this would simply put her in emotional debt to him and flip the axis of power in his favor. She didn't trust people to do good things to her if they had the upper hand. She had no way to get ibuprofen, like she usually took for cramps, so during the three times that she had to revisit the bathroom to wash the socks and dry them again to the best of her ability, she tried to relieve the pain. She splashed cold water on her face and on the back of her neck to thwart the sweating. She contorted herself into different positions, hoping that one of them would take the edge off of the sharpness of the ache.

The pain had created a deleterious state of mind and she saw Taylor through it. She watched the people walking by him. She watched people pretend that he didn't exist. She watched people scream at him to get a job. And she watched him shoulder the dehumanizing treatment in the same determined way as he maintained his affability even when everyone seemed perturbed by it and pushed him away. She felt a fondness growing for him. Because his sexual inclination was toward other men, there was something pure about the link between them. People had deceived her before and people had disappointed her even more times than that. But with Taylor, it seemed the only ulterior motive he had was to feel like he had someone in the world to exist with. It occurred to her while she was watching him that she might actually have a friend.

By the time it got dark, Taylor's efforts had resulted in a few coins over $7. They decided to walk to the closest store they could find. Having spotted the giant blue letters and yellow spark logo of a Walmart, they cut through the crowd of other shoppers dallying in the aisles until they reached the pharmacy section. They examined the shelves for the cheapest solution to Aria's predicament. Aria soon realized that she would have to choose between them eating that night and buying pads. She evaluated whether she wanted to be clean, or whether she wanted to be full.

"Let's get something to eat instead," she said dejectedly.

"Well, what are you gonna do?" Taylor chided, as if suddenly broken from the rhythm of his mission. "I don't want you to have to be bleeding everywhere."

Aria mustered up a look of enthusiasm to mask her true feelings and responded, "Nah, I'll figure something out. It's not like I can just come in here every time I have a problem. Besides I'm starving, aren't you?"

Taylor looked at her suspiciously, but soon agreed to walking to the other end of the store. After some deliberation about what to buy, they decided in favor of practicality. They eventually walked to the checkout stand with bananas, the cheapest protein bar they could find and a can of tuna on special.

After setting out on foot again, Aria and Taylor sat on a strip of lawn outside the Walmart, watching the cars come and go. Taylor struggled with his pocketknife to open the lid of the tuna can. When it finally opened, he offered some to Aria but she declined and peeled back one of the bananas instead. She was determined not to give up her principles for the sake of her own survival. She could not find it in herself to choose her own wellbeing over the death of another being. She was already thin, but, looking down at her forearms, she could see that her hunger had stripped away all unnecessary flesh. It had worn her down to the sinew, and, having seen her face in the bathroom mirror so frequently that day, she knew her face was gaunt.

Not wanting to take the risk of ending up somewhere worse than where they were already, Taylor and Aria spent the night behind the Walmart, hidden between a collection of blue crates, topped with compacted cardboard boxes. Aria left Taylor sleeping and made trips to the bathroom to wash out her socks that were serving as a substitute menstrual pad.

Later that week, Aria got more creative. When they passed a Starbucks on the way to the library, she worked up the courage to pop inside and ask one of the men behind the counter for a few packets of plastic utensils. He handed them over with quizzical slowness. Aria pulled a pile of napkins free from its dispenser and went to the bathroom with them. She unwrapped the plastic package from the utensils and placed the napkins on top of it, so that if she bled through the napkins, it would collect in the plastic.

Aria had to deliberately plan her week around whatever restrooms were available to the public. A couple of times, other women who visited the restroom at the same time looked at her as if they had guessed that she was homeless. Aria hated that. She abhorred being looked down on. There were times on the street when she watched everyone else rushing around the world like they were caught in one big hamster wheel. At times like this, she felt better than them, possessing a self-government that they severely lacked. But, at other times, she felt subhuman and humiliated to be looked at like a pest or pitied.

Beaten by the trials of the week, Taylor's optimism had diminished to a sanguine commitment to do the best he could with whatever he had. Aria had figured out by the second day what it took Taylor the week to accept. She could tell that he was deluded: sure that the person he considered a friend was in fact a friend, when the truth was she wasn't. Sure that he would have support and opportunities once he made it here, but he didn't.

After a close call with police, who were placing notices to vacate on camps in one of the places they tried to stay for the night, they trailed a couple of the men when they packed up to leave. Taylor had the idea that perhaps the men would lead them somewhere where the chances of getting hassled by police was lower. And if not, the worst that could happen was that they would discover other potentially useful places in the city. Instead, they ended up on a street that made them both all too aware of their inexperience.

When the Union Rescue Mission in LA opened its doors in the 1800s, people without jobs, hobos and transient workers congregated there because it was the last train stop in the country. Naturally, the infrastructure that built up around it catered specifically to both transience and poverty. In the late 1900s, the city adopted a "policy of containment" whereby the services for the homeless and needy were moved directly to the places where they had already naturally collected. The area was called Skid Row.

The scene that greeted Taylor and Aria was one they'd have expected to see on the television after a national disaster in a third world country – not on an ordinary night of the year in the United States. The street was lined with disheveled tents and makeshift plastic tarps, propped up over piles of clutter. Hundreds – maybe even thousands – of men, woman and children, rotting under the iron hand of poverty.

Shopping carts full of every possession that their owners had. A paralyzing smell. Urine and feces stained the sidewalks, but people didn't seem to care, or couldn't care because there was nothing they could do about it. Drunk and high, or having succumbed to the decay of hunger, people sprawled out against the pavement and chain-link fences. Luxury lofts rose above the blighted lane, like specters cruelly reminding the people below of the luxuries that they would never have. Aria could feel the precarious overcast of crime lurking just underneath the patrolling eye of the cop cars that seemed to be making supervising rounds throughout the area. Concerned with criminal justice instead of human rights, they felt more like sharks ready to attack at any moment.

An internal warning of danger screamed at her through her nerves. She couldn't stay there. "I can't do this," she said, expecting to be met with resistance. But there was none.

"Yeah, fuck this, let's just go back to Walmart tonight, this is disgusting," Taylor said. They did an about-face and walked back the way they had come, hoping to go unnoticed. During the walk back to Walmart, the initial shock of the experience compelled them to exchange remarks back and forth, in search of mutual validation about how bad the place had been. And then both Taylor and Aria fell into a self-preoccupied silence.

Now that her period had started, Aria was regretting running away more than ever. Suddenly the problems that had caused her to run away seemed minimal in comparison to what she was facing now. The details of her former life seemed sweeter than she had originally believed. So many things she had taken for granted. The memory of them moved in slow motion, like a scene from a movie deliberately trying to be nostalgic.

She was in torment. Before finding a hiding place to lie down for the night with Taylor, Aria sat in a stall in the Walmart bathroom and cried.

CHAPTER 11

Bravery had a way of finding Aria, where mercy would not. They say a woman can't be until a girl dies, and the girl inside Aria was dying. Either that or she was retreating into the dark recesses beyond her reach. Her innocence was not welcome in this new life. Like all women on the streets, she had been forced to accept that there were people who found beauty only in broken things, people who hid their secrets behind the voiceless. But these people did not admire what was already broken; instead, they broke things to create that pleasure for themselves. They did not confide in people who would keep the shame of their demons safe because of vulnerability. They placed the stains on their conscience inside those who could not speak for themselves, instead of cleansing them.

Aria was learning the hard way that life for anyone on the streets was not as free as she had once imagined because life on the streets was not safe. It was even less safe if you were a woman. Hypothermia, heatstroke, rape, violence, infection, sunburn, arrest, insanity, injuries with nowhere to go to treat them, hunger and malnutrition seemed to follow you when you lived out on the street, like an invisible vulture, simply waiting for you to take a fall. And choosing a companion who was as out of place and flamboyant a target as Taylor made it even less safe.

They decided to spend their day at the closest library they could find to seek a safe refuge. Upon arriving, they went their separate ways inside the building. Taylor went to look for jobs online at the computer lab and Aria found a corner with a collection of chairs. She picked up a large cookbook with which she intended to conceal the fact that she was napping. She weighed her exhaustion against the chances that doing so would get her in trouble and decided that she still looked more like a student who was not preoccupied with her appearance than someone who had come in off the street. She hoped that anyone who saw her there would find the fact that she had fallen asleep more endearing than offensive. She drifted off into a dreamless sleep that was far deeper than she had intended.

She was awoken by a hand on her shoulder. "The library is closing," a woman said in a tone that suggested she felt bad for having to wake her up and send her on her way. It didn't matter if the woman seemed to be fine with the fact that she had fallen asleep. Aria's body felt like it had been dropped out of thin air, consumed by the fiery flush of both embarrassment and adrenaline. She nodded in acknowledgment and jumped to her feet so fast that she didn't notice the torn piece of paper upon which Taylor had written in undeniably poor handwriting: *I'm going to a temp office, I'll be back as fast as I can. Wait here for me. Love Taylor.* The note fell to the floor and under the chair she had been sitting on. Taylor had found her sleeping and, having decided not to wake her, placed it on her lap.

The lights in the library had dimmed. The stores in the foyer had closed their doors for the night. Aria was confused, having been suddenly jarred into a reality where it seemed that she had missed so much. After exiting the building into the congregation of other homeless people who, along with her, had suddenly been ejected from their sanctuary, she looked back through the windows to see if she could find Taylor still inside. She felt her stomach sink. Not knowing what else to do, she sat down on the grass. *Did he fucking abandon me here?* she thought to herself.

Aria had been wrong about people before. But this just seemed so drastically out of character, especially given that they both seemed to be each other's lifeline. She felt sick. Her world was spinning. Her mind was flailing to reach for ideas about what had happened and what to do now, as if those ideas were buoys in the middle of a deep ocean full of sharks. After about half an hour, that all-too-familiar feeling of bad luck got the better of Aria. She was doing her best to stay in the light from the street lamps and blend in with the crowd, which was largely ignoring her. Since she was a child, it had dawned on her that some people are lucky. They see themselves in the faces staring back at them. They are not strangers in the world. Some people feel the warmth of connection; they are not worn thin by wariness. But to Aria, her own voice sounded like a wolf's cry in a chorus of bleating. She was a stranger in this world. She had no one and she had nothing to belong to.

Aria had resigned herself to accepting that as if things could not get any worse, now she was alone, when Taylor's voice rattled across the distance from nearly a block away. "Aria!" he was yelling again and again. He walked toward her rapidly.

The relief of hearing his voice was ineffable. But the closer he got, the more that relief turned into resentment. She would have confronted him about simply leaving her there to think she had been abandoned without saying a word, but she saw that Taylor was walking toward her with someone else in tow. The rupture between them, known only to Aria, was left unmended because it was suddenly less important than the approach of a total stranger – and his dog.

"This is Luke," Taylor said, before he had even reached her. And once he did, "This is Aria," he said, waiting for the pair to shake hands. Luke took the initiative in a way that suggested that he respected the necessary distance that Aria's body language implied she required from him.

Aria looked down at his dog, who was held close to him with a striped, dirt-stained bungee cord. "This is Palin," Luke said, with a chuckle. Aria later learned he had named his dog after Sarah Palin, the politician who had run for vice-president. It made him laugh to have displayed his disdain for her as a person and for her policies by "keeping her on a leash like the politician's pet that she was." He also considered it to be a brilliant way of advertising his liberal political persuasions to anyone who he happened to meet on the road. It was a great way to sort out potential foes from potential friends.

It was obvious that Luke adored her. Unlike so many of the dogs Taylor and Aria had seen who lived with their owners out on the street, Palin was in perfect condition. She looked a bit like a border collie, simply taller. Most of the long hair on her body and ears was black. But the tip of her tail, her legs, underbelly, shoulders, neck and face were white with black freckles of all different sizes. White eyelashes accented amber brown eyes, which looked far too human to be dog eyes. In fact, everything about her seemed more human than dog, especially her facial expressions. Her intelligence was palpable, making for an equal personality mix of sweet and sassy. Aria reached down to pet her and she closed her eyes with pleasure under the touch.

"We met at the temp office, he has somewhere we can stay." Taylor's voice cut through the moment of connection.

"Yep," said Luke. "Are you hungry?"

Aria nodded, still hesitant to fully let him in. Luke took off his tall, metal-framed camping backpack and rifled through the compartments. He shoveled her out a few handfuls of bulk trail mix from a plastic bag. Aria almost laughed out loud, but, afraid to be rude, she smiled instead and said, "Thank you."

"No problem, man, don't worry about it," Luke responded, pleased with his capacity to help where help was needed. Everything about Luke seemed stereotypical to Aria – and the trail mix was the epitome of cliché.

Luke was a "Crusty." That was the not-so-affectionate term given to people who were homeless not through circumstance, but by choice. He had abandoned the 9-to-5 lifestyle in favor of train-hopping, hitchhiking and panhandling. Luke's homelessness was a statement against "the man." He despised the government and he was not afraid to let everyone know it. His life on the streets was a form of passive activism. And his rebellion made him feel free. But Aria knew what he did not. She knew that a Crusty's rebellion was not freedom. It was not choosing a life for what they wanted. It was choosing a life *against* what they did not want.

As they walked, Aria listened to Luke, and studied him carefully. Unshaven and unwashed, he hid his blatant irresponsibility beneath a head of sandy red dreadlocks that fell just below his shoulder blades. It was not that she disagreed with his opinion on things. In fact, she agreed with pretty much everything he said. It was just what he had decided to do with that opinion – that was where they parted company.

She could not work out whether she liked him or hated him because of the mixed message of his entire state of being. She felt guilty for the resistance that she felt toward him because he was being so incredibly friendly. In fact, when she thought about it, the friendliness he exhibited was advocacy. This made her feel simultaneously supported and looked down upon. It became clear to her that he saw people like her as the underdogs in society. And he had joined them with the same forced philanthropy and imposed-but-false equality as the whites who had joined the Black Panther movement in the 1960s.

She hated feeling pitied. She hated it when the surface of things did not match what was underneath. It was clear that Luke's sense of equality with everyone else on the street was just a surface veneer and that under it, he saw himself as their hero – and maybe their savior.

Aria followed just behind Taylor and Luke, next to Palin. She watched them talk and agree with one another about the plethora of conspiracy theories that had caused Luke to abandon his mainstream life. She could feel the rapport building between them. Taylor was thrilled to have someone to talk to. It was obvious to Aria, watching them talk, that she had deprived him of his need for verbal stimulation with her tendency to be silent. In Luke he had found someone in the world even more apt to dominate a conversation than himself.

Though dirty and full of holes, every item he was wearing from top to bottom and every item in his possession, from his North Face backpack to his outdoor-enthusiast hiking boots, was of the highest quality. At one point, when they stopped to take a rest, he folded his legs in such a way as to perfectly expose the label on the waistband of his pants. Aria laughed out loud when she saw the capital letters Georgio Armani.

Taylor and Luke stopped to see why she had laughed but she passed it off by saying "It's nothing" and let them resume their conversation. By now, Aria had him all figured out. Luke was a rich kid who couldn't do right by his daddy. Their high standards and workaholic tendencies had driven him to want to find some connection that couldn't be found in his tennis matches or piano lessons. He obviously failed to conform to what his father wanted. So he got fed up with it one day and threw it all away. Aria felt no sympathy for him at all. To her, it was blasphemy for him to believe he even knew what suffering was. She could not shake the feeling of irritation she had toward him. She was glad that both he and Taylor seemed oblivious to it.

After a couple of hours, they had reached a part of the city that seemed to bleed into the arid nature that surrounded it. Luke showed them where to sneak through the chain-link fence and scrub trees surrounding what appeared to be an abandoned auto shop. Through the dark, Aria could just make out that the red and yellow stripes across its exterior had faded from neglect. Peering through the inky fog of night that had settled across the city, she could see that the large lot around the shop was cluttered with broken-down cars, many of which were missing wheels, hoods or other parts. Having not been washed in years, they looked like they had been salvaged from a natural disaster. Interspersed between the cars were a few tents and the occasional blue tarp, covering collections of clutter underneath them. There was no one to be seen apart from a boot belonging to one of the camp's inhabitants that was sticking out from underneath a blanket.

Careful to be quiet, they followed Luke to his tent. Like everything else that he possessed, the tent looked like something only a rich kid would have. Aria asked Luke if there was anywhere to use the bathroom. He pointed to the

left and told her, "We mostly just find a place in the woods."
She left the boys to walk to the perimeter of the property and
climbed over the fence into the scrub sage and stunted oak
trees surrounding the lot. Making sure that there was no one
around to catch her, she peed in the tall grass before climbing
back over the fence to find Luke and Taylor again.

Luke guaranteed them, even though they never asked, that
tomorrow he would help them to find a place there to establish
their own camp if they wanted. But that night he invited them
to stay with him. Aria watched him hurry to push everything
in his tent over to one side to make room for them. His
lengthy conversation with Taylor had not ceased, it simply
buzzed through exaggerated whispers. Even though Aria had
slept almost the entire day, she was still so tired that when she
lay down on the other side of Taylor, who was thrilled to be
sandwiched between her and Luke and Palin, the airy sound of
their voices quickly lulled her to sleep.

Aria was glad to be taken under someone's wing, even if
that someone was as obnoxious as Luke. She was glad that
the deafening noise of the city could only be heard as a breath
in the distance. She was glad to have the pressure of Taylor's
incessant need for conversation temporarily taken off her. She
was even more glad that, contrary to what she had feared just
hours earlier, she was not spending the night alone.

CHAPTER 12

The metallic twang of an old Martin guitar being poorly tuned pulled Aria from her slumber. The sun had been up long enough that it had made the condensation on the inside of the tent tepid. She listened to whoever was playing the guitar stop and start again and again, trying to master a song that she had never heard before.

Palin stood up and stretched out across them, waking up both Taylor and Luke. Luke pulled her on top of his body, smothering her in affectionate kisses and baby talk. Palin was snuggly in the morning. She seemed to bathe in the re-establishment of closeness that took place when people came back from the short parting of dreamtime to greet her. When Luke had moved his attention to changing his shirt and pants for the day, not thinking that anyone was watching him, Palin made her way over to repeat her snuggle routine with Aria. She flicked Aria's face with her little black nose while being prevented from licking it. Aria held her muzzle still and planted a kiss on it, making the dog exhale a little sneeze. Aria was in heaven running her fingers through her cottony hair and feeling the weight of Palin's perfect trust against her.

Luke unzipped the tent just in time for Taylor to sit up straight and stretch his arms across both of their faces. "Who lives here?" Aria asked Luke, wanting to get a feeling for what she was about to be met with before exiting the tent.

"Well, it's just a group of us who decided to create a little community, I guess you could say," Luke explained. "That over there is Mike." He pointed to the man who was playing the guitar. His white hair was tied in a ponytail behind his head and shrouded by a black trucker's hat. "That over there is EJ," he said, indicating a thin man who was sitting half in and half out of a broken-down black Camaro. "That's Ciarra," he said, pointing to a woman who was watching herself brush her hair in the wing mirror of a giant purple van. Then he pointed to a tarp on the right. It was tied between the fence and two trees. "Anthony lives there. He's on a trip so you'll meet him later."

By this point, Aria couldn't take everything in. But Luke continued anyway, and she didn't stop him. "That place belongs to Robert. He's a great guy, you'll like him," he went on, pointing to a lime-colored one-man tent with a bike near the perimeter of the lot. "Oh, and that's Wolf," he said, pointing to a Native American-looking man walking across the lot. "And that place over there belongs to Darren." He gestured to an abandoned RV.

Aria counted them and said, "So eight of you live here?"

"Well, nine because Ciarra has a son, and ten if you count Palin." Luke petted her head as an affirmation of her importance.

"Do you all know each other?" she asked.

Luke answered her with an air of humor that said everything his words did not. "Some of us did before. We all know each other now. I wouldn't say that all of us are friends. But we're like roommates." He switched topics despite Aria's curiosity. "Are you guys hungry? I know a place if you are."

"Hell, yes," Taylor replied, looking at Aria like he had hit the jackpot by meeting Luke. He gathered his things as if he intended to take them along.

"Nah," said Luke, "you don't have to take your stuff. That's the benefit of living here – we sorta watch out for each other, ya know? You can leave your stuff here, no one's gonna take it."

"Oh, cool," Taylor said and dropped what he was doing. Aria wasn't so quick to trust the other people in the camp. There was only so much you could trust desperate people with. She pulled her backpack on and scooted out of the tent, waiting for Luke to take the lead again.

"Hey!" She heard a voice cut across the car lot. "Who you got?"

The woman who had been brushing her hair in the wing mirror was walking toward them. Aria was caught off guard by her gregarious nature. She was wearing a pair of cut-off jean shorts and a purple tank top. Her stringy brown hair was streaked with highlights whose roots had grown out a long time ago. Her skin was mottled with purple acne scars.

"I'm Ciarra," the woman said, extending a stiff hand directly at Aria, like a knife meant more to establish dominance than affinity.

She accepted the handshake as fast as she could. "I'm Aria."

"I'm Taylor," Taylor interjected enthusiastically, giving her his hand to shake.

Ciarra turned her focus back to Aira. "I like your hair," she said, crossing all the usual boundaries of social etiquette to touch it. Aria was noticeably uncomfortable, but let Ciarra do whatever she wanted to establish that she was not to be considered a threat.

The dance of hierarchy that so often played out between women, which was playing out now between herself and Ciarra, was exhausting Aria. She could tell that Ciarra had no interest in her except as an opportunity to establish her superiority. Luke's voice cut through the tension. "I met these guys yesterday. They're good people. They're gonna stay here for a while."

Ciarra pursed her lips and raised her eyebrows, nodding up and down as if to say, "Just who do you think you are to make that sort of decision?" But she simply said "Ah, OK. Well, tell me if you want to go shopping, I know all the good places, and make sure to introduce them to everyone else so no one tries to shoot 'em." She winked at them in a seductive manner, satisfied with having elicited fear.

Aria watched her walk back to the van. She was intimidated by Ciarra. But she was also envious of the way Ciarra seemed to tame the world around her. That was not something Aria felt able to do.

Taylor, Luke and Aria walked a long distance until they reached a church that Luke had promised contained a food pantry. Aria had expected to find a soiled storeroom with various canned goods, which she would then have to try to figure out how to open. But to her surprise, the line that they found themselves in led up to a plastic table where a woman was handing out sandwiches wrapped in plastic wrap. Luke and Taylor each accepted one. She paid no attention to them. But when Aria reached the end of the line to take the sandwich being held out to her, the woman said, "There you go, darlin'," with an almost southern drawl that owed more to cultural upbringing than it did to geographical location.

This unexpected bit of intimacy confused Aria. It both comforted her and contradicted her sense of reality. Aria had come to expect cruelty or at least self-centered altruism from people. This sense of genuine kindness was like a shock to the system and she couldn't quite decide whether she liked it or not. Given the strange nature of the interaction, Aria read the lettering on the woman's name tag. Her name was Imani. On that cold June morning, Imani was simply someone who had been unexpectedly kind; Aria could not know then that she had met a friend.

— * —

That day Taylor and Aria followed Luke endlessly to different parts of the city. Aria was beginning to feel the same way Taylor did: that they had hit the jackpot by meeting him. After visiting shelters and locating a mission that allowed a 15-minute shower for each of them, by the time they were headed back to the car lot, Aria felt better than she had in a long time. She had found a sleeping bag in a donation pile at one of the shelters. She was holding it under her arm like a treasure. And, except for her clothes, which hadn't been laundered for weeks, for the first time in weeks she felt clean.

When they got back to the car lot, the sun was almost setting. A few of Luke's "roommates" eyed them suspiciously as Luke led them around the lot, looking for a place for them to set up camp. Seeing as neither of them had a tent, the obvious option was to see if one of the broken-down cars could serve as a temporary shelter. They settled on an abandoned white Land Cruiser because it had the most room, all of its doors were still mounted and its windows were intact. The metal on its front end was still crinkled from the accident it had never recovered from. And it was missing both of its front wheels. Still, later that night, when Luke said goodnight and left them to their own devices, climbing onto the gray fabric of its interior felt like luxury.

Aria got into her sleeping bag and lay flat across the back seat. Taylor reclined the front passenger seat as far as it would go over her legs. "I like it here," he said, watching the other inhabitants of the abandoned car lot go about their business before turning in for the night, and Aria agreed with him. "Luke told me some places I could find a job tomorrow. I think I'm gonna try and get a bus ticket or somethin' and maybe go see if I can get into that acting program." She realized that meant she would be alone for the day but Taylor quickly added, "You can come with me if you want to, I just don't know how much fun it's gonna be."

They were both aware that since she was still under 18, she had to lie lower than any of the rest of them, and Aria guessed he didn't like the risk that her being underage posed to him. It would be safer for her to stay there. "That's OK," she reassured him. "I can stay here tomorrow. Maybe Luke can show me around some more."

She wasn't really excited to spend more time with Luke, especially one-on-one, but the idea of not walking anywhere for a day was enticing. She wanted Taylor to go chase his dreams, no matter how unrealistic they were. Watching his zeal for the future, which once had been so irritating to her, now felt like watching a flower grow among the weeds. His fervor for life was a scarce form of beauty that life on the streets tried to strip from him every day. And Aria wanted him to keep it. She wished that she could have some of it herself.

She patted Taylor's arm before she fell asleep, to soothe away his worry about whether she felt hurt by his intention to leave her behind the next day. She remembered the terrible posters with empowerment quotes at the group home. One of them said, "You can learn something from everyone you meet." She smiled to herself because regardless of how obnoxious it was, she was finding it to be true. Taylor had taught her something. He was teaching her how to cut her losses without cutting loose her hope.

The last thought that went through her head that night before falling asleep with her blankie was, "You never know, something could get worse. And you never know, something could get better."

CHAPTER 13

Past the anemic pallor of discarded surgical gloves, the cigarette boxes and the beer cans torn and crushed, a shallow stream cleaved the woodland by the car lot. Luke led Aria upstream, past where the people in camp who cared less drank, did laundry and occasionally urinated. He said next to nothing. The careful progress of his footsteps was occasionally impeded by whatever lawless path Palin's nose took her down, her tail curled up over her loin. Occasionally, she would lie flat on her belly and hold her head low in the grass, staring straight ahead as if stalking a phantasm neither Luke nor Aria could see.

When they stopped, Aria stuck her fingers deep into the cold air hovering inches above the flowing water, deep into the mellow of the earth's own breath. The green of better days was brighter than the green that flavored the landscape. The sun's hands ran over everything, the wet wings of a moth as they opened and closed, the crown of oak leaves and the water that was older than the flow of human blood.

They quickly and silently confirmed their mutual comfort level with nudity. They washed their clothes with a mint green bar of pumice lava soap that Luke carried with him in a ziplock bag. Almost no discourse floated between them. Aria mimicked Luke, draping her clean clothes over the branches of one of the nearby oak trees. The heat of the sun censored the chill of the air.

Aria sat on a rocky outcropping near the stream, waiting for her clothes to dry. She watched Luke run the bar of soap across the scope of his body forcibly. The water below him was tainted with a streak of powdery white from the soap. He used his hands to cup the water and saturate himself. Aria felt warmed by the primal image of him. Luke was a traveler. His body and dreadlocks had been chiseled by the necessity of migration. In many ways, when he was naked, he looked how she imagined a primitive man might have looked thousands of years ago. She smiled, picturing him hunting through the woodland with a loincloth and a spear.

When Luke came to sit down next to her, the river spray still shedding from his skin sparkled against the right side of her body and caused her to flinch. They sat in the awkward but pleasurable silence of unresolved sexual tension until Aria couldn't sustain it any longer. "So what's your story?" she asked. Though she was convinced she could most likely write the story of his life without him even telling her, the fact that they were sitting there naked had softened her judgmental attitude.

"What do you mean – like, what was my childhood like, or …?" He didn't finish the sentence.

"Well, yeah. I mean, people don't just end up out here for nothing," Aria replied.

Luke paused for a moment, looking down at his feet. "Well, I was born out here in LA. My dad was a surfer. He met my mom on a scuba-diving trip. He was the instructor. According to him, she was the one that came after him. Who knows." He paused as if trying to sort through something in his mind and picked up where he left off. "According to my dad, my mom didn't even want us. But he wouldn't marry her unless she agreed to have kids. She told him that if they got a divorce, he was the one taking the kids. But that wasn't at all how it turned out. My dad said that on the delivery table, my mom grabbed me and said 'mine.' And then she wouldn't let him touch me until she was ready to let go of me. After they got married, my mom wanted to move away from here. So they took us to Park City, Utah. I would have been a surfer too, but I learned to ski instead. But that's where everything went to shit."

Again, Luke paused as if trying to untangle a knot in his head. It was clear that whatever had happened had cast him into a state of confusion.

"Did you have any brothers or sisters?" Aria asked.

"Yes. I had a younger brother. His name was Alex. He died. He ran his bike into the back of a parked van and died," Luke replied. He fell silent again.

"Did your parents get divorced?" Aria asked, trying to help him start back up with his story.

"Yes. My dad started drinking. They hired us au pairs and pretty soon, my mom started making all the money. She didn't respect him anymore. She fought him for custody of us, which made him drink even harder. And then it was kind of like we were dropped into thin air. My mom got married like five or six times, each time to a richer and richer man, and my dad developed this habit of driving drunk. He ended up in jail.

"When I was eleven and my brother was ten, my mom was off on safari and my dad put us both in the car when he was drunk. Thank God he was arrested. But we sat there at the police office for hours while they tried to find someone to come pick us up. Finally a family friend came and got us.

"Needless to say, my brother started having drug problems and so my mom sent him away to a boys' camp in Sedona. When he came back, he was different. And one day, he just decided to ram his bike into the back of a van."

Luke stopped as if that was the end of his story but Aria wanted to know it all now.

"How did you end up out here, though?" she asked.

Luke started speaking again, but this time, he told his story as if recounting it were a chore. "Well, I could never do anything right by my mother. And yet, I was her favorite. So it was really confusing … I fucking hate my mother. Um, I went to college for a little bit, but I didn't know what I was interested in, so I just signed up for a bunch of music classes. I was playing trombone. I was interning for the local legislature. And one day, I met this girl and totally fell in love with her so we moved in together. But my mom didn't like her. She treated her like shit. And she said that if I kept living with her, she'd stop paying for my college. Obviously I refused. So she called the IRS to report me. Basically she had been claiming the money she spent on my college tuition as salary for an employee that didn't exist. So they came after me for all the money. She expected me to just cave in. But I was so sick of her bullshit that I told the IRS what she'd really been doing. Even the IRS agent thought my mother was a bitch. Anyway, I stopped talking to her. I haven't talked to her since."

"What happened to the girl?" Aria asked, suddenly terrified for the answer.

"She died," Luke said flatly. "I was driving across an intersection and a huge black Suburban hit the wheel well and she wasn't wearing a seatbelt. My lung popped. They told me in the emergency room that she had died. I wanted to die too. It was me that killed her.

"I was hysterical. By the time they let me out of the hospital, I had eighty thousand dollars' worth of medical debt and nothing to go home to, so I just put everything I needed in my camping backpack and paid for a flight out here."

"That's so fucked," Aria said when Luke finished. It was all she could say. She was unable to break through the rough persona that she had manufactured over the years. But inside, she was speechless. She knew the contours of grief well enough to know that saying "I'm sorry" would have been a slap in his face. She felt guilty for having judged him so wrongly to begin with. She felt like holding him. Instead, she held the heaviness with him just sitting in the quiet, sharing his burden for a few minutes.

Luke didn't ask Aria anything about her life that day. He was the kind of man who hated to ask anything of anyone for fear of their rejection, even details about themselves. Instead he filled the space with his political theories.

Once their clothes were reasonably dry, they put them back on. Having clean clothes again felt like heaven to Aria. Another simple pleasure that she had taken for granted before now. They sat down again to take in a few more minutes of the peace being offered by the nature around them. Luke got out his bag of trail mix and rolled down the sides of the plastic far enough for it to resemble a flimsy dish. He offered Palin part of a sandwich he hadn't finished. The dog devoured it and then sprawled herself across their legs, exposing her belly to the sky as a solicitation for affection. The glee with which she did it made them both laugh. Together, they fussed over her as if she were a maharaja.

It struck Aria how strange life can be. One second, your life can fall apart to the degree that you don't want to go on living. And the next, a pleasure as simple as a dog can bring the breath back to your life again. Aria could see that Palin had picked up where the woman of Luke's life had left off when she died. Palin had brought him back to life again. She had given him a reason to live and she had loved him like his mother had not. She wondered if maybe the reason Palin felt so human was because she wasn't really a dog, but an angel in a dog's body come to save this man.

Taylor didn't return to the car lot until Aria was already asleep. Despite his less-than-graceful movements, he tried to get into the car quietly, so that she wouldn't wake up. Unbeknownst to him, his attempt failed. However, instead of saying something, Aria surveyed him through a hole in her sleeping bag until he had fallen asleep.

— * —

Taylor was noticeably distraught. He had slipped out before first light and bummed change off of people at the closest bus station until he had enough to buy a fare. He had taken several buses to the studio whose flyer he had been carrying around in his backpack, thinking it would be his promised land. But when he got there, he had been told that all the work/study positions were currently filled. They asked for his number so they could call him if one opened up, but he didn't have a cell phone. Instead of admitting to his current situation, he simply told them he would check back every week.

The studio was nowhere near the offices that Luke had referred him to for temp work. On top of that, he made the mistake of taking a wrong transfer on the bus system and found his efforts opposed by the masses of people visiting Universal Studios. So he only had time to visit one temp office before they had all shut down for the day, and that office had nothing for him. He was too proud to mow lawns for a landscaper. He felt humiliated at the idea of being a janitor at a manufacturing plant. He couldn't lifeguard because he couldn't swim.

Taylor could not accept the reality of where he was in life. He had imagined himself being instantaneously scouted once he came to LA. He had come here to be an actor. Compared to that, every job that was available felt beneath him. The day had been just one more exercise in disappointment in his life. His stomach throbbed with emptiness, both emotionally and physically. So much so that it was hard to fall asleep. But eventually, he did.

CHAPTER 14

In the morning, their sleep was shattered by the sound of tapping on the window. At first, they quailed, expecting to see a police officer or some other person who posed an equal amount of threat standing above them. Instead, two blue eyes peered over the lip of the car door.

"Aston, get away from there!" Mike yelled at the boy who was staring through the window. The boy took the stick he was holding and ran back toward him as if the trouble he had created for himself had not fazed him. The kid was stocky, oversized for the five years he had accumulated on earth. Though the tragedy of his life was obvious by virtue of him being there, his demeanor defied it. Instead of collapsing, he had turned into a brave little warrior, already at war with life. But, that warrior nature made him either a little hero or a bully, depending on the day.

When Aria and Taylor emerged from the vehicle they now called home, Mike motioned to them to join him by his army-green ridge tent. They made their way across the lot apprehensively.

"Hey, I'm sorry about that, I didn't mean for him to wake you. He's a little rambunctious sometimes."

Aston had found a place in the dirt and was digging at it with his stick aggressively. "I heard you playing guitar the other day; you're good," Aria said.

"Oh thanks, it's just something I picked up along the way. I'm not really very good, but I enjoy it. Would you like some coffee?" he asked.

"Um, OK," Aria said, not because she actually drank coffee, but because the way he asked implied it would be a rejection of him instead of the coffee if she were to refuse.

Mike was a man of few words. He talked the way that Aria imagined the cowboys of Wyoming would talk. She liked it.

She found herself asking him questions just so she could hear the way his voice sounded. He warmed up the coffee on a little Coleman gas camping stove and poured them each a cup in a pair of blue metal mugs. "Have you met Ciarra yet? She lives just over there," he said, pointing to the purple van.

"Yes," Aria said.

"She's my daughter. We named her Cameron, but she changed it to Ciarra for whatever reason," Mike said with a smile. Just peering out from underneath his trucker hat, he seemed simultaneously embarrassed and proud to claim her as his own. "I watch Aston for her when she's on a night shift. She doesn't stay here that often. Only when she breaks up with one of her boyfriends," he said, making light of a situation that he obviously disapproved of.

Mike didn't feel like he had the right to exert much authority over Ciarra. Aria gathered that this was because she had spent the majority of her childhood with her mother and had only reconnected with Mike after she dropped out of high school to live with him.

A large rectangle of cardboard was leaned up against the mouth of his tent. There were three lines written on it that read: No job. Willing to work. God bless. Mike noticed Aria looking at it.

"I'm not a beggar," he said. "I only use it if I can't find a job." Aria smiled back at him to lessen his obvious shame about it.

Mike explained that he did not see himself as homeless any more than he saw himself as a beggar. As far as he was concerned, he was just a man without a job looking to get back on his feet. He took any work that was offered to him. The only problem was that not many people wanted to hire a man his age, especially for the manual labor jobs that were most widely available to people in his particular situation. For Mike, asking for favors was only a back-up when temporary work, pawning off possessions or collecting plastic bottles had failed. He was a proud sort of man. It was a trait that his daughter,

Ciarra, had inherited. And part of that pride was evident in his decision to help raise his grandson Aston, despite having next to no experience in childcare himself.

Taylor was uncharacteristically silent that morning. Aria could tell by how slowly he was sipping his coffee that he, too, was drinking it out of courtesy.

Two men approached the tent. Mike greeted them submissively and, obviously wanting to make them feel welcome, motioned to them to sit down on two foldable camping stools. They said hello and waved at Taylor and Aria without introducing themselves, and began to talk as if the young people weren't there.

"You wouldn't believe the line down at JWC yesterday," one of them told Mike. He was an older man, whose toothless mouth was drawn into a smile that paled in comparison to the smile of his eyes. They gleamed with pleasure under the gray whiskers serving as eyebrows. His nose was bulbous and far too big for his face. But it made him all the more endearing to look at. Silver stubble covered his chin and what was left of his hair was wafted into Einstein-like tufts on top of his head. Even though she had only just met him and had not yet even been introduced, Aria knew she could love this man. She had an image in her head of a grandpa bouncing his two grandkids on his knee with a Christmas tree glittering in the background. This man looked like he had come straight out of that vision and into real life. The instant affection that she felt for him made her all the more shy toward him.

Mike became uncomfortable with Aria and Taylor's exclusion from the conversation. "Hey, let me introduce you to these guys." He pointed first at the less vocal of the two of them. "This is Darren, and this is Bob."

"Robert, but you can call me Bob," the older man corrected him with a humble wave in Aria's general direction. Darren just nodded his head, obviously leery of the youngsters' sudden presence in a spot that was clearly a ritual meeting place for them. Despite the introduction, Darren and Bob resumed the conversation purely with Mike.

Darren was dressed in a green camouflage coat over long blue jean shorts. On his head was a brown camouflage baseball cap that said "US Army Veteran" under a seal of a bald eagle that looked to Aria like it had been flattened like a pancake. His now graying hair had been strawberry blond once. It came down to his collarbones. His mustache met his beard in a perfect open-ended frown of a triangle, making his already dispirited poise seem all the more somber. His right leg was lacerated with a network of purple scars and his left leg was missing. In its place was a dirty prosthetic. The stump of his leg was capped with a gray sock and suctioned into the socket. A steel pole the size of a shinbone fed into a black tennis shoe.

Aria guessed that the three men were friends and that they had probably relocated here together. Contrary to Aria's assumptions, as she later found out, they hadn't known each other at the start. Robert had come to the abandoned car lot first, and nobody knew how he found it. He had invited Darren to stay here with him after the two met at a holiday meal program just over three years ago. Robert was 68 years old. He had worked all his life as a mechanic to retire. Like so many seniors on the street, he relied on social security checks, but they put him in a position where he had to choose between eating *or* paying rent. He did everything he could to keep his apartment in Santa Monica until the relative who was living with him, and who he depended upon to keep the place, died five and a half years ago. He had been living out of a backpack, with his bicycle and one-man tent, ever since.

Darren had invited Mike to the camp one year later. Mike had served four years in the army, which granted him immediate rapport with Darren, who, unlike Mike, had made a career of the army. That is, until the last time he was deployed to Iraq, where he crossed paths with an IED that made mincemeat out of his legs. He had been referred to a mental health program as part of his recovery but had ended up on the street when their attempts to alleviate his paranoia, flashbacks, night terrors and chronic pain had failed when compared to alcohol. Still trying to make it through the day with PTSD, and now alcoholic, Darren had turned the inside of the abandoned RV he now occupied into a vault of trash. Darren had become a hoarder.

Aria felt wrong for having arrived in a place where such established connections already existed. She imagined herself to be an imposition there, even though they never indicated that they minded it. So she made the effort to engage with them, with an air of exaggerated friendliness. When the conversation died down between them, Darren and Robert started asking Taylor and Aria their stories. Except for the occasional interruption by Aston coming into the tent to announce and re-announce his boredom, Taylor and Aria took turns telling their tales and answering questions until there were no more questions to be asked.

Taylor and Aria learned a lesson the hard way that day, too: never drink coffee if it is the only thing you get to eat on a given day. After they left the three men, their efforts to find discarded food in a dumpster behind a grocery store produced nothing. Both feeling jittery and sick to their stomachs, they lay down against the door of the loading dock until they felt good enough to make the trip back to the car lot. Aria threw up, which made her feel better, and drank enough from one of her plastic water bottles to feel full.

Aria couldn't get the meeting with Mike and Darren and Robert out of her head. She recycled it in her mind. They had parted ways that day feeling the nearness brought about by hardship, which, like superglue, closes up the cracks that would normally separate people from such different walks of life. She could not work out why, no matter where some people seem to turn, their lives have no door leading anywhere … Dead end after dead end after dead end of pain. The inevitable rain of loss had soaked them all. It had left them all destitute.

There was so much uncertainty in life. Aria wanted some certainty. But so far, any certainty that people seemed to establish seemed to be ornamental anyway. Despite her youth, Aria already knew that all ornament would be lost in death, just as Luke had lost his brother and girlfriend. It would disappear like shadows into light.

It was a thought that usually made her feel uneasy. But tonight, it made her feel glad that she currently had so little to lose.

CHAPTER 15

The air smelled of gasoline. Two streets away, a couple of men sat on the curbside, sipping their deaths through a bottle hidden in a paper bag. The unlit street lamps stood over their heads like pallbearers. The day was so hot; it seemed like the sun looked to cremate everything in sight. Ciarra, who already had a cigarette in her mouth, handed one to Aria and lit it. At the very least, it took the edge off the adversity that no amount of nicotine could fully drown out. Every time a car passed, Ciarra would lean forward to look inside the windows to ascertain whether the driver was a prospective client or just some passerby who wasn't worth her notice.

She had lied to her father, for obvious reasons. Ciarra wasn't working night shifts at a bar. Ciarra was a nightwalker. She slept with men for money or for blow.

Almost two weeks had passed since Luke had brought Taylor and Aria to the abandoned car lot. Luke had taken Palin up the coast of California to attend a festival of some sort. Without him as a go-between, Taylor and Aria had been forced to converse with the other inhabitants of the lot. Though they all lived very separate lives, the connection formed by common circumstances had already garnered them a certain level of acceptance in the group.

One night, before the sun went down, Aria noticed someone flailing and moaning in the old broken-down Camaro. When she approached the car, she found EJ in withdrawal. His bone-thin body was writhing in pain. Sweat stuck the loose strands of his black hair to his forehead. His eyes were rolling behind his eyelids and he was breathing as if he was having a seizure. Aria sat in the driver's seat and tried to soothe him. Under her touch, he quieted and tears started to roll down the side of his face toward his ear, which was pierced with a hoop earring.

Even though he was 23 years old, he reminded her of a small child stricken with the flu. EJ, who was an acquaintance of Ciarra's, was addicted to fentanyl. He was used to injecting every five hours, but hadn't managed to get his hands on a dose. EJ never spent the day at the car lot. He came and left, so absorbed in the cycle of his addiction that he was a mystery to everyone, more like a ghost that slept among them. The day after Aria had been with him through such a vulnerable moment, he went back to acting as if he didn't know her at all, or perhaps didn't remember.

Aria had also met Wolf. In truth, they had been introduced to one another by Robert and had only shaken hands. He didn't sleep in a car or in a tent or beneath a tarp like everyone else at the lot. Except for when it rained, he would sleep out underneath the open sky, preferring to have nothing between him and the world. His real name was James, but everyone called him Wolf and it was the only title that was fitting. Out of everyone at the lot, Wolf intrigued Aria the most. He seemed to hang around the lot less because it was a home base and more because it offered a poor substitute for a missing sense of tribe. Aria watched him disappear into the woodland for hours and even days, as if on some sort of solitary vision quest. When he returned, he would sit with Robert and talk for hours, or throw a stick for Palin until she was too tired to fetch it anymore. And more than a few times, she saw him sitting with EJ in his car.

On one of those days, Aria had thought they were smoking weed. But, after watching them long enough, she realized that Wolf had gathered a tiny bundle of sage and was smudging EJ with it. Whether EJ was open to Wolf's guidance or not didn't seem to matter to Wolf. He appeared to be heavily invested in EJ's recovery. He had imposed himself as a mentor to usher EJ out of his lost-ness.

Aria loved the feel of Wolf. He had a distrustful way of being. But his poverty and his ill-fitting clothes could not conceal what was truly magical about him. Aria could hear the pulse of the earth itself in his footsteps. She could hear its rivers in his veins. He seemed to carry both the earth and sky within him. His skin was the color of coffee. His 40 years upon this earth had only just begun to trace chicken-foot wrinkles from his eyes to his temples. He wore his long black hair in a ponytail that was tied just above the back collar of his shirt. His hands and arms were covered in tattoos, most of them representing some part of his life that he considered to be a rite of passage. Some of them, spiritual messages to himself, were etched into his skin so he couldn't forget them. There was no way of telling where the black of his pupil ended and his iris began. The whites of his eyes were yellowed. Palin's eyes looked more human than his did; and the consciousness behind them, more familiar.

Wolf was N'pooh-le, a tribe commonly known as Sanpoil. He had been raised on the Colville Indian Reservation in Okanagan County, Washington. His father had gotten into his beaten-up pick-up truck and disappeared when Wolf was eight. Most of his memories before then were of his father beating him and his mother. He remembered the days spent by himself, trying to fill up the vacuum of boredom with both his mother and father passed out cold in whatever part of the house their chronic drunkenness had left them. He never knew where his father went. And his mother never quit drinking.

In most ways, Wolf took up the place in his mother's life where his father was supposed to be until he was 16 and she died of liver disease. His childhood had birthed a dream within him of reuniting the tribes. He saw the loss of their way of life as the reason for all their suffering. For a couple of years after his mother died, he dedicated himself to this vision, thinking that everyone would be quick to commit to the old way of life of their people if only he led them back into it. But he was wrong. They had given up. They had given in to the fissures that existed between each other and between themselves and that old way of life. So he left, bitter. He lived his life up and down the Pacific coast, looking for some tonic for the anger he felt toward himself, toward the white man and also toward his own people.

It was not uncommon to see Native Americans on the streets. Most of them had thrown their traditions away in favor of alcohol and chew. Equally, they seemed less ruined by life out on the streets. Perhaps because, having been stripped of their culture, they had lost everything already. Or perhaps it was because living nomadically, relying on whatever bounty could be hunted or found, was in their blood already. Their lives did not seem as devastated by lack of possessions. And the sun did not seem to wear them down the same way. The tragedy was in their extraction from the land. It was in the annihilation of their culture. It was in the loss of their tribe. Wolf did not find it as easy as others to accept what had happened to his people. The tragedy of it was heavy upon his back. He felt eaten alive by it. Wolf would vacillate between a modern embodiment of a medicine man and dissolving into suicidal crisis. When Aria watched him, she felt like maybe he helped people so that one day they might just turn around and rescue him from this torment that he seemed to carry with him everywhere he went.

Apart from Robert and EJ, the person Wolf spent the most time with was Anthony. He was a scrawny man, who lived beneath the blue tarp affixed to the chain-link fence on the far end of the lot. He had attended one of Mike's morning coffee socials, which Aria had yet again been motioned over to attend. The seam just between the brim and cap of his olive-green baseball hat was stained with sweat. He had small, dirty-green eyes with so much sclera that they reminded Aria of shark eyes. His sandy blond hair was cut short, his beard and mustache trimmed. After years of harsh treatment, his body was stiff and weathered. His skin bore the corrupt color of a permanent sunburn. His hands, graceless in their movements, were covered in cracks and callouses.

Anthony had killed a man. When he was young, he had been a bucker at a logging company in Idaho. When he found out that his wife had been cheating on him with a man who worked beside him every day as a faller, he drove over to the man's house in a rage to confront him. The screaming match escalated until the other man threatened to call the police on him for trespassing. When Anthony didn't leave, the man pointed a rifle at his face. This made Anthony so angry that he grabbed the gun and wrestled him for it. When he ended up with the gun, as if overtaken by something other than himself, he pointed it back at him and shot twice. Anthony tried to skip town, but was arrested two days later. He was charged with voluntary manslaughter and was sentenced to 17 years in prison.

His parole papers had been signed off years ago. But to get a job, or buy a car, or qualify to rent an apartment, as a convicted felon had proved to be impossible. So, he turned to robbery and had spent his time since then in and out of jails. On occasion, he would intentionally get himself arrested to escape the cold of the winters before deciding to come out west to California.

Anthony found life outside prison unmanageable. He no longer felt wanted in society. There was no way to transition from life behind bars to life outside them. Perhaps Wolf offered him a sense of tribal belonging that society would not afford him. Perhaps Wolf was on a mission to save the part of himself that lacked a tribe externally through Anthony. But unless Wolf had sunk into the intentional isolation of one of his downward spirals, the two were inseparable. Anthony followed Wolf around like a beta member of a two-man wolf pack.

Ciarra had tried to bum a smoke off of Aria one day the previous week. When Aria told her that she didn't have any, Ciarra had put two and two together and realized that Aria didn't have any money. Suddenly the tables flipped from "you help me" to "I'll help you." She promised Aria that she could find work for her and that it didn't matter how old she was or wasn't.

Without Ciarra needing to say what the work was, Aria knew. There was no other reason to beat around the bush about it. Before she accepted, Aria weighed the burden of her circumstance against her conscience. She felt the malaise of the stigma that came along with prostitution. She didn't want to wear the scarlet letter of it. But at the same time, she wasn't particularly identified with her body. It had been used on multiple occasions by men already. She found herself unable to care about something that never felt like it was hers. Besides, it wasn't like she would be spoiling something that was pure to begin with. In fact, part of her liked the modest kick of empowerment that she felt in response to the idea that as opposed to giving it away for free, she would be getting something in return for it. If they didn't care about her at all, at least she'd be able to use them mutually in order to buy food and clothes and eventually get a place.

What made Aria hesitate was not her conscience; it was knowing that Ciarra was no philanthropist. Ciarra's "love," like so much of the "love" Aria had been given throughout her life, was more like a spider's web, designed to ensnare. She could feel the sense of forced allegiance in the pretense of caring that Ciarra had fashioned to disguise her own need for power and control. Aria did not want to give in to it. But she was also in a lose–lose situation. To turn Ciarra's help down was to establish herself as a foe from the get-go and to suffer the consequences. Aria eventually accepted Ciarra's offer, hoping not only to get a leg up on life, but also to stay safe from the covert fascism of Ciarra's social game.

Now, here she stood, in a nylon pink miniskirt and a cut-off tee that Ciarra had coerced her into wearing. They had been standing there for less than half an hour before a man in a BMW pulled over to the side of the street. He had stopped for Ciarra, whose attempt at a plaid naughty-schoolgirl uniform had been attracting men like moths to a flame. Ciarra seductively leaned her arms on the frame of the lowered passenger window. Aria couldn't hear what she was saying, but she knew that Ciarra was trying to sell the man on the idea of sleeping with her instead. Ciarra had promised to get her hooked up with a "john," the depersonalizing word they used for a client, before leaving with one of her regular clients that her pimp had arranged for her that afternoon.

Ciarra's regular john was sitting in his parked car a block further on from where they were standing. His engine was turned off. Aria could see him watching through the rear-view mirror. His name was Larry. He was a gentle ogre of a man who was missing most of his hair. He wore a "God Bless America" t-shirt over the bulk of his severely obese body. The way he was smiling while he waited for Ciarra made Aria pity him. He was so clearly unaware of the level of Ciarra's deception.

Ciarra had been complaining about this regular of hers while they were on their way there. "I don't know, he's sweet but sometimes it's like, what the fuck do you want to pay me for?" she said, laughing at how ridiculous it was to her that most of the time he just wanted to talk and take her out to dinner instead of to fuck. "I don't know whether he's lonely or what the fuck is goin' on. Maybe he's in love with me." She winked at Aria when she said it.

As she explained to Aria, Larry was the kind of man who had so little sense of real wealth within the world that his stable salary and bonuses made him feel like a king, especially when compared to these women of the night. And, desperate for affection, he was committed to spoiling them with it. Really, he was buying the way they looked at him when instead of telling them to suck his cock, he took them on a shopping spree, or at the very least focused on trying to get them to orgasm instead. They would fake it every time, but he was too naive to know it. Instead, he deluded himself that they loved spending time with him and that he was the only man who had ever cared about them. It was a hero fantasy that Ciarra played straight into. "You gotta love the guy," she said. And maybe some part of her did. Not in the way a woman loves a man, but in the way a girl loves a puppy or a kitten. His blatant naivety made her feel safe. And safety was a hard commodity to come by.

Aria shifted her attention back to the negotiation taking place between Ciarra and the man in the BMW. Ciarra's flirtations ended. She pushed herself back from the ledge of the car window and turned in her tall boots toward Aria. For a minute, Aria expected the man to drive off. But instead, the car stayed parked by the curb. "Come on, bitch, hurry," Ciarra yelled affectionately at Aria. She opened the car door, ushering Aria inside as fast as she could.

"Hey," the man said. Aria said hi in response and smiled at him, trying to mimic Ciarra's sexual flair, albeit unsuccessfully. He drove away from the curb, attempting to draw as little attention to himself as possible. Through the side mirror, Aria watched Ciarra strut toward Larry's car and get into it before her own car turned the corner.

The car pulled into a parking spot just in front of the outermost motel room on the bottom level of a cheap, two-story, U-shaped motel. Inside, the carpet, left over from the 1970s, was stained, as if its putrid orange color weren't off-putting enough already. Two beds took up the room. They were arranged against a wood-plank wall and covered with floor-length orange bedding. Above them were two cheap-looking reproduction paintings of a group of sailboats. The sharp fetor of chain-smoking hung so thick in the air you could taste it.

Aria didn't want to know anything about this man. She didn't even want to remember his face, so she didn't focus on it. She intentionally tried to ignore everything about him. He put $150 in small bills on the bed stand, then sat on the bed as a ploy to get past the awkwardness between them. Ciarra had warned her to make sure he had the cash as well as the cock, and now the end was in sight, Aria took control of the situation, hoping that by doing so her feeling of susceptibility would subside. She got down on her knees in front of him and started unbuckling the belt holding up his pants.

She stroked the insides of his thighs, occasionally kissing them and letting her breath graze the bottom side of his erect penis, which smelled like fish and urine. He hadn't even bothered to wash his cock first. He watched her unwrap and roll a condom to the base of his dick, not touching her at all at first, as a method of increasing the grip of his sexual tension. It took only moments for the tension to get so high that it eroded his calm. He grabbed Aria's forearms and used them to twist her face-first onto the floor. The aggression with which he pulled her skirt up and pulled her underwear to the side left red marks on her skin. After struggling for a moment for lack of wetness, he impaled himself inside her and began hammering.

Eventually, he was not satisfied with doing it doggy style and pushed her face-down flat against the floor. He tucked her hands underneath her hips to aggrandize her submission. The weight of him made it so Aria had to sneak in breaths between his penetrations. The thought about what people had tracked across the floor that her cheek was now pressed up against crossed her mind as a distraction from the trespass of his dick inside her. It took her back to Mr Johnson. She had become an expert at this point of dissociating from the burn. Aria could feel the icy sensation of liquid exposed to air on the side of her face that was turned to him, instead of to the carpet. She assumed it was spit, but it was blood. "Oh shit," he said, realizing that the force of the intercourse had given him a nosebleed. But he didn't stop. He let it trickle down his lip and onto her face, occasionally sniffing to reduce the flow.

"You're a fine fuck ... yeah, you're a fine fuck, aren't you?" he whispered forcefully, less to her than to himself, trying to turn himself on even further. Eventually, his body went stiff. Gripping her thighs to hold himself inside her, he exhaled the almost painful-sounding moan that Aria had come to expect when men came. Breathing heavily, he went limp, not caring that the weight of his body was given over as a burden to Aria's. She managed to shift out from underneath him, the rash of carpet burn now on her face and the front side of her hands. "That was good," she said, breathing heavily and smiling, hoping to give him the impression that she'd actually liked it. He petted her while he caught his breath. She focused on the pores of his face, instead of the features of it. She still didn't want to remember this man or take note of anything about him.

Despite having just fucked her, he closed the door when he went to use the bathroom. She yelled through the door, "I'm gonna go catch a bus."

"Nah, I can take you back," he responded.

"No, it's fine, really. I need to get to a place that's closer to here anyway."

"OK," was all he said.

Aria paused to see if he was going to say anything further. But there was only silence. So she folded the $150 and put it in the right cup of her bra before stepping out into the parking lot of the motel, closing the door behind her.

She started jogging. The impact of her feet against the pavement made it impossible to quell her tears and so she started crying, using the tears to wipe his blood off of her face until there were only smears left. She sat down on the first patch of grass she could find until she had collected herself well enough to walk back to a bus stop on the Orange line, where she was able to get change for a bus fare.

She didn't tell Taylor where she had been or what she had done that day. When she got back to their car, before he and Luke showed up for the night, she used one of the water bottles from her backpack to wash the crime off of her face so there wouldn't be any evidence.

When Ciarra returned to the car lot, she greeted Aria with ardor. "How'd it go?" she asked.

Aria handed over the money that she had made. Ciarra took half of it to give her pimp and gave the rest back to Aria. "It was OK. It's not really my thing," Aria replied. She had prepared to defend herself against a fall from grace, but no defense was necessary.

Ciarra seemed infinitely more satisfied with Aria's failure to do what she herself did so well. She laughed at Aria with a hair flick and said, "I get it. Not everyone's got it," then winked at her as Aston fussed for her to pick him up and onto her hip. Ciarra left their short meeting feeling self-satisfied. And that self-satisfaction bought Aria some time outside the scrutiny of her focus.

Aria tied Taylor's little flashlight to one of the grab handles in the back of the car and wrote in her journal.

"I fucked a man today. I am forever poisoned by it. No … imprisoned by it. To be loved instead of fucked must taste like so much freedom that the lack of bars and chains alone would make you bleed. I'm not doing it again … At least I hope not. I guess you never know what might happen. I have seventy-five dollars now, which I can't let anyone know about. It seems strange that homeless people steal from each other but whatever. There isn't anyone around to hear me cry about it. There is nothing special about fucking. I don't get why men like it so much. I want love. But I got stuck in the intestines of misfortune too young. The acid has become my home."

She closed her journal and put it back into her backpack before turning off the flashlight. She was glad of the $75. It would buy her a full stomach long enough for her to find another way of making money.

CHAPTER 16

Aria closed her eyes and listened to the harp, whose fairy-like plucking stood out against the melody of the classical orchestra. She imagined the musician's hands and fingers stroking across the strings. Her body knew every note of the song. Then again, everybody's did. The song was "Silent Night." The speakers in the mall had been playing an endless rotation of Christmas songs for a month now.

She had come to the mall to use the public restroom and dig through the dumpsters behind the stores, which promised to be full because it was Christmas Eve. She found herself sitting in the common area of the mall, between the rows of kiosks, watching children pose for pictures on Santa's lap.

Aria felt ambivalent about Christmas. For her, and so many of the other people in her position, there were two sides to the story of Christmas in their lives. In one way, Aria could feel what might have been. She could see herself as a child in a different kind of home. It was as if she were looking through a window onto that life she never had. The glass was partially frosted. Inside she could see her younger self with her mother, Lucy, looking healthy, with a responsible and gentle man who took care of them by her side. She could see a younger sister or brother there too. The family dog was wearing a Christmas sweater. They were reading *The Night Before Christmas* on the couch in front of a giant Christmas tree. Every ornament on the tree was glamorized by the creamy glow of the Christmas lights. She had memorized every one of them. She had felt the nostalgia of taking each ornament out of its wrapping with this imaginary family each year. She could taste the thickness of hot cocoa against the roof of her mouth.

Every smell associated with Christmas contained a story of its own, a thousand years of festivity. Aria loved those smells. She loved the idea that the notes of each Christmas carol had the potential to restore those positive memories and those feelings of love and belonging to full bloom. She loved the look on the children's faces, overwhelmed with the magic of presents appearing in their stockings. She loved the way that people seemed to be stricken with a sudden sense of kindness during Christmas. Instead of fighting their way through the crowd, people were smiling and making way for each other. They were wishing each other a happy holiday. Aria imagined she would love the tradition of Christmas if that tradition had been anything good.

But the other side of the story of Christmas in Aria's life was the reality: that Christmas wasn't good. It was watching her mother draw a Christmas tree on a paper with crayons because it was all she could afford to do. It was the time of the year that Lucy was most aware she couldn't give her daughter the life she wanted to give her. It was watching her mother struggle to buy or steal her one toy each year. It was playing with that toy by herself, watching Lucy drown away that feeling of shortcoming with a needle. It was the fucked-up way the foster parents or staff at the group homes tried to make them enjoy a holiday designed specifically to celebrate the very thing that all of them had lost.

Aria knew that the man who was pretending to be Santa most likely had the stain of alcohol on his breath. She knew that the shops were just looking to Christmas for one more way to tease the money out of people's purses. She knew she had no home to go home to. And because of all this, Aria wished that Christmas didn't exist. The interminable build-up to Christmas was like never-ending foreplay leading up to an experience that she could never have. The outward hatred she showed for Christmas was her way of hiding the painful fact that, like everyone, she wanted to love Christmas, but couldn't because of the reality of her unlucky life.

It had been nearly five months since Aria had come to Los Angeles. Though she had found a sort of base camp in the car lot and with the people who lived there, it had been a breadth of hardship. In that time, Aria had learned the true value of a dollar. She had learned how to disappear into the tapestry of the city. She had learned so much the hard way, like where not to walk at night and where not to walk during the day. Her life had been a surfeit of near misses. Finding programs for people in her position that posed too much of a risk for her to try to join.

Taylor hadn't had it much better. He had taken a handful of temp jobs and lived off of the dollars he made until he had none left, but it was never enough to rent a place. He had attended a few publicly advertised cattle calls for actors, but had never gotten a part. He had slept with more than a few men, but it never amounted to anything more than a booty call. Some days he went out on behalf of both of them with a cardboard sign to solicit charity. It made Aria feel guilty when he did it, but she was still 17. She couldn't take the risk of getting caught.

Luke and Palin, forever nomadic, had been off to a dozen festivals. Occasionally he brought back a gutter punk or two that he had met there. They would park themselves at the car lot for a day or two before leaving on the boxcar of some train, headed to whatever places anarchists go. Though her almost patriotic devotion was to Luke, Palin had grown close to Aria. Scratches now scuffed up the side of the broken-down Land Cruiser from Palin trying to coerce her to come out and play.

Aria's hair had grown longer. She had bitten her nails down as far as she could chew them. As far as food went, some days she was luckier than others. The unpredictability of sustenance made it difficult for her to concentrate sometimes. She welcomed the mental fogginess because it made her stop thinking about her life. Her gums were sore. With the lifeblood stripped from her immune system, it seemed like she had fallen sick at least seven times in the past months. She was so skinny that people might have been expected to guess the truth about her situation. But because her youth would not give her body the permission to decay, people simply assumed that she was anorexic.

No matter how many times she managed to find a place to wash them, her clothes seemed to be eternally soused by the fumes of sports cars that passed her by. Aria had never cared about fashion. But she found herself missing the feeling of wearing something just because it looked good. It was asking for trouble to be on the streets and wear something for any reason other than that it was practical.

With no phone or calendar, and LA having no real seasons to demonstrate the passing of time, the days blurred into one another. If society was a rat race, most of its members were stuck in the wheel. The people on the street believed themselves to be free from that rat cage, but the stasis in which they lived was just another kind of rat cage. Their marginal existence was the wheel of surviving day to day. Never getting ahead, every day starting over at zero. Aria had the feeling that if she got off the street and came back to these same places, she would see the same people doing the same things in one year, five years, 20 years … assuming that they hadn't died first. If you weren't insane before living out here, the living here would make you insane. It would kill you, but not quickly and not painlessly. It would wear you down at the edges before scooping out your core.

Last-minute shoppers swarmed through the corridors of the mall: frenzied people quickly bouncing from store to store with bags in their hands. The buttery smell of toasted almonds, coated in cinnamon sugar, was laced through the air. Aria wove her way through the crowd to get outside the building behind the food court. She waited until no one was passing by and grabbed the first thing that her hands could reach out of the dumpster. It was a styrofoam takeaway box with a divvy of partially eaten lo mein noodles. Instead of standing there, she took them to a corner of the bustling parking lot and ate them with her hands. Whoever had finished the first portion of the noodles had drowned them in soy and sriracha hot sauce. It made her mouth and stomach burn, but she ate them anyway before heading back to the car lot.

Luke woke them up in the morning by knocking his elbow against the glass. In his hands, he was precariously holding two paper cups full of instant hot cocoa. He had taken the packets and cups from a bank office three days before with Christmas morning in mind. Like almost everyone else, Luke had nowhere to go this Christmas. But in typical fashion, he had taken it upon himself to prevent them all from sinking into sorrow.

Taylor opened the door and took the cups from him. "Merry Christmas. It's cocoa," Luke announced. "I'll be back in a second."

Taylor handed one of the cups to Aria. It was so hot that the film of wax on the outside of the cup began to come loose on her hands. They watched Luke go back into his tent and carry little cups to every person in the car lot, except for Ciarra, Aston and Mike, who had been gone for two days to visit a relative somewhere in Hemet, California. When he got around to Anthony's tarp, Anthony refused to respond. He was not asleep; he simply didn't move. He stayed where he was, lying on his stomach, staring off into a chasm of depression that only he could see. Luke placed the cup of cocoa in front of his face, where it stood the least chance of being knocked over but where he would be forced to see it.

Luke came back to the Land Cruiser with his own cup of cocoa and Palin in tow. They both got into the back seat with Aria, forcing her to slide over to one side. "Mmmm, a subtle note of cherry, maybe some oak and definitely some chocolate undertones," he said, jokingly sipping his cocoa as if impersonating a wine sommelier.

They laughed out loud. The joke was all the more funny because the cocoa he had managed to make them on his little camping stove was anything but gourmet. The saccharin sweetness of synthetic chocolate was enough to give them all a headache. But it lifted their spirits anyway. "So, what the fuck should we do today?" Taylor asked them with a tone that denoted defeat.

"Ah, dude, today's the best day to go downtown. People give out mad loot, man," Luke responded.

"What do you mean?" Taylor asked.

"It's Christmas, the only day people actually give a shit," Luke responded with a pandering smile.

As it turned out, Luke was right. He, Taylor, Aria and Palin sat under the façade of a building on a street close to the three biggest missions in the city. Aria was glad that being in California meant there would be no snow for Christmas this year. It wasn't that she hated snow; quite the opposite. But it didn't feel quite like Christmas without snow, and so the holiday didn't hurt as much as it might have otherwise. Christmas lights didn't look or feel the same without the backdrop of powdery white.

The streets were crowded with people like themselves, looking to take advantage of the habitual alms that they could expect to receive on Christmas Day. In a slow and virtuous swarm, families and couples passed by in their brand new Range Rovers, Ford Fusions, Porsches, Teslas and Toyota Priuses. Every so often, one of the cars would stop and open the trunk to gather an allotment of whatever they had decided to hand out to the homeless that year. They would walk the items over to whichever recipients they had singled out and hand them down to them with righteous smiles on their faces.

Aria felt uncomfortable in her own skin. The entire display made her lose even more faith in humanity. It was her poverty that forced her to consent to being there, where her pride could not. This was a poison called philanthropy. The reality was that people did not care. Every other day of the year, these same people would yell at them to stop loitering in front of their buildings or to go get a job. Every other day of the year, these same people would pass them by, dousing them in the ordure of their car fumes. But today, with the Christmas spirit upon them, suddenly they all acted like they cared. Aria would have been glad for this sudden shift, were it not for the smug looks on their faces. Contrary to popular opinion, it was not Christ-like at all. She could see that this giving was not really giving. It was taking. It was a transaction. People like herself accepted whatever they were handing out, and in exchange, they could revel in a sense of their own moral goodness. It was a display of self-gratification. People love nothing more than seeing themselves as good, even if it is by definition entirely self-centered.

By the end of the day, Aria had begrudgingly accrued an orange, four water bottles, mouthwash, shaving cream and a razor, four pairs of new socks, a pack of sanitary wipes, a bottle of hand sanitizer, two toothbrushes with toothpaste, a packet of gum, chapstick, five hand warmers, a packet of mixed nuts, four granola bars, a comb, a packet of cheese and crackers, $10 and some beef jerky which she couldn't eat. When neither Luke nor Taylor was close enough to see, she fed the jerky to Palin, who inhaled it. Palin seemed overwhelmed with the excitement of the unforeseen change of atmosphere and the energy between people in the air. Each time a person had approached them, she submissively flattened her ears and crawled toward them, anxiously wagging her tail. Only one person leaned down to pet her. The rest simply assumed that because she was in the company of a vagrant, she must be carrying some kind of disease.

Having caught wind of a turkey dinner that was apparently offered every year to the homeless and hungry at the United Methodist Church, Taylor and Luke decided to follow a fellow drifter there. Aria declined to join them. Instead, she walked the long distance back to the car lot alone. When she arrived, she could see that Anthony had not moved from his original position. The cup of cocoa that Luke had placed beside him had been spilled. Aria assumed it had been knocked over intentionally. Aside from Anthony, there was no one else at the lot. They had probably all gone out to take advantage of the many opportunities that existed as a result of this sudden Christmas caring.

Aria sat in the mute atmosphere of the back seat of the Land Cruiser. Here, away from the self-gratification of the people and the diminishment she felt because of it, she was glad for her little pile of charity items, where she hadn't felt glad before. She spread them all out on the seat of the car. She was conscious that the way she felt, looking at them, was similar to the way she'd felt on the few occasions when one of her foster parents had taken her trick-or-treating. She felt replete. At least for a little while, she wouldn't have to go desperately searching to meet an immediate need.

Stripping down to her bra and underwear, Aria used a few of the hand wipes to give herself a kind of provisional sponge bath. She pulled the comb unforgivingly through the length of her hair. She was grateful for the comb most of all. Since her brush had gone missing when her backpack was stolen on one of her first days in the city, she had been using her own hands to untangle her hair every morning. Leaning her legs out the opposite side of the car from where Anthony's camp was situated, she used one of the bottles of water, the razor and the men's shaving cream to shave her legs for the first time in ages. She didn't know why she did it. Perhaps it was stupid. There was no reason to shave her legs in the life she was currently living. In fact, doing so might make her more uncomfortable once the hair started to grow back in. But she was sick of feeling decrepit.

Because it was Christmas, she allowed herself to separate the orange and the packet of cheese and crackers from the rest of the stash, which she stuffed deep into the main compartment of her backpack. The sweet-sour taste of the orange segments was tainted by the bitter pith that still glazed her hand from when she'd peeled off the rind. She spread the cheese on one of the crackers with the little red stick that was provided in the packet. It tasted chemical, but it felt luxurious to eat. When she had finished, she threw the orange rind and the little tangle of hair that had come loose in her comb over the fence of the car lot.

Waiting for Taylor and Luke to return, Aria found herself loosely watching over Anthony's little denigrated arbor. The blue tarp over his head was contorting with the lift and release of the wind. Aria imagined that he must have actually had good Christmases once. It made her sad to imagine them. She could see him younger, wearing a ridiculous Christmas sweater and sitting down at a long table with so many family members that he would have to shout to be heard over the chorus of voices. Of course, she didn't know if what she imagined was anything like his actual Christmases. But she could conjure up no other explanation for his catatonic state.

For most people, Christmas was a time of celebration. It was a time for gifts and family and feasts. But for people like herself and Anthony, whose ostracization had led them straight into the back alleys of life, Christmas was anything but that. Watching him, Aria began wishing that if people were actually capable of caring about the people in society who were damaged or down and out of luck, they would act every day like they did on Christmas Day. Then again, if they did, she doubted whether anyone would be living on the streets in the first place.

CHAPTER 17

Home was not a person. Home was not a place. Having
dug up their roots so many times, Taylor and Aria were
beginning to wonder if people like themselves were homeless
less because no home existed and more because neither of
them even knew what home was. Other people seemed to
know. They'd found it somewhere. Those people lacked the
anxious searching that polluted Taylor and Aria's lives. The
pair debated the concept of home on their way to the church
where Luke had taken them the day after they had met him
so many months ago, hoping to find the doors open for
lunch once again. Aria was conscious of how good it felt to
walk down the street in new socks.

Something that Aria had come to find out is that when
you are homeless, suddenly wealth is determined by a pair of
new socks. They keep you warm, they keep you clean, they
prevent a whole host of different ailments that occur when it
seems like all you are doing with your life is walking. And as
she had found out the hard way, when push comes to shove,
they can serve many other functions than that which they were
originally intended for.

The $10 that Aria had gathered on Christmas Day had run
out. When Taylor had gone out to the city looking for jobs,
which he had done every day the previous week, Aria had
waited for him to leave before setting out on her own. First
she spent some of the money at a grocery store on a packet
of cigarettes. Then she bought a bus fare so she could save
herself from walking. She spent the rest of the money on a
carton of plain rice from a Chinese fast-food restaurant. Part
of her felt guilty for having spent money that she could have
saved for emergency situations. Contrary to what people
often say about people on the streets, it was not in her nature
to spend money all at once. But having nice things and

HUNGER OF THE PINE

having money on the street is more dangerous than spending it. It would have made Aria a target. And she already knew what it felt like to save money only to have it stolen. So she decided it would be better to spend it on herself than to potentially lose it all.

On their way to the church, Taylor and Aria paused at a stoplight near a shopping center, waiting for it to turn green. Aria felt her heart jump a little at the familiar sight of Darren, who was standing across the intersection from them, panhandling. When the light turned green, Aria held Taylor back so they could spy on him without him noticing. He was sitting on a bench with his battered crutches laid out in plain view. A sign propped up in front of him read "Homeless Vet Support Your Troops." His prosthetic leg was intentionally displayed.

In the months they had spent at the camp, Aria had come to understand Darren. His entire presentation was meant to guilt people. He was angry. The lack of opportunities that he'd had in life were opportunities that the army had promised to give him. He had enlisted with a sense of national honor and pride. Back then, he felt like he belonged to something bigger than himself. But that honor and that pride were now timeworn. They had frayed out from underneath him, exposing instead a void of terminal aloneness.

Darren now felt as if the very country he served had turned its back on him. And he was determined to make the country and its ungrateful, idiot civilians remember him. He displayed the sacrifices he had made for them in plain view as if to say, "Shame on you, look what I sacrificed for you, now give something back to me for it."

Aria felt conflicted watching him. On the one hand, his sense of entitlement and the shame he used as a tool of extortion were enough to make you hate him. Many of the citizens he was now guilting, including herself, had never wanted him to go to war in the first place. It's hard to feel grateful for a sacrifice you never wanted or asked someone to make. But on the other hand, he was right. Aria imagined that in his position, she would be angry too if she had offered up her life for someone or something else and in return had ended up losing everything; reduced to constant pain both emotionally and physically. The country had turned its back on him, especially the very institutions that had promised him belonging in the first place. Like a broken Springfield Model civil war rifle, he was now a forgotten symbol of war. Patched together and gathering dust, he was no longer a tool the government could use for the violence of their foreign policy.

Like that broken gun, Darren was less devastated to be on the shelf than he was to be considered worthless now, his dignity abolished by every passerby that ignored him.

Taylor and Aria decided to cross the street perpendicular to where he was sitting. They did so without him ever noticing that they were there. When they reached the church, the line was shorter than it had been the last time they had come there. The big black woman, Imani, was manning the table once again, her rich, welcoming smile pulling people down the line. She seemed happy to see Aria again, which took Aria by surprise. "How you two doin'?" she asked, ladling chili into two paper bowls on the table in front of her.

"We're OK ma'am, how are you?" Taylor answered, suddenly reverting to the manners that were beaten into him in his youth.

"Well, I'm fine today, just fine," she responded, pausing to collect two care kits from a cardboard box underneath the table before continuing to speak. "We've got these here for you today. Some deodorant, some hand lotion and chapstick and some baby wipes. The kids made 'em themselves." She pointed to each item as she listed them, all of which had been carefully packed in a plastic ziplock bag.

Taylor and Aria paused awkwardly, not knowing if they should take the bowls and care packages from the table themselves or whether they should wait for her to hand them over directly, until Imani broke that pause. "You know I'd been hopin' to see you here again. I wrote the number down to my office in case you ever wanted some help with anythin'. We've got some great programs you might like." She handed Aria a business card, which advertised the church. On its back, she had handwritten her phone number and her name.

"Thanks," Aria said, trying to disguise her distrust with openness. She put the card into her pocket.

"You two come back and see me now," Imani said, carefully handing each of them their chili and care packages.

"Thank you, ma'am," Taylor said. Aria just smiled and nodded her head to indicate that she had heard her. Imani felt the relief of knowing that her first attempt to establish connection with Aria had successfully landed.

Imani was a social worker on a mission, on several missions in fact. Her sense of purpose in the world had replaced the conscious need for a partner or any other form of support for that matter. She was a member of the church, where she handed out lunch to the homeless on most days of the week. Every morning and also at unexpected times, when crises occurred, Imani had her hands full with her work at a family services center in one of the worst parts of town. In the afternoons, she went home to her two-bedroom apartment, to take care of her family members that were incapable of taking care of themselves, much less each other.

It seemed to Imani that all she did was manage crises, whether it was in her professional life or in her private life. In fact, handing out food to the homeless and attending church were the two most stress-free facets of her life. When the state found Imani's sister to be unfit to take care of her three kids, their custody was passed to Imani's mother, the children's grandmother, who was progressively being rusted through by both diabetes and heart disease. Now, one year later, Imani found herself sleeping on her own pull-out couch and caretaking all of them. Because of this, Imani had no spare time to speak of. She had no other choice than to be strong. Her moral heart had made self-sacrifice its bedrock. The fact was that Imani took care of everyone in her life.

In common with many of her background and culture, Imani was a God-fearing woman. But she wore her faith with more self-effacing grace than others. She believed in every fiber of her being that Jesus cared for all his children and did so in mysterious ways. Her faith was so deep and unshakable that she was not troubled with doubtful questions about the ways in which this "care" happened. When tragedy struck, which it so often did around her, she knew it was not God that was mistaken but she that could not grasp the full picture. In her wallet, she carried a paper, now crinkled from years of use, that said, *Faith only occurs in the absence of knowing*. It was her favorite quote and she lived her life by it.

Imani had worked out the first time she saw her that Aria was homeless and that she was underage. But she also knew that calling the police was not the solution. "You just gotta love 'em," she thought in her head. That first time, Aria had been with Luke. Imani had seen him in the line before. She knew him to be a man who could be counted on to take advantage of all the benefits the church could offer. Like nearly everyone else, she could tell that he had chosen to be homeless and because of this, his entitlement drove her crazy. Still, she hoped that because Luke had been the one to lead Aria there, he would bring her back and gradually, she might be able to connect Aria with the necessary resources to get her off of the street.

Imani had no way of knowing whether Aria would do anything with the connection she'd tried to make, or whether she had been too damaged at this point to recognize opportunity when it was handed to her. But Imani could rest in knowing that she had done what she could do for now. She also knew that the best way to get Aria to trust her was to put absolutely no pressure on her at all. These kids who had no home to go to were like stray animals. You had to be patient and not react or trap them, and stay consistent while they tested you again and again. Sometimes Imani felt like they were actually *trying* to get her to act in such a way that they could prove to themselves that no one loved them. It was like playing a game of chess where what these kids didn't get was that winning this game meant killing their own best interests.

The slurry of flavors scalded Aria's nose before she had even tasted it. It was not the best bowl of chili. It probably wasn't even good. But Aria's current circumstances elevated her appraisal of it. The way the sharp musk of cumin coated her throat, and its heavy sustenance, made her feel cradled on the inside.

Taylor and Aria ate without talking. A warm meal had been so hard to come by that it was a pleasure worth the silence. Having become accustomed to one meal a day and some days none, Aria struggled to finish the chili. By the time she fished the last bean from the bowl, her stomach was sore. Taylor, who finished before she did, announced he was going to take a short nap and to wake him up whenever she was ready to go. He lay down in the grass and covered his face with his jacket.

Aria leaned back on her elbows to try to relieve the ache of being too full. She watched Imani serving the other people in the line. A young man had made himself at home on a cardboard box beside her. He was slumped over his bowl of chili, spooning it into his mouth boorishly and laughing. From the familiarity of the body language and talk between them, Aria guessed that they must know each other personally. His head was covered in a purple do-rag. He wore an oversized puffy blue coat and oversized jeans that rode so low they didn't quite cover his boxers. The knock-off gold watch he was wearing on his left wrist made the brown skin, under the jungle of black tattoos on his arm, look copper. He had thick lips and wide-set dark eyes. Even from a distance, Aria could see that his eyes caught so much light, the reflection in them made his pupils look white instead of black. In fact, the reflection made his eyes look like he was crying even when he was smiling. Underneath his carefully constructed image of bravado, Aria could see the child still alive in him inside his eyes. A five-year-old boy looking at the world as if he was still watching his father leave him.

He seemed to be forever crying without crying at a loss still unresolved within him.

Aria switched her attention to the cook. Imani seemed to her to be the epitome of a big black woman. Her skin was the color of hickory. The entire length of her coarse hair was regulated into box braids, two of which she had tied together in the back, as if in a last-minute attempt to keep them out of her face and to tame the rest. She spoke with a twangy paralanguage common to the African-Americans who had spent their youth on the South Central side of the city. The way she moved her body was both slow and loose. This mannerism of casual familiarity made people feel at ease. She wore a pair of black-rimmed prescription glasses and a loose-fitting blouse with stretch pants over her heavy curves.

After a time, the young man got up and gave Imani a sideways hug. "You be good now, don't you be gettin' into any trouble!" she yelled after him when he turned away. He afforded her a sideways smile and a wave before bounding across the street. He held the belt of his pants up as he jogged.

Aria watched him check and recheck his watch on the side of the street until an iridescent black low-rider car drove up behind him. She watched him get into the car and drive away without ever knowing whether they had anything in common with each other. Without ever saying hello or waving goodbye.

She poked at Taylor's side and said, "What do you want to do?"

Taylor pulled the coat down from his face, squinting against the sunlight. "I don't know," he said, realizing that neither of them had thought past trying to seek out a meal. "There's a temp office like ten blocks away. They might have gotten something new in for me." He said it like a question more than a statement.

"Yeah, that's a good idea," Aria said. "I can stay here and wait for you to get back if you'd like."

Taylor was taken aback, having assumed that she would go with him and wait outside the office instead. "Don't you want to come with?" he asked.

"No, I don't want to just stand around outside. Besides, I can talk to her about whatever she was talking about before," she said, pointing to Imani.

Taylor suddenly seemed insecure about the idea of wandering the city alone. But he didn't want to risk being pushed away by pressing her to accompany him. "OK," he said. "It'll only take me like two hours. I'll meet you back here and we can go back home."

He pulled his backpack up onto his back and, before navigating his way to the sidewalk, he said, "Cross your fingers for me." She smiled and gave him a thumbs up. The way he walked was so obviously gay that she caught herself worrying about his safety, strutting down the road in this part of town unaccompanied. She felt compelled to join him to avoid the guilt she would feel if anything happened to him because she wasn't there. But Aria wanted to talk to Imani away from Taylor's tendency to blindly trust people and accept their assistance, no matter the hidden consequence. She wanted to see if Imani's offer was legitimate or truly full of shit.

Aria watched Imani, waiting for what looked like a good time to cut in. That time never came. By the time she was about to make a move to go over and talk to her, the woman had disappeared inside the building, leaving a younger girl in charge of the table, and didn't come back out for so long that Aria decided the opportunity had closed. She walked briskly in the same direction as Taylor had gone, hoping that if she walked fast enough, she would be able to catch up with him. Soon she found herself standing at an intersection two blocks away from the church, not knowing which way he had gone. She stopped to lean against an inhospitable brick wall for long enough to decide whether to continue looking for him or to go back and idle at the church, waiting for him to come back.

In front of Aria, there was the Super Sun Market, or so it said in red 3D lettering affixed to a yellow stripe of paint above the door. It was a corner store on an unpeopled street. Despite the new year having come and gone, Happy New Year was still written across the front windows, surrounded by doodles of poorly drawn fireworks. Its door was propped open as if begging for customers to come in. For some reason unknown to her, instead of immediately walking back to the church, Aria decided to heed its invitation. As she stepped through the door, the smell of the place gave away that it was a store that belonged to immigrants. In addition to the usual things that can be found in any small general market – candy bars, medicines and overpriced refrigerated goods – there were items that Aria had never seen before. She paused in front of a stack of bags containing what looked like little orange beads. The packages said Masoor Dal, beneath the icon of a flaming genie's bottle.

Aria peered around hesitantly, trying to locate whoever was tending the store. There were a few closed doors that clearly led to other rooms or closets and a staircase that led to a second floor, which didn't look like it was intended for customers. Aria took advantage of the absence immediately, attempting to trick any potential security cameras by pretending to look at one item with one hand, while using the other to steal things away in her jacket pocket. She had taken a candy bar, a packet of gum and a packet of peanuts before she heard the heavy, hurried footsteps of someone coming down the stairs.

"Hello, welcome." The man's voice preceded his entry into the room. He nearly fell through the doorway to the stairs in his eagerness to greet her. For the briefest of seconds, Aria thought that she had been caught red handed. But instead, the man looked ashamed that he had not been there to tend to her needs when she had first entered the store. He had been raised with a strict sense of customer service, which he had clearly fallen short of by leaving the store untended for a few minutes. He must have mistakenly assumed that no one would show up in the time he had given himself to use the bathroom.

The man who stood before her did not appear to be much older than herself. He was thin and tall. She could not tell if he was Middle Eastern or Indian. Bushy eyebrows framed his almond-shaped eyes. They were the color of melted chocolate. They peered down at her from an almost uncomfortably close distance. They were as trusting as they were curious. His face was almost childlike, only a hint of stubble gracing his chin and upper lip. Even though his long nose, prominent ears and thin upper lip made it so that he would not be what most people would consider handsome, there was something that Aria found stately and tempting about him.

"Do you need help finding anything?" he asked.

"Nah, I'm just looking around," she said.

"OK. I am Omkar," he said, putting his hand against his chest. "Tell me if you need anything." His accent stressed the syllables rhythmically, the words almost entirely spoken in the front of his mouth. She liked the way he put emphasis on the wrong syllables. It made him all the more endearing.

He looked almost disappointed at her rejection. She couldn't work out whether the let-down she felt was due to the fact that he had worked out that "just looking around" meant "probably not going to buy anything." Or whether it was because he was lonely and desperate for the discourse implied in showing her around the store.

Aria felt bad for having stolen anything from a man who was so obviously nice. But it was too late to change her mind now. She wandered through the aisles to deceive him into thinking she had looked around without finding anything interesting to buy. She was fully aware of Omkar restlessly waiting behind the checkout stand in case she was to indicate the need for his assistance. Aria was impressed that so much of his personal energy filled up the room. His essence was so thick it nearly sucked the breath out of the room. This was not the kind of place that a man with such obvious charisma would normally be found.

After a few minutes, she made her way to the door and said "thanks" before stepping outside of it. She heard his voice yell out behind her, "Thank you, come back again." Aria felt strange leaving, as if by stepping into the store, she had exited her own life and entered his. She hadn't realized how her own story had faded into the background of the thick smell of Punjab spices when she was walking around the shop. Suddenly, the street outside felt colder and her loneliness more bleak. As she walked back to the church, she used the momentum of her body to emotionally push through and past the way the feel of him haunted her.

— * —

Taylor arrived long before he had promised. The temp office had told him that they had no new listings and so he had turned back as quickly as he'd come. Aria felt like they were occupying two different worlds despite their physical proximity. Taylor, who didn't mind the surface chitchat that took place between them on their way back to the car lot, was oblivious to the distance between them.

When they arrived back at the lot, there was a commotion taking place. Aria and Taylor watched at a distance, sensing the tension in the air. Ciarra was screaming, "Get the fuck outta here you sick fuck," as she threw a handful of dirt in the direction of a man who had parked his Chevy Beretta on the street just outside the lot. The man wore an ill-fitting flat-brimmed hat over a mullet. The top of his too-tight jeans was hidden beneath the bottom of a loose-fitting gym tank that he obviously wore to show off his muscles. He stalked toward his car in a rage. His cowboy boots kicked up dust under his angry footsteps.

Ciarra continued to cry and scream at him and throw rocks long after he was out of range. When he drove away, she got into the purple van, slammed the door and sobbed against the steering wheel.

Taylor and Aria walked with trepidation through the gate toward the white Land Cruiser. Luke called out to them before they reached it. Palin came bounding up toward them, her tail wagging and her ears pinned with elation, curling her body like a fish under their hands.

Aria coddled Palin with endearments, ecstatic to see her again and feeling the heaven of being so obviously wanted by someone. They went over to sit with Luke in the doorway of his tent, leaving their legs just outside the door instead of taking their shoes off. Luke smelled of campfire smoke and sweat. He had obviously not taken a shower in a long time but was oblivious to his own stench. "Dude, that was off the hook," he said referring to his recent travels. "There were so many people there, dude. There were bonfires every night and dancing and chanting and just magic people, you know?"

Taylor took the bait and started asking him questions. Even though Aria was barely listening, Luke spilled the details of his journey that he so obviously wanted to tell the both of them as if they were listening equally.

Aria let his voice fade into the background. She was petting Palin when a sound near Ciarra's purple van caught her attention. It was Aston indignantly digging holes in the dirt with his stick like he so often did, there being nothing else to preoccupy himself with. Aria's stomach sank when she saw him. She was close enough to see that the brow on the left side of his face bore a cleaned-up cut. A bruise that covered half his face had swollen his left eye shut.

She knew that marks like that on a child so young could never have come from a school fight or an accidental fall. She knew that Aston had been beaten. She wondered if that was the reason Ciarra had ended up in the fight they had just walked in on.

Aria was consumed by fury that she could do nothing about. She watched Aston sit alone in the dirt, his mother having closed the door on him, drowning in her own self-pity. It reminded her of her own childhood. The many times she watched her own mother cry her eyes out over the very person who was ruining their lives. Her body went numb with the memory of it.

But she didn't approach Aston because she knew the kind of mother that Ciarra was. She would abandon her son but consider any person who tried to take her place an enemy. And Aria couldn't afford that. At least not right now. She was terrified of Ciarra. In fact, she hated her. But her safety depended upon Ciarra never knowing it.

Aria knew that the man who had stormed off in a rage was Aston's father. A deadbeat who showed up like a hero to take his son somewhere only rarely, whenever his band was in town. He lived in Las Vegas. One of two electric guitarists in a heavy metal band that got few gigs, he had a day job doing assembly at a manufacturing plant. It was not enough to pay child support. Or, more to the point, he said it wasn't, and Ciarra was so afraid of him stealing Aston as retribution for taking him to court that she never forced the issue. But on more than one occasion, today being one of those occasions, Aston's failure to please him during one of their outings had resulted in a beating under the disguise of discipline.

Ciarra couldn't find it in herself to be a mother. The agony of being left to fend for the both of them and the deprivation of having no support made it impossible for her to comfort Aston, who she knew was sitting on his own just outside the door. She knew it wasn't fair to him. She also knew he hated her for it. But she couldn't blame him because no matter what she said, she knew that she deserved it. She hated herself for it, too. There was nothing more painful than knowing she had to be a mother, but not feeling capable of being one. It was always the same. She hated herself for thinking that today would be any different. How many times had they been through this? He would stroll into their lives unpredictably, promising that this time would be different. But it never was. They would never be a family again, not that they ever were. But Ciarra couldn't stop herself from hoping that, by some miracle, their dysfunctional liaisons would transform into the picture she had in her head of a white picket fence and meals together at the dinner table.

Ciarra dreaded the aftermath. She knew that she couldn't take Aston to school that week. She had made the excuse that he had fallen or gotten into some kind of accident one too many times. She also dreaded how her father would react. Mike would come back to find Aston bruised and battered, and he'd lecture her, like he always did, about her poor choices in life and how unfit she was to be a mother. She couldn't face it. So instead, she decided to take Aston away.

Aria watched Ciarra get out of the van and grab his arm to come with her as if he were in trouble. She watched her pick him up and walk straight out of the car lot and disappear down the adjacent street. Ciarra wouldn't return for over a week, staying with one of the other girls who worked for the same pimp until she ran out of money and had to rely on Mike to watch Aston again. It had happened before. It would happen again.

Aria felt the all-too-familiar seduction of her usual way of coping with emotions at times like this. She tried for a while to defy it until she couldn't do so any longer. She needed the release. The release of pain.

She told Taylor and Luke she was going to pee and went out into the woods to a place outside of their visual range. She found the sullied shards of a broken beer bottle and, buzzing with adrenaline, drew the edges that were sharpest across her arms. The electric sting that sliced through her forearms as she cut them again and again was more powerful than her overwhelming feelings. The glass, now coated with her blood, became slippery as she used it. She started crying. But the multitude of splits in her arms were still weeping more than she was. The sharp sting had climaxed to an overall burning sensation that induced her body to start shaking. She watched her body forming clots to stop the flow of blood. She could feel the disunity in part of her wanting to be punished and another part, whatever part was forming those clots, wanting her to thrive. She watched her blood fall into the dust and laminate the grass blades.

Aria could see herself in the bruises that hugged Aston's face. It was a tragedy to be hidden. A cycle of perpetual let-down that neither of them could find a way to escape. It was not even the pain of yesterday that mattered. It was that the pain was back again today.

She wanted there to be a sunrise on the darkness of his life. But she couldn't make one for him any more than she could make one for herself.

CHAPTER 18

Aria had developed a cold again. Her body ached and her throat was sore. The pressure in her head made her feel disconnected from the world and it seemed like her voice had risen up into her sinuses. Taylor had gone out looking for work and had promised to try to bring something back for her to eat.

In predictable fashion, Ciarra had returned to the camp with Aston a few days earlier and Mike was watching him again. The bruises on his face had diminished and turned yellow-green. Aria didn't want him to get sick, but she was playing with him anyway because of how sad she felt for him. Aston had spied a way out of his boredom when Aria had exited the Land Cruiser and sat down beside it, looking to get some sun. He had brought his little collection of Hot Wheels cars over to her and asked her if she wanted to play.

"Not like that, like this," he said, dissatisfied with the method she was using to scoot one of the cars across the dirt.

"Vroom!" Aria sounded, trying to make an engine noise to bring life to their game of pretend. But Aston cut her attempt short.

"They don't make that sound. That's the wrong kind of engine. They sound like this … *zzzzzz*."

He repeated the sound for a couple of minutes, taking breaths in between his buzzing. He drove the car up onto Aria's legs and back down again into the dirt.

It was sad to Aria how in his own world his play was, even when he had someone to play with. She began copying him. A bright smile lit up his face and he stared at Aria with a playful, innocent look, which was uncommon to him. She showed him how to drive the car up and over the actual cars in the lot, pretending that they were huge mountains to climb, until Ciarra showed up, having been gone all night, and called him over.

Ciarra ushered him into the purple van and Aston continued the game that they had been playing across the inside of the car, while Ciarra climbed into the bed of the van and fell asleep. It was enough to break Aria's heart.

She sat down again beside the Land Cruiser. Luke waved at her on his way out of the lot with Palin. She smiled and waved back. Aria had come to find that just like Taylor, Luke had a tendency to imagine a rapport that didn't actually exist between himself and others, including the people who were currently inhabiting the car lot with them. In fact, Aria and Taylor were now more generally accepted than he was.

Despite Luke's friendliness, Mike, Robert, Darren and Anthony barely tolerated him. To be voluntarily homeless was an insult to those who had no other choice. Aria read between the lines of their obvious annoyance when he was around. They saw him as both irresponsible and pathetic. Though tolerance was a long way away from friendship, it seemed to be enough for Luke to set up camp and imagine himself to be welcome there.

Still, she couldn't help but like him. Her original dislike of him had been replaced by fondness. She felt that fondness when she watched him and Palin leave the lot to walk together toward the heart of the city.

In the afternoon, she wrote in her journal, then tried to take a nap. She grew sick of waiting for Taylor to return with nothing to do in the meantime, so resolved to walk to find a place where she could watch some television for free. In the previous weeks Aria had devised a clever way of accessing free entertainment. She would make herself look as presentable as possible, then find a restaurant with a sports bar and tell them that she needed a table for two, and ask them to sit her in a place where she had a good view of the television because the guy meeting her was a "sports buff." She would sip her water and keep telling the waiter that she didn't want to order until her date showed up. Eventually, when she was ready to leave, she would lead them to believe that she had been stood up by whoever was supposed to meet her there. She would leave without ever ordering anything and without them having any idea as to why she was actually there. On one occasion, a waitress had given her a cheesecake on the house out of pity. The only problem was, she could do it only once for each cycle of staff in each location.

As with so many homeless youth, no one noticed Aria or guessed that she was homeless. Being so young, she did not *look* homeless even though she was. Though unnaturally skinny, she was not weathered like the people who had been on the streets for years. So as long as she made sure not to be seen by police after curfew, or go to certain places when she should have been in school, she blended in to society. She blended in to the background of people's various assumptions about her, all of which were wrong.

Aria walked over to Robert's tent, hoping that he might know of a place with a television nearby that she hadn't tried yet. His bike was leaned against one of the broken-down cars, indicating that he was most likely inside his tent instead of out on the town. Getting closer, she saw his shadow inside the tent, echoing his movements. "Bob!" she called to announce herself tentatively so he wouldn't be startled by her sudden approach.

"Yep?" he said, ceasing his task to see who was calling his name. Seeing Aria's face peek in through the door of the tent, he looked unsure about her visit.

"Do you know of anywhere close to here that I could watch some TV?" Aria asked.

"Hm, not off the top of my head," he said. "Let me think."

Aria loved to hear him talk. The fact that his mouth was almost entirely toothless gave him a lisp that made him sound harmless. Coupled with his disarming personality and forgetfulness, he reminded her a bit of Winnie the Pooh.

"Why don'tcha come in here for a minute and let me think?" he said, still straining to search the outer reaches of his memory to come up with a suitable answer for her.

Aria sat down on a camping mat that was covered in little wood shavings. "I'm makin' a donkey for Darren, cause he's stubborn as a horse's ass," he explained, erupting into wheezing laughter that forced Aria to laugh too.

"I didn't know you were a carver," Aria said when their laughter had subsided.

"Oh yeah, been doin' it all my life actually. You wanna see some of my other pieces?" he asked, immediately charged with the idea of someone appreciating his craft.

"Yeah, I'd love to," Aria said.

Robert convinced his aging body to cooperate with his enthusiasm and contorted himself, reaching for a giant canvas duffle bag that was leaning against the corner of the tent. Without getting up, he dumped its contents out onto the mat beside her, an assembly of little wooden sculptures. "I know a guy that lets me sell 'em over on Grand Avenue and I done a couple of art fairs."

Aria lifted them up one by one to examine them.

Robert went back to whittling, the sound of his knife gnawing into the piece of butternut wood in his hand. She ran her fingers across the satin smoothness of their contours, admiring the curves and lines of the little details he had added to them. Except for a few naked women, children's movie characters and trees, most of them were carvings of animals of various sizes. Animals like big-horn sheep and bears and fish and horses and snakes and birds. "They're beautiful," Aria said, feeling like her rather clichéd sentiment didn't do justice to the way she felt about them.

"Thank ya," Robert replied, keeping his focus on his carving.

Having realized that their conversation about the carvings had erased Robert's memory of her original question about TV, Aria thought about asking him again, but quickly decided against it. Instead, she began putting the sculptures back into the duffle bag for him. "You can pick one if you'd like," he said.

Aria was taken aback. "But you have to sell them," she retorted.

"Eh, I'm so old you never know if I'm gonna sell em' or die tryin'." Robert erupted into laughter again, the sheer size of his smile taking over the expanse of his face.

"I really do like them, but it makes me feel guilty," Aria protested.

Robert countered it: "OK, well, if you won't just pick one, I'm gonna have to come over there and pick one for ya."

Aria abruptly became aware of the opportunity to have something special, inherent in his jest. "Actually, I'd love it if you'd pick one for me," she said, staring up at him, the open bid for his affection now in plain sight between them.

"You sure?" he said, assessing her level of certainty and getting up from his seat before she answered, "Yeah."

Robert picked through the wooden figures, occasionally stopping to scrutinize one of them, and muttering little sounds to himself as he did it. Eventually, he handed her a little carving of a beaver that he had made out of black walnut wood.

Aria ran her fingers up and down against the texture of its ligneous fur. She didn't immediately understand why he had chosen a beaver for her. It seemed a strange pick to Aria. It was not an animal that she had a relationship to already, nor was it an animal that she felt any personal connection to.

Robert maneuvered himself stiffly back to his station and resumed whittling. To Aria's relief, he began to explain himself. "The most important thing to the beaver is his home. It seems to me that home just might be the one thing you spent your life wishin' for, am I right?" He didn't wait for her to say anything because he already knew the answer.

"Home doesn't come easy to the beaver, though. He's gotta put hard work into it and interrupt the flow of nature around 'im to do it. But in the end, because he's determined to do it, he builds himself a home and then he gets his lady friends to move on in and has himself a family."

Robert chuckled, turning the rather serious weight of his sentiment into humor.

Aria was frozen to the spot. Her eyes began to well up with tears. She had to intentionally think about something entirely different than where she was in order to prevent it from showing. She knew that this was Robert's way of conveying what he wished for her future. It was his version of encouragement.

In that second, this little beaver became the most special thing that she had in her possession. It carried with it the meaning that he had ascribed to it. It carried with it her own deepest desire, which Robert had perceived without her ever saying it. And it also carried with it the quiet, internal caring that Robert felt for her. That care might never be overtly demonstrated, but because of this little interaction, they both knew it was there.

Aria got up off her knees, holding the sudden treasure in her hand, and kissed him on his cheek. "Thank you so much for this," she said.

Robert was surprised to be kissed, but smiled back as she got up to go and said, "Well, you're very welcome," before returning his focus back to whittling.

Aria walked over to the Land Cruiser. She sat in the car with the door closed, holding the little carving of the beaver in her hands. She imagined soaking in its energy. She had never loved an object so much in her entire life. She found the hidden pocket in her backpack and placed it inside for safekeeping.

Later that night, after Luke had returned from town, he and Aria were sitting face to face in his tent, engaged in a theosophical conversation, when Taylor came bounding toward them. "Oh my God … Oh my God, you guys will never believe what happened," he said, crashing into the tent to sit with them. His own excitement had taken his breath away. "You know how the studio said they were all full, right? Well, I went back today, it's like the hundredth time I went back there. And they said they have an opening for me!"

He clapped as he said it, not leaving a window open for their response. "So I'm gonna go to the studio twice a week now. One time for a work shift and one time for my acting class … Oh my God, you guys, I'm so excited."

Aria was happy for him, but she was not happy for herself. She was sick of seeing him disappointed. She was sick of watching him struggle through an experience that so far had been the exact opposite of the success he had imagined it would be. But she was also afraid. She felt him getting closer to his dreams and she felt those dreams pulling him further away from her. Unexpectedly, she found herself afraid to be left behind by him. She and Luke offered congratulations, but neither man noticed the sudden drop in Aria's mood.

Taylor reached into his backpack and produced three packages of ramen noodles. Luke had to cook them sequentially because his cooking stove was only large enough for one serving. Aria watched him pull out the propane base of his little stove, assemble the other parts around it and start cooking. To her surprise, when he was done with his first batch, he handed it to her.

Unable to wait long enough for them to cool down, Aria scalded the roof of her mouth. She ate them with a fork that Luke unfolded from his pocketknife. The all-too-familiar flavor and scent of the noodles soothed away the anxiety she felt in response to Taylor's news. She loved the wrinkled texture of them against her tongue. Taylor had picked up the theosophical conversation with Luke where she had left off. And so she resumed her usual observer role and listened to them while she ate. When he had finished, she let Palin lick the remaining broth off the edges of the bowl.

Taylor, who usually had an easy time sleeping despite any kind of disruption, could barely sleep that night from excitement. He tossed and turned, unable to stop his mind from running down the corridors of what good things might happen because of his sudden positive twist of fate. Aria, on the other hand, was not kept awake by the same ambition. She fell asleep with her hands cramped tight around the reassuring shape of the beaver statue that Robert had given her. The sudden threat of being left behind by Taylor had caused her to want a home now more than ever.

PART THREE

SONATA APPASSIONATA

CHAPTER 19

The way the light filtered into the giant hallway made the marble flooring look like it was covered in glass. The gloss of it hurt Omkar's eyes as he walked down the hall. Students sat around the round tables that were scattered to either side, their heavy textbooks stacked beside them. No one looked particularly excited. Each student seemed to be absorbed in the drudgery of what they had to get done in order to attain their chosen degree.

Omkar joined them. He sat down at a table with two other students. Only one of them looked up to acknowledge his presence. He thumbed through the polished pages of a calculus textbook until he found the pages that corresponded to the professor's daily assignment and began resolving equations with his mechanical pencil.

Omkar was in his second year at college. He had chosen to major in civil engineering. Even though he didn't know it yet, his choice of major had been determined the year he was born.

Omkar wasn't always an only child. He used to have two older siblings. His parents had not been planning to have another child and so Omkar had been totally unexpected. They had a son, Ajit, who was 20, and a daughter, Shashi, who was 16. Ajit had recently moved from where they lived in Chandigarh to Bhuj in the state of Gujarat to work for a textile export company. As fate would have it, Shashi had gone to visit Ajit, accompanied by her aunt, for Republic Day. But that day, an earthquake hit that turned out to be one of the deadliest earthquakes in the history of India. The earthquake destroyed 400,000 homes. Twenty thousand people died that day. Omkar's brother, sister and aunt were among them.

Having only just been born when it happened, Omkar didn't remember his parents' reaction when they heard the news. He had no memory of his sister or brother. But the tragedy was like a thundercloud always hanging over the family. His mother kept their pictures on the wall. She clutched Omkar tighter because of the loss of them. She clutched him so tight, he could barely breathe. It was as if his parents had placed all of themselves in him and in his life's trajectory, which they tried to control every part of.

After the tragedy happened, they spent five more years in Chandigarh before deciding that they couldn't take the pain of trying to feel like a family again in the same house that Ajit and Shashi had been raised in. They considered moving to a different house in the same city. But it would have been the same way of life. They wanted a new life altogether. So, when Omkar was seven, they decided to move to America. They chose to move to Los Angeles because of the weather and the dreams they imagined they could make a reality there. Although he had been a market research analyst in India, the only job that Omkar's father could get in America was in a little convenience store called the Sun Market. He worked hard and saved money until he offered to buy the place from its owner, who wanted to retire. He renamed the place the Super Sun Market. The family had been both working and living there above the store ever since.

Omkar wanted to be a civil engineer in order to design and construct buildings that could withstand any earthquake. This goal was the North Star of his life. The Gujarat earthquake lasted just over two minutes. In those two minutes, the entire course of his family's lives was changed. It was tainted forever. Three members of his family had been lost. And some people had an even worse fate. Some that were there, who did not die themselves, lost everything and everyone. Omkar couldn't live with the idea that in a matter of minutes, something like this could happen. He had so many reasons for having this goal, but deep down, part of him felt like if he just figured out how to resolve the issue that had killed them in the first place, the dark cloud over the family might lift.

When he was done with the assignment, Omkar got up from his place at the table in the great hall. He tried to make as little noise as possible collecting his things. Before driving home, he bought a burrito, which he ate in a solitary corner of the cafeteria, watching other students contemplate their purchases. Despite coming to America, Omkar's family only ever made Indian food. He knew that his mother would have some waiting for him when he got home. It wasn't that he didn't like her cooking; he loved it. It was that eating American food sometimes made him feel less foreign. And today was one of those days where he wanted to feel less foreign. Despite having been in America for almost 12 years now, he hadn't managed to lose his accent, and as a result, he felt like people couldn't see him at all. All they saw was the stereotype of an Indian exchange student. Omkar hated that people couldn't see through that stereotype almost as much as he hated how unfortunate it was that he fit that stereotype so closely.

And he wanted time to think. Omkar was haunted by his encounter with Aria. The day she'd come into the store, he had raced downstairs expecting to find one or two of his parents' friends standing there, waiting to scold him for his poor service and irresponsibility. He had thought her to be the most beautiful thing he had ever seen. He had found it hard to hide the shyness he felt in her presence with the usual "greet-the-customer routine" that his parents expected him to execute perfectly. He couldn't get her out of his mind.

He'd allowed her to swim around in his head, letting the idea of her distract him from the boredom of the store. He extended the meeting in his own mind. He imagined her life in the suburbs of LA. He imagined her mom and dad and sister and brother. He imagined her at college and wondered what she was studying there. He had no idea how wrong about her he really was. But there was something about her loneliness that mirrored his loneliness and promised that they might find what they both lacked together.

He would most likely never see her again. But the fact she existed made him feel like maybe a woman existed out there in the world who could tame his loneliness. And he let the promise of it comfort him.

— * —

The unpredictable chords of the overly dramatic soundtrack from a Bollywood soap opera dominated the room. Omkar's mother, Jarminder, was glued to the screen as usual, fully immersed in the storyline. Her figure was the very epitome of an Indian mother. Her curves softened into the subtle corpulence of middle age. A furrow of displeasure was always written across her face. Despite the overacting, these soap operas were her drug of choice. And except for the fact that it gave him temporary relief from her constant micromanagement, Omkar hated them.

Omkar was bothered by so much about his mother. He didn't understand why they had come to America in the first place if they planned to bring so much of India with them. His mother still wore a salwar kameez every day of the week. To be fair, the silk fabric was more beautiful than what people of the Western world wore, but it was just one more thing that made fitting in impossible for the Agarwal family. Jarminder hated speaking English. Frequently, she would speak to Omkar and her husband in Punjabi and they would respond in English at home. She was as irritated with this behavior as they were irritated by her refusal to speak the language of the country that they were still trying to make into a home. It made her feel like she was losing herself.

Omkar's father, Neeraj, also bothered him. Though he had demanded that they all learn perfect English, he too had defiantly brought his customs with him. Every day he would wake up and tediously wrap the navy blue fabric of his traditional Sikh turban into an aggressive peak. This was the image of his father that Omkar would always remember. His *kara*, a cast iron bracelet he wore on his right wrist, would slide across the surface of his arm as he pulled and folded the fabric of his turban across his cheekbones. In traditional Sikh form, as a sign of his acceptance of God's will, he did not cut the hair from any part of his body. The bottom half of his face was claimed by wild black facial hair, which had long since been transforming into gray.

Omkar stood in the kitchen looking down over the street. He filled up a water glass, failing to turn off the faucet before it began to overflow onto his hands. "*Dhi'āna rakhō*," his father said in their native tongue. It was a warning to be careful. Neeraj had taken it upon himself to bring Omkar's feet onto solid ground. His son's dreamy nature didn't make him feel confident about his capacity to work hard enough to carve out a life for himself. The sound of Neeraj's voice was deep and authoritative. Sometimes his father reminded Omkar of a warrior who had retired into the retail business. After all, the Sikhs had been warriors.

Omkar stared at the glorified painting of Guru Nanak on the wall. The look on his face and the way he had his hand lifted in the painting always made Omkar feel like he was messing up. Neeraj had aspired to fashion himself after Nanak's virtue. As a result, Nanak always reminded Omkar less of a guru and more of his own father.

Though Omkar wore a thin version of the traditional *kara* bracelet, he had chosen when he was very young to shave, cut his hair and abandon the traditional Sikh costume. Sometimes, this made him feel guilty. Neeraj and Jarminder still felt invalidated in their lives and beliefs by his decision. They wanted Omkar to be proud of his faith and most of all proud of the culture that had forged the marrow in his bones. But they also knew that faith could not be forced upon their son. They knew that the tighter they held him, the more he would rebel, and they were afraid that rebellion might just lead him to reject their culture entirely. And so, there was a tension in the house that was never directly addressed. You could only feel it sometimes in sideways comments and in the emotional distance between them.

Neeraj sat down on the couch beside Jarminder. The companionship of his wife could only be accessed at times like this by joining her in her fixation on the screen. He asked her for an update on the plot line. Irritated at the possibility of missing something, she caught him up in a fast and exasperated tone before settling into the pleasure of having someone to experience the rollercoaster of intrigue with her.

Omkar, who had only come upstairs for a drink during his shift watching over the family shop, sidled back down the stairs. The store seemed emptier than ever. He stood behind the checkout counter staring at the products, whose packaging advertised only to the emptiness in the room. It felt like a waste of life doing what every good Indian boy should do with the family business. "How much more of a cliché could I be?" he wondered. But he didn't want to hurt his parents any more than they had been hurt already. Omkar hadn't yet carved out his own life because of the fact that he would have to leave his parents' lives to do it. He couldn't face the severity of the shame inherent in doing so. He couldn't choose to betray them by becoming one more thing that they had put all their energy into, only to lose.

With no customers to serve, he pulled out his laptop computer and went back to his schoolwork until out of the corner of his eye he caught the silhouette of someone about to come through the door. Omkar felt an alarm go off inside himself, the ecstatic shock of seeing her again. It was the girl who had come into the store a week or two ago. Despite his shyness, he stood up and immediately welcomed her back.

— * —

Aria was almost upset to discover that the strange feelings she had felt for the man who stood before her were back. She afforded him a bashful smile and began looking through the aisles. It felt wrong to have come back there, but once again, Aria was desperate. Her period, being predictably unpredictable as usual, had rebounded back into her life. Aria was mad at herself for not having spent some money on provisions when she had it. But since it had not been an immediate need, she had not prioritized preparing for it.

Having used her socks again and spent most of the morning sitting still, she imagined that the woman at the church, Imani, might have some way to help her out. But she had arrived too late for the meal service and Imani was nowhere to be found. That was when the idea of coming back to the little market had popped into her mind. Aria had hoped that, in keeping with the first day she had visited, the store would be untended long enough for her to steal what she needed. There was a deeper part of her that wanted the man who had been there on the first day to be there again. But necessity trumped the degree that she currently cared for him.

Omkar desperately searched for the least awkward way to approach her to ask for her number as Aria scanned the aisles until she found what she was looking for. Resorting to her go-to technique of looking at an item with one hand and putting another in her pocket with the other, she took a mini-pack of tampons and slid them in her pocket. That jolted Omkar out of the romantic interlude he was planning for them in his mind. Because he liked her, he was paying special attention to the security mirror in the corner of the room, hoping to learn something about her from her purchase choices. And so he had seen her take the item off of the shelf.

He felt his excitement drop as if hurled from a ten-story building. Maybe he'd been wrong about this girl all along. She didn't seem like the type to shoplift. He had imagined that the connection he felt between them would certainly mean that she wouldn't do something like that to his family. He tried to rectify his impression of her by telling himself that she didn't know the store was owned by his family. Perhaps she just thought he worked there as a clerk. He felt dizzy, not knowing what to do. He could hear his father in his head, yelling at him to call the police. He didn't want to do that to her. But he didn't know what to do, so he stood like a statue, in shock, doing nothing.

Aria picked out the cheapest packet of gum she could find and walked toward the checkout counter. For a second,

Omkar hoped that she would take the item out of her pocket and pay for it as well, so he could go back to seeing her in the way that he did before tonight. But she didn't. Instead, she took a handful of spare change out of her pocket for the gum, hoping that the purchase would serve as further disguise for what she had taken. The noise from the cash register took up the space where their words did not. Aria was disappointed by his suddenly withdrawn demeanor; he had been so friendly before. But all she could think of was getting out of the place quick enough to avoid being found out. So when he handed her back a dime and some pennies, she pivoted and walked back out the door.

Omkar stood at the counter in shock for 30 seconds before the idea of following her shot into his head. The rush of the decision had already taken hold of him. "Papa, Papa, watch over the store for me!" he yelled upstairs, throwing his jacket over his shoulders and struggling to get his arms through the sleeves fast enough.

Neeraj came downstairs with a worried look on his face. "What is this?" he said, equally concerned and perturbed at his son's request.

"It's something I forgot at school. It's very important." Omkar's apology was inherent in the way that he said it. Neeraj was visibly frustrated by his son's immaturity in having forgotten something so important, but he nodded consent and Omkar sprang out the door.

He looked frantically both ways down the street as far as he could, searching for her. As fortune would have it, he could just make out the patched design of her camo pants and the edges of her hair being played with by the wind as she walked away from him. He began to follow.

It was one of the most exciting things he'd ever done in his life. Keeping the perfect distance to survey her every movement, but also making sure never to be noticed, made him feel like a character in one of the action movies he loved so much.

After 30 minutes had passed, the feeling of excitement began to crumble at the edges. It was confusing to him that she was still walking. They had walked so far, Omkar was afraid of not being able to find his way back to the store. He felt more worried now than intrigued. But he continued to follow her down the dismal, crowded streets and through alleyways, stoplight after stoplight impeding the flow of her progress toward wherever she was going.

After two hours had passed, Omkar knew he would have to call a cab to get back home. It had also started to rain. He was following Aria with a knot in his stomach. At first he had imagined the spy mission to be fun. But it wasn't fun anymore. He had assumed that, because she strolled into the store on foot, she must live in the neighborhood, especially given that she'd showed up twice. He was now plagued by confusion about why she would ever walk so far. He was bothered by the idea that a girl shouldn't be walking alone on the streets of any city, much less for so long. Omkar was now committed to the mission of finding out where the hell she was going, more out of concern than a sense of curious adventure.

The distance between the houses and buildings began to grow larger. The sun had given up on their journey, casting an indigo hue over everything in sight. Omkar watched Aria take a side road. Following her down it, through the haze of the rain, he watched her duck under a broken stretch of chain-link fencing. He saw her walk over to a car in a broken-down car lot and get inside it. Careful to go unnoticed, Omkar waited before exploring further from a distance. He walked a full circle around the car lot. By the time he was done observing the tarps and tents and clutter, he was soaking wet. But Omkar had ascertained enough to understand what was truly happening. He watched Aria and a few of the other people at the encampment until his view was too severely obscured by night.

Omkar dueled with the branches of the trees and bushes in order to get back to a main road without being seen. Instead of immediately calling a cab, he sat down on a curb, letting the hum of the cars pass by him. He had assumed that Aria had stolen the pack of tampons because of some habitual pattern of defiant rule-breaking. He had expected to follow her to some suburban home which belonged to two parents, much like his own, whose rules were strung too tight for her to breathe. So tight that she had to break rules somehow, even if they never knew that she had broken them. But that was not what was happening at all. It was clear to him that she had stolen the tampons because she literally had to.

Omkar didn't know what to do. He loved her even more now. He was conscious of loving her when the thought of loving her more now crossed his mind. He was in love with this girl, who he knew almost nothing about, a girl he had never officially met. He wanted to go back and rescue her, but take her where? And what if she didn't like him? What if the way she looked at him was just a strategy to be able to steal what she needed to live?

When Omkar finally did call a cab to go home, he did his best to memorize the route between the car lot and his family's store. It felt so wrong to leave her there that as he was driving away, every cell in his body revolted. One day the minutes of his boring life had been ticking away and now, he could not fall back in line with those minutes. His mind was possessed with the image of her and all the unanswered questions he had about her.

— * —

Totally unaware of her new admirer, Aria smoked a cigarette, hoping that it would alleviate the pain of her cramps. She cracked the door open so as to not submerge them both in smoke and leaned against it.

"You shouldn't be doin' that," Taylor said from the front passenger seat.

At first Aria thought he was referring to the cigarette she was smoking. "Dude, I'm fucked right now, could you just get off my back?" she said.

"No. Fuck it!" Taylor yelled, turning around with tears in his eyes. "She's not good company and you don't need her fucking up your life too. You don't need to go doin' things with her like that."

It took Aria a second to realize that he was referring to Ciarra and her one-time attempt at hooking.

Taylor had arrived early and had rifled through her backpack, looking for the pocketknife that Luke had recently given her. Despite the protests of his conscience, he had read her journal, including the entry she had made about having prostituted. It had plagued him for the last few hours. Coming back to the car lot to find her gone had made him assume that it was not a one-time thing and that she was at it again that night.

Unaware that he had read her journal, Aria imagined that Ciarra had said something to him about it.

"Dude, I only went with her one time and it didn't work out … Why the fuck do you even care?" Aria yelled back, taken completely by surprise by his outrage, especially given that he didn't bother to consult her about the trajectory of his own life.

"Because you're better than that. You're better than her. You don't need to go doin' that shit."

Taylor turned back to face the windshield, his arms crossed to protect his vulnerability. He was quietly crying.

Aria felt judged, but beneath that judgment she could clearly see from his reaction the attachment that he had to her. Feeling loved to that degree made it impossible to defend herself with an attack.

"I only did it once and it didn't work out. I swear to God I haven't gone back, it's too fucked up," Aria countered.

"You swear to God you aren't lying to me?" Taylor said, turning around to face her again, scanning her face to determine her sincerity.

Aria said nothing further. She looked him straight in the face. Taylor started to cry again, pulling her head toward him with the crook of his elbow so as to hug her as best as he could, given the awkward position of their bodies relative to one another.

Taylor considered her to be like a little sister and the idea of her falling prey to predators behind his back was more than he could bear. "OK, just promise me," he said, wiping the tears away from his cheeks.

"I swear to God," Aria said, trying to wiggle out from under the pressure of his request.

"OK, 'cause I love you," Taylor said, waiting for her to reassure him in return.

"I do too," she said. It was not an impressive response, but it was enough for him to turn back around and position himself to go to sleep.

Aria was as uncomfortable with the pressure Taylor put on her to live up to his expectations as she was with the sudden realization that he cared so much about her. That pressure, though uncomfortable, made her feel warm inside her chest.

Instead of immediately falling asleep, she looked out the window at the broken-down RV that Darren had turned into his garrison. Whatever light source he was using cast just enough glow for her to see the chaos of clutter among which he lived his life: piles upon piles of items he had found and brought back here. For Darren, these things had become a safety signal, a way to buffer himself against the soreness of his own vulnerability. It was a life's worth of people who were so inconsistent, unreliable and impermanent that they could only be counted on to use and take things *from* him that had made him this way. It was safer for him now to attach to things rather than people. It was the only way to predict and control his life. It was the only way to feel good.

Darren could look at anything and imagine a potential time when he might need it. The piles were the closest he could get to closeness. They felt cozy to him. The physical distance between objects, which is created when people organize things, felt cold and isolated to him. He didn't want that separation.

That organized separation between objects reopened the wound of emptiness and isolation. Besides that, Darren hated space. For Darren, space meant exposure, where attack could come from anywhere at any moment. Having clutter around him offered him enclosure and padding from potential threat.

When Darren had returned from war, he began to identify with trash. There was a day before he ended up out on the streets where he was about to throw away a milk carton and suddenly he saw himself in that milk carton. It was suddenly something that he had used and was about to throw away the same way that the army had used him up and thrown him away. He couldn't stand it. So he washed it out and filled it with soil to use it as a pot for a dandelion he dug up from the lawn outside the house. Seeing the value in anything and everything was the best way he could find to resolve the wound of being treated as if he no longer had any value and of being used and discarded himself.

Though the seemingly careless and unsanitary way that he kept his possessions suggested a lack of caring, that couldn't be further from the truth. Darren was terrified of losing his things or having someone take them away. The very idea of it threatened to reopen the scab covering his wounds. He could not face the idea of needing something and not having it, or even worse, not being able to get it. He could not face that emptiness of the emotional neglect that he had filled up with things. He could not face the idea of himself being discarded. He could not face the panic of exposure. To lose his things was to lose the only relationships in his life that he felt like he really *did* have.

Aria felt sorry for Darren. Her own wounds allowed her to clearly see his. Like her, he was just doing the best he could with what the world had refused to give him. Like them all, he drained the soul from the cigarette between his lips, as if begging for mercy from a God that had cursed him. The indifference with which people passed by his noiseless cry was a sin in and of itself. He had built his life on the shoal of their insults and spare pocket change. Aria knew that this was probably how he would live out what was left of his life and that this was most likely the way he would die. And despite the bramble of his character, it nearly broke her heart. She distracted herself from the strain of watching him anymore by lying down and thinking about the man from the store. He had told her his name on the first day they had met and she tried to remember it, but couldn't.

Aria imagined what it would be like if she had met the man under different circumstances – if they had been classmates together, or had met at a party somewhere. Almost any other circumstance seemed to guarantee her more dignity in their meeting. Aria fantasized about the certainty of love exchanged in a moment, finding each other face to face in some revolving door. She imagined herself to be more glamorous than she was now, a woman of class and fortunate circumstance. That certainty felt more beautiful to Aria than the uncertainty of the sudden passion that she felt for him and the inevitable lack of passion she was convinced that he would feel in return if he knew anything about her.

CHAPTER 20

The three of them sat beneath a noisy underpass. It was the best place they could find to avoid the rain, which by noon was so heavy that it looked to drown everything in sight. Aria had found a giant blue rain slicker at a pre-Christmas clothing donation drive at one of the homeless shelters on the outskirts of the city nearly a month ago. She was gladder of it now than ever.

Aria, Wolf and Taylor had visited a food pantry on their way from the public library back to the car lot. Wolf slid the hooked end of the can-opener blade on his Swiss Army knife across the lid of a jar of baked beans, breaking the metal tediously as he went. His long hair, not tamed into a ponytail like usual, blew in the wind as if it were caught in a water current. Aria stared at the veins that were woven like tree roots just under the surface of his hands. When he managed to open the can enough, he slid his fingers under the razor-sharp edge and forced the lid, still attached, to bend open. He handed the can to Aria, who began to spoon the contents into her mouth with two fingers. It confused her senses to be eating beans cold like this. Taylor had upended a plastic container of applesauce and was patiently trying to drink it so as to avoid getting his hands dirty.

Taylor was in such fabulous spirits that the curve of the overpass might as well have been the curve of a spiral staircase in a palace. Due to his willingness to do anything and everything that would get him closer to his dreams, he had proven himself to be so useful to the acting studio that they had asked him to come four times a week now instead of two. Aria watched him in awe. Here he was, sitting underneath an overpass, no money, no car, no home, eating his only meal of the day, with a smile on his face as if he were a king. She was envious of his buoyancy.

Having lost focus for just a second, Aria felt the acute sting of the lid of the can carving a small split into her knuckle. She winced, sucking in her breath loudly enough for Wolf to hear her. She watched the blood well up and weep down the topside of her fingers. Wolf dropped what he was doing, grabbed a handful of the dirt that had not yet been soaked through by rain and released it softly right over the top of the wound. The cardinal red of her blood mixed with the dust to make a muddy paste on the surface of her hand.

"Just keep it there, it'll stop the bleeding," Wolf said, returning to what he'd been doing.

"Thanks," Aria said, trying hard not to think about whether the dirt he had used was clean or tainted by road filth or some other vagrant's alcoholic urine.

Their hunger made the effort of talking an expense that none of them seemed willing to afford for the most part, until Taylor grew anxious with the silence. "My class is putting on a play of *The Little Prince*."

He was talking to Aria, but Wolf was the one to respond to him. "That's a good story," he said.

Both Taylor and Aria were taken aback that someone like Wolf would even know what that was, especially given that even Aria had no idea what the hell Taylor was talking about.

"You know it?" Taylor asked, lit up with the potential for conversation.

"'It is only with the heart that one can see rightly what is invisible to the eye.' Yeah, I know it," Wolf responded. Taylor stared at him, waiting for an explanation. "It was one of the books we read in one of them Head Start programs on the rez. The main character kind of reminds me of you, in'it?"

"Really? I wanna know why?" Taylor pleaded, excited at the idea of being recognized by someone.

"The little prince was kind of an alien, in'it?" Wolf said in the native cadence of his thick rez accent. "He doesn't belong anywhere. And he's got this big imagination, even though none of the other people do. He gets lost in this desert and, kinda like a vision quest, he learns about himself there. And he meets this rose and this fox and learns how to be responsible like a man and about what love really is. And the story kinda makes it good to imagine, like you always imaginin'. He even kinda looks like you, in'it?" Wolf's teeth sparkled when he was finished explaining himself.

"Hey, thanks," Taylor said, so thrilled with the knowledge that he was significant enough for Wolf to have taken notice of him that he was oblivious to the sweet but subtle insult that his parallel contained. "I always thought I was so good, but goin' to these classes makes me feel like intimidated, like I'm more insecure than I thought I would be. And when you're acting, that just makes you look like an idiot."

"You just gotta find a part of every character you play inside you. And then it's easy 'cause you're not really acting and you're not afraid to do it wrong 'cause it's real," Wolf told him.

Taylor stared at Wolf in total shock, willing to soak up his obviously good advice. "Did you act or somethin'?" he asked.

"No, it just makes sense. Besides, acting is all us Injuns are doin' anyway. I've got to act and dress like a white man every day." Wolf chuckled at his own humor.

"Wait, I don't get it." Taylor said, staring squarely at Wolf as if his entire acting career hung in the balance of understanding the concept.

"Let's say you've got to be a character that's really angry. You just gotta find the part of you that's really angry and let it out," Wolf said in between bites from a can of cold ravioli.

Instead of indulging Taylor's obvious desperation for tutelage, Wolf allowed what he had said to act as a tide, pulling him deep into the ocean of his own angst. He addressed Aria and Taylor as if they themselves had been the offenders. "The killin' of us has been so effective that many of us Natives can barely say a word in our own language, much less recite the prayers the ways our ancestors did. This is what they did to us. The pain and the anger is so deep and ancestral that I got no idea what the fuck's going on inside me or how to deal with it. But our perspectives and truths are met with deaf ears. The futility and hopelessness in all the people of Turtle Island is a wild fire destroying us from within."

Wolf beat his chest as he spoke. He paused for a moment and then went on, letting his anger spill forth from wherever it was stored within him.

"It's been like this ever since the moment they set foot on Turtle Island over 500 years ago in 1492 … when that murderer and sickened spirit Christopher Columbus stepped foot on the continent that's been our home for thousands of years. He and his conquistadors tore Arawak babies from their mothers and fed them to their dogs alive. Tortured and raped our women in front of our Native men to break our spirits. We became infected with 'em."

Aria and Taylor had stopped eating and were instead watching Wolf guardedly. Neither of them was sure whether they were entering into a conflict with him or were simply watching a process of self-implosion. In truth, they had unintentionally wandered into a war that he had been waging long before meeting them, one that had started long before he was ever born.

"We speak the same words from our mouths as the white man, but the language of the heart and how we communicate to the web of life is different," Wolf continued. "It is a language the white man don't possess. We are invisible to 'em unless we are used as their sports mascots or slaves. They exploit our medicine, ceremonies, culture and textiles. They sell us. They label us as Indians, Redskins and Savages, and change our tribal names to bastardized references so it better suits their ignorance. We Natives have so many ways of being, but we are seen by the white man only one way … as warriors on horseback with our shirts off and with long dark hair … with painted faces and buckskin and bows and arrows. They force us to play roles as the villains in every story told where the white cowboy is always the hero savin' the day. Even the Lone Ranger's sidekick is named 'Tonto' which is a word that means stupid. They call us savage and simple but they are the savages. They annihilated over 100 million of us. Ten times more people than Nazi Germany killed.

"We call the white man 'Little Brother.' Because it's the Little Brother that needs to be taught. He doesn't know how to work with nature anymore, including his own nature. He has to be reminded of how to take care of himself and all existence again. But Little Brother is a stubborn, defensive little shit and blind to the death he causes to the natural world. We have lost countless animals, tribes and holy grounds to extinction because of his 'modern world.' The heat even rises in our atmosphere and still Little Brother doesn't believe what the wisdom keepers have been warning us about. We are banished or exiled by the white man into reservations and barrios, and those places don't give us a place to belong. All that's left is anger. We rot out there in the abuse, the alcohol, the poverty, the religions and the broken way of life that has been forced on us by the white man. We had to practice our own spirituality in secret until 1978."

Wolf fell silent. His soliloquy suddenly turned inwards against himself. The most deafening war within him was being fought because Wolf was a mixed breed. The rape, pillaging and slavery brought to his people by what Wolf called Little Brother meant that he, like so many other Natives, had both the victim and the villain in his veins. Many of his suicidal downswings were initiated by the fact that he had turned against his own blood. The white man was once a demon that had come to them. Now, he and his people faced new demons. Most of them, the kind that resided within. Wolf wanted the earth and its people to return to what it was before those demons had landed. The brawl against the modern way of life was a varnish covering the fact that he knew deep down that life would never be that way again. To Wolf, every rock and tree and animal and stream was not only family, it was himself. He dreamed of coexistence. He dreamed of Tribe.

But he could not seem to create it. He screamed against the sickness that they had been infected with. That sickness was not smallpox. It was separation.

Aria and Taylor said nothing and just let Wolf's words wash over them. Both of them knew that Wolf was right about everything he said. But at the same time, neither of them felt that it was fair to be resented to such an obvious degree for crimes that they themselves had not committed. Nor did it feel fair to be expected to pay the price for what their forefathers had done. Especially given that they never asked to be related to them in the first place. Even if there was a way for someone to repair the damage done, Aria and Taylor were in no position to help themselves, much less sew together the patchwork of a fragmented past. The crimes of those who came before them, who bore the same skin color as their own, were like a yoke around their neck that they were born with. They would forever be seen as the villain for what their ancestors had done to people of other races, colors and creeds. Both Aria and Taylor knew that the resentment would immediately convert to both fury and ridicule if they were to say anything about the mutuality of pain inherent in being just as incapable of changing the color of their own skin. They were both aware that expressing the pain of the unwelcome inheritance of the stigma of being white was taboo. And so, they kept silent.

For a few minutes, Taylor searched through the confusion of his feelings about what Wolf had said, until he recalled the original lesson that Wolf had meant to convey to him about acting. He looked for a part of himself that was as angry, but his search was cut short by a noise coming from across the street. A man, engulfed in multiple layers of clothing, had begun throwing handfuls of mud and rocks at the cars passing by. His sanity had been corrupted into a fight that he was having with the thin air. They watched him lost in the distressed pattern of muttering to himself before screaming an outburst of profanities and flailing his body around as if warding off imaginary attackers.

The presence of the man made all three of them nervous. Aria tried to pay attention to something else, sensing that if this man felt the pressure of her attention on him, she might show up on his radar enough to make him cross the street. He was trapped in an alternate reality, where everything and everyone was just a part of the world that only existed in his own mind. Aria did not want to show up in that reality. She knew that if she did, she would exist there as something other than herself. He would fit her into his story *about* her, and if that story about her was a bad one, he might become violent toward her.

After a few minutes, a police car rolled up to the curb and two officers stepped out. The man began rocking back and forth. Aria felt her chest begin to ache. It was obvious that the police were trying to help him, even while they were getting him to stop throwing rocks at the cars. But she knew that the man had already fit the two police officers into his reality, the poisoned game of unintentional pretend that was taking place in his own mind. It was a false reality, where everything and everyone was out to get him. They were powerless; there was no way to avoid directly playing into his disordered storyline.

Aria watched as one of the officers managed to convince him that he had come to take him to a safer place. The man rocked his willowy body over to the police car, shouting one more time at the cars on the road before getting into the back seat willingly.

When Aria saw the cop car make a U-turn, she jumped behind Wolf, suddenly afraid that they would see her and Taylor, who looked younger than he was, and try to bust them both for truancy. But instead the car drove right past them. She eyed it until she couldn't see it any longer and instead began to worry about what might happen to the man.

Making sure the coast was clear, they got up and walked in the direction of the car lot. By the time they reached the lot, the moisture in the air, mixed with the brine of their sweat, had made their clothes adhere to their skin. Aria convinced Taylor and Wolf to walk to the stream in the woods, where

Luke had taken her. Despite the overall chill of the day, being put off by the scent of herself, Aria had it in her mind for them to launder some of their clothes. She left Taylor and Wolf standing outside the fence, waiting so she could go see if Luke wanted to join them.

When she approached his tent, it was empty. Though the door was zipped closed, she could tell that he had left with Palin for the day. But when she turned back around, something strange caught her eye. It was a little collection of items lined up on the hood of the Land Cruiser.

Aria approached the broken-down car, which she now considered a home, with hesitation. She wasn't sure if it was a practical joke or a cosmic blessing or even if she was seeing clearly. A packet of baby wipes, a water bottle, a pair of new socks in a plastic ziplock bag, three granola bars, fruit snacks, a new toothbrush and toothpaste, a burrito wrapped in silver foil and a Snickers bar. Aria stood in front of the hood, confused. She didn't know if the items that were placed there were for her or for Taylor, or if, by some bizarre circumstance, someone else had left their personal stash there. She didn't want to unintentionally find herself in a conflict, but she also didn't want to lose an opportunity where one had presented itself, so she collected the items and stuffed them inside her backpack as fast as she could. She decided that if Taylor or anyone else came looking for them, she would pretend that she had taken the items for safekeeping. Until it was clear that no one would come looking for them, she would not allow herself to get excited or even to consider them hers.

She rejoined Taylor and Wolf. They spent the rest of the day at the river, which had grown irascible and swollen with the California winter.

— * —

Omkar had pored over various articles online about the things that homeless people need. He had searched the landscape of his conscience for an argument against taking items from the family shop and giving them to the girl he was in love with, but in the end, he couldn't find one that was good enough. During his next shift, he collected the items in a little plastic bag and waited until he could find a perfect time to drive back to the car lot, hoping that she would still be there. Omkar had never intended to walk up to her and give her the items. He knew she would probably be embarrassed. He had always planned to put them somewhere for her to find.

Sneaking into the car lot made him nervous. To him, the people who occupied these kinds of places seemed like animals. He was afraid of them. But he pushed through the fear, willing to take the risk that one of them might attack if they saw him. He had watched the lot for long enough to see that the girl wasn't there. He lined up the items on the car that he had seen her get into, and ran back the same way he had come.

Omkar knew there was a risk that one of the other people living in the lot might take them. But he justified the risk by telling himself that even if they did, it was because they needed it. He crouched behind the trees for so long he was almost ready to leave before he saw her walking down the road with two men beside her. He watched her tell them to wait and walk over to the car. He watched her look around and stuff the items he had placed there into her backpack. It reminded him of scenes he had seen in nature documentaries on television – those scenes where a wild animal finally takes the food that someone is offering, and the relief of knowing that the animal might then be OK.

As he watched her, it occurred to Omkar that a man could stab a girl without making her bleed. He could break her heart without hearing it shatter. It was clear to him that she had been both stabbed and shattered, but that the affliction had not weathered the lily of her face. Unlike those men, he both saw and heard that pain.

The assault of the worry that he felt for her was pacified by her immediate acceptance of the things that he had given her. To be a man, taking care of a woman, even to this small degree that she would currently let him, made him feel a strength that until this point had been unknown to him. He felt that strength spill through his muscles. He felt it fortify his spine.

Omkar could not rationally explain his feelings for her to himself or to anyone else for that matter. She was still unknown to him and yet she was more known to him than his own breath.

He smiled from ear to ear. He tasted the value of that smile. He felt its symmetry against his lips. Once she was out of sight, he walked back to his car. The sound of his footsteps was no longer the sound of his movement forward in life. There was no longer a destination. Omkar knew he was exactly where he was supposed to be.

CHAPTER 21

Aria traced the scores lacing her arms. The cut marks she had made had been reformed into purple scars beneath the confines of her coat sleeves. Though raised, they were smooth to the touch. One part of her was ashamed of them. Another part wanted them to be her voice. She wanted them to scream for the rescue that she couldn't. She waited until she was finished peeing, wiping herself with a leaf that she had pulled from the soil, and stood up from her squatting place in the woods.

Having done some research on edible plants at the library recently, Aria had been scouring the cracks between sidewalks in the vicinity of the car lot looking for purslane. And she had found some. Not in the dense mats that they are so often found in, but she found more than a few solitary patches crocheting the cracks in the cement. Its tiny jade-like leaves stretched outwards on stems whose red tint made them appear to be dyed with cherry juice. She had wandered off into the woods with a handful to find a spot to eat them. The tart flavor of the weed reminded her of watercress stained by citrus.

Aria was inspirited by the potential of foraging. Until recently, the idea was something she had never contemplated. It wasn't until her body started breaking down that she began to value the freshness of natural foods. So much of the diet she had access to on the street was restricted to what contained enough preservatives to not need refrigeration, what cans of food were available at food banks and what uneaten leftovers could be salvaged out of trash cans. Her diet was causing her to crumble and her body told the tale. The idea that edible plants and especially weeds could be growing in abundance all around her, but that she didn't know enough to recognize them yet, opened up a whole new realm of possibilities. It opened up the possibility of feeling good. It opened up the possibility of not panicking about where her next meal would come from. And it opened up the possibility of not having to entangle herself so deeply in the humiliating, and strings-attached, dependence on other people's charity.

After such a successful mission, she resolved to return to the library soon to learn everything she could, and she walked back to the car lot in high spirits. Feeling passion again toward anything at all was like a tonic to her veins.

Climbing over the fence to the car lot, she felt happy to see that Taylor had arrived there first. He was sitting in the front seat of the Land Cruiser, looking through the black and white mesh of words in a local newspaper. She opened the back door to get inside. "You would never guess what I found," she said. "There are plants growing all around the city that you can just eat. It's so cool."

Taylor smiled at her, more enthusiastic about the uplift of her attitude than he was about the actual subject matter responsible for that uplift.

She had brought him back a sprig of purslane to try. She handed it to him. Taylor put it in his mouth skeptically, twisting it around with his tongue and scrunching up his nose in disapproval of the taste.

"Oh my God, stop it. It's good," she said in response to the faces he was making and they both started giggling.

"Hey, do you know why these things were on the hood of the car?" Taylor asked nonchalantly, lifting a small collection of items from the area beside his feet. He expected Aria to give him an obvious answer. He handed them to Aria. "These newspapers were on the car too," he added. Aria examined the items; a bottle of sunscreen, a pack of feminine hygiene pads, two juice packets and a gift card to the fast-food restaurant that was closest to them, which just so happened to be a Subway sandwich store.

"I literally have no fucking idea," Aria said.

"Seriously? Hm. Maybe Luke put them there," Taylor said, throwing the paper down to go ask him.

Aria watched him walk over to Luke's tent and crouch down to pet Palin, while he asked Luke about the items. The confused look on his face did not dissipate. He came back to the car. "Nope. He's got no idea either. But he saw 'em there before I did and was about to tell us how dumb it was to keep our stuff there out in the open for everyone to see."

Aria thought about telling Taylor about the first items that she had found in the exact same place, but decided against it. "I'm totally keeping this, then," Taylor said, lifting the sunscreen into the air. "I'd like to avoid looking like a tomato, thank you. I'm so white I'm practically see-through." He stashed it in his backpack. "Oh, and this. I have to keep this because you never know when that shit's gonna start," he said, framing the feminine hygiene pads between his hands as a joke. Aria started laughing and so did he. "Come on, I know what we're gonna do today!" he said, displaying the Subway gift card between his fingers.

Taylor began to open the door of the car, taken by the wave of the impulse to walk with Aria straight to the store. "OK, wait just a minute. I've got to go ask Mike about something. Give me ten minutes," Aria said.

"OK, hurry up 'cause I'm hungry." Taylor said, lifting the newspaper back up in front of his face.

Mike was cleaning the dirt off of a pair of Carhartt working boots. He stopped what he was doing when Aria approached him. "Hey, did you see anyone put stuff on the hood of our car?" she asked.

Mike peered around her in the direction of the Land Cruiser. "Nah, I can't say that I did. Course I's gone most o' the day." He went back to his work on the boots as if their conversation were over.

"Do you know if anyone was here today?" Aria asked. Given the proximity of his tent to the Land Cruiser, Mike was her best chance at finding out who was leaving things on the hood of the car, so she was grasping at straws.

"Ya might try Bob. I don't think he went no place today."

"OK, thanks anyway," Aria said, running over to Robert's tent instead. True to form, he was there, whittling away on a little wooden statue of a bluebird. "Hey, did you see anyone put stuff on the hood of our car?" she said, startling him out of the asylum of his artistry.

Robert stopped to think. "As a matter of fact I might've. There was a willowy fella here earlier today. I figured he was one a' Luke's friends or somethin' 'cause he ran over toward his place."

"Well, can you remember what he looked like or anything?" Aria pleaded.

"Well, lemme think. He was a tall, skinny fella. He was dressed proper. And he might'a had dark skin. But it could'a just been cause the light was shinin' in my eyes. Ya think it might'a been a friend o' yours?"

"I don't know," Aria said. "If you see him again, can you stop him and ask him who he is?"

"Sure thing," Robert said, smiling at Aria with his toothless smile, pleased to be included in the sudden intrigue of the mystery afoot.

Aria ran back toward the car, knocking on the passenger window to indicate her readiness to go.

The Subway store smelled like Elysium. The yeasty smell of freshly baked bread turning from white to golden brown made both Taylor and Aria feel buttoned up in warmth. The gift card had $10 on it. They ordered a foot-long veggie sandwich and deliberated over what makings to add to it while the man behind the counter slid it down the bar. They took it, with a bag of salt and vinegar chips, to one of the tables and each took half of it.

They indulged in silence until Taylor decided to throw in casually, "I met a guy. I mean, it's prob'ly nothing, but whatever."

"You're just now telling me this?" Aria asked, amused.

"He came into the studio a couple of times this week. And when I was on my break, he took me to go get a coffee. He looked at me all weird 'cause I ordered an orange juice.

He took me home after my shift was done and I fucked him." Taylor lifted his eyebrow and opened his mouth wide; impersonating the look of self-congratulatory shock that he imagined Aria would feel hearing the news.

Aria smacked his arm affectionately. "Well … what's his name?" she asked.

"His name's Dan," Taylor said, his mouth full of food.

"Do you like him?" Aria asked.

"Yeah, I mean I guess. He's good so far," Taylor said, sorting through the way he really felt about the sizeable gap in their age difference and life circumstances.

Taylor had been working at the front desk the day that Dan came into the studio. Dan was in his fifties, a retail real estate executive with an affinity for buying houses at auction and flipping them. Except for the impeccable fit of his black turtleneck sweater and perhaps the tightness of the way he strung his words together, nothing about him would lead someone to guess that he was gay. His penchant for real estate was surpassed only by his penchant for stage acting and for younger men. In the first two minutes of their meeting, Dan had told Taylor that he looked like a Roman statue come to life. The hunt had already begun.

They had coffee at a café a block away from the studio. Instead of asking Taylor about his life, Dan had lamented how many men in the past had broken his heart. Dan could not figure out why the lavish lifestyle that he afforded each of his conquests was not enough to make them stay. In his mind, they had all taken the expensive gifts and Broadway musical shows and trips to Venice for as long as they wanted to milk him for it until they ran away with other, younger men. He could not see that by sitting down with Taylor at the coffee shop, he was marching to the heavy beats of the exact same drum.

When Taylor divulged that he had slept with Dan after just having coffee, Aria couldn't help but tell him a joke. "You want to know why gay men have sex so much faster and so much more often than straight men?" Not pausing for him to answer, she went on. "Because the only thing standing between a man and sex is a woman." She laughed out loud.

Taylor's laughter rose up to meet hers. "That's a good one," he said.

Dan had driven Taylor to his house in upper Laurel Canyon in his powder blue, convertible Bentley. Taylor had never seen a place like it in all his life. He tried to act unimpressed so as to not give Dan the upper hand. But underneath the impression he was trying to give, it took his breath away. The modern design of the house opened up on an infinity pool with an uninhibited jetliner view. A metal spiral staircase swirled up through the air. When Taylor walked into the kitchen, he stood in disbelief that it boasted two ovens instead of one. The countertops were made of glittering white quartz. And all through the house were relics from old movie sets. Many of them related to Audrey Hepburn.

Dan had disappeared into the bathroom to use a douche bulb before inviting Taylor to take his clothes off and join him to fuck bareback in the steam shower. In truth, Dan had liked it more than Taylor did. He was already smitten with the new lover he had found in Taylor. Taylor did it more to guarantee himself a dram of security with Dan as well as to secure himself a position of power over him. Something about it felt like a protective measure, except that protection worked both ways. If he could secure Dan's attachment, he would have some measure of safety and control over with Dan himself. He could also use Dan and his wealth as a kind of shield protecting him from the world. The fact that Dan had traveled the road of being gay and of making a success out of himself in the world long before Taylor had made Taylor feel less vulnerable. In order to fuel Dan's interest, Taylor had declined to stay the night, but promised to see him again and took off on foot before the sun had begun to sink below the horizon.

When Aria and Taylor finished eating, they parted ways. Having spotted a donut shop, Taylor decided to go in to ask if they had any day-old goods they might be willing to part with before he went to the nearest gas station in order to elicit spare change from the customers. Aria went back to the car lot. On her way there, a thought crossed her mind. If someone had managed to sneak into the lot to put items on the car, that meant they were probably watching to see when she and Taylor left. So, the surest way of finding out who the person was would be to fake that she was leaving and make a stake-out in the woods to watch over the car.

On the first day that Aria faked leaving the lot, only to hide out and watch over it, no one came. She regretted having wasted a day that she could have spent out finding food. But curiosity drove her back to her hiding place the next day. The sunset had turned the clouds a violent fuchsia. The trees had become soft silhouettes against it. Having sat so long waiting, Aria's mind wandered to some imaginary landscape in which it could entertain itself, until movement in the car lot arrested her attention. She squinted in an attempt to see more clearly and could not believe her eyes. The man who was jogging toward the Land Cruiser, a bag of items in his hands, was none other than the man who had been tending the little market by the church. Overwhelmed with dizziness, she watched him line the items up across the hood of the car.

The man ran back even quicker than he had come. Aria was frozen in the shock of a million contradictory emotions. She raced toward the car, collecting the items before anyone else could lay their eyes upon them, and sat in the potpourri of her dismay.

Aria was embarrassed. She felt ashamed that he had discovered things about her life that she never wanted him to know. She was embarrassed that she hadn't known someone was following her the last time she had seen him. Aria hated that because of his generosity, it felt like she owed him something. But despite that shame and imagined indebtedness, she also imagined that if he had discovered these things about her and had continued to come back, he must not have rejected her for them. This confused her more than anything else, but it also made the fondness she already felt for him grow. No one had ever done something for her in secret, because giving her something had always been a ploy to get something in return.

When Taylor came back later that night, bouncing with excitement that he had managed to procure over $35 from his efforts standing on a curbside with a cardboard sign, Aria said nothing. She listened to him talk, giving the impression that she was listening when half of her was not. She was fighting with her burgeoning feelings for the mystery man. Her wishes and fears ran through the hallways of the house of her hope. She followed them out of grace. There was no way of knowing whether any of what was happening between them would lead to anything good. But she could not kill the promise growing within herself. Like a weed, its roots had wound themselves deep into her heart, and it scared her.

She knew she had to confront him. If not to make the decision to let the flowers of that weed blossom, to decide to kill it dead. Either way, she had to see him again.

CHAPTER 22

The bell on the door serenaded her entrance. Aria looked around to see if he was there, but he wasn't. Instead, the man who was tending the counter at the Super Sun Market was an older man with a turban and fierce features that had been cushioned by age.

"Hello, welcome to the Super Sun Market, what are you looking for today?" the man asked.

"Um, is there a younger man who works here sometimes?" Aria asked him, stepping far outside her comfort zone by doing so.

"Yes, that is my son, Omkar, why? What has he done?" the man asked with the immediate assumption that his son had made a mistake or committed some offense against her.

"No, no, he didn't do anything, he just promised to help me figure out some stuff about Indian cooking the other day, and …"

Neeraj cut her off before she finished her sentence with a condescending laugh. "Omkar doesn't know what I know about Indian cooking. Come with me," he said, expecting her to follow as he turned to take her straight over to a shelf lined with little packets of spice.

"One of the things that people find intimidating about cooking Indian food is the vast array of spices used. I find that as soon as people are able to identify and understand the spices we use, then suddenly this cuisine is not as hard to make after all. Most of the spices are dry-roasted to release their essential oils before being ground into spice mixes."

He picked up a box filled with little sage-colored pods which Aria thought resembled immature green pea pods that had been set out to dry. Letting her examine it, Neeraj continued his sermon. "There are two kinds of cardamom used in Indian cooking: green and black. Green is the more common variety, used for everything from spice mixes to lassis to Indian desserts. The flavor is light and sweet. Green cardamom can be blended whole when making spice mixes, like garam masala. However, when using them in sweets or desserts, what you would do is to pop the pod open and lightly crush the fragrant black seeds before using. Black cardamom, on the other hand, is very powerful and smoky, and needs to be used with extreme carefulness. Normally only the seeds would be used, and if using the whole pod, it's best to pull it out before serving the dish, or it won't taste good to bite into."

Aria allowed Neeraj to pull her from aisle to aisle, explaining the ins and outs of the ingredients used in Indian cooking and how to use them, until he had exhausted his medley of products to show her. Even if she had come to the store interested in information about Indian cooking, the speed at which he expected her to absorb the information was unreasonable. But she found enjoyment in his passion for it all. "What recipe is it that you are wanting to make?" he asked.

"Oh, I don't actually know. I guess I was gonna make up my mind about that after I came in here," Aria responded, proud of herself for a moment for having lied so seamlessly.

That moment was short-lived. "One minute, I have something," Neeraj said, turning to search behind the checkout counter. He walked back across the store with a small, brightly colored flyer advertising the store. Holding up the reverse side for her to see, he said, "This here is a beginner's recipe, very easy. You can try for yourself and maybe you will like it."

He stepped back, folding his arms with satisfaction. Aria looked at the recipe for chicken tikka masala, which was printed on the page. It was one of the Agarwals' small ways of introducing people to the superior taste of their country and culture. "Thanks," she said, wondering whether she should just leave or work up the courage to ask him when Omkar would be back. Not able to let the opportunity pass, she trampled over her apprehension. "Um, do you know when the man, I mean Omkar, will be here again?" she asked.

Neeraj was taken aback, suddenly distrustful of her interest in his son. "He's coming back tonight, but he is very busy with his schoolwork. Why do you want to know?" he said, hoping to deter her.

"No reason, never mind," Aria said, wanting to get out from under the pressure of his distrust as fast as she possibly could. "Thanks again," she added, walking backward a few steps and waving at him with a smile.

"You're very welcome," Neeraj answered her, wanting to leave her with a good impression before she left, despite his suspicion.

Aria walked briskly out the door and down the street. The bell on the door made a riot in response to her exit. She had already made up her mind to wait for Omkar to return the minute the man in the store had hinted that he would be back that night. Trying not to make herself conspicuous, she crossed the street and sat against the side of a building in an alleyway with a view of the store. She didn't know how long she would have to wait, but she couldn't let it deter her. So she let her mind wander, making sure to act nonchalant when anyone passed by and always keeping an eye on the store.

It was dinnertime in homes across the city. Aria could hear the buzz of the tail end of rush-hour traffic on a distant highway. She could feel people slowing down for the day and picking up last-minute items to bring home to eat. The sun still had half an hour left in the sky. Out of all the cars that had passed during the three hours or so that she had been waiting there, only one car interrupted its straight-line trajectory and pulled up to the curb just beyond the store. It was a compact car, an ash-gray Honda Fit. (Neeraj had bartered with a man at a used car lot to buy it for Omkar the year he'd been accepted to college.) Because of the sun's reflection across the driver's side window, Aria couldn't see it was Omkar until he stepped out of the car, his hands full of books and papers that he had not bothered to put into a backpack.

Aria rushed across the street toward him, not wanting to give Omkar's father time to notice that he had arrived. Omkar was oblivious to her until she was standing right next to him. He jumped back, startled, and almost dropped the books he was precariously balancing in his forearms. In a fluster, he put them on the roof of the car and turned to face her. His cheeks flushed and he could hardly breathe. "Um, are you into me?" Aria asked, cutting straight to the point.

Omkar took a deep breath and put his hand against his temple, his mind stuttering over what answers he could give her, and finding none.

"Well, I saw you leaving stuff for me and I wanna know why," Aria said, pleading with him to answer.

Omkar was seared with embarrassment at having been caught. For a minute he teetered on the precipice of manhood before deciding to take charge of the whole situation and play it as cool as he could. It was his best shot at getting her to like him back.

"My name's Omkar," he said, redirecting the conversation and extending his hand for her to shake. Aria was confused by the sudden topic change. But she took his lead and placed her hand against his palm. Her hand inherited the warmth of his hand. Its strength carried her for the briefest of moments.

"I'm Aria," she said.

Omkar loved the ladylike intonation of her name. For whatever reason, it reminded him of a bird's wing. He realized he wouldn't be able to avoid her questions, so he decided to confess. "You must be wondering what is this, what am I doing or whatever. But I just want to express this ...

"Ever since I saw you, I couldn't get you out of my mind. Don't take me wrong. I never meant to chase you or stalk you or whatever. I'm not a creep or something. I'm not the guy who is going to do anything bad or wrong. I just think I must be in love with you or something. And I was curious about you. When I found out where you live, I just wanted to show you I love you. That's why I left you those things, I swear."

Having conceded so much, Omkar stood over her, waiting for her response. Part of him was relieved to no longer have to hold the pressure of keeping the feelings he had for her secret.

Aria couldn't believe her ears. Despite suspecting that he might have feelings for her, she had expected him to tell some story about leaving the things because he felt sorry for her. She stood there as if she had been put on pause. Discomfort etched a half-smile across her lips. She didn't know what to say.

Again, Omkar took charge of the ungainliness of their conversation. "Look, will you go on a date with me? I swear I'm not the guy who is going to do anything bad."

"OK, yeah. I guess I'd like that," Aria said. She had spoken without thinking, as if some unknown part within her had answered on her behalf.

Excitement coursed through his veins. "OK, well, can you go out tomorrow?"

Aria smiled at his urgency. "Yeah," she said.

"Do you want to meet here or should I come pick you up?" Omkar asked, careful to maintain a respectful distance.

"Ah … I can meet you here. What time do you want me to be here?" she asked.

"How about five o'clock? Is that too early or …?" Omkar said, ready to adjust himself to any time she specified.

"Nah, five is good," Aria said.

Omkar and Aria stood there on the pavement of the street, neither of them wanting to be the one to rupture their proximity. Eventually, Aria gained the strength to step out from beneath the reassurance of his shadow. "OK, I'll see you tomorrow, then," she said, shyly moving her body away from him while still looking him in the eye.

"OK, see you tomorrow, then," he said, standing motionless and watching her start to walk down the street. "OK, five o'clock. Thank you!" he yelled out after her, suddenly feeling the need to remind her of the time they had agreed upon as if she had already forgotten.

Omkar turned and placed his arms and forehead against the cold steel of the top of his car. No longer trying to act collected because of her presence, he let out a sigh of relief.

When he opened the door to the store, carrying his heavy load of textbooks and papers, Neeraj criticized him for not using a backpack to carry his things, and Omkar realized his father hadn't seen Aria and him talking. He had probably been too busy looking through the spreadsheets, which he insisted on printing out instead of reading on a computer.

Omkar went straight upstairs. Without taking his shoes off, he lay down on his carefully made bed and stared at the ceiling. His heartbeat hammered against the walls of his chest. With his mind, he traced the lines of her. He memorized the music of her voice. He knew the hours between now and five o'clock tomorrow would be the longest he had ever spent.

For the rest of the night, Aria wrangled with the part of herself that wanted to hope. She could hear her inner voice make a hundred and one excuses for why it wouldn't work between them. She suffocated that excitement beneath a blanket of pessimism until the wrestling match she had been playing with herself was put to rest by Aston running up to her through the dark.

"Where's my mommy?" he asked.

"I don't know. Why don't we go look for her?" Aria said, taking his hand to lead him toward the purple van.

Aria cupped her hands to look inside. The van was cluttered, but empty of life. So she led Aston over to Mike's tent. But it too was deserted. "When did you see her last? Did she say anything to you about where you're supposed to be?" Aria asked, kneeling down to face him at eye level.

Aston's usual bullish demeanor had been reduced to the suddenly fragile mien of a child that had found himself abandoned. "Mommy put me to sleep in there and told me that when I woke up, I should go to Grampy's," he said, pointing first to the van and then to Mike's vacant tent.

Aria felt the anger rise up inside her in response to her intuition about what was really going on. It was an all-too-predictable pattern. She didn't care if it was knowing neglect or miscommunication on Ciarra's part; it was damaging either way. Before confirming her suspicion that Aston had been left at the lot completely unattended, she walked with him, scanning the other encampments for any sight of either Ciarra or Mike.

When their search turned up nothing, she brought Aston back to the Land Cruiser and did her best to distract him. It was a method she had learned from the many social workers she had seen working with young children at the group homes. She pulled one of the juice packets that Omkar had left for her from her backpack and watched him sip it in between his running commentary about cars. When Aston finished, she tried to wind his energy down by singing to him like she used to do to her younger siblings sometimes at the Johnsons'.

"Hush little baby, don't say a word, Mama's gonna buy you a mockingbird. And if that mockingbird won't sing, Mama's gonna buy you a diamond ring. And if that diamond ring turns to brass, Mama's gonna buy you a looking-glass. And if that looking-glass gets broke, Mama's gonna buy you a billy goat. And if that billy goat won't pull, Mama's gonna buy you a cart and bull. And if that cart and bull turn over, Mama's gonna buy you a dog named Rover. And if that dog named Rover won't bark, Mama's gonna buy you a horse and cart. And if that horse and cart fall down, you'll still be the sweetest little baby in town!"

Aston began to quiet under the soft stroking of her fingertips against his arm. "Again," he begged when she had finished and she repeated the song again.

Rhythmic breathing eventually governed his little body. His innocence was painted in the dirt stains on his face. When Taylor came back for the night, Aria shushed him as he opened the door and explained what had happened in a whisper just quiet enough not to wake Aston up.

Before she fell asleep, she avoided the inclination to think about Omkar by staring down at Aston as he slept against her. Aria unexpectedly began to miss her younger siblings. She wondered what story they had been told or had told themselves about her disappearance. Aria felt more guilty for running out on them without explaining herself than she felt for anything. Her body remembered the weight of them leaning up against her, like Aston was doing now.

She took Aston's limp hand in hers and thought to herself, "In this hand is the power to open or to close. And every moment is a crossroads. I hope he decides to open this hand instead of close it." Aria could see how the bankruptcy of compassion that had plagued Aston's life might make him choose to be hard and closed off to love and to life. After all, she was tempted to close off to it herself some days. But meeting Omkar had made her glad that she couldn't find it in herself to do it.

Looking down at the baby fat still ornamenting Aston's face, she wished that same failure upon him. Despite her youth, she had already found there to be more strength in softness after all.

CHAPTER 23

Cars flowed down the highway. The tall palm trees bordering the roads were coddled by the wind. Aria and Omkar were headed for the ocean. Omkar was trying his best to focus on his surroundings and the navigation system on his phone, which was in the habit of barking directions a second too late for him to follow them. It was difficult to focus through the elation of having Aria next to him.

Aria was reserved because she was embarrassed. The truth was that she had never seen the ocean. The closest she had ever come was visiting Lake Michigan as a child. And since coming to LA, she had been so forced to focus on survival day to day, on foot, that she had not had any opportunity to travel west to see the ocean. Of course, she had not admitted it to Omkar because it made her feel classless.

"Are you too cold?" Omkar asked, his hand on the dial of the air conditioner, ready to make an adjustment.

"Nah, I'm OK," Aria said, growing uncomfortable with the quiet between them. "Wanna play a game?"

"Yeah – I mean, yes, what kind of game?" Omkar asked.

"OK, it's a fun game that I used to love to play when I was at school, except I used to be the one guessing for other people. Basically, I'd sit in my desk and think about what thing people would be."

"What do you mean?" Omkar asked

"You know the game where it's like if I were a car, what kind of car would I be; or if I were an animal, like what animal would I be? It's like that game. But we have to guess for each other," Aria said.

"No, I've never played that particular game," Omkar said, excited to give it a try.

"OK. I'll start. If I were an animal, what would I be? You have to guess for me and I have to guess for you," Aria said.

Omkar thought for a considerable amount of time with Aria staring him down, waiting for an answer. Eventually, a smile crossed his face. "You'd be a jungle cat."

"Why would I be a jungle cat?" Aria asked, curious about his impressions of her.

"A … maybe because you look a bit like them. You remind me of a cat, but not like a small cat and not like a lion. You seem very independent and mysterious and majestic and a little bit wild," he said, teasing her affectionately.

"OK," she said, "let me think." Aria paused for even longer than he did, scanning him for any resemblance he might have to any specific animal. "Ah, I got it," she yelled. "A bush baby."

"Oh my God, it's because of my ears, isn't it?" The embarrassment Omkar felt for the way his ears protruded was suddenly revived. Despite the dark shade of his skin, she could see the redness appear in his cheeks and neck.

"Maybe a little bit," she said, holding up her fingers to demonstrate an inch to tease him before explaining her choice further. "Oh come on, they're cute! And they are really smart but kind of silly too. Plus, they can see through the dark, I mean you saw through me!"

The sudden sentiment made him adore her even more. He had to remind himself to look at the road instead of at her face. They played the game back and forth, telling each other what fruit and vegetable and car and celebrity they thought each other would be, for as long as it took to reach a parking spot at the public beach.

When Aria got out of the car, the long roar of the ocean greeted her. Like a breath, its exhalation pushed water up onto the shore and its inhalation pulled it back again. Aria suddenly understood why people made such a fuss about the ocean. Its beauty was free from the bondage of the words that one could use to describe it. Little birds bounced around in the white foam at the edge of the waves, sticking their beaks like sewing needles deep into the sand.

She had not imagined the ocean would have a smell, but it did. At first she thought it might be the smell of fish, but that wasn't quite right. It was something else, something she had never smelled before. Maybe some ancient breeze of kelp and salt mixed equally. She searched the curve of the entire horizon, unable to find any land, and felt the power and vastness of the water, which seemed to have a consciousness in and of itself. It seemed to be alive. It was a power that could not be shouldered by coral or bone.

The breeze kicking up off of the water played with her hair. It seemed to move in slow motion. The allure it afforded her beauty was not lost on Omkar, who stopped unfolding the blanket for the picnic site in order to stare at her.

Aria rolled up her pants and walked into the surf. The water was a shock. The cold of it caused a dull ache to rise from the soles of her feet past her ankles. She giggled to feel the way the sand was pulled out from under her by each wave, making her legs sink deeper and deeper. The Pacific did not feel like a friendly, loving ocean. It felt wild and impassioned in its depth.

A pelican interrupted her congress with it. She looked up to watch it looming through the air. It looked like a feathered dinosaur that had been granted amnesty from extinction. It was unlike anything she had experienced in all her life.

"Hey, come over here," Omkar called to her, not wanting to abandon their belongings on a public beach in order to join her. Aria walked back from wet to dry sand and sat opposite him in front of the picnic items he had taken great care to display before her. He had already opened a few Tupperware containers. They were filled with some kind of homemade food that Aria couldn't recognize. There were two sodas, two bottles of water, a few rustic-looking slabs of bread wrapped in paper towel and a blue package of Oreos, waiting to be opened.

"Did you make this stuff?" Aria asked.

"Actually, my mother made these. But I *can* make them." Omkar felt shy to admit it. The truth was, he had taken some of the food his mother had made for dinner and told her he had to attend a late-night study group. "If you don't like them, we can go get something else somewhere."

He handed her a slab of bread. Demonstrating what to do with it, he tore through the structure of the bread with his hands, removing a piece from it. He used it to spoon some of the curry from a Tupperware container into his mouth.

Aria copied him gingerly. When she placed it in her mouth, she was in disbelief. The tomato was creamed; its flavor was heavy in her throat. It was suffused with spices that contained all the memories of a foreign land within them, all the celebrations. It tasted like pure indulgence, like luxury and wealth on the tongue. "What is this?" she asked him.

"This is chapati," he said, holding up the bread in his hand. "That's tikka masala." He pointed to what she had just eaten. "And this is tadka dal," he added, indicating a yellow curry in another Tupperware container.

"Where is all this from?" Aria asked him. The emotional feel of the food had made her suddenly curious about his heritage.

"This is Punjab food. Which is part of India, close to Pakistan, where my family's from. Do you like it? You can tell me if you don't like it, it's OK," Omkar said.

"No, I love it. Can I try this one?" Aria asked, reaching toward the yellow stew.

"Yes," he said, dipping his bread into it first to show her it was OK.

The second stew was both chalky and creamy; its filling consistency reminded Aria of split pea soup. But it was sunrise yellow. Toasted cumin hid in its thickness. It was comforting to eat and Aria imagined it would be even more comforting if it were a familiar flavor, like it must be for Omkar.

The chapati was slightly blackened at the edges. It reminded Aria of Mexican tortillas, but it didn't taste like tortilla. The dust from the flour glazing it came off on Aria's hands. She nibbled around the edges. One of Aria's little quirks was that she had always loved the flavor of burned bread. Aria pulled open one of the little bubbles in the bread and imagined herself inside it. She imagined what it would feel like to live in the soft light of the little dough cave. The bread was unmeasured. It felt rustic. As with all the food in his culture, the amounts of the various spices and ingredients were determined only by the fingertips of the cook. It was an emotional art form, not a science. Aria could taste his grandmother's hands in the bread. The war of potent flavors in the food that was laid out before her had reconciled into a harmonious dance.

Although it made her feel shamefully unsophisticated, eating Omkar's food suddenly opened up a whole new world to her. It had never occurred to her that every culture and country might have its own foods; foods which, unless someone traveled to that part of the world, they would never see or taste in a lifetime.

"Have you ever tried Indian food?" Omkar asked, surprised by the way that Aria was acting.

"It's kinda embarrassing, but no. I mean, I've seen Indian restaurants and stuff, but no one has ever taken me in one," Aria responded. She felt ashamed to admit it, afraid of how Omkar would see her once he discovered just what kind of unsophisticated life she came from.

Omkar sat back, watching her relish the food like a hungry animal. He guessed she ate with such fervor due to hunger as much as because she liked the taste of the food.

"So tell me about your family," he said. Aria felt herself at a crossroads. She could skirt the issue or she could tell it to him straight. Aria wanted him to love her. She wanted him to hold her in high esteem. But then again, she would rather have him decide to reject her *now* rather than *after* she had already become attached to him. So she threw the truth at him as if it were a test for him to pass.

Omkar stayed silent as she spoke for over an hour.

"Well, I guess you could say I don't have one. I mean, I don't even know if my mom's alive, and I never met my dad. No one ever chooses to end up like this … like me … Poverty fuels the whole system. Anyone who says otherwise is fucking stupid. People who can't make ends meet just end up coping in whatever way they can. No one can take care of kids when they can't even figure out how to survive themselves. But no one helps them. They just come down and take their kids away, and that doesn't help them. It just makes their lives even harder 'cause now they're dying both inside and out.

"Then they throw you in a group home, which is just a modern orphanage. You're under constant surveillance by the social workers and psychologists and courts, but none of them really care about you. You're just one big charity case that most people take advantage of so they can feel good about themselves. It's nothing but rules and regulations instead of love. Some foster parents are OK – the good ones just want you to behave yourself and act like everything is fine now – but a lot of them are even worse and more abusive than the parents they take kids away from to begin with. No one hears you or cares what you say you want or need. They decide your life for you and they tell you you're gonna see your parents again, but we all know it's a goddamn lie. And when you're like eighteen, you just age out of the system with no support and no skills, so a lot of 'em just end up repeating the same cycle. They follow in their parents' footsteps because there aren't any other footsteps to follow. The entire system is fucked."

Aria told him the truth about her mother and Travis, the truth about the state taking her away, the truth of what it had been like in foster care and group homes, and the truth of what had made her run away.

Omkar did not break his focus from her. Instead, he leaned toward her, letting the surges of painful truth after painful truth hit him so as to not leave her alone in them. When her confession came to an end, he held her head against his chest and said, "I'm so sorry."

There was nothing more to say. Nothing he could say would have been good enough. So he let the comfort of his body do the talking and Aria let him hold her. Though she didn't cry, she felt some small child within her crying. It was crying with the release of finally being contained between the protective walls of a person who would claim her.

"I lost my brother and sister in an earthquake. My aunt died in it too," he told her. Though he knew the story of his own tragedy could never compete with hers, Omkar saluted her willingness to be vulnerable by offering up his own vulnerability in return.

She listened to him tell her about the earthquake and the dark cloud over his family, about the oppressive constraint of his culture and about moving to this completely foreign country, with one ear against his chest. When he had finished speaking, she listened to the sound of his fingers stroking and playing with her hair.

Without them noticing, the sun had already set upon their time together. The glow from the city lights made the churn of the ocean water sparkle. Underneath the excitement of the romance, their bodies had found a home in each other, a sense of belonging that Aria had only met once before, while watching a part in a movie. When she was little, she had seen a Disney movie called *Fantasia* in which there was a segment, accompanied by the *Pastoral Symphony*, with a group of female centaurs of all different colors bathing and preparing themselves until the music changed, signaling the arrival of all the males. One by one, each female was united with the male of her corresponding color. But a blue male and blue female hadn't found each other yet. They were sitting alone, feeling like they were the only ones without someone to belong with, until the cherubs drew them in each other's direction and they saw each other for the first time.

Aria had spent her life feeling like that last centaurette, waiting for someone to belong to, until today.

Before it was so late that his parents would have grown concerned, Omkar drove her back to the car lot. Pulling up there, and knowing that she would be spending the night there in that reality, threatened to pollute the fantasy of their time on the beach. But he didn't have an alternative, and he hated himself for consenting to drive her there.

Before she got out of the car, he wrote his phone number down on a piece of paper towel he pulled out from the picnic bag and handed it to her. He worked up the courage to kiss her cheek. "Thank you so much for tonight. I had a wonderful time, truly." Aria smiled at him lovingly and closed the door behind her. He watched her walk away until he couldn't see her anymore and pulled away from the curbside, feeling like his life had finally begun.

— * —

It had been the best day of Aria's life. As in Taylor's situation, the squalor she found herself in seemed more like treasure because of the promise of the way her life could feel with him in it. She walked toward the Land Cruiser with the intention of lying awake, preserving the feeling of being with him for as long as she could before falling asleep. But the bestial cruelty of the reality of her life thwarted her intention.

There was a scuffle of panic near the broken-down black Camaro. Sensing the urgency of crisis instead of conflict, Aria ran toward Anthony and Wolf, who were crowded around the open door of the car EJ had claimed for his own. "He's OD'ing!" Wolf yelled out to her. "We've got to get help quick."

Though still breathing, EJ was unresponsive, his body occasionally tensing up and going loose again. Wolf was holding him half out of the car and yelling at him to wake up. The sides of his face were tarnished by the acid of his own vomit and he was making choking sounds. Even through the dark, Aria could see his already pale skin turning the color of clam flesh. "We gotta get him somewhere fast!" Wolf yelled, pulling EJ from the car with the help of Anthony. Both of them held one half of his limp body, and they started carrying him as fast as they could in the direction of the city.

It was a sad reality that all of them knew without having to communicate it to each other. None of them owned a phone, but even if they had, they couldn't risk calling the attention of police to the car lot. It would put every single one of them at risk. So they were rushing him away from the car lot as fast as they could to find help. Aria felt the pit of doom in her stomach. She had a feeling that EJ wouldn't survive if they took so long.

She looked back to where Omkar had dropped her off and realized he had already left. "Stay on the road and keep walking!" she yelled out to them, turning to run as fast as she could. She ran as fast as her legs could take her toward the city streets she knew would have some life still left on them. The shops and restaurants had all closed for the night. The stale light made them look cadaverous.

Her chest burned and her legs spasmed but she kept on running, flailing her arms to try to stop any cars that passed her, but no one pulled over. She ran across a street, against the red light, toward a group of people waiting to get into a bar. "Help, we need help, someone's in trouble, I need a phone!" she yelled at the group of startled people.

There was a hiccup of hesitance before a man approached her and asked her if he should call 911. "Yes," she gasped, completely out of breath. She watched him dial the number and tell the dispatcher that someone was in trouble before he handed the phone to Aria.

She did her best to answer the questions being asked by the pacifying voice on the other side of the line. She described the emergency, telling them the name of the street that Wolf and Anthony were carrying EJ down and some of the buildings that were defining features on it. She described his condition. But when the woman asked Aria for her name and address and phone number, Aria went silent before hanging up the phone. She couldn't afford to tell them. Part of her was terrified that not staying on the line would cost EJ his life, but she was fairly certain that they had already sent an ambulance.

Aria thanked the man, who was standing over her, confused about why she had handed him back the phone so soon, and started running back in the direction she had come. By the time she spotted her friends in the distance, the red and blue flash of ambulance lights illuminated their figures. Aria stopped and watched, not wanting to be caught up. She watched the police officers and paramedics crowd around EJ, long enough to see him take a huge gasp of air and begin to cough uncontrollably in response to the naloxone being squirted up his nose.

Anthony had run away at the first sight of police cars, afraid to be locked up again, and Wolf was standing against a length of chain-link fencing. He was out of breath, but giving information to the same officer they had seen take away the mentally ill man who was throwing rocks at cars the other day. Even at a distance, Aria recognized the way his glasses and his chubby face seemed to strip him of the ruthless authority that other cops had in spades.

Wolf lied to him by saying that he didn't know EJ, but that he had seen him collapsed on the sidewalk. He gave the officer his address back in Washington and told them he was visiting a relative nearby. The truth was Wolf had been trying to extricate EJ from the crepuscule of his downfall for months now.

To Wolf, EJ was a lost brother that he had taken it upon himself to rescue. He knew that EJ had lost his way. He wasn't always this way. EJ used to be a catcher on his high school baseball team. He had lived with the nagging pain of his parents' divorce and the pain of never really feeling understood. It was pain that no one ever saw to begin with. He hid it beneath the bark of his popularity until he had suffered a sprain and labral tear in his shoulder. The doctor prescribed him OxyContin and when he took it, he noticed that it didn't only take away the pain of his shoulder, it also numbed the emotional pain that he had grown accustomed to living with. For a while, he faked still being in pain and took to doctor-shopping so he could keep being prescribed his medication until he had to find another way to fuel his addiction. He bought painkillers off of other kids at school, and then he fell in with a group of other addicts who knew a dealer who could supposedly get him anything.

Once he had touched the euphoria of fentanyl, there was no going back. EJ had thrown his entire life away for the haze of opioid addiction, using again and again to avoid the agony of withdrawal.

EJ had run away from home years ago and couch-surfed before his first night on the streets. The night he ran away, he took three of his mother's sleeping pills to try to hold him over long enough get his hands on a fix. Instead of sending him to sleep, they had put him in an altered state of mind. He put a pot of macaroni and cheese on the stove for two hours and nearly burned the house down. His girlfriend, who lived with him in his parents' house, had woken up to the sound of the smoke alarm. When she confronted him, he found his father's handgun and because of his inebriation, was lucky enough to shoot a bullet into the wall instead of through her. His father came downstairs before his mother did. He tackled EJ and called the police on his own son. When EJ was released from the police station, forcibly sobered up, he had no memory of the incident. He didn't trust himself to be around people anymore. So he came back to his parents' house just long enough to break up with his girlfriend and to collect a few of his things.

— * —

The sound of the double doors being closed when the stretcher was loaded inside the ambulance was inaudible from where Aria was standing. The flashing lights, unaccompanied by the wail of the siren, felt eerie. Aria missed the sense of urgency in the sound.

She'd sensed irritation in the paramedics' body language instead of concern. Not fully understanding the pain that someone has to be in to end up like EJ, they were frustrated at having to put effort into someone who was so determined to destroy himself.

She watched the ambulance pull away from the curb, do a U-turn and drive right past her. She tried to catch a glimpse of EJ through the back window as it drove by. His addiction rode the chassis of the ambulance with him like a phantom. It was a demon he could not exorcise from himself even for the sake of those who loved him. Though it was invisible, she could almost see it lurking there, knowing it would inevitably come to this.

EJ would come back and say he was sorry. He said it every time sobriety found him in between the wave sets of his life. He said he would try, but never hard enough to withstand the crucifixion of the way getting sober felt. His soul cried out every time he'd swallow a pill or jam a needle into another vein, but he ignored it so long he could no longer hear the scream. Watching the ambulance disappear over the horizon, Aria stared down the invisible phantom that both was and wasn't him, long enough to see that it wouldn't be content until EJ's life was a life that was wasted, until his breath was a breath that was gone.

CHAPTER 24

Just over a week had passed since Aria had seen the ocean for the first time. Just over a week with no word about EJ. That was how it was in this life where relationships were forged only by the commonality of circumstances. One day someone who had been a prominent figure in the mural of your life was suddenly gone and you might never hear of them again.

Omkar and Aria had seen each other every day but one. On one of those days, for the first time in almost two years, Aria had gone to see a movie in a movie theater. Though the theater wasn't fancy by any means, compared to all the places Aria had been for the last year, it might as well have been an opera house. She felt underdressed and self-conscious walking through the foyer. Omkar had taken her there on a date when his attempt to convince Aria to meet up with a friend of his had failed. There was an off chance that his friend might have let her stay on his couch for a while until Omkar could come up with a different solution, a better place for her to stay. But when he made the suggestion to Aria, she refused to entertain the notion. Aria was uninterested in favors. She didn't like the feeling of owing anything to anyone, much less someone she had never met before. She found the whole idea humiliating.

It was a terrible movie, with all the underwhelming drama of a decidedly burned-out sequel to a movie that Aria had never seen. But she didn't care. She watched the changing light from the scenes displayed on the screen, turning Omkar's face dark, then illuminating it again. Aria had found some dandelions to eat off of someone's lawn, but she hadn't planned her day well enough to find anything else to eat. As a result, when Omkar bought her a bag of popcorn, she had gorged herself on it until her stomach hurt too much to eat anymore.

At first, Omkar was shy and formal about the date. Aria had to graze the outside of his arm with her pinky finger to

encourage him to lift up the armrest between them and take
her hand. When he did, the dew of sweat started to accent
the heat between their hands. Omkar was nervous and elated.
But he felt frustrated with himself that no matter how many
times he saw her, he couldn't force himself to act cool. Instead,
he felt like an immature schoolboy, devoured by the anxious
limerence of puppy love. He found his own reaction all the
more frustrating because he knew it wasn't puppy love. What
he felt for Aria was something much deeper. It was something
that he could not name.

Aside from the movie date, they managed to see each other
for an hour or two in between Omkar's classes and work shifts.
For the most part, sustained by the little items that Omkar
would bring her, Aria spent her time at the car lot, counting
down the minutes between their time together. But today,
knowing that they would not meet up until after sundown,
Aria had decided to follow a tip that the St Francis Center
offered a warm breakfast to those who needed a meal.

Aria looked down to watch the blur of her high-top
sneakers carrying her across the pavement. The walk, which
she had started while it was still dark, had already been
longer than she had anticipated. It had taken her through
shopping centers, past highways and into industrial parts
of town. She was beginning to wonder if she had taken a
wrong turn somewhere. Wandering into unfamiliar territory
was always a risk for anyone on the street. It was a risk that
made her regret coming alone. But with Taylor gone an hour
before her to the acting studio and both Luke and Wolf
gone the night before to an art walk event, she hadn't had
a choice.

Up ahead, Aria could see the bright orange sign belonging
to a Home Depot. The sun had not yet touched the painted
stalls of the parking lot, which before business hours were
vacant. A group of nine or so men were standing near the
inlet where people pulled into the lot. Every morning men
who were out of a job, or unable to get work for one reason

or another, would stand there to see if someone with a construction project would hire them and pay them cash for the day. For the most part, though hardened by manual labor, the men looked benign enough. Still, Aria felt tense when she passed them. She felt herself walking quicker to try to get out of range.

The hair on the back of Aria's neck stood up as if she were being hunted. None of the men had made a sound when she had walked by. They had not cat-called, like she had prepared herself for them to do. They had simply watched her pass intently.

It all happened so fast. By the time she felt the eerie feeling of predation and had turned around to check behind her, the man was already close. Upon seeing her notice him, he broke into a run in her direction.

Aria bolted as if on automatic pilot. Panic and adrenaline sprinted through her veins. She tried to run sideways to evade him, but he was faster. Aria had unintentionally cornered herself.

The man pushed her from behind, trying to throw her to the ground. But instead, the force threw her against the wall of an industrial warehouse. Her face buffered her fall. She did not notice the burn of the scrape, or the way the peak of the pain subsided when blood began to flow from her lips and nose, until after everything was over.

Aria didn't defend herself as the man had expected her to. She had been trained over the course of her life not to. Fighting the futility only put her more at risk. Instead, she froze and smiled at the man, hoping to pacify him or at least get it over with, with the least amount of violence possible.

Caught up in the convulsion of whatever carnal instinct had been triggered, the man said nothing to her. He spoke only with the terrorism of his body. His fingernails carved red marks into the skin of her hips as he tried to rip and pull her pants away from them.

The frenzy was interrupted by two of the men running toward them across the street. "*Para ahora! Para ahora!*" one of them yelled over and over.

When they pulled the man off of her by the back of his t-shirt, he wouldn't let go of her jeans. Aria's legs were pulled high into the air before he let go and they smacked the asphalt hard enough that her heel was badly bruised.

Her attacker swung a punch through the air at one of the men who had come to her rescue, but because he ducked, it only grazed his arm.

"Go on … Go on, get outta here!" the new arrival yelled defiantly in her attacker's face. Both of the men stood ready for a fight. Instead of taking them on, the first man ran. "Go on, get outta here!" the man yelled again, hoping the words would chase him even further from where they stood.

He reached down toward Aria. "Hey, you OK, miss?" he asked in a heavy Mexican accent. "You're cut up pretty bad."

Aria let him pull her up to standing position and she adjusted her clothes, which had been twisted by the scuffle. She was too shocked to respond. Her body started to process the trauma by shaking.

"Hey, you need to call somebody?" he asked, still holding her arm and worried. Aria shook her head no. "Hey, I know somebody who could help," the man said, still waiting for any verbal sign from Aria.

Aria wanted to run away from this place. She wanted to take care of the aftermath herself and unburden the men who had come to her aid. But she thought about the fact that should any concerned passerby or cop drive past her, a bloody face would draw attention to herself, which just might land her in more trouble than she was already in. So she said "OK," expecting them to point her in the direction of whatever place they were about to suggest. Instead, the man began to lead her away from the building and down the street. The other man followed them at a short distance, looking less than thrilled by the idea of leaving the opportunities they might miss at the Home Depot parking lot.

"I'm Pedro," the man eventually said, pointing to himself. "This is my brother Consuelo."

"I'm Aria," she said, trying to meet the man's friendliness with welcome. "Where are we going?"

When she snapped out of the shock of what had happened, she was surprised at herself for simply deciding to blindly trust these men.

"We know somebody who owns a store up there," Pedro said, pointing further up the street. He seemed mildly insulted by the sudden distrust in her voice. He imagined her distrust owed itself to the fact that he was brown and she was white.

The men led her to one of the little authentic Mexican stores that Aria had come to notice littered the city. Case upon case of cakes and breads were displayed in front of her. Half of an entire wall was covered with a succession of fresh and dried green and red peppers of every different size and shape. The entire ceiling was cluttered with piñatas, their tassels reaching low enough to brush Aria's forehead.

The smell of the place was overwhelming: a congregation of scents, from the sting of industrial cleaner to the hearty scent of Maseca corn flour, all of which were smuggled into the scent of cardboard boxes whose contents had leaked through them in the heat, permeating the trailer of whatever semi truck they had taken to get there. The slightly cheesy accordion strokes of an upbeat Mexican *norteño* band was playing across the speakers. Aria stopped to listen to the basic and repetitive guitar notes and the voice of the man singing passionately over them in Spanish.

When they entered the store, Pedro greeted an older woman who was fussing over an assortment of tamales that were being held in a heated metal basin. They greeted each other with such geniality that Aria imagined them to be related. "Hey, come over here," Pedro called to her. "This here is Doña Lolita. She's a good woman. You can trust her."

It was obvious that Pedro had told the woman what happened. Concern and anger were evident on her face. "Come here, *mija*," she said, leading Aria behind her through the crowded aisles. She opened a door to a tiny bathroom in the back of the store and ushered Aria inside, closing the door behind her as if she alone were taking charge of Aria's chastity.

Aria looked at herself in the mirror before cleaning herself off. The damage done to her face looked to be just on the surface, despite the blood and split in her lip. She waited for a while for the water to run hot, before deciding the place probably had no warm water. She wiped her face clean with the cold, chemical city water being pumped through the pipes, then rejoined the woman outside.

"Have some *pozole, mija*," the woman said, setting a steaming soup down in front of her on the table with a little side plate of raw, shredded cabbage, raw onion, dry oregano and a golden plain tostada. Guessing that Aria had no idea what to do with it, she took her hand and sprinkled some of the cabbage and onion into the soup and stirred it around with Aria's spoon.

"Thank you, but I can't pay for it. I have nothing with me," Aria said.

The woman scoffed as if insulted by the fact that Aria presumed she would have to. "Don't worry, *mija*. You're so skinny you need some food on those bones of yours," she answered with a laugh.

Doña Lolita looked to be in her late fifties. Her coal black hair, which was entirely gray at the roots, was pulled into a tight bun. Her thin lips were coated with hot pink lipstick, far too bright for her complexion. Her eyebrows were pencil drawn on top of the gray eyeshadow that was poorly applied to her eyelids. Her brown eyes were the color of cola. They sparkled out from the mayhem of her makeup and acne scars. The lard-rich food she had cooked all her life had made her body and face plump. The feel of her was a strange mix of discipline and mothering.

"You can have this, too … And this," she said, placing three more items she collected from around the store in front of Aria.

"Thank you so much," Aria said, looking her straight in the face, totally overwhelmed with (and even more guilty about) the care she was being shown.

"OK, is everything OK?" she asked, wanting to know if she could leave Aria to eat on her own.

"Yeah, it's wonderful," Aria replied.

Satisfied with her efforts, Lolita went to sit with Pedro and Consuelo at one of the other little tables in a corner by the meat counter. She had fed them too. At another table, a group of four women sat playing cards.

Aria watched the men eat and talk to her. They were speaking in Spanish so she couldn't tell what they were saying.

Pedro and Consuelo bore furrows on their faces. Their clothes and skin were covered in splatters of bright white paint from whatever job they had been able to find yesterday. Their jeans and work boots were coated with cement dust and their calloused skin and bodies were beaten by manual labor into a kind of crudeness where all elements of mercy were lost. Pedro was friendly. The cruelty that life had shown him had not corrupted his propitious attitude. Consuelo was less congenial. The luster of his heart and inherent goodness was withheld behind a cautious demeanor. He spoke absolutely no English and followed his brother around as if doing so meant the difference between life and death.

Aria could tell from their body language that this was not a lighthearted conversation. They were talking about how to navigate worst-case scenarios in case the police got involved with what had happened to Aria. In the emergency of the moment, Pedro and Consuelo's conscience had trumped the care for their own safety. Both Pedro and Consuelo were illegal immigrants. They could not afford to exist in the eyes of the state.

Pedro had come to the United States first, nearly ten years ago. A bad harvest season had made the owners of the farm where he lived and worked lay off nearly all of their workers, including Pedro. As a result he could not feed his wife and three children. Growing up in a little town just north of Jerez, Zacatecas, he would often see families whose relatives had moved to the United States, wearing fancier clothing. And at least some of their kids could afford to go to school. Pedro was illiterate. He had never had a pair of new shoes in his lifetime, much less been able to go to school. With no skills other than farming, he found there were no jobs available to him there. The threat of starvation made the risk of crossing the border, to try to work on a farm in California, a risk he had to take. A family friend in the States vouched for him by promising to pay a "coyote" the $5,000 he required to illegally transport Pedro across the border.

Pedro kissed his family goodbye, promising to send them money, and got into the back of a semi truck transporting huge rubber truck tires. Five of them crossed the border in that truck. Aside from a few stops to get out and relieve themselves in the middle of the desert somewhere, each one of them was made to lie as flat as they could against the inner lining of the tires. This way, if anyone opened the hatch of the trailer, all they would have seen was merchandise. Pedro's tears that day were tainted by the unnatural smell of rubber. Like the men who had made the journey before him, he did not take the risk lightly, simply on the promise of opportunity. Instead, he was torn in half. On one side the heavy doom of the deaths of the family he was responsible for. On the other, the only chance he had at preventing that fate from occurring.

Pedro had taken jobs on several farms over the years before someone told him that he could make more money in a day than he made from farming in a week by standing outside Home Depot and taking the temporary jobs that people who came looking for cheap workers could offer him. Like everything in his life, he had thrown himself into it with no schooling. Having lied that he knew what he was doing so people would hire him in the first place, he had learned how to paint and lay concrete and put up drywall out of pure necessity.

Pedro now found himself in another chapter of powerlessness different from the one he had faced back in Mexico. He lived his life like a fugitive. He couldn't rent a house because his name couldn't be on record. And even if he could rent a place from someone who would do it off the record, he would have to decide between his family's survival and his own. If he rented a house and paid the bills and got groceries, nothing would be left over to send them down in Mexico. So Pedro hopped from place to place, staying with people according to their proximity to each job site that he worked on. No matter how hard he worked, he could never make enough to pay the price for someone to transport his family across the border to be with him. It had taken him three years to pay off the coyote that had brought him. And even if he could, it was too dangerous.

Pedro didn't have a spouse, parent or sibling living legally in the United States, so no one could sponsor him to get a green card. Even if he had, the price of becoming legal, as set by the American government, was more than $20,000, which was more money than any member of his family could ever dream of accruing. And whoever sponsored him would need to prove that they had an income of more than $30,000. No employer would pay him salary and insurance plus the legal fees necessary to legitimize him for work. And the American government would not recognize him as a refugee in need of asylum. With no options, Pedro had been living his life between the cracks of American society, wiring money to his family back in Mexico whenever he could.

So many men, like Pedro, had left to find work that many of Mexico's towns and cities had been reduced to ghost towns. Only old people and wives with children remained. Deprived of life and the animation of commerce, the dust of the desert was eating them away. Crime was a last resort for people who had no other way to make a living, and like roaches, men looking to make a living on that crime inherited the forgotten towns. Consuelo was Pedro's younger brother. Being too young to leave with Pedro to begin with, he had stayed in Mexico to help take care of the family, including the wife and children Pedro had left behind. When he was old enough to work, Pedro concocted a plan to get Consuelo to the United States so that together they might make enough money to bring the rest of the family across the border.

Pedro had sent him some money to pay a man to guide him across the border on foot through the Sonoran desert. Five men, three women and four children had crossed the 80 miles with him. In the 42-degree heat, with the mother screaming on the bankside, Consuelo had watched one of the children drown in a river they had been forced to cross. When Consuelo arrived, he was harrowed. The terror of life in Mexico had been replaced by the terror of living in a completely foreign land. The terror of getting caught and having the chance of a better life obliterated. Consuelo felt like an outsider. He and Pedro had manufactured their lives with a mindset of survival. An achievement mentality was a luxury not given or taught to them. Success was a new pair of shoes, a liter of Pepsi, the money they could wire back home. Despite leaving their country behind and the stoicism with which they conducted themselves, because of that terror, they clung to all the familiar parts of their culture for dear life as if trying to turn America into a new and improved Mexico. With the ongoing threat of a wall being built between America and Mexico, and the increased vigilance of the feared ICE immigration agents, their lives could only get worse.

Aria looked around the room. On the wall in the corner was an altar topped with religious relics. A green and orange statue of the Virgin of Guadalupe stood front and center upon it, her virtue and blessing presiding over the store. The altar below her had been draped with a bright yellow mesh scarf. Beside her was a collection of fake flowers displayed in a vase. A gunmetal rosary hung off of the corner so as to display the Catholic cross at its base, and beside that, a long green candle in a glass container with a painting of San Judas Tadeo. The candle had been turned upside down. As per tradition, the candle would remain that way until the wish that Lolita had made on that candle had come true. She had wished for a kind and responsible man to come into her life and never leave her.

To Aria's left, at another of the small tables, a group of four women sat around a game of *loteria*. Like bingo, the little place cards were arranged in front of them with pennies covering what squares had already been called. Aria could just make out some of the "tarot meets tattoo parlor" drawings on the squares. The women were betting on the game with quarters piled in the center of the table. Despite it being a game based entirely on chance and luck, they parlayed the money they would win, buffering the unpredictable and uncontrollable reality of the game with superstition.

Aria worked her way around the chunks of chicken to lift the large kernels of hominy onto her spoon. The broth was spicy, the tomato base disguised by the heavy flavor of oregano and the richness of the chicken fat that glazed the top of it. When Aria had finished what she could of the soup, she opened the little fluorescent orange package of Gansitos that Lolita had placed on the table in front of her. The smell of them reminded her of Hostess cupcakes. She bit into the synthetic sweetness, white sponge cake with a stripe of strawberry jelly and pastry cream coated in a film of chocolate and topped with chocolate sprinkles. She ate both of the cakes in the package, trying to savor the taste of them.

Watching her struggle with her drink, Lolita came over with an opener and popped the top off of the bottle of mandarin-flavored Jarritos soda. "*Mija*, let me do that," she said, taking the metal cap with her to return to the table with Pedro and Consuelo.

It felt sinful to chase cake with soda. The bright food coloring and carbonation were unsympathetic against her tongue. The sweetness of it made her teeth hurt, but it tasted reassuring.

Aria felt like she had taken a turn down a street and wound up immersed in a completely different country. Had it not been for the specific situation that had brought her there, she imagined she would have been much less warmly welcomed. Her mind was not disquieted by the incident that had led to all of this. She was used to it. Violation was just an unlucky part of life and Aria felt like there was no point in dwelling on what could never be changed. Instead, she pretended to be on vacation. She tasted the foreign flavors and smelled the foreign smells. She let her eyes take in all the things in the store that she had never seen before.

Eventually, Pedro and Consuelo got up to leave. Aria didn't know where they were headed to, maybe back to the Home Depot parking lot to see if they had missed their chance to land a job or not. Pedro paused after hugging Lolita, but before walking out of the door, he called out, "Hey Aria, you be careful eh?" as familiarly as if she were his sister.

"Thank you, guys," Aria called back at him, extending her hand toward him in thanks through the air. Consuelo tipped the brim of his baseball hat and the two of them ducked out the door.

Lolita was uneasy. She looked over at Aria as if trying to decide what to do with her. The look made Aria feel like she had worn out her welcome. Not wanting to burden her any further, Aria took the lollipop that Lolita had also given her from the table and placed it in her coat pocket. She got up and asked, "Should I put these anywhere?" referring to the mess she had made at the table.

"No, *mija*, it's OK. It's OK, I'll take care of it," Lolita said, coming over to usher away the mess herself.

"Thank you, really, thank you so much for everything," Aria said, not knowing how to repay the generosity that Lolita had shown her.

"Just be safe and don't get yourself into any more trouble."

Aria shrugged and nodded her head.

"Let the *Virgen María* guide over you," Lolita said, patting Aria on the sleeve of her coat.

Aria walked through the aisles to the door of the store. "Thank you again," she said, extending one last appreciative look in Lolita's direction.

She decided to walk a different way back toward the car lot, having to backtrack a few times because the route was unfamiliar. The idea of waiting to see Omkar in the boredom of the empty car lot was usually tedious, but after the intensity of the day so far, it felt soothing. She pulled out the Rebanaditas lollipop from her pocket and tore off the yellow wrapper. Aria was confounded to see that the lollipop was covered in a dust that looked like chili powder. She didn't know whether to expect it to be sweet or savory. She stuck out the tip of her tongue to find out. It was salty. She could not find any sweetness beyond the taste of salt and the sting of the hot pepper. "How strange," she thought to herself. But she put it in her mouth anyway. Overwhelmed by the off-putting taste of pure hot chili powder, she held it in her mouth for a few seconds before the faint flavor of watermelon candy peeked through. She smiled to herself because the experience was symbolic of the day so far, which had started off unsavory and turned out sweet.

Up until that day, Aria had been afraid of Mexican men. She had thought them to be venal and barbaric. Never did she imagine that two of them would be the preventers instead of the perpetrators of a crime against her. It felt strange to know nothing about them aside from their names, even stranger to ponder the webbing of life. It never ceased to amaze Aria to imagine people's separate lives and to see how the threads of their life paths were suddenly woven together in one place for one singular experience.

Perhaps those life paths would stay woven for a while, like hers and Taylor's had. Or perhaps they would never cross one another's paths again. Either way, Aria could feel some cosmic orchestration at work in the world at times like this.

CHAPTER 25

A couple of hours had come and gone since Aria returned to the car lot. The afternoon sun was high and harsh. Only Robert and Anthony were milling around their camps.

Aria was writing in her journal in the shade offered by the inside of the Land Cruiser when a commotion outside stole away her attention. It was Ciarra returning to the lot with Aston in tow. But she wasn't alone; she was followed by a black man that Aria didn't recognize. The man was tall. His shoulders were slightly hunched around a concave chest. The bones of his face were chiseled. A stifled mustache sat atop his thick lips. Even from where Aria was watching, the large diamond earrings that pierced both of his ears were clearly visible. His perfectly trimmed hair looked like a thick mat of black moss. He was wearing a neon lime sport jumpsuit and impractical black high-top Jimmy Choo sneakers that were an obvious status-driven fashion statement.

Aria cracked the cruiser door open quietly so she could try to hear what they were saying. She could just make out a word here and there, enough to gather that the man was Ciarra's pimp.

Ciarra had met the man when Aston was still a baby. After Aston's father had abandoned them for his flop of a music career, Ciarra had been suffocating under the financial and emotional weight of having become a single mother at 19. On one occasion, a friend offered to watch Aston for her so she could release all the pressure for a night. She could be irresponsible and be her own age again. So she went to a nightclub with a friend. It was there that she met DeShawn. He spent the night buying her drinks and dancing and exploiting her low self-esteem. They slept together for a week. During that week, DeShawn paid her bills and took her shopping. He promised to take care of her and said she would never be alone again. Though it was just his process of recruiting hoes, Ciarra imagined it to be the start of a relationship. She believed herself to be in love. During that week, he also introduced her to blow. The first time she snorted the powder with him off of the kitchen table, it was during Aston's naptime. In the beginning, she complied in order to endear herself to DeShawn. But before long, she was addicted. Now, it was just one more hold that he had over her.

The first day that DeShawn sold her for sex to another man for money, he convinced her that because she was having sex already, there could be no easier and better way to become financially successful than to make money doing what she was already doing for free. Slowly DeShawn changed the game. Ciarra had slipped into the trap and he began to season her. Cocaine wasn't the only addiction that had a hold over her. His intermittent reinforcement did too. Compliments were replaced by insults. Now he was nice to her only if she did exactly what he wanted. He used violence to threaten her when she wouldn't comply. He collected whatever money he could from what she made, to deprive her of it. He deprived her to create dependency and used the giving or withholding of her material needs to motivate or to punish her. Before she even knew what happened, she had slipped under the tyranny of rules, quotas and performance incentives. Now, if she wanted the bills to be paid or wanted to eat or if Aston needed anything, she would have to go out and make him more money.

When he was working, DeShawn went by the name of Ghostbuster. But he required his women to call him Daddy. It was a tradition in the community he grew up in, which was saturated with prostitutes, including his mom and sister. Becoming a pimp was simply a normal and achievable way of making money. It was a road to glitz and glamor as opposed to the squalor of welfare.

DeShawn preferred to recruit and manage white girls because he found them easier to manage. They could blend into a variety of environments, from rich to poor. And the younger they were, the easier they were to manipulate, the harder they worked to earn their money and the easier they were to sell.

But now Ciarra had become a liability. In the years since he recruited her, he had rethought his stance on using drugs as a way to keep his dames dependent. His women who were addicted were unreliable and a danger to themselves. He worried that it could threaten earnings if a woman was willing to charge a lower rate behind his back in exchange for narcotics. It was this unreliability that had led him to the car lot, looking for Ciarra.

"Look at this here. You's supposed to be with a date." DeShawn tried to impede her path toward the purple van. His "bottom girl" (the most experienced woman in his lot, who had been given the job of training new girls, keeping the peace and monitoring what he could not) had called DeShawn to report Ciarra's recent lax behavior.

"I just need to sleep. I'm sick, just let me sleep it off and I'll go out tomorrow, I promise," Ciarra said, trying to pull Aston past him. "Plus, I got no one to watch him right now. My dad's supposed to be here, but he isn't." She kept her eyes averted just like he expected, but waited for him to grant her permission.

"You know what I'm gon' have to do? I'm gon' trade you down," DeShawn said bluntly. "I can't have no bitches actin' this unprofessional. Fuck you. I don't need you, don't no one need a low bitch like you." He expected his threat to trade her to another pimp to motivate her to comply. But instead she managed to get by him.

He yelled out after her. "You know dat money you need for the abortion? You ain't gon' get it now. Not from me and not from nobody. I'm gonna give it to another girl in the stable. I'm gonna give it to Carley. You out on your own now, you a renegade … You out of pocket. Watch and see how far ya get wit'out me! You wanna be a lot lizard or you gonna get the fuck back out on the track?"

DeShawn was the only person Ciarra had told that she was pregnant. Though DeShawn made sure his "bottom" took all his girls to a clinic to get on birth control pills, he couldn't be there to make sure each one of them remembered to take them every day. Even though he expected the men hiring his women to use a condom, he couldn't take any chances. Sometimes, due to the irregular hours she worked, Ciarra had taken the pills randomly. With a few of her johns, she had allowed them to pay her more to fuck her without a condom.

It was a decision that had come back to haunt her. She was just over two months' pregnant, a reality that threatened her livelihood. Out of the money Ciarra made, DeShawn had allowed her a smaller share, with the understanding that he was saving up that money until she had earned enough for the bottom to take her to an abortion clinic and deal with her "little problem." It was just another one of the little problems Ciarra had tried to forget by freebasing or shooting cocaine.

Ciarra had shot cocaine several times that day before picking Aston up from school. All day, as always, she had been trying to chase the feeling she'd got from the first injection. Not able to get it from a reputable source, she had bought it from a stranger out of desperation and had only realized, when stirring it with water didn't make it go clear, that it was cut with something else. She shot it anyway.

Once, Ciarra had been afraid of needles. The first time she shot up instead of smoked it, she had to have someone else do it for her while she looked away. Now she was addicted to watching the blood draw back in the needle. It was the rush of knowing that once she saw it, she was guaranteed to get that amazing feeling that would wash every last scrap of her pain away.

The second it hit her bloodstream, the taste of ether took over her mouth. The sound in her ears changed to a ringing and throbbing. Her heart started pounding like a piston, pumping a wave of energy through her being. For once, she felt like she could do anything and go anywhere. She felt like she had been lifted out of the prison of life and instead was on top of the world. But the sound in her ears scared her. She had been told that the sound in her ears was what you heard right before you were about to OD. Being unfamiliar with the blow she had procured, she had overestimated her tolerance. Ciarra was afraid that if she sat down, she would die, so she didn't. She spent hours running around and doing things until she was sure the risk had passed. But now, in the low of the comedown, those hours had caught up to her and she felt even worse than usual.

Aria watched Ciarra stumble toward the van as if fighting a vapor of exhaustion trying to suck the life from her veins. It was obvious that she was high. The shackles of the futility in her life, which the cocaine had freed her from, had been put back on and were heavier. Ciarra didn't care to live anymore. She couldn't care about anything. She felt like giving up. All she could do in a state like this was sleep.

DeShawn jogged to catch up to Ciarra, slamming the driver's side door that she had just opened, preventing her from getting inside it. She spun around to face him with her back against the side of the car. "You get the fuck back on the track," he yelled, pointing a finger so close to her face it grazed her nose.

In an attempt to defend her, Aston tried to get between their legs and push DeShawn away from her. "Don't hurt my mommy!" he yelled. DeShawn immediately punched the side of Aston's head, knocking him to the ground.

Aria watched him turn his attention back to Ciarra, preventing her from getting between himself and Aston. The boy struggled to get back up off of the ground. When he did, again he tried to get back in between them. DeShawn yelled something Aria couldn't hear at Aston and proceeded to beat him.

"No, stop it! Oh my God, stop it! OK, I'll go back out. Oh my God, stop!" Ciarra screamed at the top of her lungs, too afraid of him to take a step forward to physically stop him.

DeShawn backed off of Aston, who was lying motionless in the dust. By this point both Anthony and Robert were watching the scene from within their tents, like frightened rabbits peeking out at a predator from their burrows.

Ciarra ran up to DeShawn, desperate to make amends. She looked for him to cosset her. Her body language indicated compliance. "OK, where's the date? I'll go right now. Just as soon as I get him in the car," she said.

"A'ight. That's my girl. You go out to the cathouse now by the kiddy stroll. You see what you can pick up. But that little trick you pulled is gonna cost ya. I ain't losin' no revenue."

Ciarra nodded in agreement, knowing she would have to work to pay off the money he would have made if she had shown up to whatever "date" she had been expected to service.

Satisfied, he put his arm around her neck and planted a kiss on her forehead. Aria watched him walk over and kneel down next to Aston, who was dazed to the point of not being able to get up. DeShawn pulled Aston to his feet and brushed the dust off of his pants and shirt, stabilizing the boy's drunken sway, which had been initiated by his dizziness. "You love your momma, don'tcha? Yeah, you're a good boy, ain'tcha. But your momma gotta work. If you let her work, one day I might teach ya to be like me. You'd like that, wouldn't ya? You'll be good with the ladies, yeah, I can tell you gonna be good with the ladies."

He handed Aston's hand over to Ciarra, who pulled the boy tight against her legs. "I'll take you back out on the track," he said as a final order, not bothering to wait for a reply. Mother and son stood motionless against the van, watching DeShawn walk back toward his customized black Lincoln Navigator.

Ciarra got them both in the car and rushed, despite her stupor, to clean the blood off of Aston's face with a wet wipe. Though she heard nothing, Aria could see him crying through the windshield as she did it. Then Ciarra stripped down to her push-up bra in the front seat, changing her clothes as fast as she could to put on something sexier. When she got out of the van, she grabbed Aston and put him on her hip. The heels she was wearing wobbled when she walked across the uneven ground. Aria watched them get into the back of DeShawn's car and disappear behind the tinted windows.

Ciarra hated herself for the wounds that yet again distorted Aston's face. But her guilt wouldn't allow her to extend herself so far as to coddle him. Instead she stared out the window at the city passing by. The humbling darkness of her existence, which was hardly an existence, tumbled her with its claws. The company she kept had proven itself to be a synagogue of hell. She would take to her grave the way she judged herself for it, the way she blamed herself for having been so stupid and desperate to have fallen for it all in the first place. But she was stuck now. As far as she could tell, she had not only sold her body to meet their basic needs, she had sold her soul, too. Now her life was a blasphemy against those who had wished for her to do well. And now, the only thing strong enough to drown the shame she felt was cocaine.

One of the other girls at the cathouse would watch Aston while Ciarra worked in another room. She hated when circumstances forced her to do that. She could never relax when he was out of her sight at a place where the dangers of the game were always lurking.

— * —

Aria couldn't take it anymore. No one knew better than she did that the system was broken. She wouldn't wish it on anyone. But a broken system seemed better than the neglect and violence of the hands currently in charge of raising Aston. She found herself between a rock and a hard place, but had to make a decision.

She had been in the system herself long enough to know the protocol. The fire of being fed up with watching Aston being bruised and battered and left alone, on top of the fury of seeing Ciarra high, like her own mother had been so many times, launched Aria into motion. She crossed the city blocks swiftly, to the first place she knew of with a pay phone. It took her a few minutes to find enough willing people to give her the spare change to make a call.

"Hi, I'm calling to make a report," she said, waiting for the woman on the other end to indicate she was ready to take notes. "It's a little boy, about five years old. His mother is an addict. She's keeping him in an abandoned parking lot. He gets beaten pretty regularly and also left by himself when she goes out to prostitute. I don't know if he's being fed. He got beaten up pretty bad today and I think someone should go get him."

Hearing her own voice, Aria could hardly believe what she was doing. Some part inside her was bellowing that she was making a serious mistake. But the part of her that was louder was the part that had dialed the number to the Department of Children and Family Services. Though the woman on the phone pressured Aria to reveal her identity, Aria refused and insisted on reporting anonymously. She gave her Ciarra's and Aston's names and explained their whereabouts, only hanging up once she was certain that someone could find them.

On top of the guilt that Aria felt for reporting them, she felt guilty that she had revealed the whereabouts of the car lot. Though fairly certain that the police would escort a social worker there – someone who would only be concerned with the welfare of the child – she had no way of knowing if she had just put herself and everyone else there out of the closest place any of them had to a home. But Aston was a child. It was a risk she had to take. Though Aria already knew all too well the agony that Aston was about to face, she knew she could not live with herself for standing by and watching.

Knowing that the authorities would have to decide whether her report indicated child abuse before initiating an investigation, Aria walked back to the lot to wait for Omkar to show up after his classes were over for the day. The words she had spoken into the phone were a eulogy of her innocence and youth. Aria played through possible scenarios of the cops showing up to look for Aston. She practiced how to go undetected and escape in each one of them.

The atmosphere when she got back to the lot was a warring absence. Despite the loss of her youth, her decision had left her like a child standing alone in the desert. She had sucked the stone of humanity's indifference as dry as she could. Now there was nothing more to do but wait ... Wait for the priest that followed the beast of mankind's cruelty, looking to clean up after him.

Doubt whispered that her life was a room full of errors; that the proud pyramid of her virtue would fall. But it was a call she had already made.

CHAPTER 26

Omkar ran the smooth tips of his fingers over the cuts on Aria's face and, reclining the driver's side seat, held her against him. The air conditioner of the car blew an unnatural wintergreen chill across their faces.

Both of them said very little. Aria didn't tell him the full story about the incident outside the Home Depot, or her time in the Mexican store. Nor did she tell him about reporting Ciarra and Aston. Instead, she simply told him, "Some people out here are kinda territorial. If you go too close to their things, they chase you." She explained away the injuries adorning her face as resulting from a fall, so she could put it behind them. She wanted to soak in every last drop of the peace that his closeness granted her before he left. They would sit in the parked car like this and talk or not talk for as long as they could before Omkar was forced to return at a time that allowed him to avoid rousing any suspicion in his parents.

The next day, Aria spent most of her time with Taylor and Luke. She had been carried back to a place of anticipation about what might lie ahead, rather than the hope she had briefly felt.

— * —

At the other end of the city, Ciarra sat on the edge of the bed in a hotel room that her regular john, Larry, had purchased for the day. It was a Saturday. Having taken Aston back to the car lot to be watched by Mike, she had met Larry there in a last-ditch effort to try to exploit his affectionate nature and get him to pay for her abortion behind DeShawn's back.

Ciarra told Larry that she was pregnant with his child. She had expected him to grow long in the face and begin to brainstorm about how to get her out of the mess entirely. But that wasn't at all what happened. Instead, a heartwarming smile spread across his unbecoming face.

"Really? I mean, are you sure? Did you take a test?" he asked. Ciarra nodded. Larry paced the length of the room once before telling Ciarra to wait just a minute and rooting around in his duffel bag. He walked back toward her with an item he had found inside it, concealed in his palm. "Well, as you already know, I think you're just about the most beautiful girl in the world. And I've been waitin' to do this for just the right time. But I guess that time's gonna be now."

In shock, Ciarra covered her mouth with her hand as he struggled despite his weight to drop to one knee on the ground in front of her and begin to speak. "Ciarra … Baby doll, I love you. Since the first time I laid eyes on you, I knew you were gonna be something special in my life. The only thing more beautiful than you is your heart. You're such a special woman to me. I know I'm not the best to look at. But I plan to take care of you. You can quit this and love only me. What do you say? Will you marry me?"

Ciarra watched his eyes well up with tears, in a state of complete disbelief. There were too many thoughts and feelings to sort through in the seconds granted to her, with his life lingering on the precipice of her reply. "Yes," she said, letting him slide the little cubic zirconia solitaire onto the ring finger of her left hand.

Larry leaned in for a kiss, bracing himself against the gloss of her knee-high white go-go boots. For the next hour, instead of getting swept up in the commission of her seduction, Larry lay on the bed with her and held her close. Ciarra was careful to give him the impression that she was happy and in love with him too. He could not see or feel beyond the walls of her façade. Larry was in his own little blissful world alone.

In Larry's world, Ciarra loved him. In Larry's world, he wasn't taking advantage of the women he paid to have sex with him. He was engaging in a transaction that served them both so he could get the affection he so desperately needed, but that no other woman would grant him willingly because of the way he looked. In Larry's world, he had come to Ciarra's rescue and would give her the care a young woman deserves. He could already picture her in the morning, cooking him breakfast in the newly decorated kitchen of his little house. He had always wanted to be a father. Sadly, no woman had been interested in choosing him to sire her child. As he lay there on the bed, happier than he had ever been, he imagined it would be a boy. He pictured the green field of the Dodger Stadium and the look on his future son's face when he called over the man selling peanuts.

Ciarra's world was different. Her profession required her to treat Larry like he was the only man left in the world. She had petted and pampered him. She had listened to him talk for hours about himself. She had sucked his cock whenever it was time to leave in order to go in search of her next client. She wasn't in love with him in any way. Larry had no idea that she already had another child. It wasn't something that a girl like her brought up in between the role-play and the fuzzy handcuffs. So why had she said yes? It was because of the inescapable heartbreak of her life. It was because she was desperate to square up. This was the best chance she had at any of it, at exiting the game, at escaping the constant tension of survival, at giving Aston the life that he deserved. Love was nothing next to survival. Love was nothing next to the promise of a safety she had never touched in all her life.

From underneath the weight of his arm across her, Ciarra felt her sorrow for Larry rise, and maybe a hint of guilt for the fact that she had lied to him. The father of the child that was now living this abhorrent life inside her was most likely not even his. It could belong to any of the several men she had slept with unprotected. She didn't plan on keeping the child, even if she married him and so got Aston and herself off of the streets. If push came to shove, she would steal money from him to get the abortion when he was away at work one day and tell him that she had lost the baby.

The paradoxical gratitude and disgust she felt for Larry stirred like gossamer spice in her chest when she kissed him goodbye and promised to call him the next day. He blew her kisses as she walked away from him. She boarded a city bus and rode it to the bus stop closest to the car lot. The sinking feeling she had felt in her heart when she said yes to marrying Larry had been displaced by heartening thoughts of the way hers and Aston's life would improve. She jogged toward the car lot, excited to tell Aston about their sudden turn of fortune. Excited to tell him about the fact that soon, he would live in a real house.

Ciarra was an expert at running in high heels. She jogged forward despite their waver until the sight of a cop car near the lot made her stop dead in her tracks. She began to walk toward it timidly, hoping to ascertain the situation at a distance far enough to decide if she should run in the exact opposite direction. Two police officers and another woman and man (who appeared to be with them) stood in a huddle with Mike and Aston. At first, she panicked that the two people with the cops might be the owners of the little car lot. Maybe they had called the cops to come kick them all out, to make way for a new business plan. But then she remembered the state of Aston's face and she started running. The adrenaline coursing through her body was enough to make her vision blurry.

She ran toward them, no longer caring if the defensive rage she felt would get her arrested. "What's going on?" she yelled out to them, slowing her pace once she got close. The huddle opened up as if they had all been waiting for her to arrive. Dismay was written across Mike's face. Aston was examining the wiggle of one of the loosely sewn-on eyes of a teddy bear that the people had brought him.

When the police car had pulled up to the lot with the two people who worked for Child Protection Services, Anthony and Wolf had scattered inconspicuously into the woods. Aria, Taylor and Luke had already been gone for hours in search of somewhere to get food. And Darren had left early to plant himself somewhere in the city beside his little cardboard sign. The only people who stayed put when the police approached were Robert, Mike and Aston.

In Ciarra's absence, they had interrogated Mike about his daughter and grandson. They had searched the van that she had been living in. Once it was obvious to them that Mike was both naive and not the person to blame for the crime that had covered Aston in bruises, they had told him the truth about his daughter. They told him they had reason to believe that Ciarra was both an addict and a prostitute. That she was doing other things with her time and resources than working night shifts at a bar to try to get their lives back on track. Mike felt crushed, a failure, the faith he wanted to have in his daughter reduced to ruins.

The police and the pair from CPS had already made up their minds. There was no way they could justify allowing this child to stay in the conditions he was obviously in. Unlike the usual, the situation they had found themselves in was an exigent one. None of them confused poverty with neglect or abuse. They would not even need a court order to take Aston away.

Once Aston had given Ciarra's legs a hug, the male CPS officer ushered the boy away from the conversation, distracting him with questions about his favorite things and asking Aston to show him a game he liked to play. The female CPS worker spoke for all of them. "The reason we're here today, ma'am, is because we needed to investigate a report we received of your son being in an unsafe situation. Do you have any idea who might have done this to his face?" she asked, trying to give the impression that she was on Ciarra's side instead of against her.

"No one did that to his face, he had an accident riding his bike the other day," Ciarra said belligerently.

"Would you be able to show us that bike?" the social worker asked, knowing full well that Ciarra, who was too poor to afford a place to stay, would not be able to produce one.

"It was a friend's bike so it's at another house. What exactly are you accusing me of?" Ciarra asked. She tried to remind herself to stay calm and not get defensive, but she could not control the storm of her emotions.

"Ma'am, we know that a fall from a bike didn't do that to his face. The more cooperative you are with us, the better this is going to go for you and Aston," the woman said in a warning tone.

Ciarra refused to say more.

"Does Aston's father maybe have a number that we could call to talk to him?" the woman asked.

"No. I don't know where he is. He's a musician and he's on tour," Ciarra said. The way the woman looked down at an envelope she was holding made Ciarra see red with panic. "This is a violation of my rights. It's unlawful what you're doing. You have to get a warrant or a court order to search my home," she challenged.

The woman, who had already lost her patience with Ciarra, barked back at her, "A broken-down vehicle in a tent city does not qualify as a home, especially if that vehicle is not even yours. We can do this the hard way or we can do this the easy way. I'm going to ask you again to cooperate with us. Do you happen to have a phone number where we could reach Aston's father?"

Ciarra could not control herself. She was locked in a fight to keep her own child. In defense of the terror and shame she felt, her blood boiled hot in response to the transgression. "You can't prove anything. I love my son and I'm a *very* good mom!" she yelled.

Mike broke his silence in response to her argument. "Ciarra, I think you oughta cooperate with these folks."

Her rage turned in the direction of her father. "What the fuck, Dad, now you're on their side? They're tryin' to fucking take Aston away from me, don't you see that? They're trying to take Aston away."

She directed the fight back toward the social worker. "Who the fuck told you he was getting abused? I want to know who called you."

The social worker cocked an eyebrow. "Ma'am, I'm not allowed to tell you who gives us a referral. But we do need to take Aston to get a medical exam. The law allows us to take custody of a child in this situation."

"No fuckin' way. No fuckin' way am I gonna let you take my son away."

Ciarra started to walk toward Aston, intent on claiming him away from the man who was preoccupying him. One of the police officers, who had been standing like a guard statue, spoke up. "Ma'am, if you intervene, you may be lookin' at arrest. I may have to arrest you."

Ciarra yelled, "This is bullshit. This is such fucking bullshit." Her anger gave way to uncontrollable sobbing.

Mike interjected. "Well, what if I take custody for a while? I'm his granddad."

The woman shook her head regretfully. "We can't let Aston stay in a place where we can't be sure that he has access to running water or food. Whoever has custody of him has to be living in a suitable residence."

Mike looked down at the floor, his hope expended by the grief that he dared not overtly show them.

"What the fuck about all those people down on Skid Row?" Ciarra asked. "They have fuckin' kids. Why the fuck aren't they getting their kids taken?"

The way they reacted to her question denoted that they had no explanation to offer her. Ciarra collected herself and tried, despite her despair, to make herself the victim. "We've had a hard time, that's all. It's just me and him, you know? His dad don't give us any money. We don't live here. We're just here temporarily so my dad can watch him when I work."

Ciarra was pacing up and down. The social worker thought about asking her about her work, but seeing as how she already knew the answer and knew that Ciarra would lie, she didn't bother. "Ma'am, because of the hour right now, I'll be taking Aston to the office. We are going to do Aston's physical tomorrow morning. Unless for some reason the physical goes on all day long, which it shouldn't, I'm going to pick him up from there and drop him off at school. Within five days, you can request a visit with him and we can have someone supervise that visit. During that visit, we are gonna need you to do a urine test just to make sure that there are no drugs in your system. I can update you any time if you want to call me. Do you have any questions before we take him with us?"

Ciarra's rage took over her terror again. "I don't appreciate these fucking allegations. How the fuck would you feel if someone just came into your house in the middle of the day and took your kid away? How the fuck would you feel? Yeah, I feel pretty shitty, obviously."

Mike walked over to the purple van and put Aston's toy cars into his little school backpack, along with a jacket and a toothbrush. "Can we at least say goodbye to 'im before you guys take 'im?" he asked, handing the backpack to the social worker.

"Yes, you can definitely do that," she said.

Mike kneeled down in the dust in front of his grandson. "Hey Aston, you're gonna go with these nice people for just a while, so Mommy and I can find you a house, would you like that?"

"No." Aston shook his head.

"But if we could get a house, we could get a dog. Wouldn'tcha like that?"

The dejected look on Aston's face brightened. "Can he be like Scooby Doo?" he asked.

"He may be a little different than Scooby Doo, but we can look for one the same color," Mike said, uncharacteristic tears welling up in his eyes. "Go say bye to your mother," he added, guiding his shoulder to turn toward Ciarra.

Ciarra gave a sigh of defeat and put a hand against her forehead, turning around to try to repress her tears. Aston jumped up on her, completely unaware of what was actually occurring. She picked him up and held his head flat against her neck. "Hey Mommy, Pop Pop said I could get a dog. Can you find a house soon?" Aston asked, suddenly more excited about the reason for needing to go with the strange people standing in the lot than apprehensive.

Hearing Aston use his pet name for her father made the burden she usually felt toward Aston vanish. All that was left was the torment of losing something she loved so much. She started crying. "I love you, buddy," she said. "You be good, OK? Mommy's gonna come get you as soon as I can, OK?"

Aston sat up to look at her. He put his fingers into the wet of the tears on her cheek. "Mommy, why are you crying?" he asked, confused at why such good news had made her act so sad.

"Mommy is just gonna miss you, that's all," she said.

"It's OK, Mommy," Aston reassured her naively. "You don't have to miss me, you can see me every day." His blatant innocence about what was going on made her cry even harder. He walked toward the man he had been playing with and let the man lead him out of the lot.

Everyone stood there watching him walk away willingly until the sight of the car door closing behind him restored Ciarra to her original state of uproar. The woman social worker handed her a piece of paper that she didn't bother to look at. "I'm gonna fuckin' sue you for this. This is a violation of my rights. I am a good mother! Fuck you. Seriously, fuck you."

The woman and the cops stayed completely calm in response to her outburst. When they were certain they had said everything they legally had to say and had given her all the information they legally had to give her, they left.

Mike stood motionless as Ciarra paced. "Who the fuck do they think they are … Fucking pigs. I'm gonna fucking sue them, I swear to God!" she yelled, talking as much to the universe as she was to her father.

"We can get us a house and then we can get 'im back," Mike told her, as unable to moderate her distress as he was his own.

Ciarra sank to the floor, kneeling with her legs splayed. She cried against the complete powerlessness that she felt until she couldn't take it anymore. She ran to the purple van to get her coat and then took off on foot. Mike didn't know where she was going, but he guessed, especially after what the CPS workers had said, that she was going to find a dealer.

The entire thing had been like a concussion grenade going off in their little camp. Mike explained what had happened to Robert, who had been minding his own business in his little tent since finding out that the police were only there to find Ciarra. Though buoyed by Robert's encouragement, Mike felt like it was entirely his fault. He re-evaluated the kind of father he had been or not been. He wanted to have faith in Ciarra, but he couldn't. He made himself a cup of coffee as a comfort.

The only consolation he could find was in the plan he was hatching to get a more stable job. A job where he could afford a house with steady paychecks arriving in the mail. Once that happened, he would try to get custody of Aston for himself. He would make up for the poor job he had done in Ciarra's childhood by giving them both a stable place to live. Tomorrow, he would go to ask for a job at every trucking company he could find.

CHAPTER 27

"I used to put it down to the fact I wasn't fit enough or I didn't look good enough or how big my nose was or that my legs look like chicken legs or whatever. But I really think all that had nothin' to do with it. I was just avoiding the bigger issue."

Taylor was eating an oatmeal cookie that he had saved from the free lunch he had been given at the church. He chewed it while he talked. "I mean, I knew there was somethin' wrong with me when other boys wanted to start hangin' out with girls and I just wanted to hang out with them. I basically did everything in my power not to face it. I think I just felt so much shame I couldn't admit to it until I kinda had to, you know?"

Aria was listening to him from the back seat of the car. The rest of the car lot was void of movement. Everyone else had already turned in for the night. "There was this boy in middle school, Brian Meyer. He was the first boy I ever kissed. I don't know, he was prob'ly just having fun. Straight guys like to do that sometimes. But I was so in love with him I used to write my name and his, and then my name with his last name in my school notebook over and over. I was stayin' with this real Christian family at the time. The mom found my notebook and kicked me out of the house 'cause of it. I guess the idea of movin' in with someone is just scary 'cause it means I kinda have to own it, you know. Like I still feel like maybe it's somethin' I gotta do in secret. But if I'm living there then everyone kinda knows."

Dan had been pressuring Taylor to move in with him. Aria had known about Taylor's resistance to doing so for weeks now. But tonight, she tried to relieve the boredom of trying to fall asleep – neither of them was tired – by digging deeper about the real reasons why. To Aria it made no sense at all why someone in Taylor's position wouldn't jump at the first

247

opportunity to get off the street, especially given everything Taylor had told her about Dan so far. With Omkar in her life, Taylor's frequent absences felt less like abandonment than they did before. Given how effeminate he was and how out of the closet he seemed, it shocked Aria that Taylor was still so ashamed for people to know that he was gay. She tried to counter his shame by telling him there was nothing wrong with it, but nothing she said seemed to sink in. Eventually, the conversation slowed and she heard the louder, labored breathing of his sleep.

Later that night, the shrill sound of Palin's bark startled them awake; the hysterical alarm of her intonations sent a wave of dread up and down both Taylor's and Aria's spines. They threw off the weight of their sleeping bags in preparation for conflict before they even knew what the conflict was. It was Taylor who realized first what was happening.

"Holy shit … Oh my fucking God, we gotta get out of here … Quick!" he yelled to Aria, flailing to collect whatever things he could in time to escape.

The entire car lot was alive with fire. Its molten veins had already claimed Mike's tent as well as the Camaro where EJ used to stay. And it was reaching to swallow everything else in sight. Before Aria could make sense of what was happening, she grabbed the shoulder strap of her backpack and pulled it free from beneath the seat. She yanked the hood of Taylor's sweater to make him run with her, so tightly that he was forced to abandon most of his things.

The heat from the fire had veiled the air in an elemental static that distorted vision. They ran through the only visible break and climbed over the fence as fast as they could, unable to make out whatever it was Ciarra was screaming. When the cold began to offer solace, Aria knew that she had run far enough to ensure that she could stay beyond the span of the flames. She turned back around.

Aria's imagination was plagued by worst-case scenarios. She tried to decipher who was and who wasn't OK through the turbulent screen of fire. Anthony was pouring his last two bottles of water onto a group of flames that were nipping at the edges of his tarp. It was an exercise in futility. He tried to untie the ropes that affixed it to the tree before giving up his efforts and running toward them. Wolf, who had woken up Robert just in time, was yanking the older man to safety. Robert was visibly in a daze. Already mauled by age, he was lethargic and still half asleep.

It took them all a minute to comb through the dizzy collage of disbelief in order to accept what was occurring. Luke ran to what tents and cars that he could, checking to see if anyone was still in them before he couldn't access them anymore. Palin's crazed barking cried out above it all. She was barking in the direction of Ciarra, who was manically squeezing the liquid from a small pile of white jugs of lighter fluid before throwing them toward the fire. "I know one of you fuckers did it … Come out and show yourself!" she screamed, before throwing another one. "I know you're all fucking narcs."

The holocaust of her fury was painted across the car lot as the fire that was decimating all of it. From the spaghetti-like trails that the flames followed, Aria could see that while they had been sleeping, Ciarra had poured lighter fluid in a deranged maze across the expanse of the lot.

Terrified that Mike had been killed by Ciarra's rage, Aria scanned for him frantically until she found his outline. He was standing just outside the fence behind his tent, watching it burn to the ground. He did not intervene in the destruction. He watched everything he had to his name evaporate into smoke and ash, as if he deserved it. His arms were folded in defeat. He made no attempt to respond to Ciarra, who continued screaming insults and fueling the fire until there was no more lighter fluid left. Watching her tantrum, Mike thought about how much Ciarra was just like her mother. From the years he had been married to her, Mike had learned that confronting either of them once they had tipped over the edge like this would only add fuel to the fire.

Ciarra abandoned the scene before a fire truck arrived but only made it a few blocks before she was arrested. Aria, Taylor and Anthony eventually ventured around the perimeter of the chain-link fence to reunite with Luke, Robert, Wolf, Mike and Darren. But once they did, they barely talked. Instead, they all stood in the darkness just beyond the reach of the light being discharged by the fire; watching the firemen scamper around the lot, watching everything turn black. There was nothing to be done.

The fire that had taken everything was a flicker compared to the forest fire of guilt that Aria felt, knowing that in a way, because she had been the one to report Ciarra, she was the one to blame for all this. The people standing next to her were the people in the world who were already the most powerless and already the poorest. Now, because of her decision, the only thing they had was their lives and whatever items they could grab before running.

Darren was the one who anguished her the most. Because of his gruff, military demeanor, before tonight Aria had not imagined that he could cry. But Darren was crying. He stood in front of the rest of them, chaotically pacing back and forth. Each time he stopped, it seemed like he might run straight into the flames toward his camper. Each time he stopped, he re-evaluated the reality of his powerlessness to save his things. What shard of safety he possessed had been taken from him. The only relationships he had, which were with his things, were lost. Since he was a hoarder, it was a thousand times worse for him than it was for the rest of them.

Eventually, he went down on his knees and elbows in the dirt. He held his head with his hands and started rocking back and forth. Except for Palin, who by alerting them had most likely saved all of their lives, no one went to comfort Darren. They felt as powerless to comfort him as they felt about the fire. He began to hyperventilate and pull sticks and handfuls of soil toward himself and hug them as a barren replacement for the things that he had lost. The sight of him doing it made Aria start to cry.

With nowhere to be, once the ground had given way to ash and only the heat of what happened remained, they divided up. Luke, Wolf and Anthony took Darren deeper into nature to spend what was left of the night there. Robert and Mike started walking toward the city. But they didn't sleep that night. Instead, they found a gas station, sat on one of the picnic tables outside and spent the night trying to help each other make sense of what had happened.

Taylor's resistance to staying with Dan had been cremated along with the rest of his things. He took the fire as a sign from God that he was meant to move in with Dan, so he called him on the phone that the older man had recently given him. The phone had felt like an unwelcome leash until he had needed it tonight, Dan's way of keeping track of him. But now it felt like a lifeline instead of a chain.

Aria had taken again to the streets. When Taylor offered to talk Dan into letting her stay with them, she had lied that she was going to follow Luke and everyone else. Instead, she headed in the direction of the Super Sun Market. She planned to wait across the street for him to emerge from the store in the morning.

— * —

Omkar was locked in the kind of dream that would make no sense upon waking, despite it being all too logical and real while he was in it. The low, repetitive buzz of the vibrator on his phone eventually drew him out of it.

"Hello, sir, this is Officer Hawkes. I have an Aria Abbott here," the pleasant male voice told him. "Sir, am I correct in understanding that you have assumed responsibility for Aria while she is in town?"

"Yes, sir," Omkar replied automatically. Having been taught well to fear authority, Omkar was hardly breathing. He listened like a soldier, waiting for orders.

"Sir, I don't know if you're aware but we have a curfew for anyone under eighteen. They cannot be out between 10pm and sunrise unless accompanied by an adult. Can you tell me your exact address?"

Not wanting his parents to be involved, Omkar recited the numbers belonging to a house three doors down from the store. Hearing the address, Officer Hawkes realized that the address was only six blocks away. As far as Officer Hawkes was concerned, because he was wasting his time doing juvenile sweeps anyway, instead of going through the hassle involved with taking her into the station or driving her the six blocks to the house, he decided to delegate the task. "Sir, I'm gonna have to ask you to come pick her up," Officer Hawkes said. "I can't let her out of my custody until an adult can come get her."

"OK, sir, I can definitely do that. Where can I pick her up?" Omkar asked, listening to the policeman relay their whereabouts, with the phone pressed between his cheek and shoulder so he could swiftly get dressed. When Officer Hawkes hung up, Omkar climbed out of his second-story window and dangled off of the ledge of the windowsill before dropping in order to avoid waking his parents up.

A year or so earlier, a string of nighttime shootings had made the city councilmen call for police to enforce a teen curfew in the city. Even though all the shootings had involved only adults, the police were directed to use every law enforcement tool they could to crack down on the recent spike in violent crime. On this, one of only two nighttime shifts he worked, Officer Hawkes and a group of other officers had been sent out on a juvenile sweep. Hawkes knew the routine well. He was expected to arrest them and either take them home or take them to a law enforcement post until their parents could come pick them up. It had been a rather ironic stroke of bad luck that Aria was spotted walking across the city exactly on that night. But her bad luck was offset by the fact that Officer Hawkes hated curfew law. Not only was there absolutely no evidence that it did anything to prevent crime, he found it to be an embarrassing waste of law enforcement resources. Most of the kids he ended up arresting were Latino or black, and every time he put the handcuffs on, he could feel the already strained relationship between law enforcement and minority groups worsening.

When he had spotted Aria weaving in and out of alleyways and under overpasses, he had considered whether to simply let her go. He worried more for her safety than that she was up to no good. But he decided to give her a scare in the hope that it would discourage her from running amuck at this time of night. Aria didn't run. When she saw the police car sparkle its lights once from behind her, she stopped dead in her tracks.

Aria was surprised at first to see the officer that stepped out from the car. This was the third time she had crossed paths with this same cop. Though she had seen him act kindly, that did not fool her into forgetting that he was a cop and she was an underage runaway. Aria pretended to be ignorant of the curfew law and told Officer Hawkes that she was visiting a friend here because she was from out of town. She had expected to be arrested. She had half expected the karma of what had happened at the car lot to make today the day that she was caught and sent back to Illinois state foster care.

Officer Hawkes had heard excuses like hers before, but to his surprise, when she presented him with her ID and he shone his flashlight across it, he could clearly see that the license was in fact an out-of-state license. Instead of arresting her and forcing her to call her parents, who obviously would not even be able to pick her up, he asked her for a number so he could call whoever she was staying with in Los Angeles. Aria pulled out the number that Omkar had written on the scrap of paper towel from her backpack.

While they were waiting the few minutes for Omkar to arrive, Officer Hawkes asked her trivial questions about things like where she went to school and what it was like where she came from and how she liked her time in Los Angeles so far. Aria hated it when police tried to act so friendly. It always seemed to be a contrived attempt to make themselves come across like good guys instead of bad guys. No cop had ever made her life better. Plus, she found it hard to accept a cop as a benevolent keeper of the peace with a Beretta and handcuffs visibly displayed on his belt. She wasn't compliant or nice to him while they waited out of an actual liking for him. She was compliant and nice out of fear of what would happen if she wasn't.

The feeling of sitting down in Omkar's car and being enclosed inside it was ineffable. No longer having to keep it together in the face of a situation that could very probably have separated them, Aria started to cry. She could not believe any of what had happened or how close she had come to the very thing she had spent nearly a year trying to avoid.

Omkar pulled away from the curb and drove out of sight of the cop car before pulling back up and turning the engine off. Despite his multiple attempts to quiet her tears and find out what was happening, Aria kept weeping. Omkar noticed when he hugged her that her clothing smelled distinctly like smoke. He was forced to wait for her to offer an explanation. When she finally did, Omkar felt out of his depth. He knew he had lived a sheltered life and couldn't understand the pressures she had been under. He tried to release her from the guilt of having called CPS.

He felt a ton of responsibility for her wellbeing. Aria had no place to go. And Omkar could not live with the idea of handing that responsibility back to her. While she talked, his mind raced for possible solutions. He settled on a temporary one. He would sneak back into the house and set up some blankets on the floor of the storeroom in the shop before sneaking Aria in for the night. He could set his alarm and leave with her before his father even got dressed in the morning. It would at least buy him a day to come up with another plan.

Both of them were almost bewildered when the plan worked. Their entry had solicited no stirring from upstairs. The blankets Omkar had found smelled like him. Aria breathed them in when she lay down in them.

Omkar sat down against the wall behind her, pulling her back against his chest. Aria apologized again for inconveniencing him. If she had known that he would end up having to pick her up anyway, she would have called him from Taylor's phone. But Omkar did not feel inconvenienced. He felt good to finally carry the weight of her welfare. Though he did not yet know exactly what to do with it, it felt like there was suddenly more space for him in her life. The smell of smoke in her hair caused him to imagine what it would be like to take her camping and to roast marshmallows. Omkar stayed as long as he could without raising suspicion.

Aria would not normally have been able to sleep after the sequence of events that had taken place that day. She would have writhed, reliving the torture. But Omkar's presence was laden with consolation. Being near him caused Aria to feel the strange juxtaposition of being completely overwhelmed and at the same time, calmed by the cottony refuge of Omkar's being. Eventually, it was that refuge that coerced her into sleep.

When Omkar finally climbed back up the stairs, his anger toward the prejudice of his own culture climbed the stairs with him. Leaving her in the unfurnished starkness of the storeroom made Omkar feel like a fugitive in his own house. He wanted to keep her with him. He didn't want to have to hide her or the way they felt about each other.

PART 4

CODA

CHAPTER 28

The way you date as an Indian in America can be summarized in two sentences. In the eyes of your parents, either you are too old and you should be married already. Or you are too young and you shouldn't so much as look at another boy or girl until you are ready to get married.

Relationships were yet another thing that made Omkar resent his culture. He found himself straddling the divide between two cultures that couldn't be more different if they tried. In American culture, dating could be casual. Parents let their children date young and didn't seem to intervene when they did. In Indian culture, children were not allowed to date. Most Indian kids growing up in America were simply sent off to college socially stunted. It shouldn't have been a surprise, therefore, that many of them failed to meet someone to marry on campus. Yet it always did seem to come as a surprise. When their son or daughter would turn 26 or 27, parents would panic and take matters into their own hands. There was nothing casual in Indian culture about forming a relationship with the opposite sex. The entire thing was a carefully orchestrated arrangement, which for the most part was conducted by parents. And marriage was considered to be the most important part of a person's life.

Omkar's parents had met on their wedding day. Their parents had selected them as a match for each other with the idea that it would be the best thing for both of them. Like the vast majority of marriages in India, theirs was an arranged marriage. It had been several days of pre- and post-wedding ceremonies and parties. Now they fully believed that the blessings they had sought from God when they bowed before the holy script had been granted. Theirs was a happy marriage. Time had seen them grow to love one another.

It was a fact that Jarminder reminded Omkar of daily. "Our marriages are much more successful than those of the Westerners, Omkar," she would say. "Parents have lived longer, we know how the world really works. So we will make a better decision."

It always made Omkar queasy when she said it. Not because he disagreed with her entirely. In fact, Omkar was not against the idea of having a wife chosen for him, provided that he could meet her enough times beforehand to decide if he liked her or not. What scared Omkar was that he had liked girls before, none of whom met the criteria his parents had so clearly set out. He lived in desperate fear that one day he might fall in love with a woman to whom they would not consent … To find himself caught between the sense of duty he felt toward his parents' happiness as well as the approval he so needed from them, and a woman his heart could not give up for either of those things.

Omkar had not been allowed to date. His parents were afraid of him marrying a girl from another culture and they had not been the kind to hope that he would meet a nice Indian girl at college. Because they no longer lived in India, the pool of suitable matches for Omkar was small. They were looking for a girl who came from the same religion, caste and subculture. They wanted her physical appearance and her educational and/or professional accolades to be impressive.

Being in America, they had no large community of girls whose parents they knew well. They also had no matchmaker. As a result, they had toyed with the idea of taking Omkar back to India to try to find him a wife, before deciding first to turn to computers to serve the role that a matchmaker might have served before. Their plan, the minute that Omkar graduated from college and secured his first salary, was to put him on the market.

Neeraj and Jarminder had persuaded Omkar to cooperate in helping them to create a Bio Data profile on him. They were doctoring it and tempering their impatience by sending it to a few people they knew in the hopes that the day wouldn't come where he would graduate and they would have to cast it out to a wider audience of families they didn't know.

A Bio Data was rather like a job application, except it contained all kinds of details about the color of Omkar's skin tone, his star sign, religion, caste, hobbies, education, achievements and the details of what kind of female the family would prefer. His mother had designed it like the menu of an Indian restaurant, complete with a peacock feather and a reddish orange backdrop. He had just managed to squeak by without putting a turban on for the picture of himself on the upper right side.

Omkar had done with Aria what most Indian boys did when they found themselves in love with a white girl: he had said nothing to anyone about her. He had snuck her into the folds of his life. He had hidden their romance under the disguise of late-night study groups and errands he needed to run for the sake of maintaining the upstanding reputation that he held in his parents' eyes. But all that was about to come crashing down around Omkar's feet.

Neeraj walked from his bed to the bathroom, leaving Jarminder asleep under twisted covers. Not yet awake, his aging body felt stiff. There was so much less energy there to motivate his movement than there had been years before. His grogginess dulled the crispness of the way things looked. When he went to sit down on the rim of the toilet seat, he pushed his hair out of his face. It fell to the middle of his back. He scoffed with irritation, noticing that only remnants of toilet paper were stuck to the cardboard roll. Jarminder had finished the roll of toilet paper and not replaced it. It was one of those petty irritations that he had learned, over the many years he had been married, to let slide instead of confronting her about it. He stood back up and searched the cupboards for another roll. Another wave of frustration hit him and he muttered to himself, realizing that he would have to go downstairs to the storeroom to get another roll. He put his bathroom robe on and made heavy footsteps walking past Jarminder. It was a passive-aggressive attempt to make her feel guilty for the fact that he would have to go all the way downstairs because of what she had failed to do. But the sound did not wake her.

He walked down the stairs the same as he did every day. The stale air in the shop was still. He made a quick survey of a shelf whose presentation filled him with dissatisfaction before opening the door of the storeroom.

The sound of the door opening jolted Aria awake. Both Neeraj and Aria jumped, startled by one another. A deep freeze of shame washed over Aria's surprise while his was replaced immediately by anger. He swore in Punjabi and then switched to English. "What are you doing here? Why are you here? I recognize you. Did you steal something? I'm going to call the police."

Giving her no time to answer, he walked toward the phone. Aria shot to her knees and started packing her few things into her backpack. Adrenaline coursed through her veins. She felt terrible that because she had stayed there, she and Omkar's father had started off on such a vile foot. But she couldn't afford to stay around to try to fix it. In case the police showed up, she decided to run.

Neeraj was in the middle of dialing on the archaic landline phone that he had insisted on keeping in the store when Aria walked past him. "I'm sorry, I didn't mean anything, I'm sorry," she said, her eyes lowered in shame.

"Don't you go anywhere. Stop. Stop where you are!" Neeraj yelled, hanging up the phone and picking up a magazine to follow her out.

The clang of the bell on the shop door when she unlocked it woke Omkar from his sleep. At first, he thought he had dreamed the sound. The wave of terror did not crush against him until he heard his father's voice yelling on the street outside.

Omkar nearly bowled his mother over as the sound compelled both of them to rush down the stairs toward the conflict at the same time. He already knew what had happened before he saw either of them. He was already chastising himself for it.

"Papa, stop. Aria, don't go, please, both of you … Just let me explain."

"This girl was stealing from us. I found her in the shop. What do you want me to do?" Neeraj said, pointing the rolled-up magazine in her direction.

"I was not stealing. I was asleep," Aria retorted.

Jarminder stood on the sidewalk in her satin robe, shocked and confused by the situation.

Omkar tried to de-escalate the tension. "Papa, Mama, this is Aria. She's a friend of mine. We were out so late last night that I decided to have her stay here. It wasn't her fault. If you want to blame somebody, then blame me," Omkar pleaded.

"You expect me to believe that you made some friend of yours sleep in the storeroom? So stupid. Just how stupid do you think we are? Why are you covering for this girl? What is she to you?" Neeraj demanded.

Omkar tried another approach, hoping that by appealing to their compassion, he might resolve the conflict. "Look Papa, she has nowhere to go. She's not like me. She doesn't have a good family to go home to. Her family treats her badly. You taught me to be a man who doesn't just stand by and let bad things happen to people. You taught me to do something about it."

"You are not a man, you're a little boy. You're a little boy who lies to his family!" Neeraj yelled. He paced up and down, suddenly aware of the embarrassing position they were all in, standing out on the street in their nightclothes.

Jarminder appealed to Omkar in Punjabi. She told him that he should know better than to lie to his family. She told him that it was not his place to interfere in another family's business, especially the business of an American family. She explained to him that because an American family is so different to an Indian family, he could never really know what was going on. But even as Jarminder talked, she tried to ignore the nagging feeling that some other truth lay hidden beneath his explanation. You could call it a mother's intuition.

She could feel something between Omkar and the girl now standing before them on the street. She could feel it in the carefulness her son extended toward her.

"Omkar, go back inside. It's time for your friend to go back home," Neeraj said, walking back toward the door of the shop in an attempt to set an example. Omkar could feel the ghost of the truth inside him lurking in the corner of his being, howling to be heard. Each time it welled up, he pushed it deeper until he couldn't suppress it anymore. Now facing the fate that he had been trying to avoid, Omkar found himself in a lose–lose situation. If he admitted the truth, he risked losing everything but Aria. But if he maintained the lie, he would have to continue to live it. There would never be a time in the future when they would suddenly be OK with her. The pressure of avoiding the potential consequences of them finding out had become unbearable. With an air of penitence, Omkar decided to tell the truth. His first words stopped both Neeraj and Jarminder dead.

He turned toward his mother. "Actually, I have to tell you the truth. Aria is not just a friend. She is my girlfriend. Do you remember what you always told me, to listen to everybody but to do what I consider right? I have listened to you and Papa. I know why you think it is right for me to be with a girl who you would choose. But for me, Aria is right. I know what I am saying is going to upset you, but I can live with that. But the one thing I cannot live without is this girl."

Omkar walked over to Aria and pulled her by the hand toward them, as a statement of his commitment to his decision. "This is Aria Abbott. She is the girl I love." He waited, like a soldier, for their resistance.

Neeraj eyed Aria from top to bottom. Jarminder refused to look at her. Instead she looked Omkar straight in the eye and said, "No son of mine could make such a decision without our consent. I forbid it. I forbid this utterly and completely. You have to focus on your schooling. You are too young to know what love is, do you hear me? This can't happen! Do you know

how hard we have worked so you could have a better life –
now you want to go and throw it all away on some girl?"

"She is not some girl, Mama, she is the girl I love."

Jarminder turned her back on him as a demonstration of
her disgust. "Do you even know her family? Do you even
know what kind of girl she is? What kind of family lets their
daughter spend the night at a boy's house? We should never
have brought you here. We should have stayed in India. We
never thought that if we gave you a good education and all
these opportunities, you would do something like this …
That you would lie to us. That you would bring home a girl
like this, a girl who is not one of us. A girl who does not even
know our culture, who cannot speak our language, who we
know nothing about."

She felt deafened by the death knell of the life that she had
planned for her son resounding. As far as she was concerned,
only hardship awaited her son if he were to take the path that
he was headed down.

"Mama, you don't know her," Omkar pleaded. "If you
did know her, you would know that she is smart and she is
beautiful and she is good and I love her."

Neeraj tried to find a middle ground between his wife and
son. "Omkar, I know you believe you love this girl, but your
mother is right. You are too young to know what love is. The
game of love is slippery. And by lying to us, you have proven
that you are too immature.

"This has got to end now, Omkar. The kind of love that
lasts is the kind that is slow to bloom. If love comes fast, it
will disappear just as fast. Is that what you want? Do you
want to throw your life away for something that will end
soon anyway?"

Omkar fumed at his parents' blatant refusal to consider the
reality of his love for Aria. As usual, the control they confused
for love gave him no room to breathe.

Aria was petrified. She was not the sort of person to stay
where she wasn't wanted, and being so obviously unwanted

made her want to run as fast and far as she could. But Omkar held her tight and she let him hold her there, out of some dim hope that his parents' sound rejection would wither. Aria had imagined that the only reason Omkar had made her sleep in the storeroom was because of his parents' strict stance on sex; the reality now revealed made everything depressingly more clear. She said nothing, but continued to listen to them talk about her as if she weren't there.

"I can do nothing about it if you refuse to accept that I love this girl," Omkar said. "But I'm disappointed in you. You have raised me to have an open mind, but now, when I ask you to have an open mind, you keep yours closed."

Omkar's confidence was quickly countered by his father. "Don't disrespect us. Don't talk to us that way," Neeraj yelled, puffing up his chest and turning a shoulder to Omkar as a warning. "Whose son is this? We have not raised a son to act like this and to think this way and to talk this way. We have not worked so hard to give you this life so you could wreck it. We forbid this match, Omkar. I am your father and because I am your father, I can tell you that this girl is not right for you. And I expect you to respect that. Now come inside."

Neeraj motioned to Jarminder, who began to follow him back inside. Omkar hesitated a second before the futility of convincing them strengthened instead of weakened his resolve. Taking a final stand, he yelled, "Alright, I can see that you don't respect what I have said. I can see that you do not respect that I love this girl. I can see that you do not believe you have raised a son who can love this girl. So maybe I'm not your son. Maybe you will disown me. I don't care because I do love this girl, Papa, I love her whether you accept it or not."

When the pause led to no compromise on either side, Omkar told Aria to wait outside. He walked past his parents and back into the store. Neeraj and Jarminder followed him, relieved. Despite his last words, they were convinced that he was going back into the store because he had given in to their reasoning. However, in the time it took them to walk back up the stairs to put the conflict entirely to rest, Omkar had dressed in the first outfit he could find. He had grabbed all the things he needed for class; he had collected his wallet and was now looking for the car keys.

"Omkar, Mama needs you to drive her to *gurdwara* this morning on your way to school," Neeraj said, walking toward his room.

Omkar was further enraged by the way the obvious conflict was swept under the carpet of their plans for the day. He lacked the tolerance to stay there a moment longer. Keys in hand, he walked back out of his room and straight past his parents, ignoring his father's comment. It was a disrespect that he had never shown them before. It felt both liberating and catastrophic.

Neeraj and Jarminder were so taken aback that by the time they yelled out after him, he had already reached the bottom of the stairs. They followed him, but by the time they got outside, Omkar had already ushered Aria into the passenger seat of his car. They watched him turn on the engine and drive away.

The pair took to arguing when Omkar's absence left them nothing but each other to fight against. They were angry but Jarminder quickly collapsed into tears. Her anger at Omkar's insolence could not compare to her fear of losing the only child she had left. She felt guilty. Maybe she even doubted herself for the things she had said. The fear that Neeraj felt could not be seen, though it was there inside him too. He held himself together like he had been trained to do. He looked at the empty road where his son had been and held his wife like a stem supporting a petal that was wilting.

The guilt that had taken over his parents affected Omkar too. After apologizing to Aria multiple times, his voice had been stripped away by it. It blew through him like white smoke, snuffing out the air in his lungs. He could feel the numbness it carried in his left hand, which gripped the steering wheel, and in his right hand, which held Aria's. He knew that the love he felt for Aria, and his choice to be honest about it with his parents, was right. He never doubted that for a second, which was why it was so confusing to feel so wrong about doing something that felt so right. The wrongness of displeasing his parents was ingrained in him, like salt in the ocean. He could not separate himself from that indoctrination, much as he wanted to.

Despite what his parents had projected on him, Omkar had no plans to throw his life away. He had three classes to attend before figuring out their next steps, and so, once he made sure that Aria was willing to wait on campus for him to be done for the day, he drove them both to the crowded parking lot of his college. He bought Aria a container of breakfast hash and a pudding and led her to an open space on the green lawn just outside the cafeteria. He opened the lids for her. Watching her eat made him feel settled. Omkar was afraid that the way his parents had reacted to her would make her change her mind about him. He could tell that the impact of being so harshly unacknowledged and renounced had made her withdraw inside herself. It was true; Aria had been wounded by it. But it had also been the story of her life. It was a sensation she had unintentionally become an expert at holding, being passed from temporary home to temporary home, none of which was a family.

Omkar coaxed her to lean against him. He pulled at the silk of her bangs with his fingers. "I feel really guilty. I should have explained about my culture to you before. Indian parents have a hard time accepting that times have changed. No matter how old you are, they treat you like a child. In my culture, most marriages are arranged by our parents and it's kind of a big deal to them to make sure that the girl comes from a certain caste and a certain family and a certain culture and a lot of other things."

"Well, what do you want to do?" Aria asked, not wanting to come between Omkar and the life to which he belonged.

"I don't know. For a long time, I thought I might actually prefer for my parents to choose who I should marry. But that just isn't the path my life went on. Part of me thinks it might be destiny that my parents moved here, because I was meant to meet you. But it doesn't really matter, because I am in love with you, so it doesn't matter who my parents want me to marry or if it's a good idea or not."

"But I don't have a family. I know how bad it is to be without a family and you don't. I don't want to be the thing that ruins your relationship with your family. That would fuck up our relationship so much worse than you realize," Aria argued.

"Are you the one saying you won't accept my family?" Omkar said. It was more of a statement than a question. "No … they are the ones that won't accept you or me for that matter. You aren't the one not accepting my family; they are the ones not accepting you, so they are the ones separating me from them, not you. You need to trust me. I won't let anything ruin us."

Aria rested on the belvedere of his reassurance until it was time for him to go to class. After he kissed her forehead and she hurried across the courtyard between the buildings, Aria realized exactly where she was. She watched the students file past her and felt intensely out of place.

Unlike her, these students had been sheltered. For them, the future was a risk they were excited for. College was rather like a low cliff over dark waters. A diving board off which they would jump into the real world, hoping they could swim. And of course they would. Their success was obvious to everyone but them; much like a baby taking its first steps with trepidation.

Aria had never been given the luxury of wondering whether or not she could swim. She had never been given the choice to jump or not to. There was something in the weakness of their buffered lives that she both despised and envied. For the first time in months, she thought about the school she had dropped out of. Dropping out had proven to be a conflicting move. On the one hand, it made her both freer and therefore more empowered than her peers. It was like she had broken out of a prison that the rest of them had chosen to stay trapped in. On the other hand, she could clearly see now how everyone else was being funneled down the road of success. They were both supported and led. She was now forced to fend for herself in a world that she had not been ready for. Nothing about her future was a guarantee, least of all success. Aria's graph was measured by an axis of pain.

Sitting on the green, Aria felt bad about herself. Though the other students would see her as indistinguishable from themselves and probably mistake her for one of them, Aria could not forget the differences between herself and them. She felt classless. It was strange to her; given that she found school so embarrassingly cumbersome, dumb even, that seeing herself as a dropout would cause her to feel so bad about herself. She chased the feeling away by finding a bathroom and washing her face with cold water.

The threat of failure chased the students like a specter toward their chosen majors. It made them run from classroom to classroom and study from dawn to dusk. Only the occasional student looked to have ended up there by accident, or to have been placed there because of the prestige belonging to their parents, who viewed their attendance there to be critical. Academic prestige lingered over the buildings, whose prime had come and gone. The words belonging to the books read and exams taken there for over a hundred years were written heavy on its chaptered stone.

Aria leaned against that stone, waiting to see Omkar's face again. Waiting for him to take her somewhere less pretentious, somewhere that wouldn't serve as such a somber reminder of her shortcomings.

CHAPTER 29

Their love was in the color of conviction. It was in the weightless communion of their lips and nectared smiles. The light coming through the window of the motel room was blanched. It teased its way through the over-starched curtains to spill across their faces. They did not answer its call.

Omkar had rented the room for a night. It was only natural for Aria to expect him to make love to her there. But to her surprise, Omkar had initiated nothing. Instead, when she stripped down to her underwear, he kept his clothes on for good measure and pulled her backward against the curve of his body, like a pearl against the bend of a clamshell. She could hear the excitement in his breathing; it was like a sea sliding when the ocean wants to claim something on shore for its own. But he would not allow his body to follow suit. They slept a fitful night, churned in the stimulation of being so near each other. And now, it was the morning.

His fingers adored her. They slid across the silk of her, cherishing each freckle and pore. They traced the lifted pathways that had been carved into her arms by glass and steel. Omkar could not imagine the kind of pain that could drive her to such an action. All he could imagine was to rescue her from it. He carried the grief of her scars with the tribute of his fingertips and the kisses that he placed on them. He was not trying to arouse her with his touch. Instead, he was calming her. There was a poem in his touch and the verses of that poem spoke of solace.

Aria knew what to do with herself when it came to sex, but not to this. Not to being loved by a man. Aria was conscious that she loved the smell of him. She listened to those verses he spoke through his touch as if they were spoken in a foreign tongue. She was out of her element and out of her depth. When they spoke to each other, their words felt so shallow compared to the conversation of touch.

"Did you sleep OK?" Omkar asked her. Aria nodded. "Did I crowd you?" he asked.

"No," Aria answered. She wanted to thank him. She wanted to tell him that spending the night next to him had made it the best night of her life. She wanted to tell him that he was the first straight man who had slept with her without "sleeping with" her. But those deeper words wouldn't come. They would make her so vulnerable that some part of her would not let them out.

By the time they sat up, the sunlight had turned from white to yellow. The city had already long been marching around them and the breakfast hour had ended. Omkar picked up his phone and started listening to the messages he had received over the course of the night. His parents had called him 23 times since the incident the day before and they had left 16 messages. At first, the messages were angry. Then they were worried. They were worried even before Omkar did not come home for the night. Now, in two of the messages that his father had left in the early morning, Omkar could hear his mother in the background crying and telling Neeraj what to say.

Omkar set the phone down and looked at Aria. "I think I should go talk to them. They are really freaking out. They sound like they might be willing to at least hear me. I can pay for another night and you can stay here until I come back if you want."

Aria thought about asking to go with him, but decided against it. She didn't want to feel the pierce of whatever they might say about her. But sitting in an antiseptic motel room felt isolating. Some part of her was afraid that Omkar would come back through the door later that night, having been talked into following their advice, and tell her that he couldn't see her anymore. She didn't want to sit there waiting all day under the vulture's wing of that potential.

"Um, actually, there's a church up the street from the shop. Is it OK if you drop me off there? I have a couple people I might want to see there," she said.

"Yeah, OK, sure," Omkar said, happy that in his absence he would not have to carry the guilt of her waiting on him. "Are we supposed to take these to the front desk?" he asked, holding up the little plastic cards that served as room entry keys.

"I don't know," Aria said, giggling at their naivety.

"I'd better just take them to the front just in case. I'll be back in just a minute. When I knock, let me back in, OK?" Omkar said, tying the laces of his shoes before exiting the room to return them.

When he returned, Aria heard the polite rapping of his knuckles against the doorframe. She started laughing to herself instead of getting up to open the door. Having decided at the last minute to pull a little prank on him, she acted like she didn't hear him. When he tried to peek inside the window, Aria hid behind the door. She tolerated a few of his attempts to yell at her that he was there and to open the door before she opened it. Upon seeing her laugh so hard, Omkar understood it was a joke that she had played on him and began to chase her around the room. Eventually, after making him chase her up onto the beds, she intentionally gave up and let herself be caught by him. The humor of the moment was dissolved by the way his breath capsized against her and the way his devotion hunted her. Because of his height, he loomed over her. Though nervous, Omkar leaned down and pulled her upwards by the small of her back. The features of their private passion were formed of fondness. He claimed her lips as his and sipped the rosy pigment from them. Their youth was bent by that kiss. It was bent by the fever of loving each other so much they could break.

When Aria opened the door of his car to step out onto the lawn of the church, Omkar grabbed her hand and kissed it. It was something he had seen in the movies and had always wanted to do. They both smiled, aware of the unoriginal (though endearing) nature of the gesture.

Aria didn't watch him drive away. Instead, she walked toward the church steps with a mind to wait there for the lunch service to start. Only a few people were milling around the building, like actors in a play before the stage was set. She had been sitting there for only a few minutes when a man came bounding toward her, holding up one side of the belt of his oversized jeans. Aria had seen the man here before, talking to Imani while he ate his lunch.

"Hey, what a do?" the man said, with his deep voice. "You know when this place opens up?" He pointed loosely toward the church.

"I think it's open now," Aria said.

"Nah, I mean when they start servin' food," he said.

"Not exactly, what time is it now?" Aria asked.

The man looked down at the face of his knock-off gold watch and replied, "It 10:55."

"Well, I imagine they might start at like 11:30 or 12, but it's just a guess," Aria said.

The man looked around, as if dissuaded by her answer. "Min' if I sit here until it open?" The man sat down beside her roughly, before Aria could start indicating no.

"So what's your name?" he asked, folding his arms across his raised knees.

"Aria," she responded.

The man extended his very large hand toward her. "Good to meetcha Aria, my name's Kendrik."

Aria stared at the purple of his palms when she shook his hand. "Are you friends with Imani?" she asked.

"Ah yeah. I known Imani for a long, long time. She's a good woman, definitely a good woman."

"Do you have a job or why do you come eat here?" Aria asked.

Kendrik laughed at the bluntness of her obvious insult. "You think just 'cause I'm black that I ain't got a job?"

Aria hadn't even realized her question could be misinterpreted in that way. "No, shit, that's not what I meant. I mean no one comes to eat at these kinds of places unless there's some kind of story ... Like, I don't have a place to live or a job, for example."

"I could have a job. I'm just lyin' low for a while. Plus I'm on probation."

"On probation for what?" Aria's bluntness got the better of her again.

Kendrik cracked a one-sided smile, amused by the lack of social sense inherent in her question. "Nothin' big, just stealin' some stuff. What about you, Little Miss Thing, shouldn't you be in school or somethin'?" He asked the question as a friendly strike-back.

"I already graduated," Aria responded.

Kendrik cocked one of his eyebrows in doubt. "OK, whatever you say."

She felt bad for lying to him, especially seeing as Kendrik seemed obviously the last person on earth who would ever turn her in.

Kendrik's phone rang in his pocket. When he answered it, he turned slightly away from Aria. "Baby, your brother ain't gonna do shit cause he broke. Baby, you know nobody got it worse than he do ... No, I gotta wait 'til I get off work ... OK, love ya baby."

Aria tried to interpret his conversation through his short, one-sided replies. "That's my girlfriend," he said, putting the phone back into his pocket. "You got a boyfriend?"

"Yeah, actually. We haven't been together very long, but ..."

"You got nothin' else to do but tell me about 'im," Kendrik said, prying further.

"Well, he's Indian ..." Aria began and was stopped.

"Wait, you mean like an Indian Indian or like one of them cowboys and Indians types?" he asked.

"Like an Indian Indian."

Her response made Kendrik erupt in laughter. "I did not see that comin' ... OK, so he's an Indian Indian. What else?"

"He's in college, studying to be an engineer," Aria replied.

Again, Kendrik erupted in laughter. "Oh my God, you just pickin' the low-hangin' fruit, ain'tcha?"

Though the humor of the stereotype of an Indian boy being in engineering school was not lost on Aria, she didn't laugh with him.

"Wait, wait, this here's my woman." Kendrik pulled his phone back out of his pocket. It took him a second to find a succession of pictures of his girlfriend in the gallery.

Aria swiped through them. In almost every picture, her face was turned at a flirtatious three-quarter angle. Her hair was straightened and dyed purple-red. Her eyebrows had been drawn on to match the color of her hair, and big fake eyelashes framed a sassy look in her brown eyes.

Kendrik watched Aria scan through the pictures proudly, waiting to hear a comment on her beauty, which he knew he could expect. Aria giggled when one of the pictures she clicked to was a topless one. Kendrik jumped to take the phone out of her hand. "You don't needa see those. They be triple-X." He paused for a minute, trying to figure out how to cut through the embarrassment. "She Brianna. She work at Foot Locker down in Crenshaw," he announced.

"She's pretty. How did you guys meet?" Aria asked.

"Her cousin be a friend o' mine. Yeah, I met her at a kid's birthday party. She was tryin' to hit this piñata and was swingin' the stick all around. It was pretty cute." Nostalgia was heavy in his smile when he remembered it.

"Are you from LA?" Aria asked him.

"Yeah, I been here all my life." Kendrik's response trailed off when Imani caught his attention. "Hey, I gotta go say hi to Imani over there," he said, standing up. Aria nodded. "Nice talkin' to ya," he said, again holding one side of his pants while he bounded across the lawn to Imani.

Aria watched them hug and Kendrik proceed to help Imani set things up on one of the foldable picnic tables. For the most part he was talking and she was listening. Aria missed his company when he left. The conversation had served as a welcome distraction from her worry about what was happening between Omkar and his parents just a few streets away. She also liked him. The macho impression that he gave was like a gloss he didn't want people to see past. Underneath it, he was friendly, and she could feel the gravity of his caring.

Jarminder heard Omkar's car pull up to the curb first. Neeraj had opened the store, but was not tending it. Instead, he had spent the morning failing to console his wife. Neither of them had slept the previous night. They had called everyone they knew, looking for Omkar. In her mind, Jarminder had run through every different version of them crying and running to hug each other if he came home, as she'd seen in all her favorite Bollywood movies. But in reality, when he showed up, the suffering she felt in his absence again turned into anger.

She sat on the couch and folded her arms. "I don't want to speak to him," she said in Punjabi.

Neeraj knew his wife beyond the wall she was presenting. He walked downstairs and opened the door for Omkar as he approached. "Hello Papa," Omkar said, walking through the door.

Neeraj contained his relief at seeing Omkar standing before him perfectly OK, masked by his stern demeanor. "Your mother is upstairs," he said.

Omkar walked up the stairs and saw her sitting on the couch. She defiantly turned away from him as punishment for what he had put them through. "Mama, I need to tell you something." She didn't answer.

Neeraj sat down beside her and spoke for her. "What is it, Omkar? What is so important that you have to treat us in this way?"

Although his mother showed no sign of yielding, Omkar began to speak. "You have always told me that a happy marriage is one where both partners want to be together. Otherwise, it feels like death. Mama, if I was with anyone but Aria, it would feel like death. I am not doing this to be funny. I am not doing this to disrespect you or Papa. I am doing this because I love her. I want to marry her some day.

"You also always tell me that there is no place that will give me as much comfort as my own home will. But Mama, that isn't true. The comfort that I feel when I'm with her is better than anything I have ever felt. How can that be true unless she is my home, Mama? I love you. I don't want to see you upset like this. But I need you to love what I love. A learned person is honored, except in their own house. I have learned something in this country. I have learned that a life without the person that you love is no life at all and it doesn't matter if that person you love is black or white or brown or a man or a woman. This is not respected in this house, but it should be. Don't make me choose between you and the person that I love. Mama, you can't say that you love me and ask me to choose."

Neeraj's arms were folded across his potbelly. "Omkar, look at what you are doing to your mother," he said.

"I'm not doing anything to Mama. She is doing this to herself. Love should be celebrated and she's acting like somebody just died."

They sat in silence for a few minutes before Jarminder broke that silence by yelling in Punjabi. She scolded him about the cruelty of his character and guilted him about his selfish capacity to discard the wishes of his family, using cultural sayings as scaffolding for each argument. Her outcry bled her clean of the life she had always imagined for him until the only thing that was left was her fear of losing him.

Jarminder started to cry. Neeraj handed her a tissue to blow her nose, but she continued to sniff. "I am your mother. All I ever wanted was your happiness," she said.

"I know, Mama. My happiness is Aria. Mama, she is the light of my life and I cannot live without her, please understand me." There was silence for a few moments.

"Where did you meet her? Where is she from? Who are her parents?" Neeraj asked, surprised at himself for being interested.

Omkar looked at the carpet, knowing that what he was about to say would not be received well. "I met her here at the shop. She came in one day and I started talking to her. Papa, it was love at first sight."

Neeraj was surprised at his son's answer. He had assumed that Omkar and Aria had met at school. Suddenly, he didn't know whether he felt good about Omkar tending the store after all. He certainly hadn't expected it to be the family's undoing.

Omkar continued, "Aria doesn't have parents. I knew this was going to upset you. But it isn't her fault, Papa. She lost them just like we lost Ajit and Shashi. Papa, it wouldn't be fair if someone thought badly of you because they died. It isn't fair to think badly of Aria because her parents died. She was sent here to live with an uncle, but he started abusing her, Papa. When she refused to sleep with him, he kicked her out of the house."

Neeraj was disgusted. His pride in the honor and decency of his own culture swelled within him. Only in white culture would a child be abandoned to a person like that. At the same time, his sense of Aria began to change. He could see that in contrast to his original impression, Aria was pure. Her chastity obviously meant so much to her that she was unwilling to trade it for her basic needs. Neeraj respected that quality in a woman. Despite his desire as a parent to remain dismissive of her, it made him feel protective of her.

Omkar felt guilty for lying to his parents. He could not tell them the complete truth about Aria's past. They would not understand it. They were too conservative to accept the idea that he intended to marry a woman who had a drug addict for a mother and who never knew her father, any more than they could accept that she had dropped out of school or was currently living on the streets. He would have to talk Aria into upholding the lie as well.

"Is her uncle looking for her?" Neeraj said, wanting to steer clear of involvement in a potentially dangerous situation.

"No ... he said that if she wouldn't sleep with him, he doesn't care if she lives or dies." Omkar felt himself winding them deeper and deeper into the lie he was telling to corrode their resistance to Aria.

Much as she might not want to admit it, Jarminder could feel some empathy toward Aria. She wiped tears away from her eyes with the tissue. "Well, one thing would be good ... I wouldn't have to share my grandkids on holidays."

The three of them started laughing. "I'm not saying that I'm happy about it yet. You can't expect that from me," she said.

"Does this mean you are OK with it?" Omkar asked, knowing his life was flailing on the hook of her next statement.

"I'm saying we'll live with it, Omkar. We want you to be happy. But don't you dare ever, ever do that again!" she said, referring to Omkar's disappearance.

Omkar rushed in to hug her. Her consent spoke for both his parents. It was more leniency than he had imagined either of them to be capable of.

In truth, in the hours of torment since Omkar and Aria drove off, they had already had it brought back to them with explosive force what it felt like to lose their children. When you lose a child, you never ever forget, but it's something that over time can sleep in your mind because of the pressures of day-to-day life. Omkar's absence had reminded them that as long as he was alive and happy, it didn't matter what school he graduated from or even whether he graduated at all. It didn't matter if he got a good job or didn't. It didn't matter if he married the sort of girl they wanted him to marry or even if he got married at all. Faced with the threat of losing Omkar from their lives, they realized that when you love your child, everything that you think matters no longer matters in comparison to having them be a part of your life.

Omkar went to the kitchen to do the dishes that were layered in the sink. Neeraj and Jarminder followed him. "What are you working on at school?" Jarminder asked him, still sniffling the remnants of their conflict away from the surface of her expression.

"I'm taking a physics course that's really challenging. But I'm also taking a class on wave propagation in solids, and so far I really like it. Did you know that when an earthquake happens, the earth's crust ruptures and it creates elastic waves in the earth? So essentially an earthquake is a wave."

Omkar's enthusiasm was met with protest. "Don't talk to me about earthquakes, Omkar. I've had enough for one day."

The soapsuds began to make Omkar's hand itch so he turned off the water and scratched the top of his hand. Jarminder noticed him scratching. It was a good omen. "Ah ... look, you're going to receive good luck," she said.

Omkar rolled his eyes and went back to washing. Superstitious as she was, it gave her comfort. She imagined it was God giving her the message that maybe her son was right in choosing Aria. "Omkar, why don't you bring her for dinner tonight so we can meet her the right way? I am making *sarhon dā sāg*. Do you think she would like it?"

It had never occurred to Jarminder until this minute that she might be cooking one day for a daughter-in-law whose tastes differed from their own. She felt the very real fear that if Aria disliked her cooking, she might not have any other grounds for a relationship with her.

"Yes, Mama, I think she would like that very much," Omkar replied, throwing the dishtowel over his shoulder.

"You're not going to let this get in the way of your studies?" The question was more of an order she barked at him.

"No, Mama. I promise," he said.

When Omkar hugged them both to say goodbye after settling on a time to come back that night with Aria, he walked down the stairs light with excitement and heavy with maturity. Omkar felt like a man. Aria had a way of calling those dormant qualities out in him. He felt like he was taking his place in the world of men. Aria had been like an angel who had come to awaken him to himself.

As he got into the car to drive toward her, he remembered an old Punjabi saying. "If a man expects his wife to be an angel in his life, then he should first create heaven for her." He finally understood that saying. It was now exactly what he planned to do.

CHAPTER 30

When Omkar and Aria opened the door of the Super Sun Market, the air was heavy with the smell of onion and ginger. Omkar's mother was crouching in the kitchen, using the floor as a counter. She was making *makki ki* rotis while a curry of mustard greens sweltered on the stovetop.

"Hello, Mama," Omkar said, placing a pile of mint that they had purchased on the counter. Not knowing how to act around the two of them together, Jarminder barely acknowledged them with a nod of the head when they came in. Instead, she directed her energies to what she felt confident in doing: her cooking.

Neeraj emerged from his bedroom to join them. He was no longer bellicose. Though he still maintained something of a graceless attitude, a smile just peeked out from beneath the bramble of his beard when he greeted Omkar.

Omkar introduced him to Aria as if they had never met before. Though Aria found it strange to pretend as if nothing had ever happened between them, she went along with it. When Neeraj took her hand, he held it instead of shaking it. Without thinking, she responded by doing a miniature curtsy. It made her feel like an idiot. A dense awkwardness trespassed between them. In response to it, they all put their focus on the cooking.

Jarminder pinched off a piece of dough from the rest and rolled it in her hands. She smacked it against her palm while rotating it again and again until it was flat and circular enough to her liking. She placed it on an unoiled griddle and turned it from one side to the next. Just like a tortilla, the bread began to blacken in spots. Just when Aria thought that Jarminder was about to put it on a serving plate, she took the griddle off of the flame of her little gas stove entirely and held the roti with a pair of tongs over the open flame. The roti responded by puffing up so it was no longer flat, like a pancake filled with air. When Jarminder took it off the flame, she ladled a spoonful of clarified butter onto the roti and spread it across the surface with the back of the spoon.

Omkar took Aria over to the living room in order to show her some of the items in the house. He made her touch the yellow flush of the curtains, which had been sewn by hand by his grandmother. He showed her a pair of ornately embroidered fabric shoes, called *jutti*, on a shelf and joked that they were his mother's best weapon in the house when he was growing up. He explained the portrait of Guru Nanak as well as the sheathed sword, which was mounted on the wall beneath the painting. There was no plan behind the decoration of the house. Oil marks still stained the wall in rectangles where pictures used to hang. The items that served as decoration had been added over the years one by one and as a result, it boasted no aestheticism. Like a nest for a magpie who had been collecting things, the house served as a personal treasure box for Jarminder. And Neeraj had let her do whatever she wanted with it.

Omkar pulled a photo album out of the bookcase and started flipping through it for Aria to see. Most of the pictures had yellowed; the plastic covering them had lost its flex. They cracked with stickiness when Omkar opened the pages. Aria found it painful to see so many years of a life that he had lived before her. She watched him lose his baby fat, learn to ride a bike, spend his first years in America and every birthday that had passed before she'd met him. She saw his aunties, who, according to Omkar, could give the FBI a run for its money when it came to keeping tabs on everyone they knew. She saw the faces of his brother and sister who had died. The tragedy had projected sorrow over their smiles.

"I thought your last name was Agarwal. Why does your name here say Singh?" Aria asked, pointing to the names written beside the pictures.

"Actually, it isn't a last name, it's a kind of middle name. Every man in our culture has the same middle name, which is

Singh, which means lion. And every woman in our culture has the same middle name, which is Kaur, which means princess," Omkar replied.

"Ooh, that's sexy, the lion and the princess," Aria whispered under her breath, softly enough so that Omkar's parents wouldn't hear her or see her wink at him.

When the food was ready, they all sat down at the tiny dining table beside the kitchen. Neeraj and Jarminder studied the lines of Aria's face. They found it beautiful, but distrusted the motives beneath it. The conversation that happened at the dinner table was a concerted effort to avoid sitting there mutely. Though they had set the table with utensils, they ate with their hands instead. Aria copied them, leaving her fork untouched, which made them smile.

Omkar spent the time offering up details about Aria that he imagined would convert his parents to some shade of approval of her. Aria was so nervous that once she finished eating, she realized that she hadn't even really tasted it. When their plates were empty, Omkar insisted upon doing the dishes, despite Jarminder's protests. Neeraj turned on the television to watch a cricket game and sat in front of it, finding it hard to take his mind off of what was happening in the kitchen. Jarminder allowed herself to be consumed by a project that required her to carry things up and down the stairs from the store to their apartment at least a dozen times.

Aria stood next to Omkar with a cold glass of mint *chaas* in her hand. She sipped on the freshness of the mint, cumin and green chili in the cream of it while watching the look of worry play across the side of his face. Omkar spoke low enough that his parents couldn't hear him over the chatter of the television. "I'm sorry if all of this is a little weird. Some of this stuff we do is kind of stupid. When we moved here, my parents never got it that we live in a different country and they just kept doing the same stuff they did back home in India."

Aria was surprised by his apology. "Are you kidding me?" she said. "Omkar, you should never be ashamed of your culture. It is so cool. You guys are like exotic warriors or something. You guys have been telling me about your culture all night and it's been making me think and I don't think we even have a culture. I mean, unless you call backyard barbecues and football games a culture."

Omkar laughed and said, "That's the thing: you never think you have a culture until you leave the place where your culture is the *only* culture. If I took you to India, you would all of a sudden know what American culture is. It's like a fish that spends his life swimming in water. The fish doesn't know how to tell you about water until he is suddenly in the air."

Omkar's culture was like an exotic spice that ran through his veins. Aria could smell that spice in every word he spoke and in everything he did. She found it erotic. She felt the stoic power in the line of men and the sensual mysticism in the line of women that had lent their lineage to him. Unlike her, his belonging was never questioned. He could resist that belonging, he could try to talk and act like something else, but it was something he could not wash himself clean of. The culture he came from was like a flavor that permeated the way he felt to her. It was so much a part of who he was and perhaps even part of what she loved so much about him.

"Can you drive me back to the lot tonight?" Aria asked.

Omkar shot a confused and dejected look down toward her. "Why do you want to go there?"

Aria was equally confused. "Because you know I don't have anywhere else to stay," she responded. To her, it was obvious that the reconciliation between Omkar and his parents would mean they wouldn't be spending the night at the hotel again. And given their culture, it was obvious that she couldn't stay with him there.

"No, you don't understand. It's OK; Mama's been doing something to fix things," Omkar said and yelled for his mother. Jarminder shouted something back up the stairs in Punjabi. "Just a minute and I promise I'll show you." Omkar said, leaning against the counter with a satisfied look on his face.

Jarminder arrived at the door and motioned for Omkar and Aria to follow her back downstairs. She opened the door to the storeroom feeling a mix of anxiety and pride.

It was no longer the barren cement room that Aria remembered. The floor had been covered with mismatched carpets. A twin mattress had been laid on the floor and a bed had carefully been made with lavender-colored sheets and pillows. The cement foundation ridge that ran through the room now acted as a mantle for an ornate statue of Ganesh, with its head of a white elephant and body of a human with four arms. Every wall had been covered with unfolded saris. Their colorful and opalescent silk lifted and billowed when the door opened. A frail stream of smoke, carrying the scent from a stick of sandalwood incense, rose from a little bronze incense burner near the door.

Aria could not believe what she was seeing. "You can stay here. My mother made it up for you," Omkar said.

"Are you kidding me?" Aria asked.

Jarminder thought the question implied that Aria had been insulted that they would put her in a storeroom and so she sought to justify herself. "I'm sorry, it's just that we don't have any more rooms upstairs."

"No … No … It's lovely," Aria said, realizing that Jarminder had misinterpreted her. Ignoring the air of formality that she'd felt until then between herself and Jarminder, as well as the way Jarminder went rigid when she did it, Aria rushed in to hug her. "Are you totally sure?" she asked.

"Yes, yes, we're sure," Jarminder said, wobbling her head back and forth instead of up and down. "The sheets are new. If they are stiff, I can just wash them," she said.

Aria was quiet in disbelief. "I'm going to stay down here with her to talk for a bit, Mama," Omkar said, indicating his readiness for her to go back upstairs.

"OK, you can use the bathroom upstairs, but no hanky-panky," Jarminder said, pointing her index finger at Omkar.

Aria sat on the end of the bed, listening to the stairs creak as Jarminder climbed them. Omkar sat down next to her. "You've got to be fucking kidding me," she said again, looking to Omkar for an explanation about the strange turn of events.

"My parents are good people, even though they don't exactly act like it sometimes," Omkar said. "They could never feel good knowing that you don't have somewhere to stay. Plus I told them that I wanted to move out and get a place with you and they sort of freaked out. Indian parents can't stand the idea of not living with their kids." He giggled.

"Are you totally sure? I don't want it to be weird for me to be here or whatever," Aria asked again.

"Yes, my God, it's totally fine, I promise," Omkar said, although he knew he was failing to completely convince her.

He stayed downstairs with her until Neeraj yelled down to them, "Omkar, it's time to go to sleep now, you have school in the morning." It was his way of making sure his son wasn't being irresponsible in more ways than one.

Omkar kissed Aria on the cheek and said, "Sleep well tonight. I'll be thinking of you all night just up there." He pointed at a corner of the ceiling before running up the stairs.

Aria waited until she could hear no more sounds in the house before tiptoeing upstairs, with all of the clothes she had in her backpack, and sneaking into the bathroom. Turning the water pressure on only halfway so it would be quieter, she let the hot steam asperse her skin. It was a feeling she had sorely missed.

She washed her clothes by hand with shampoo and threw them all over the bar of the shower curtain before soaping herself. It was the first time since running away nearly a year ago that she had taken a shower that wasn't timed and watched by an attendant. The feeling of being able to enjoy the water and brush her teeth inside the shower felt like a luxury beyond measure.

When she went back downstairs, she draped the damp clothes over the top of the door and took out the little beaver statue that Robert had given her. She placed it by the statue of Ganesh. She did not realize the symbolism of having done so. She did not realize that the beaver was telling her that it, and she, had found home. Instead, she thought of Robert and all the other people at the car lot. She wondered whether they were OK or not. She wondered if they had all found some other place to stay. She reminded herself that the meaningfulness of her relationship to them might be entirely one-sided. Still, Aria made the decision that she would go back to the car lot the next day, when Omkar was at school. There was some closure she needed, even if it was to stand before the empty lot and to realize that she might never see any of them again.

Aria turned the lights off and lifted back the top sheets of the bed to crawl between them. Her body felt the shock of there being no plastic between herself and the mattress. Every time she had stayed in a new house like this, it had been in a foster placement or a group home. They always put plastic on the beds to prevent damage from potential bed-wetting. The noise and feel of the plastic always made Aria feel bad, as if they expected her to be like a stray dog that wasn't potty-trained. "This is how other people feel," she thought to herself.

She felt grief for the pain of her childhood as much as she was celebrating how good it felt to be trusted and welcomed enough that Jarminder had put the sheets directly on the unprotected mattress. The feeling of that trust that was placed in her put as much pressure on her as it took away. Pressure to stay in their favor. Pressure to earn her keep. Pressure to make them never regret it.

When morning came, Aria cracked the door open wide enough to see that she had awoken before the sun had risen. She wasn't accustomed to going to sleep so early. While everyone else was still asleep, she forced some of her damp clothes back over the shape of her body and looked around the store for ways to repay the Agarwals' kindness. But because Neeraj was so careful about the upkeep of his store, Aria could not find much to do. She took the window chalk markers and rewrote the fading letters that spelled "New Year's Sale

On Items" on the front window before organizing the piles of papers and items stacked behind the checkout counter. She wrote a thank-you note to Neeraj and Jarminder and left it there. Then she wrote a letter to Omkar telling him to meet her at the car lot after he got off of school and signed it with a heart. She made her bed and left the letter on it.

Once Aria had collected everything except her wet clothes back into her backpack, she left, holding the bell attached to the door when she opened it so it wouldn't announce her exit. The air outside was crisp. The irrigation system in the neighbor's lawn hissed from beneath the thick and newly cut buffalo grass when she passed it. One of the neighbors stopped her minivan with three kids in the back to ask Aria if she wanted a ride to the school bus stop. Aria thanked her, but declined, suddenly feeling insecure about how young she must look in comparison to how she felt and the life she had been living.

As the morning sun touched her with its un-sugared rays, she turned back to look at Omkar's window. Thinking of this new chapter of her life with him, she thought, "Has your life already spent its shade and has it stained you?" She stopped on the side of the road to write the verse in her journal. She did not know if any love or hope could wash the shadow from a person. But she hoped that maybe Omkar could love her with that ineffable stain she felt because she knew that now, without him, life would always be so much less.

CHAPTER 31

They were in the deserted doorways, their cardboard boxes erected like monuments to commemorate their anguish. The irony of their lives written in the sign on those boxes reading "this side up." Their thirst could not be quenched by the water they didn't have. Their hunger could not be satiated by the food they could not afford to buy.

No one thinks they will end up like this. No little five-year-old boy or girl sits on the carpet of their kindergarten class during sharing time and says they want to be homeless when they grow up. Before Aria had become one of them, she had always looked at homeless people like they were "those people." Now, she understood that a life on the streets was just a hair's width away from almost anyone. Given the right cocktail of conditions, anyone could find themselves here. They were not a different species, even though it comforted people to think of them that way. To separate themselves from "those people" who were homeless made folks feel further away from being homeless themselves. But the truth is, "those people" were people just like you or me. They, the outcasts of mankind's ambition; the carriers of the shadows that no one truly wants to face.

There was a pining in their movements. A boundless yearning for a kindness they had either tasted or never tasted. A deep hunger for love they might or might not ever find. Their lives were the *hunger of the pine*.

Aria walked toward the car lot, through the parts of town that served as a cocoon for those without a home. She felt a knot in her stomach when she got close enough to turn off onto the side street that would lead her there. At first she saw no movement and imagined that she would find herself standing before a deserted lot. But that was not what she found. They were living there, like a graft over the scar of the fire-damaged earth. With nowhere else to go, having been able to do nothing else, some of them had stayed there. EJ had not been seen since he had been taken away in the ambulance. Aston had been taken away by the state and Ciarra had been arrested. Taylor, who had moved in with Dan the night it happened, had not returned. But she could see Robert, Anthony, Darren and Wolf there, rebuilding their lives from nothing on the deflagrated landscape. Their tents and tarps had been turned into smoke. Only the frames of the broken-down cars remained; their windows gone, their colors turned to black. Darren, who usually marched through his disciplined daily routine as a replacement for the regimented life of the army, was passed out cold on the dirt under a tree. He had used the bottles of alcohol, which crowded him like debris from a shipwreck, as an anchor. He had tied his anxieties of having lost all of his things to the liquor and had sunk them deep into a drunken slumber.

Anthony, Wolf and Robert were sitting against the fence, talking. Out of everyone – perhaps because of the sheer relief of not having been hassled by police, or because he laid claim to fewer possessions – Anthony seemed the least affected. He and Wolf had spent the night after the fire in a shelter before deciding that the shelter felt less safe than the streets and certainly less safe than the quiet of a charred car lot. So they came back to the lot to see if it had been reclaimed by the city. Finding it abandoned once again, they started over where they left off. Wolf seemed the same as he always did. The fire had reinforced the opinion he held about the world already.

When Wolf caught sight of Aria, he lifted an arm against the sky as a salute to call her over. Robert cracked a toothless smile. "How ya been?" Anthony asked her, extending an arm up from where they were sitting for her to shake. When she took it, he shook it once firmly and folded his arms again.

"Um, OK I guess. How about you guys?" Aria asked. They all chuckled as if in chorus.

"Oh, you know, life's been better." Robert said. They chuckled louder because of his response, which was aimed more at them than at Aria. It egged Robert on so he continued. "The good news is, I've been thinkin' … people pay lots o' money to go camp out under the stars at them national parks and we get to do it for free." His joke was met by an uproar of laughter and it egged him on even more. "I've been thinkin' about those people who go camping with RVs … It's like they start packin' and at some point they go … what did I forget? Oh, I know … My house!"

Again, his joke teased laughter from all of them, including himself. The way he talked, because of his missing teeth, added an additional layer to his humor. Though it lifted the mood, Aria could see that it was also his way of coping. Having lost all of his wood-whittling tools and figurines in the fire, it was obvious that he was at a loss for what to do with the hours of the day.

"Is Darren OK?" she asked, looking over at him.

"Oh, you know, he's gettin' on," Robert said, conscious that in truth he wasn't. But they could no more help him than they could help themselves.

"Where's Luke?" Aria asked.

"He said he was comin' back here right after goin' to meditate," Wolf said, winking at Anthony as a nod to their inside joke about how ridiculous Luke was. Though Wolf knew the value of both vision quests and sage, both he and Anthony hated that meditation and sage seemed to be the only tools Luke had at his disposal for dealing with things. Because of his mannerisms and life choices, they couldn't see Luke as a man and often teased him about his various new-age habits.

"What about Mike?" Aria asked, worried about what the response would be. The area where his camp had been was picked clean. There was nothing left to indicate that he had ever been there.

Robert was the one to answer her question. "Oh, he came back here yesterday, said he was goin' down to Hemet to stay with a relative and see about a job." He looked suddenly somber. It was obvious that he considered Mike a friend. The telltale signs of missing him were carved deep into his demeanor.

"I think for a father, seein' your daughter that way just kinda does suhum to ya. Plus I think he's feelin' kinda responsible for it all. I told 'im you can't do nothin' about the way some kids turn out, but it doesn't matter what I tell 'im." Robert quickly changed the subject, hoping to put their focus on something less doleful. "You been stayin' outta trouble?" he asked Aria.

"Yeah, I've been OK. Actually, I met a boy and his parents have been letting me stay with them."

A smile crept across all of their faces. "He ain't that fellow who came sneakin' in here before, is he?" Robert asked. He was already certain of the answer. In his mind, the only reason that a young man would bring gifts for a girl, especially in secret, was if he was in love with her.

"Um, yeah," Aria said, her cheeks flushing.

"Well, you can't just drop somethin' like that and not say nothin' else about it, in'it?" Wolf said.

Robert explained. "Aria here had a secret admirer. But it looks like he ain't so secret anymore."

"His name is Omkar. I met him in a shop he works in, actually," Aria said, hoping her lightweight answer would satisfy their curiosity.

"Omkar ain't sound like a normal name, in'it?" Wolf asked.

"No. Actually, he's from India," Aria said.

Wolf's white teeth shone when he smiled at the idea of her being with someone who wasn't white. Even though he felt a duty, if he ever settled down, to preserve his dying race by marrying another Native, knowing that Aria had fallen for a boy who wasn't white made him feel one step closer to love. He let the conversation rest at that.

An hour passed before Luke returned to the car lot. Aria made herself a place beside Robert and spent the hour listening to the three men talk. Palin spotted Aria long before Luke did. She pranced up to Aria with her tail furiously wagging. When Aria reached out for her, she flopped upside down to expose her belly and flailed with excitement in the dirt, the ground leaving her white fur dusted with ash.

Luke started jogging when he saw her. "Hey, how've you been?" he asked, out of breath.

"I've been OK, how about you?" she asked.

"Dude, that was some crazy shit. I've been seriously worried about you," Luke said. It surprised Aria that Luke had even thought about her. On the streets, you could never be sure if the people you spent time with really saw you as a friend, or if common circumstances simply caused you to trespass across each other's lives. "Hey, there's a festival next weekend up in Portland. I got us a ride if you and Tay wanna come." Though it bothered Taylor, "Tay" was Luke's nickname for him.

"Oh, thanks. I kinda need to stick around here. I got a boyfriend now," Aria said.

"Oh really? That's great. What's his name?" he asked.

Aria told him, but Luke had asked out of formality. He was not even listening when she said his name.

The mood between them seemed immediately colder. It was a chill that was noticeable to all of them. Wolf was the first to try to remedy it. "Hey, you had somethin' you wanted to talk to Aria about, in'it?"

Luke took a stick and poked at the ground. What little maturity he had, drained from his appearance. "Yeah, you wanna take a walk?" Luke asked her.

Aria looked toward the rest of them as if asking permission. Anthony and Wolf, who took the social shift as a cue to start walking toward town in search of an open meal program, stood up. Anthony shook her hand warmly. Wolf, as if sensing it would be a long goodbye between them, hugged her and placed his palm over the crown of her head. Aria didn't understand the words he said quietly under his breath, but when he placed his palm against her, he said an ancient blessing for her wellbeing. "See you around," he said.

She turned to allow Luke to lead her wherever he had it in his mind to go. In her heart, she missed them already. It was strange to her that people could come and go so fast from her life. It was even stranger that people who came and went could leave such permanent footprints inside of her.

Luke led Aria back in the direction that he had taken her on one of the first days she had been at the car lot. Back in the direction of the stream, which was now more of a river. Back in the direction of the place where they had laid bare their life stories to each other.

Seeing a cluster of plants with leaves that looked like lily pads, Aria squealed, "Hey look, it's mallow." She plucked a few of the tender young leaves of the plant and inspected them before biting a piece out of one and holding it out toward Luke. "Try it, you can eat it. Apparently you can eat the seedpods, too, as long as they haven't gone woody. This is so exciting; I read that they didn't really grow like this until spring."

Luke took a curious bite out of the leaf. "It's not that bad," he said, suddenly stopping to hold his throat, pretending to be poisoned as a joke.

"Good Lord, cut it out. It's really good, I swear," Aria said.

"I didn't know you were into this kinda thing," Luke said. "You'd love this lady I stayed with up in Mount Shasta. No joke, she knows like everything there is to know about plants and plant medicines. She's kinda like a witch. This one time I was up there, I got such bad allergies and she collected this batch of stinging nettles. It was so cool – she poured boiling water over the leaves and let them sit there for like ten minutes and made me drink the water. I swear to God, I didn't have any more problems the whole time I was there."

Her interest in foraging revived, Aria chewed on the mallow leaves as she walked. When they arrived at the spot where she and Luke had spent the day together months earlier, Luke sat down on the same rock where they had sat before. The water had swollen beyond the confines of the bank. Aria sat down beside him, waiting for him to initiate whatever he had wanted to talk about.

"It's just kind of strange that you are just now telling me you have a boyfriend," Luke said eventually.

His obvious irritation bemused Aria. She didn't understand why he would care. "Well, it just happened, it's not like I've been hiding it from you forever," she said.

"OK, let me start over. What I was *going* to tell you was that I like you," Luke said. "I mean, I think I'm in love with you. At first when I felt something, I figured it's just that because I've done so much plant medicine that I can fall in love with anyone. But it just kind of got more and more intense and so I talked to Wolf about it and he made me realize that I just wasn't admitting to myself that I was in love with you."

Aria felt her stomach tighten. "Dude, what the fuck ... you can't just spend all this time with someone and not ever say something and never even act like it and then act betrayed when they get with someone else," Aria said.

"Yeah, I know it's stupid," Luke said. He reached into his backpack. He took out a folded letter that was surprisingly neat, given that he had been keeping it in his backpack for over a week. He handed it to Aria. When she opened it, a red tail hawk feather, which he had folded into the paper for her, fluttered to the ground. He picked it up for her and began twirling it in his fingers to distract himself.

"Do you want me to read this now or later?" she asked.

"Whenever ... No, actually, you can read it now," he said.

Aria was surprised to see that he had written the letter in immaculate cursive.

To My Twin Flame,

I know you or my heart knows you.

I don't know where my love started for you and I don't know where or if it will end ... Maybe in another life. Every night, you come into my dreams and then I have to remind myself that those dreams were only mine and I have to pretend that everything between us is normal. I don't want to put pressure on you, but I want to be with you. I want you to be my goddess. I will love you when you are a Shakti and I will love you when you are Shiva. I don't want there to be anything for us to hide. To me, you are like a powerful panther that also has the grace of a fragile doe. I know it's not considered very good to mention how beautiful a woman is because it usually makes her feel like that's all you care about, but I am going to take the risk and tell you that I think you are so beautiful that when I'm around you, I can't breathe. I want to dance and play and be one with you. I think you could become my everything and I want to be everything to you. So if you are open to being my woman, just bring me this hawk feather and I will know it means yes. If not, you can keep it. Wolf said that a hawk feather is a symbol of courage and strength, which is what it took me to write this letter and what it would probably take for you to trust me with your heart. Either way, I want it to keep you safe. No matter how you feel toward me, I want you to be happy and I want you to feel free. I want you to travel the world with me. I want us to live the way that two people in love are meant to live. I don't want to have any regrets, which is why I am writing you this letter, because if I didn't say these things, I am afraid that I would regret it for the rest of my life. My love for you is an unending journey. But I'd rather take that journey with you than in my own head. Can you love me?

With unending love,

Luke

Aria read the words of his letter with deep heaviness. She did not think of herself as the kind of girl to miss something as serious as the affection he had so clearly spelled out in pen. She had imagined that her fondness for Luke had been deeper than the fondness that he held for her. But that fondness was like the moonlight as opposed to the sunlight. Moonlight was reflected. It was pale by comparison. The love that she felt for Luke was like the light that was reflected from a greater love calling to her from the other side of space and time. Her love for Omkar, on the other hand, was like the sunlight, hissing hot of its own volition, and she was blinded by that light.

Aria was silent for a few seconds before speaking. "Luke, this is a beautiful letter. I had no idea you felt this way. I feel really bad now."

Luke stood up, still spinning the feather and running his fingers across the blade of it. He already knew the let-down that was coming. He could hear it in what few words she had said. "So that answer's no, isn't it?" he asked.

"I like you, Luke, way more than you probably know and more than I've told you."

Luke cut her off: "You *like* me, but you don't *love* me! That's it, isn't it?"

She answered him carefully, wary of the thin ice they had wandered onto. "No, it's that I've met someone that I care about so much, I can't – I just can't fuck it up. It has nothing to do with you. If you had given me this letter a few months ago, I would have said yes to it."

Luke looked up at the sky with anger, as if the sky itself had given him the bad advice to wait so long. "I don't want this to make you hate me. I don't want to lose you or whatever else might happen," she said.

He sat back down beside her and forced his way past his own disappointment to comfort her. "Nah, it's not like that. I could never hate you. I mean, I'm not happy, but it's not like I'm gonna just go from being in love with you to hating you. I'm way too conscious for that stupid shit."

Luke didn't ask her any questions about whatever man she seemed to love so much. He didn't want to know anything about him because it would only cause him to feel lonelier than he already was.

Palin was digging a deep hole to their left. She kicked a little spray of wet soil and grass roots onto Aria's legs. "Palin … quit that," Luke said, whistling for her to chase a stick that he picked up from his feet to throw for her. They sat watching the river, neither of them knowing what to say, until Luke held the quill of the feather out in front of her, intending for her to have it.

"I can't take that, I'll feel too guilty," Aria said.

"Nah, I want you to have it," Luke said. "Like I said, I want it to keep you safe and if it doesn't give you courage and strength to give me your heart, maybe it will give you strength and courage for somethin' else."

Aria took the quill from him and smelled it. The guilt she felt made her arms feel heavy. She put the letter and the feather into her backpack and sat with her chin on her knees, watching Luke throw the stick as a distraction from the discomfort that both of them felt.

When they walked back toward the car lot, Luke tried to erase what had been said between them with small talk. He told her stories from his various travels. At one point, he stopped her to look at a dull bronze-colored chrysalis, which he told her contained a painted lady butterfly. "Did you know that a caterpillar doesn't just sprout wings and turn into a butterfly?" he asked. "Actually, if you opened this thing, all that would come out is this primordial soup. The caterpillar decomposes and it gets totally reorganized back into this whole other thing!"

Aria felt the impact of his statement. As fascinating as the fact was, she knew that he was talking about himself just as much as he was talking about the caterpillar. She was unhappy to have become one more part of his story of things that had made him feel like he was dissolving.

When they got back to the lot, Robert was taking a nap. Palin ran up to him and licked his face, startling him out of his sleep. Darren had changed position, but had not come out of the vortex of his self-destruction.

Luke caught Aria by the shoulder. "I'm gonna go back out there, I think," he said, gesturing back toward the woods from which they came.

"OK," Aria said, flustered and not knowing what to say to repair the rupture between them.

Luke pulled her in for a reassuring hug. "I'm here for you whenever you need it, OK? I really like you as a person, not just as a girlfriend or whatever else," he said.

Aria hugged him back, letting her top hand slide up and down the muscles of his back to indicate her regard for him. He whistled and called for Palin. Aria grabbed the scruff under Palin's cheeks and lifted the velvet of her muzzle to kiss both sides of it. Palin snuffed and trotted off to lead the way. Luke took a few steps before turning around and saying, "Hey, if you ever change your mind with whatever-his-name-is, you know where to find me." Aria smiled and waved to him, touching the fingers of her right hand to her lips to indicate a blown kiss. Soon she could no longer see either of them beyond the web of the woods.

Standing in front of Robert, she could smell the hint of ammonia from his breath. His kidneys were not working in his old age with quite the same vigor that they had in his youth. "So are you gonna just stay here then?" she asked him.

"Prob'ly, you know me, I ain't got no place else to be," he said. "What abou'chu?"

"I'm staying over in East LA," she said. "Look, would you mind if I came and saw you sometimes?"

"Hell no, I wouldn't mind, though I can't work out why you'd want to hang out with an old geezer exactly," he said.

"I just do," Aria responded, not able to bring herself to explain her actual need for him or the amount she had grown to care about him.

"OK then, suit yourself. I can't promise I'm gonna be any fun, but you know where to find me." Robert grinned up at her, squinting against the sun. She knelt down in front of him and hugged him. The smell of his clothes was sour with neglect and city grime. He patted her back. Her embrace muffled the words he spoke to end their meeting.

"You go and take care of yourself," he said. Robert was not a man to make his sentiments known. His mutual affection for Aria was not something that he made known openly to her that day. Instead, he kept it for himself. He let his own being kindle it, like powder swallowed by flame.

Aria waited for Omkar for hours on the berm to the side of the road he would eventually drive down to find her. The tides of life that had brought her there had never warned her about the way she would care for the people she would meet. They did not warn her that a person could grow fond of a place which most would consider rock bottom. The fire that had cremated her time there had not burned the memories away. The flames could not reach them. The sovereign fingers of those that remained refashioned their existence on top of the ash because they could do nothing else with themselves.

Despite the flood of emotions she felt, there were no tears to cry. She couldn't let them fall, being so lucky compared to all of them. To cry would be to kick them twice. She was not deaf to the spring that had offered a second chance for her without offering one for the rest of them.

She wanted them so much to be happy. She wanted the wolf inside Wolf to stop its howling. She wanted Anthony and Luke to each find a woman to love again. She wanted Robert's kindness repaid. She wanted Mike to hear the childish trumpet of Aston's voice playing in his own backyard. She wanted to see Taylor's face on the billboards littering the city. She wanted to see EJ clean and sober. She wanted a man to walk into Ciarra's life and quiet the bonfire within her that continued to burn up everything and everyone in her life.

Aria wanted to celebrate the luck of her life, but the festival of it could not compete with the sorrow that she felt for all of them. Despite the hope she tried to hold for them, she knew that the odds were stacked against people like her and people like them. She knew that so many of the wishes she had for them were like waves that would never break against the shore.

CHAPTER 32

Though she didn't want to completely ignore it, Aria hated her birthday. She didn't want to plan something special to do for herself any more than she wanted someone else to. There was always this pressure to do something fun and to be happy on her birthday when no amount of pressure could change the conditions that made her unhappy year after year.

Omkar would have been upset if he'd known that Aria intentionally hadn't told him that her birthday was today. He would have been less upset with her than he would have been with himself for not already knowing. Aria had been staying with the Agarwals for a little over a week and helping Omkar with customers in the store during his shifts there. Despite Jarminder's constant urge to feed her, Aria had not wanted to feel in debt to her generosity, and so she had made an excuse to leave the house every day to preoccupy herself and to take advantage of meal programs around the city.

Aria had been to the church near the store nearly every day for the past week. On this day, she found herself there again, standing in line and waiting for Imani to hand her a sandwich. "Hey girl, how you be today?" Imani asked her before she was done serving the two men standing in front of her.

"Good," Aria said, not wanting to fully engage in conversation until there was no one in between them. "How are you?" Aria asked her once the men had dispersed to their sitting place on the lawn.

"I'm OK, I'm OK, just doin' ya know," she replied.

"You doin' somethin' special today?" Imani asked her, expecting that her answer would be no.

"I don't know," Aria responded. "Actually, it's my birthday today so I don't know yet."

She didn't know exactly why she decided to tell Imani and no one else. Probably it was because there was no risk of her trying to do anything about it.

"How old you be?" Imani asked, her long and freshly manicured acrylic nails pressing divots into the plastic wrap around the sandwich that she handed to Aria. Though they were painted bright purple, they reminded Aria more of claws than of nails.

"Eighteen," Aria replied. Imani's suspicions that Aria had been underage were confirmed but she made no obvious reaction.

Imani did not share Aria's relief about the fact that she had reached adulthood. For Aria, it meant that she could get a job and she would no longer be a target for the cops. Imani couldn't be sure whether Aria was part of the system, but she knew all too well that once kids turned 18, they aged out of the system. Aging out of the system was a nightmare in and of itself. Without a family and without any of the skills to make it on their own, the chances these older kids would graduate from school, much less college, were slim. The chances of them finding good employment were just as slim. It was like kicking a bird out of the nest when it didn't know how to fly. So many of the kids who aged out of the system just ended up right back where they started ... back in the clutches of substance abuse, back in trouble with law enforcement, back in poverty, out on the streets and with no social support. It was a vicious cycle that no one seemed to be able to stop.

"Well, happy birthday, girl," Imani said. "I swear on my mamma you don't look a day over fifteen." Aria smiled. "Let me tell you what you're not gonna do. What you're not gonna do is do nothin' ... Lemme see what I got here."

Imani started looking around, unbothered by the other people waiting in line. She grabbed an extra Rice Crispie treat and handed Aria two instead of one. Then she opened a purple plastic binder and took out a slip of yellow paper from the front pocket. She pointed at an address written on it in white lettering. "This here's a voucher. If you take this down there tonight, you can at least get a warm meal. I think they got a two-piece chicken meal and I think they even got cake some nights, but whatever the case may be."

Aria took the slip of paper from her, conscious of the impatience of the people behind her in the line. "Thanks," Aria said, trying to enhance the gratitude in the word with the look on her face.

"You have yourself a good day now, OK?" Imani said. Aria nodded and walked away from the table. The sky overhead looked like boiling cream. To the west, the white was turning an ominous purple. Aria could feel that the plants nearby had settled into an eerie stillness, like they always did right before a storm.

By the time Aria took the bus to the address written on the meal voucher, the streets of the city were more like black rivers. Each raindrop that hit the surface splashed as if it was hitting the surface of a lake.

Aria sat at one of several long rows of tables with a plate of rice, carrots, tortillas and salsa. Just as Imani had suspected, they were serving vanilla sheet cake that night. The frosting, which had been over-beaten with shortening, was almost waxy. Still Aria savored the square of it that they had given her.

She was glad that no one would be singing the happy birthday song to her before she ate it. Even though there was no candle, she made a wish inside her own mind. The wish was to stay with Omkar forever.

"Do you think any o' these poor saps know how much this shit they're feedin' us actually costs?" the man sitting next to her said. Aria had been chatting with him for well over an hour now, since they'd stood together in the line to get in; long enough to remember that his name was Mark. Aria smiled to acknowledge his question, but didn't answer it.

"You know some o' these places, they get companies to donate food or clothes and what-have-you and they charge what to most people seems like a small amount, but what they don't even realize is just how much fuckin' money these guys are makin'. You realize if someone gives me this coat for free and I sell it for six dollars, that's a six hundred percent profit? You're either the devil or a fuckin' genius to think up a business plan like that." He laughed to himself, pulling at the leather of a fruit roll-up with the front of his teeth.

Mark was one of the strangest people that Aria had ever met. Most people who didn't have a place to live or food to eat were preoccupied with money. But Mark took it to a whole new level. He was financially obsessed. Money had dominated the majority of their conversation and much of it was financial advice about 401Ks and IRA accounts and other things Aria had never even heard of before. Aria took what he said with a grain of salt, given that he was giving advice about how to be a millionaire when he himself was out on the streets. Despite the length of his unkempt brown hair and the swell of his weathered face, even Aria had to admit that he looked more like a man who belonged in a corporate corner office than a man who would be on the receiving end of a charity dinner like this.

Mark had been a self-made man. His mother was a single mom who had raised four kids on a $250 welfare check each month. He considered himself an entrepreneur at the age of ten, when he and a buddy of his had realized that all the kids at school loved reading comics that their parents wouldn't buy them. They saved up their money and bought as many as they could. Every day at school, they would charge the other kids money to read the comics they had bought. The profits they split from their little venture proved to be enough to buy himself what his mother could never afford. From that day on, he had harbored a secret love affair with money.

The first product Mark sold was investment-grade diamonds. From there he did private placement stock. By the time 2008 came around, Mark had become a banker.

In the late 1990s, banks had started taking huge risks. People were buying expensive houses with big loans that they couldn't afford because of how easy it was to have good credit. It caused the price of homes to rise and also an economic bubble. Because they had a lot of money, loan companies made it easier and easier to get loans, even to those with bad credit. They called them sub-prime loans. Many homeowners during this time refinanced their homes, which changed their mortgages and gave them a lower interest rate. Many of them took out another mortgage on their house and used it for spending money. The companies loaning the money changed their terms so that the borrower would have low interest at first and higher interest later. They called them adjustable-rate mortgages. They often used these initially favorable terms to convince people to take their loans in the first place. Unfortunately, many of the people who accepted were those who also had sub-prime loans. As long as the price of housing was high, investing in sub-prime loans would make the banks and other loan companies a lot of money on top of allowing them to offer even more sub-prime loans. But in response to the economic bubble, the housing companies built too many houses.

However, as Mark explained to her, beginning in the summer of 2006, the price of housing began to fall. The value of many homes dropped below the value of their remaining mortgage debt. Because of this negative equity, the owners were unable to sell them and move. By March of 2008, almost nine million Americans had either zero or negative equity in their homes. When interest rates rose, many homeowners were unable to make the higher payments and so, they defaulted on their loans. Foreclosures were everywhere. People lost their homes. They filed for bankruptcy. The number of houses for sale caused the price of homes to decrease even further. The homeowners who had sub-prime loans were forced to leave properties that were now worth less than they'd originally paid for them. The loans were worth more than the houses themselves. But the loan companies could not make money with those houses. Because the economic housing bubble had collapsed, the value of investments began to fall. The companies that had invested in sub-prime loans lost billions. Several begged for government bailouts. Some of the executives took those bailouts and tried to save themselves by giving themselves million-dollar bonuses. Other companies went entirely out of business. People went from being millionaires to being bankrupt. The financial losses and stock market decline of the 2008 financial crisis had been estimated to be just over 15 trillion dollars. Mark was one of the men who had ridden the wave of that economic bubble, only to be crushed by it.

When Mark was laid off, he was forced to drain all of the money from his retirement fund, taking on hefty tax penalties for withdrawing early. He racked up $10,000 in credit-card debt and large medical bills because without a job, he had no health insurance. His house, which he bought at the height of the bubble, lost its value. As a last-ditch effort to try to start from zero again, he let it go to foreclosure and claimed bankruptcy. The expensive contents of the storage unit that he had stuffed his life into when he lost the house were sold at auction. Now, only the sales pitch of his voice hinted at his previous life.

"It was nice talkin' to you!" Mark said before he left, extending her the kind of handshake you would expect to get after a sales pitch instead of from a friend. He stood up and put on his secondhand blue suit jacket. On the street, every part of life was about survival. It was impossible to think about how to get ahead instead of how to keep your head above water. The people who said "don't give a man a fish, teach him to fish" about the people who were low-income or homeless – those were the people who never knew what it was like to have all forces in life against their fishing. Still, with the knowledge Mark had, Aria wondered if the emotional crush of having gained everything only to lose it was what kept him from getting back on his feet again.

— * —

For whatever reason, Aria had enjoyed listening to him talk. She enjoyed the authority that life had not beaten from the sound of his voice. In his absence, she didn't want to sit there any longer. She dropped her trash in one of the large blue bins and started to head out of the building when she saw Pedro and Consuelo sitting at a table. Pedro had noticed her before she had noticed him. He got up from the table to walk toward her. Consuelo stayed seated, but waved from a distance.

"Maybe you think we are stalking you, eh?" Pedro said as he approached, shaking her hand but pulling her into a half hug.

"Ahh, I'm so happy to see you again. Do you guys come here often? I've never been here before!"

Pedro, who always seemed to be on the edge of laughter, put his hands sheepishly in his pockets. "Not too often, *pero* when we come here, I think it's nice. Come, come sit with us," he said, ushering her over to the table.

He introduced her to the three other Mexican men sitting with them before taking a navel orange off of his plate and handing it to Aria. "Here, you will like. I think since the season is harvest, it taste pretty good." He sat on the edge of his seat, watching Aria peel the rind away from the flesh of the orange, separate off a segment and bite into it.

Aria smiled and nodded her head. Pedro was right. It was a living example of the succulent potential that an orange could live up to. Having been a farmer all his life, he had developed an appreciation for produce. Pedro rejoiced in her enjoyment of it.

As they ate, Aria tried to understand what was being said between the men. Occasionally an English word she understood would be peppered into their Spanglish and Pedro tried his best to rope her into the conversation again and again. When the meal was over, having worked out that the house they were staying at was in the same direction as she would be walking, she accepted his invitation to walk with them instead of by herself.

The downpour had turned into a sprinkle. Aria felt safer walking with them through the roadsides of the city. When they arrived at Pedro and Consuelo's place, Aria felt sad at the idea of parting ways with them. Pedro lifted himself from the lawn onto the first step of the house. The exterior of the tiny house had been painted aqua green with a pink trim. The windows were covered in what looked like cages, painted white. "You wanna come in?" Pedro asked.

She did want to go in, but as usual she was afraid to be an imposition. "Nah, that's OK, I gotta catch a bus that won't be running soon if I don't go get it now," Aria said.

Having grown used to the tendency whites had to turn down offers when they wanted to accept them, Pedro pressured her to accept again. "Ah, come on, Consuelo needs to practice his English," he said, tipping his chin at his brother who was standing behind Aria as quiet as a statue.

"OK. You sure it's not a problem?" Aria asked.

"No, no, I love it," Pedro said, opening the door and stepping through it to announce their arrival.

At first, Aria thought that she had interrupted a party. Almost every inch of the house was crammed with men, women and children. When Pedro introduced her as his friend, they looked at her like he had brought her as the party entertainment. But it wasn't a party. Most of them were relatives or friends living there, practically on top of one another. One of the older women got up to give her a seat and asked her if she was hungry. When she said no, the woman poured her a glass of orange Fanta soda. The men sat and stood around the couch, watching the players from Pumas and Veracruz scrimmage against the green of a soccer field. They cooled their nerves with cans of cheap Tecate beer. The women either watched the men or talked among themselves, cleaning around the muddle of people. The noise in the little house was deafening. The children ran around the house like bumblebees with nothing to pollinate. But there was a coziness to the chaos of it all.

The smell of the house was an assault on the senses, a masculine mix of sweat and paint and freshly cut grass on top of the smell of breaded chicken that had recently been fried.

Despite her resistance to the intensity of it all, Aria loved the way the inhabitants seemed to suck up everyone around them into their festivities as if they had already been invited.

Pedro caught her staring at a bouquet of partially deflated balloons that had drifted into one corner of the room. "The kids like to play with them. Those are from my birthday. It was two days ago," Pedro said. "What day is your birthday?"

Aria rolled her eyes, all too aware of the irony of his question. "Actually, it's today!" she said.

Pedro put down his glass as if she had told him that the world as he knew it was about to change. "*Hijole*, no way, are you kidding me?" he said. Aria shook her head, embarrassed by his theatrics. "Hey, everyone … My friend's birthday is today. *Hoy es el cumpleaños de mi amiga, todos a cantarle.*"

Like a conductor he raised his glass, and everyone in the room, including the children, stopped what they were doing to join the chorus. They sang to her in Spanish.

> *Estas son las mañanitas*
> *Que cantaba el Rey David*
> *Hoy por ser dia de tu santo*
> *Te las cantamos a ti*
> *Despierta mi bien despierta*
> *Mira que ya amaneció*
> *Ya los pajarillos cantan*
> *La luna ya se metió.*

When they were finished singing, everyone cheered. The same woman who had poured her a drink went over to the kitchen and rifled around. She pulled a used blue candle that was left over from Pedro's birthday party from a drawer and a *concha* from a plastic bag covering a collection of various breads. Aria watched her light the candle on the stove and push it through the crust of the sweet bread, which she had put on its own little ceramic plate. Aria squirmed under the discomfort of being the center of attention. The woman placed the *concha* in front of her and said, "Make a wish." In her head, Aria made the same wish as she had before. When she blew the candle out, again everyone cheered.

Aria let the sun disappear from the sky. She talked to Pedro and allowed him to translate what he could for the people who wanted to know more about her while she drank more soda than she should have. When she got up to make her exit for the night, a few of the children had already fallen asleep on the floor and on couches. She stepped over one of them, surprised that they could sleep through the noise still echoing through the house.

"No, hey … Antonio can take you wherever you want to go," Pedro said, motioning to one of the younger men on a couch. He spoke briefly to the man in Spanish.

"Sure, sure, I can take you," the man said. He grabbed his coat and hat from the arm of the couch and led the way out the door.

"Hey thanks, I had a really great time," Aria said.

"Me too, hey thanks for coming. I hope to see you again real soon. Happy birthday!" Pedro said, hugging her tightly.

Aria walked across the room and hugged Consuelo, who blushed in response. "See you guys later, thanks," she said to the other people in the house. Though she had not met each of them individually, they all smiled and waved warmly to her when she said goodbye.

— * —

Aria directed Antonio to the Super Sun Market, knowing that Omkar would be worried when she got back. The brakes of his little Ford truck squealed audibly at every stoplight. The man, who had been born in America, spoke perfect English. He kept the momentum of the conversation going for the whole drive and, at the end of it, asked her for her number. When she explained why she didn't have one, he gave her his number instead. Aria thanked him for the ride and took the number, but knew that she would never use it because it was obvious that he was interested in her romantically.

Omkar had seen the man pull up to drop Aria off outside the store. He came outside partially to greet her and partially to challenge the other man with his presence. "Oh hey," Aria said, hugging Omkar as if getting dropped off by another man was a usual occurrence.

"Who was that?" Omkar asked, trying to not let jealousy get the better of him.

"Oh, that's just some guy that gave me a ride back here," she said.

"What have you been doing all day?" Omkar asked.

"Just saying hi to people and finding places to eat, you know." Aria tried to make her day sound as boring as possible, hoping that it would end his interrogation.

"Why don't you just eat here?" Omkar asked.

"Well, I don't want to be some huge burden here. Your mom won't let me touch the kitchen and it makes me feel so weird when she cooks for me. Even my own mother never cooked for me. It makes me feel guilty."

Aria played with the wave of hair over his forehead. Omkar's good nature returned. "Don't you know that Indian mothers love to cook for people? It's this big secret they don't want anybody to know about. All you have to do is to tell them that you love it and they will be like putty in your hand."

Omkar picked her up and spun her once around. When he put her down, he looked toward the store to make sure his parents weren't watching and kissed her softly on the lips.

CHAPTER 33

The sound of the shower towed Omkar from his sleep. Because of the strange hour, he knew that the person showering was Aria. The jealousy he'd felt at seeing the strange man drop her off the previous night had not gone away. Instead, it had festered over the course of the night. Seizing the opportunity of her room being empty, he pulled a shirt on over his boxers and ran downstairs into the storeroom. He rifled through the compartments of her backpack, finding nothing until his fingers grazed a piece of folded paper. He pulled out Luke's letter and unfolded it.

It took him a moment to accept the words that were written on the paper. The cursive that had impressed Aria infuriated Omkar. He read the signature over and over again, etching the sound of the name into his soul like a vendetta. The letter Luke had written made him feel as if the life that he had imagined with Aria was falling apart before it even manifested. The idea of another man being with her made every inch of him recoil. He wondered if the man who had written the letter was the same one who had dropped her off last night. His mind tortured him with the potential that she might have said yes to the proposition the letter contained. Whatever feather the letter spoke of was not inside its folds. He was mauled by the idea of her having given it back to him.

When the sound of the shower upstairs stopped abruptly, he shoved the letter back into her backpack and zipped it. He ran back upstairs and lay in bed. Omkar listened to every sound that Aria was making in the bathroom with his heart furiously beating. The jealousy and betrayal he felt was like a fever sickening the marrow of his bones.

That day at school, Omkar could not concentrate. Every word his professors spoke was nothing more than a mediocre copy of another person's genius. Though he felt like hours had passed, whenever he looked at the time, the minute hand had only traveled inches across the surface of the clock. He was no longer OK with Aria wandering around the city. He decided to tell her so just as soon as he saw her later that day. Having lost his appetite, instead of buying food at the cafeteria, he watched the other students in the outdoor common area. Catastrophe scenarios rose and twisted and fell like a molten swelling within him. It seemed to Omkar that everywhere he looked, all he noticed was other couples in love.

When his classes had finished, he spent a volatile 20 minutes fighting with himself to focus on one of his assignments at a table in the library before giving up. Determined to find Aria no matter where she had gone for the day, he let his feet carry him across the checkered marble floor like horses let out of the racing gate.

He had driven a three-mile-wide maze up and down the neighborhood trying to find her, and when he did, she was walking back toward the store. He parked the car and got out to open the passenger door for her.

Aria greeted him warmly at first, but quickly registered the somber mood he was displaying. "Is something wrong?" she asked, preparing herself for bad news. She scanned her memory to try to find some mistake she might have made that might have displeased Omkar's parents but could find nothing.

"I just had a really crappy day at school," he snapped.

"Well, why?" Aria asked, put off by the fact that a bad day would translate to him taking it out on her in this way.

"It doesn't really matter. I just need to go home and take a shower," he said.

Omkar parked the car directly in front of the store. He got out to open Aria's door for her when Neeraj came bolting out. "Omkar, where is the key to the safe? I tried to take the cash in to the bank today and couldn't find it."

Omkar sighed with frustration. "Oh my God, this isn't even the cherry on top of the cake. This is a rotten cherry on top of a bowl of ice cream that has melted," he said out loud. Aria started laughing hysterically at his analogy. Omkar searched his pockets and scoured the crevices of the car, while Neeraj and Aria stood on the lawn watching him.

Eventually, Omkar stood up, defeated. "I must have left the keys back at school," he said. "Look, Papa, I need you to watch the shop tonight. I have a project due and my study group is lazy so we're way behind on it. I will find you the key – I just need you to watch the shop for the night."

He stood there with bated breath, waiting for Neeraj to respond to his request. Neeraj folded one of his arms on top of his potbelly. He used the other one to accentuate his scolding. "I'm really angry at the moment ya, I'm really angry at this Western culture because it is … it is totally gotten into your mind ya. You have become totally brainless lately. Totally brainless you have become. How do you expect to have a good job or a good life with this irresponsibility? It is totally rubbish, Omkar. Totally rubbish."

Neeraj walked back into the store and Omkar, looking dejected, told Aria to come with him back to college. Even though she trusted Omkar to understand his own father better than she did, Aria was confused about how Neeraj's response could have been taken as consent.

Omkar drove back to his college, withdrawn and in complete silence, hoping that the library where he'd been studying had not yet closed for the night. There was no other explanation than that he had dropped the keys there in his haste to leave the building.

"You stay here, I'll only be a minute," Omkar said, leaving the car keys in the ignition and the engine running. Aria waited until she was sure he wouldn't turn back, then pulled the keys from the ignition switch and got out of the car to follow him. She followed him through the warren of hallways and through the door of the library without him noticing. She watched him ask a woman there if anyone had found a little collection of keys.

Aria waited for the woman to walk away before approaching Omkar. "What are you doing here? I said I was coming back to you there," Omkar said in a whisper.

"No way, I'm not gonna sit there and take orders from you, especially when you won't tell me what the fuck is going on with you. You're acting totally fucked," Aria barked.

Omkar tried to quiet her and looked around to make sure they weren't disturbing anyone. Aria's habit of swearing added an edge to her that he liked, but he still found it embarrassing when they were in public. "OK, we can talk once we're back in the car."

The woman came back carrying something. "Yep, someone turned them in. You're lucky, I was just about to take these over to Lost and Found before closing up for the night," she said.

Omkar inspected the collection of keys to make sure it contained the one that he was looking for. "Hey, thanks," he said to the woman, who had already turned her back on them. She was checking the room, making sure that everything was in its proper place for her to close down for the night.

He pulled at Aria's arm as a request for her to follow him but Aria balked at the pressure. She felt unsafe with his sudden personality shift. "No fucking way. I am not doing this. You tell me what the fuck is going on with you or I am literally gonna walk the fuck out of here and find another place to stay until you can man the fuck up."

Omkar put his hand up to her mouth and tried to shush her. She slapped it away. "OK, OK, my God," he said, leading her by the arm into the aisles of books. The argument was forced to break from their lips at a whisper. Each time the woman tending the library changed her location, they would have to shift where they were standing to stay out of sight.

Omkar didn't understand how it was possible that even though *she* had been the one to diminish the magic between them, suddenly he was now the one justifying himself. "Look, I didn't mean to, but I saw you getting out of that car with that guy last night and I just went crazy, you know?"

"No, I don't know. You can't seriously be that childish, Omkar, what the fuck. What, now I can't even get a ride from a guy without you thinking I fucked him or something?" Aria's question was salted with accusation.

"I never said anything like that. I just don't know how to trust you sometimes," Omkar said.

"Jesus Christ, Omkar, I haven't even done anything. How the fuck am I supposed to keep your trust when I never even did anything to lose it and you're acting like I did?" Aria felt like her image of Omkar as the perfect guy was fading. The jealousy that was now governing his words and actions was a whole other side of him and it wasn't one that she liked.

"Look," he said, "you're going to get mad at me, but I found the letter that that guy wrote to you." Aria looked at Omkar with a confused expression on her face. At first, she did not even remember the letter that he was talking about. "The one written to you from Luke."

He said Luke's name like the name itself was a curse. Shame shook her body like an earthquake. Despite the fact that she had done nothing wrong, she began to see the conflict that they were in as being her fault instead of his. She thought about deflecting the shame she felt by getting mad at him for going through her things, but decided against it. Even though she felt pain knowing that he had to distrust her in order to do it, it felt wrong to her that the boundaries of "her things vs. his things" should even exist.

When the lights went off and Omkar heard the last click of the door closing behind the woman whose job it had been to close down for the night, he stepped out from behind the bookshelves and into the great hall. "And just what exactly do you think I said?" Aria asked him.

"How should I know?" Omkar answered, irritated that the argument had turned into a quiz.

"Omkar, Luke is a friend of mine. He lives at the car lot. He gave me this the day I went back there to see if the place had been deserted or not. What do you need to know? Would you have rather I burned this letter?"

"I don't know what I would have wanted. I guess I would have wanted you to tell me about it when it happened," he said.

"OK, fine, I can do that but you've got to give me a break too, it's not like I've ever had someone to share this kind of shit with. Quite the opposite, actually, it's been sort of beaten into me to keep things to myself to avoid whatever consequences."

In the brief quiet that came between them, the deserted library seemed filled with an antique chill. Omkar played with the parchment binding of a book on the shelf next to him. When he looked back at her, through the dim light, Aria could see that his eyes were welling up with tears. Though she wanted to comfort him, she could not force herself to move toward him.

"I just don't know what I would do without you," he said.

"I know. I feel the same way …"

Omkar cut her reply short. "No, that's just the thing … You don't know. You don't know that you're all I think about. You don't know that if my whole life just fell apart, it would all be worth it because nothing else has mattered so much to me in all my life as you matter to me. Aria, you are my yesterday and my today and my tomorrow. And just the thought of you with another man, I can't stand it."

He walked toward the door, hoping to find that it could be opened from the inside, despite being locked from the outside. He had thought that Aria had followed him, but she hadn't. Instead, she had unzipped her backpack on the floor to find the feather that Luke had given her. When she caught up to him, at first she said nothing. She extended the feather toward him, far enough that the texture of it brushed against his arm.

At first, Omkar didn't understand the symbolism of her gesture. "'Bring me this hawk feather and I will know it means yes, you can give me your heart. If not, you can keep it.' Omkar, I am giving you this feather because I am giving my heart to *you*." Omkar looked down at the feather before he took it between his fingers. He let the feather fall, wanting instead to feel her between them.

The passion that drove his body toward her would have made resistance impossible, not that it ever existed within her. He ran his hands from the nape of her neck to the base of her spine, gripping her as if torn between one part of him that wanted to preserve her and another that wanted to consume her. When he pushed her against the bookcase, Aria braced herself by gripping the case binding of the books, and when he pulled her away from it, a few of them fell onto the floor. The heaviness of his breath licked the silhouette of her neck before the tip of his tongue could taste it. Beneath the armor of his flesh, the way that he kissed her made the lines that defined them dissipate. She could have forgotten where he ended and she began.

Omkar's mind wandered to whether or not anyone could see them. But the feeling of her hand against his cheek brought his mind back to her again. Wantonly she grappled with the unyielding fabric and buttons of his jeans. He tore his shirt up and over his head in response to her. Using his own weight to push her up against the bookcase again, he pulled the collar of her shirt just low enough to kiss the peach of her breasts with reverence.

Though her tug and stroke could not speak louder of the permission that she was willingly giving him, Omkar restrained himself from stripping the clothes from her with his own two hands. Instead, he waited for the pearl of her naked skin to be revealed to him when she took them off herself. It was far from the first time that Aria had found herself in a position like this. But the usual control that she took was something that the love she felt for him would not allow her to take this time. Whatever power she had, had been given over to the arch and bend of the light that displayed his muscles. Now that her heart was involved, like a prey animal that had been hunted down, she froze, waiting for his next move.

Omkar knelt down and placed her hands on the back of his neck. He held the back of her thigh, pressing deep kisses with his teeth into the front of it. He pulled her to the floor with him, using his arm like a cradle to buffer the willow of her body from the stone of the floor. At first, Omkar moved slowly so as to learn the notes to the melody of flesh. His skin slid pervasively over hers, so exposed that they could feel the earth's rotation. In the pause he took to assure himself of her readiness, Aria thought about the fact that they didn't have a condom. It was that moment that every girl looks back on and calls herself stupid for. But the fear of consequences did not outweigh her desire to belong to him.

Omkar reached down to insert himself inside her, his fingers sliding against the wet silk of her labia. When he entered the world of her body for the first time, Aria let a gasp egress from the back of her throat. The warmth and tightness of her fawned over the frame of his erect phallus. The instinct that drove them throbbed in waves that he thrust deep inside her. With the frailty of her femininity in the palm of his hands, the pain that he felt was the pain of not being able to thrust himself loose of the confines of his body enough for them to dissolve into one. With every thrust up to the last, it felt like he took a part of her into himself until he owned her completely. But it did not feel like a loss. It felt like she had found a home. The dew of her wanted to be taken and he had wanted to take it. The storm of their idolatry of each other had left the moon trembling in its wake. Its fragile beams streamed through the window and exhausted themselves across the shine of the floor. The virile fluid of his craving to make her belong to him was warm inside of her. Its slippery fervor had made a delicate marsh of her vulva and thighs.

Aware of the fact that the library was no place to let the tide of post-coital affection wash over them, Omkar rolled his weight off of her and pulled his boxers back on. He sat over the quiver of her pale body, stroking the pith of her skin and waiting for her to be ready to get up and follow him. The wandering boat of his life had found her. The wind had taken him to her side. The burn of loneliness that had charred holes in its decks could not exist in the climate of the smiles that she afforded him.

Having given so much of herself over to him, Aria's muscles were weak and graceless when he finally pulled at her to leave with him. Not wanting to stain her clothes and not wanting to lose the feeling of his skeet inside her, she grabbed one of her socks and used it to line her panties. Omkar had to help her summit the sill of the window that they were forced to open in order to escape. He didn't drive her home. Instead, he decided to contest the will of his parents by finding a place to park the car for the night.

Omkar put the hawk feather that Aria had given him on the dashboard and climbed into the back seat, motioning for Aria to join him. When she did, he laid her down and cradled her head like a baby in his lap. "Shona, do you feel OK about what just happened between us?" he asked her.

Aria nodded her head to say yes but then asked, "What did you just call me?"

Omkar twisted the word around in his mind, trying to find a satisfactory translation. "It's a kind of a nickname, kind of like 'gold' or 'beautiful' or 'sweetheart' … Shona."

Aria chuckled. "Those are three drastically different things," she said.

"Does it bother you if I call you that sometimes?" Omkar asked.

"No, it's fine." Contrary to what she expected, she loved the idea of having a nickname. As far back as she could remember, she had never been addressed with a single term of endearment.

After a few minutes, the hushed space between them was breached by Omkar's voice. "Thorns would have bloomed into flowers if I had loved them as much as I loved you," he said, petting her hair away from her forehead. "I always loved that line. It was in a poem from my country that I read once." He continued. "I don't really want to *not* know where you are during the day anymore."

Aria giggled and pretended to hit him. "Are you serious right now?"

"Hear me out: what if something were to happen to you? I couldn't live with myself. I'm not trying to control you," he said.

"Yes you are!" Aria said, still smiling from ear to ear at his possessiveness.

"No, I'm not – I just need to know where you are. Can you just do it for my sake?"

Aria paused for a long time and bit her lip, pretending to deliberate. She intended the suspense to tease him. "OK, fine," she said, rolling her eyes at him.

"OK, I'll get you a phone tomorrow. That way, if you ever need to call me or if I need to call you, then it will be possible."

Aria laughed again, "Good Lord, how much thought have you put into this?" she asked.

"Oh, you know, just days and days, is all," Omkar said, making fun of himself. "The phone may or may not have a tracking device."

The sound of their laughter was softened by the way they so obviously cherished each other. When Aria fell asleep, Omkar spent some time adoring the sweet form of her face. Should lanterns shine, they would all lead him back to her. In their private dark, he found himself helpless against the conquest of her beauty. In those short hours before dawn would return to them, he reminded himself of the vow he had made to make a heaven of her life, for the love that he felt for her was immortal.

CHAPTER 34

"OK, I'll see you at three o'clock," were the last words Taylor said before hanging up the phone. Aria had called him on the prepaid phone that Omkar had given her to ask if they could meet sometime, at the café on the street adjacent to the Super Sun Market. Having not heard from him in so long, Aria was excited to see him. She was walking to the church to kill the hours between now and then.

The line for the humanitarian lunch service was longer than usual. It snaked slowly down the sidewalk and there were several people that Aria had never seen there before. From a distance, she could tell that Imani's typical blithe attitude had vanished. Instead of the smile Aria had learned to expect, a frown now blemished her face.

When the line had moved far enough to place Aria in front of her, Imani greeted her with a forlorn, "How you be?"

"I'm OK, how are you?" Aria asked.

"Oh, you know, I'm doin'," Imani said, spooning a portion of egg salad into a paper bowl.

Aria was tempted to leave it at that and not risk the rejection of asking Imani what was wrong, only to be told that she didn't want to talk about it. "Are you sure you're OK?"

The question alone made Imani sigh and start to cry again. She wiped the mascara stains from her lower eyelids. "Life's just so unfair sometimes, you know it? This boy I known for a long, long time just got shot and I don't know whatta do with it." She paused before continuing to speak. "Ain't nothin' nobody can do. He a good kid though, a really good kid. It just don't make no sense at all why these things happen … no sense at all."

It felt wrong to Aria, after Imani had said a thing like that, to simply take her bowl and walk away. Instead she rounded the table to stand beside her, so that Imani could continue serving the other people in the line. Imani didn't know any details, just that the boy had been shot by police because he had pulled a gun on them. Instead, once the floodgates of her grief opened, Imani shared a torrent of details about him.

"Back when he was prob'ly ten or eleven, he foun' out this man I been datin' had left me for another woman. He made this comedy rap battle song about him and sang it in front of everybody at the center. We was laughin' so damn hard I nearly peed my pants. You know. He had it in his mind to be a rapper."

Imani had met the boy when he was five years old through the family center where she worked as a social worker in the mornings. He had been brought in to see her shortly after his father killed his mother and the boy was handed over to the state. "I got a picture o' him you can see," Imani said, wanting to preserve some part of him further by helping Aria to put a face to the name.

But when Imani handed Aria the phone after scrolling through it, it wasn't a picture on the screen. It was a news article. The man staring back at her was not a stranger, like she had expected. It was the face of Kendrik, the man who she had talked to once while they waited for the lunch service to begin. She had seen him many more times after that in passing. Aria felt sick to her stomach. "Oh my God, I know him … He comes here all the time. I even talked to him once," Aria said.

"Police Fire 54 Shots, Report Finds It Reasonable," the headline read. Aria continued reading. "It is unclear how many of those bullets struck Kendrik McCoy, a 22-year-old black man, but attorneys have said he was hit around 26 times. Police officers responded to a call about a man who had been threatening residents with a gun in Compton near West Piru Street. Officers say they saw the gun in the man's pocket and believe that he was reaching for it when they threatened him with arrest. The shooting has set off demands by the community for police accountability and an independent investigation into the entire department's training and an alleged pattern of racial profiling. City officials in April said they were inviting US Department of Justice mediators to hear from residents and create a 'community engagement plan.'"

Aria continued to read the article until she reached the bottom. The first thought that she had was about his girlfriend at Foot Locker. The locks of his prison bars had yawned loose and promised him a life that was worth living for. He had lost that promise in an altercation that had lasted less than three minutes. Everything about it felt wrong. Imani was not alone now in her incapacity to digest it.

Kendrik had always imagined that if he were to get shot, it would be by a Cuzz – another Crip assigned to kill him for trying to leave the gang. Not wanting to leave the city, because he had a girlfriend now, he had been lying low and avoiding the parts of the city dominated by the Crips. The day the cops shot him, he had intentionally wandered into Compton, which was Blood territory. The Bloods were a rival gang to the one he had pledged himself to, but because he wore nothing to distinguish himself as a rival, he imagined that he would be safest "sleeping behind the cloak of the sloobs". But Kendrik was recognized by a foot soldier for the Bloods, a low ranking member who was out "bleeding" (looking for new recruits to join the gang). Kendrik had crossed paths with the man during a conflict that occurred when a group of Bloods were selling narcotics in what Kendrik believed to be Crip territory. The man had parked his car to watch Kendrik, long enough to be sure that Kendrik was who he thought he was. He called a woman he knew and told her to call the police, to report that a man was waving a gun at people, and to describe him and give his location. It was a kind of a "slap back" at the insult of Kendrik daring to be there. He enjoyed the idea of the scare that getting hassled by the police would put into him. He did not imagine that the phone call he initiated would lead to Kendrik's death.

Six police officers showed up at the scene. When they pulled up both behind and in front of Kendrik, he panicked.

They yelled at him to get down on the floor. But while he was doing it, he reached into his pocket for the business card of his probation officer. Having been called to the scene of a man with a gun, they made the assumption when he reached into his pocket that he was reaching for a gun. That Kendrik was unarmed was a fact that they didn't discover until after the first officer had unloaded two shots, the second had unloaded six, the third had unloaded five and the fourth had unloaded 12.

Kendrik didn't trust the police. Policing was the most enduring aspect of the struggle for civil rights. It had always been a mechanism for racial control. Stories of police harassment and violence in the black communities where he grew up were common. The faces of the police officers he feared were faces that belonged to a larger system of inequality; inequality in the justice system, inequality in housing, inequality in employment, inequality in education and inequality in health care. Kendrik trusted his probation officer because, like Kendrik, Officer Kent was black. As a black man as well as a cop, Officer Kent had spent the last 15 years reconciling the warring perspectives within himself. As a black man, he had found himself on the receiving end of both profiling and discrimination more times than he could count. As a father to three black children, he had found himself having to have "the talk" about the reality of being black in America and about how to act in encounters with law enforcement so that they would be sure to leave with their lives.

As a cop, he knew how dangerous the job was. He had seen his colleagues killed on account of not pulling a gun fast enough. He knew that being a cop also came with its own share of unfair scrutiny. When Officer Kent showed up at the scene, he knew that some of the cops that had shot Kendrik that day had shot him out of implicit bias and some had not. One side of that war within him felt the honor of wearing the same uniform as the other brave public servants that served with him. The other side of him couldn't help but wonder when tragedies like this happened, why so many of the faces of those who were killed looked like his.

Aria's mood while she waited for Taylor to arrive at the café was dark. It was perfectly matched by the depressing wail of the indie music playing on the overhead speakers. Taylor arrived in his typical style, over half an hour late. He pulled up to the parking spot driving a sunshine-yellow Pontiac Solstice. He was dressed from head to toe in a tight-fitting designer suit with oversized glasses and Gucci sliders. He got out of the car in a Hollywood style that suggested there should have been film cameras about. When he reached down to hug her before sitting down at the table, Aria was engulfed in the attar of a cologne that blurred the lines between masculine and feminine.

"You look completely amazing," Aria said. Instead of a response, Taylor used his hand to frame his face and strike a pose as if to say, *I know, I know, darling.*

He got up almost as quickly as he sat down, realizing that Aria hadn't ordered anything yet. "Hey, you want somethin'?" he asked. Aria shook her head no. Taylor guessed that she had declined on account of having no money, so he winked at her and walked toward the counter to buy her something anyway.

He sat back down with an iced coffee and put an iced caramel macchiato in front of Aria. "Did you land a part or something?" she asked, having no other explanation for Taylor's sudden financial upgrade.

"I wish. No, Daddy's just rich," he said, referring to Dan. The café employee came over to the table, carrying a small plate with a cinnamon roll. When he placed it down in front of Taylor, the two of them looked at each other like two hissing cats. "What the hell was that?" Aria asked as soon as the man had left.

"Oh he's just sissyphobic. Some gay men find other gay men like me simply objectionable." He enunciated the words "simply objectionable" loud enough that the man behind the counter could hear.

"So where are you living?" Aria asked.

"Well, you remember I moved in with Dan, right? It was better than I expected. I mean, I guess it had to be 'cause I'm still living there! We're up in Laurel Canyon," he said. Aria didn't know where Laurel Canyon was, but from the look of Taylor's makeover, she could imagine the affluence of the place.

"Are you still taking those acting classes?" Aria asked.

"No … I don't know; it just wasn't really getting me anywhere. I kind of gave up acting for now," Taylor said. Aria could feel the shame in the cadence of his voice.

"So what are you doing every day then?" she asked.

Taylor laughed once before admitting, "I've been helpin' Dan with his thingy and redecorating mostly. Dan has this awful old movie fetish. I've let him keep a room all to himself so he can put *all* his collector pieces there. That way they won't be littering up the house … Oh, and I've been learnin' to cook. He's lucky I haven't burned the whole goddamn house down yet … Besides that, I've just been loungin' around the house." Aria chuckled to imagine Taylor in the new life he had stumbled into.

"Where are you livin' now?" Taylor asked.

Aria pointed in the direction of the mini market. "Just over there," she said.

"No shit?" Taylor said, turning around to look.

"Actually, I found a guy too!" Aria confessed.

Taylor grinned as a substitute for congratulating her. "Isn't it obvious now you're gonna have to tell me about 'im? … What's his name, what's he do, is he sexy?" he asked.

Aria told him every last detail, down to revealing the fact that Omkar had been the one leaving the things they had found on the hood of the car. When she had dispensed every detail, Taylor's expression had gone from cocksure to adoring. Words could not describe how happy he was for her. Still, deep down he envied her.

Taylor had abandoned the path toward his dreams because in many ways, through Dan, he had already manifested them.

As dramatic as he was by nature, his pull toward the stage and toward the big screen was really just the desire to "make it big." He wanted to be significant. He wanted a lifestyle that would take him far away from the poverty and insignificance he had experienced in his youth. He had found both significance and wealth through being with Dan.

Still, his life with Dan was not all gifts and glamor. Taylor was embarrassed to admit to being a sugar baby. People who had money or who'd grown up with it just didn't understand the idea that people like him came from less than nothing. Without the proper support systems, people like himself were forced to consent to extraneous means of digging themselves off the street.

Taylor was not naive enough to forget that for many gay men, the kind of relationship that Dan and he had usually lasted for only one night. For others, a week or a month at best. Unlike many other sugar daddies, Dan was monogamous and therefore committed to Taylor. But even so, he knew that even if they were together for years, it could end at any moment. He had become the male version of a trophy wife; only he had no marriage license to ensure his security. His significance and lifestyle came with the expectation of keeping himself beautiful at all times. It came with the expectation that he would never resist sex whenever Dan wanted it. It came with the expectation that Taylor would be a slave, at his beck and call. It was a price he was willing to pay.

Before their visit was over, Taylor drove Aria around in the flamboyant car that Dan had bought him. He told her to pick a song and blared it to show off the impressive sound of its speakers. "Don't be a stranger!" he yelled, when she got out to walk toward the store.

"Don't worry, you'll always be my Boo," she yelled back, waving.

As Taylor drove away, he watched Aria through the rear-view mirror. The envy that he felt for the love that she claimed to have found made him resent the circus of his life. Even though some form of mutual caring had grown out of the life that he and Dan were forming together, it was not love. It was not the love that Aria had found. It was a relationship of mutual use and transaction.

The love between Omkar and Aria was the inosculation of two trees whose roots had grown separately until they were destined to touch. His and Dan's, on the other hand, was a crooked rose.

CHAPTER 35

Her periods had been late before. In fact, they had never been regular to begin with. But there was something inside every woman that worried whenever there was reason to believe there might be occasion to worry.

The possibility of being pregnant had been a nagging disquiet in the back of Aria's mind for the past two weeks. It had grown into enough of a worry that she had considered stealing one of the pregnancy tests at the store. Aria didn't want Omkar to be involved unless she was absolutely sure. But it didn't feel right to take anything from the family who she was now becoming more and more a part of every day. So, she set up an appointment and took a bus to a non-profit healthcare center that offered free pregnancy tests.

The insulation of the room that the medical assistant had put her in to wait was fortified enough to make the room feel lifeless. Occasionally, she could hear the voices of doctors and nurses passing by as they discussed the patients who were waiting in other rooms. To distract herself from the isolation, Aria tried to memorize the anatomy of an ear, which was displayed on a medical chart that had been framed as if it were decoration.

The double knock on the door when the doctor finally came back made Aria jump. The doctor started talking before she had even closed the door. "Hi there. The test was negative, so you're not pregnant. I am a little concerned that you say your periods have always been so irregular, though. Some woman have good success evening out their cycles with oral contraceptives. The clinic can prescribe some for you if you're interested in trying that out and seeing how it goes?"

"I'll think about it," Aria said.

"Well, is there anything else that you need help with today?" the doctor asked.

"No, I'm good," Aria responded.

"OK then. It was good to meet you today, you have a good rest of your day," the doctor said, shaking Aria's hand before exiting the room. Aria followed her out, but went the wrong way, and eventually had to be redirected back through the labyrinth of the office to find the door where she had originally entered.

Instead of taking the bus back home, she went to the public beach where she and Omkar had gone on their first date. She didn't call Omkar to tell him to meet her there when he was done with school for over an hour. Instead, she watched the waves, trying to make sense of the deluge of her mixed emotions. It made no sense to her why she could feel so much dread at the idea of being pregnant, but when the doctor had given her the good news, it hadn't felt like good news at all. She chided herself in her head. "What the fuck, Aria … If you're knocked up, you don't want to be, but if you're not, you want to be. What the fuck is that about?" When the doctor had given her the news, it had felt like a loss even though there had never been anything there to lose in the first place … A loss of closeness or belonging, maybe.

Aria felt bad about herself again. The potential of pregnancy had made her realize the extent to which her life *wasn't* in order. The life she was living did not even remotely resemble a life that a child should be brought into, and that bothered her now, more than it ever had.

It wasn't a baby that Aria wanted; she was conscious of that. She had seen so many girls like her, who had been deprived of love growing up, having babies to try to fill the hole within themselves. They imagined that if they had a baby, there would be someone to finally love them unconditionally and be with them and give them a sense of belonging forever. But it was a fantasy. The minute the baby was born, that fantasy would prove false. Somewhere in the physical wear and tear of motherhood, they would realize that motherhood was a one-way street of having to fulfil the baby's needs even when no part of them wanted to. If these mothers made it past the phase of infancy and managed to enmesh their children into the dysfunctional dance of being there for *them* instead, it never turned out well. That same child that they looked to for unconditional love and belonging would eventually turn against them, brimming with resentment for being born only to suit their mother's unmet emotional needs. Aria didn't want to follow in those predictable footsteps.

The sadness she felt was the sadness of losing the potential of a deeper sense of closeness that she might have had with Omkar. She was just like those young mothers who lacked a sense of love and belonging. A baby felt like a knot that would have been tied between herself and Omkar, fortifying the security of their union. Maybe the guarantee that she would be cherished by him a little longer. Aria was irritated at her own unshakable insecurity when it came to connection. But then again, how could she not be anxious? She wasn't a girl who was worried about a loss she had never tasted. Loss had been the rule of her life instead of the exception.

There were no children on the beach that day, so instead of watching them, Aria imagined them playing there. She tried to study the bubble of belonging that seemed to exist around a man, a woman and their child. It caused a potent ache to paint itself against the trammel of her chest.

"Hey, what are you looking at?" Omkar said, walking up behind her and kissing her on the cheek from behind. Aria was staring off into the recesses of the ocean, trying to see with her mind what her eyes could not.

"Nothing," she said, smiling at him as he sat down beside her.

"Why did you come here? Did you miss me?" he jested, mindful of the fact that she had chosen to sit exactly where they had sat during the picnic he had arranged for her on their first date there.

"I don't know. I just wanted to see the ocean again," she said.

Omkar could feel the murkiness of her mood, and put his arm around her shoulder, burying his face in the hair that cascaded past the side of her neck. Aria broke the silence by asking, "How would you feel if I got pregnant? I mean, what would you want to do or whatever?"

He sat back in disbelief, his breathing shallow. "Do you think you're pregnant?" he asked. The entire trajectory of his life hung in the balance of her answer.

"No. I *know* I'm not pregnant. I just started thinking, since we haven't exactly been careful about it, you know … What would you think about it if it happened?"

Omkar leaned back on his arms. "What would you want to do about it?" he asked, not wanting to answer first in case his answer was the opposite of hers.

"No, you don't get to put it back on me. Can you just try to answer?" she asked.

Omkar thought about the fact that he was already struggling to juggle the pressures of school and work and having enough time left over for Aria. He thought about the wrath of his parents, were he to make a "mistake" like that. But even though there were undeniable consequences and even though the timing would not be his first choice, Omkar could not find an inch of himself that felt like those negative factors would outweigh the blessing he would perceive it to be if it actually *did* happen.

To his surprise, when he considered the question, he realized that it would feel like a consummation of the love that he felt for her. He pulled her to lay her head against his chest. Aria could hear the sound of his heart beating. "Shona, I don't want to ask you to do anything that you don't want to do. But how could it not make me happy? A child is a divine spark. It is sacred. If God wanted us to be a soul's entry into this world, how could I not be happy? I wouldn't care if it were a girl or a boy. I would want you to have the baby. I could not see it as a mistake because I love you and I know that God likes to use love to create new life."

Even knowing his heart as well as she did, Omkar's answer astounded her. She was spinning as a result of it. Omkar coaxed her from her silence. "What would you want to do?"

"I'm not saying that I want it to happen right now or anything, but I wouldn't want to get an abortion," she said, looking down at her feet in the sand.

A smile spread across Omkar's face. He leaned down and kissed the crown of her head. In the wake of the conversation, they watched the ocean with their minds far away from it. Aria let his surety carry her trust, and with the weight of her trust in his arms, Omkar started to think. By American standards, they were young ... too young, perhaps, to consider marriage. But when compared to the prospect of bringing life into the world with her, which was a commitment that even divorce could not undo, marriage no longer seemed far away. It made no sense to Omkar why, if he could consent to having a child with her, he hadn't proposed to her already. The conversation had been a wake-up call to whatever part of himself had not been diligent about taking precautions when they had made love. A wake-up call to the part of himself that knew how much he loved her and how committed to her he really was.

That night, Omkar sat with Aria until she fell asleep. Sensing that his opportunity was upon him, when he walked upstairs, instead of going to his room, he walked straight into his parents' bedroom. Jarminder was already asleep. With the side table lamp still on, Neeraj was flipping through the pages of a book on acupressure and locating the corresponding pressure points on himself.

Knowing his son would only interrupt them at night when he had unpleasant news to share, he grumbled in response to Omkar's intrusion. "Mama, Mama, I need to talk to you," Omkar said, bulldozing Neeraj's resistance to Jarminder being woken up. She opened her eyes groggily but was immediately stricken with panic that something must be terribly wrong.

"Mama, I have come to ask you for something. Do you remember what you said when Auntie Chann was going to marry that man last year? You said that if you have to think about whether or not you love someone, that isn't really love. Mama,

I was listening. I don't have to think about whether I love Aria because I do. I can only hope that in the past little while that she has been living here, you have come to love her too. Mama, you said a long time ago that when I met the girl that I wanted to marry, you had a ring for me to give to her. Mama, I have met the girl I am going to marry. And I am going to ask her to marry me. But I am asking for you and Papa to give me your blessing."

Neeraj huffed and sat up against the headboard with his arms folded. "She is a very good girl. We like her. But why are you thinking about this at your age? Why can't you wait until your schooling is finished? Why can't you behave your age? I do not believe you are ready for such a thing as you are proposing," he said.

Jarminder was uncharacteristically quiet. She stared *through* Omkar instead of at him. It was not the first time Omkar had mentioned that he thought of Aria as a potential wife. Having seen Omkar and Aria together, both she and Neeraj had come to terms with the possibility that they would one day be married. The strength of Neeraj's protest surprised her because it exceeded her own.

Neeraj continued. "Omkar, marriage is not a trivial thing. It is not something that you can pick up one minute and drop the next. I do not understand why …"

Jarminder cut him off by grabbing hold of the sleeve of his nightshirt. In Punjabi, she told him to stop. She scolded him for refusing to even hear Omkar out.

Omkar's heart leapt. He had barged into the room expecting a fight from both of them, and instead, it seemed his mother was on his side.

"Omkar, we love you very much. We want the best for you. If you want to marry this girl, you've got to be completely sure of it. Why can't you give it some more time? Why can't you wait until after you finish school?" she asked.

"Mama, I have four more years to earn my master's degree. I am not going to wait four years to marry this girl," Omkar shouted.

Neeraj and Jarminder were calculating the impracticality of their request, given the reality that he had spilled out on the table. "You and Papa were married when you were even younger than me," Omkar said, hoping to trap them into being unable to invalidate him without at the same time invalidating themselves. They said nothing, but both of them were reminded just how different the reality of marriage had been to what they had expected when they found themselves in the same position that their son was in now.

"At some point, Papa and Mama, you are going to have to trust me," he said. "You have raised me right. You have taught me right from wrong. I am capable of taking care of this girl and if you don't believe me, I'm just going to have to prove you wrong. Love should build things, not break them. You can't say to me that you love me and break my heart. If you love me, I am asking you to give me your blessing and help me to build a life with this girl because in my heart I know she is meant to be my wife."

Jarminder patted the bed with her hand for Omkar to come sit by her. She placed her palm flat against his cheek with tears in her eyes. Using his nickname, she began to speak. "Jeety, I may have no right to judge you, but I have a mother's right to worry. Aria is from a different community, a different culture, a different race. This makes marriage more difficult. But your father and I will get used to it. Everything we have done, we have done for your happiness. And if you say that your happiness is to marry this girl, then you must marry this girl."

Omkar hugged his mother harder than he had ever hugged her before and looked toward Neeraj, whose initial resistance had been worn down by seeing Jarminder cry. "Do you swear to me that if you marry her, you are not going to drop out or do anything else stupid?" Neeraj said. "If you say that you are in love with this girl, then you cannot jeopardize your future."

Omkar shook his head. "No, Papa, you know I want to get my degree. I swear I am not going to jeopardize my future. I couldn't do that without jeopardizing hers as well."

Neeraj deliberated, keeping both Omkar and Jarminder on tenterhooks. "OK. I give you my consent. But Omkar, you have made promises to me tonight. To break a promise to your father would be absolutely disgusting ya?" Omkar cracked a half-smile at his father's threat.

Jarminder got out of bed and walked over to the closet. Realizing that she wasn't tall enough to get to the box she was trying to reach, she asked Neeraj to get it down for her. With it in her hands, she walked back to the bed and put it down where Omkar was sitting. She opened the box to reveal a miscellany of gold jewelry. Jarminder brought the pieces out one by one. She showed him the *haar* and *ranihaar*, two of the traditional necklaces she had worn on her wedding day to Neeraj, as well as the *tikka*, which was an ornamental piece of wedding attire that had been draped across her forehead. Omkar played with the little string of pearls attached to it while he listened to her explain each piece.

Out of the several gold rings that were in the box, Jarminder selected one of them. "This is the ring I have promised you. It belonged to Papa's mother. I'm going to tell you what she told your father when she gave it to him to give to me ... A ring has no beginning and no end. Because of this, it is limitless. The *kara* you wear represents your unbreakable attachment to God. And this ring will represent her unbreakable attachment to you. With your father's and my blessing, may your marriage be eternal."

She hugged Omkar again and cried before she handed the ring to him. Neeraj patted him on the arm. Unlike Jarminder, his sentimentality only smoldered beneath the surface of what he would willingly show.

Omkar's parents didn't sleep much that night after their son left their room. They held each other and allowed themselves to be tossed between the vacillations of worry and excitement.

Omkar also found it difficult to sleep. Given that the dark could not compete with his happiness, he switched on the lamp beside his bed and examined the ring. A thin gold band joined up to a larger piece of gold that had been cut into a marquise shape and bent in order for it to conform to a finger. The gold had been carved with such detailed, symmetrical filigree that Omkar could not memorize its design. Emanating from a ruby set deep in the center, four inlays of watermelon tourmaline extended to the perimeter of the ring, like petals.

The moonless acres outside his window contained a thousand people just living their lives. None was as happy as he. Through the floor, he could feel Aria in the room below him. He could feel the tempered busyness of her sleep. Omkar could feel the seed of his youth cracking. Inside it, the stirrings of the man he was born to be.

The oil of his mother's tears lamented the death of his childhood. Though it was daunting, he found the pressure of love's responsibility to be divine. The summer of his life now hung on a single answer … An answer to a question that Omkar had not yet even asked.

CHAPTER 36

Six yards of royal sheen sprawled out across the bedroom. Aria had imagined a sari to be an exotically sewn garment. Instead, it was simply yards of radiant fabric.

Omkar stood in the doorway, watching Jarminder fuss over which sari to give her. She settled on one that was the color of ripe plum with gold embroidery on its edges. She handed Aria a matching blouse piece and petticoat and told her to put them on in the bathroom. When Aria returned, Jarminder kneeled on the floor in front of her, three safety pins between her teeth. She took one end of the sari and began aggressively tucking it the entire way around the waistband of the petticoat. When she had made a full circle around Aria's waist, she took the embroidered end of the fabric and began pleating it.

Watching her hands molding the fabric, Aria felt like she was peering through a telescope across the oceans to a different time and place. Jarminder's veins netted her hands like the consecrated, colluvium-laden waters of the Ganges; the invisible scar of patriarchy evident in the way that she moved them. With the pleated end of the fabric held firmly in her hand, she twisted it behind Aria, pulling it across her right leg and over her left shoulder. Making sure that the pleated fabric fell just below Aria's knee level, she stood up and took one of the safety pins she had been holding between her teeth. She pierced it into the fabric on the underside of the blouse just over Aria's collarbone, fastening it to the fabric that she had just draped across Aria's shoulder.

Again she took hold of the fabric, this time the embroidered top edge just beneath where she had pinned it. She pulled it tight down and across Aria's back, around her hips to the front again. Jarminder tucked the fabric into the petticoat, rolling it toward her to expose the underside of the petticoat. She took a second safety pin from her teeth, pinning the silky fabric of the sari to the cotton of the petticoat, and re-rolled it toward Aria's navel.

Thinking she was done, Aria moved away from her to go look into a mirror. "No, no, it isn't ready yet," Jarminder said, afraid that Aria would see her work before it was done. Aria stood back in front of her. Jarminder kneeled down again and gathered the loop of fabric that was now hanging in the front of the skirt and straightened it so that the edges of the loop perfectly matched. Just as she had done previously, she began pulling the fabric back and forth between her outstretched thumb and fingers, making sure the pleats she created by doing so were the same width and length. She took the final safety pin from her teeth and used it to pin the pleats together before forcefully tucking the section she had pinned into the petticoat and standing back to examine her work.

Aria felt like she had been wrapped in a sensual cocoon. The way the fabric hugged and pulled at her curves made her feel statuesque. She stepped in front of the full-length mirror hanging in Jarminder's bedroom. Wrapped in thousands of years' worth of tradition, Aria felt more feminine than she ever had before. Even though she didn't have a single drop of Asian blood in her veins, it was the mystic spirituality of her own femininity that was staring back at her from the mirror.

Jarminder took Aria's face in her hands and turned it to kiss her cheek. Jarminder had been acting strange the whole morning. Unlike usual, she had woken up before Aria could slip out the door. She had made breakfast already and insisted that Aria join them. Any coldness that had been there before seemed vanquished. On top of it, she had suddenly insisted on giving Aria one of her own saris. Aria, who couldn't understand the sudden alteration in Jarminder's mood, humored the sudden sentimentality without letting herself expect it to stay that way.

"You look simply incredible," Omkar said from the doorway. Seeing Aria in the clothes that the women from his culture traditionally wore made something churn inside him. Maybe it enhanced his sense of ownership. In the Western world, *own* had become a dirty word when it came to other people, especially women. It meant to have complete power over someone else and to control them. But Omkar understood what many men did not: that to exert power and control over another person was the complete opposite of true ownership. "Own people," his father had told him so many times when he had not been acting responsibly enough toward them. To Omkar, to love something was to take it as a part of himself. And doing so automatically meant it belonged with him and to him and so it was his to take responsibility for. With this kind of ownership, he could not hurt the person who belonged to him without hurting himself. He could not oppose their best interests without opposing his own. With this true ownership, the best interests of Aria were his primary concern.

Though reluctant to accept the gift that Jarminder had given her, Aria walked downstairs to her room wearing it. She unpinned the fabric and unwove it, folding it back into an untidy square. Dressing back into her common street clothes felt strangely degrading.

Omkar knocked on the door of her room and let himself in. "Hey, can you take a cab and meet me today at Griffith Park when I get off of school, around like 5:30 or six o'clock?" He put $50 down on the bed beside her.

"Jesus Christ, Omkar ... I can just take the bus there. You want me to take a cab that costs fifty bucks?" she yelled.

Omkar took the money and placed it in her hands instead. "Look, can you just do it for me today, just this one day, just go along with it? It's probably going to be rush-hour traffic and so they charge more. If not you can just keep the rest."

Aria rolled her eyes at him. "OK, are you gonna tell me why I have to drive all the way across the city?" she asked.

"Because I have a party to go to near there. It's kind of a cocktail party and we can bring a date to it. I want you to come as my date," Omkar said. Aria furrowed her brow with confusion.

"OK … Well, did it occur to you that I don't have anything to wear to something like that? Unless you want me to show up in camo pants?" she retorted.

"Good point. Here," Omkar said, pulling another $50 bill out of his wallet and putting it in her hand as well.

"Seriously, this is ridiculous," Aria said, trying to give it back to him.

Omkar clasped his hands around hers, trapping the bills inside of them. "Just stop now. Do this for me today, OK, please?" he asked.

Aria raised an eyebrow as a hesitant concession to his temporary insanity. He kissed her on the forehead and left the room to collect his things upstairs. Aria put the money in her pocket. Though she wanted to humor him, there was no way she was going to spend that much money on an outfit or on finding a way across the city.

— * —

Just ahead of her in the distance, buildings pierced the sky like steel daggers warning off the interfering clouds. In the hallowed halls of the city, people rushed in every direction. The spectral choir of cars on the network of freeways was muted by distance.

Aria was walking northwest in search of the first secondhand clothing store she could find. The street was littered with dollar stores and payday loan shops. A man pushing all of his tattered belongings in a shopping cart crossed the road where there was no crosswalk, without any concern for the cars on the street.

She stepped into a store whose windows were cluttered with manikins that looked like hookers. Each one was poorly fitted with cheap imported shirts or dresses. An Oriental man approached her when she opened the door. "Everything on this side for sale!" he said in broken English.

Aria nodded and walked over to a rack of dresses. She thumbed through the polyester fabric until she found her size in a white sundress, cased in sunflower print. She tried it on in a curtained alcove that the store owner was brave enough to call a dressing room. It was the first time she had worn a dress since she had run away from the Johnsons'. As jaded as she was about the world, the sunflower print made Aria feel the mirth that some people spoke of with regards to life. She liked how its warmth and innocence hugged her frame. Keeping it on, she went to the checkout counter and handed the store attendant the $50 bill. The man marked it with a pen to make sure that it wasn't fake and, keeping just over $12, he handed Aria back the change.

Aria felt naked without her backpack as she walked down the sidewalk in her sunflower sundress and high-top sneakers, stopping to look at the window display of any store that had one. She had scanned the displays boasted by at least a dozen pawnshops before something she saw in one of them that shot a thrill straight through her. As if by divine orchestration, she recognized the metal tips of a line of tools in a little burlap case that had been unrolled so the customers could see it. Aria ran inside.

"Are those carving tools?" she asked, flustered by the ardor of her own excitement.

"Where?" the man tending the store asked.

"Over here," she said, leading him toward the display in the window.

"Um, I don't know, let me check," he said, taking the tools in his hands to show them to the other man behind the counter.

Aria's heart fluttered, seeing the man's head nodding up and down. "Yep, they're carving tools. They didn't come in with a sharpener, though," he said, walking back toward the window to put them back in the display.

"No … I'd like to buy them!" Aria said.

"OK, then come over this way," the man said, reversing course toward the checkout counter. "That'll be ninety-five dollars," the man said.

Aria's stomach sank. "I only have like eighty-eight dollars," she said.

"I could sell 'em for ninety?"

Aria's stomach sank even further but her sense of urgency trumped her shyness. "Dude, seriously, you don't understand, I really only have eighty-eight dollars and I *have* to get these."

The man ran his fingers over the blades, deliberating. The other man in the store came over to where they were standing. "She's got eighty-eight for 'em," the first man said. The second man looked at Aria, cracking a smile most likely because of the amusement he got from how out of place it was for a girl wearing a little sundress to walk into a pawnshop and buy a wood-carving set. "OK, let her have 'em," he said.

Aria placed every dollar and cent she had with her on the counter. The man slid the coins back toward her, taking only the bills before rolling the case back around the little tool set and putting it into a used plastic grocery-store bag. When he handed it to her, Aria looked at the clock on the wall. Trying to make it to the car lot before going to Griffith Park was cutting it close, but she had to do it.

Robert had found a tent again. When Aria peered inside it, he was napping, but the pressure of her presence startled him awake. Besides Darren, who held up a drunken peace sign when he saw her, everyone else at the lot had gone somewhere else for the day.

Aria kneeled down to place the rolled plastic bag on the floor next to Robert. "Hey, I gotta run, but I got something for you. I'm putting it right here," she said. Robert twisted to look. "You don't have to look at it now, just open it whenever." She stood up to leave again.

Robert watched her shadow bounce across the outside of the tent as she ran off. She was already long gone by the time he managed to sit himself up and look inside the bag. When he unrolled the burlap case, an overwhelmed smile spread across his face. He thumbed the grain of the wood handles, whose previous owner had loved them glossless. He rolled them back up and hugged them close to his chest, lying back down again, like a child with a stuffed toy. Though Aria had disappeared before he could thank her, he closed his eyes and imagined her hearing him thank her anyway.

By the time that Aria made it to Griffith Park, she was out of breath and 20 minutes late. Omkar's car was parked on the side of the street and he was leaning against it. When he saw Aria jogging toward him with the plastic bag containing the clothes she had been wearing before she bought the dress, he bounded toward her. "Did he drop you off outside the park?" he asked, assuming that Aria had followed his directions and taken a cab there.

"Um, yeah," Aria said, needing an excuse for why all the money he had given her was spent. It was an excuse that she couldn't use if she told him the actual truth, which was that she had walked and hitchhiked there. He took the plastic bag from her, tossed it into the back of his car and locked it.

"Is this place nearby?" Aria asked, surprised that he hadn't opened the door for her to get in so they could drive to the party.

"Um, yeah, but they moved the party to later so I thought we could take a little hike up to the Hollywood sign maybe?" he asked.

"OK, yeah," Aria said, willing, though less than enthusiastic at the prospect of more exercise than she had already had that day. Omkar took her hand in his and led her toward a trail that carved a swath into the dry hillsides.

The trail snaked on for ages. To their left, the white letters of the Hollywood sign promised to be just up ahead, only to tease them by always staying just a little bit farther. Some of the tourists who had set off at the same time as Omkar and Aria (determined to reach the same destination) turned back around, making fun of themselves for how out of shape they were.

Omkar asked to take a rest and Aria teased him, toeing him part of the way up the next hill. With the bed of the entire city laid out below them, a group of horses came past them from behind. Aria wanted to touch them, but restrained herself. Instead, she inhaled their fragrance as they passed . They had a unique fragrance. To Aria, nothing in the world smelled as good as horses, but there was no way to describe their scent. They didn't smell like anything else because a horse smelled like a horse. The tourists they carried clung sloppily to their saddles as they plodded lazily down the trail that they had been down so many times, they could walk it in their sleep. Omkar, who was uncharacteristically pensive on the hike, tried to read the words of an advertisement being flown on a flag behind a prop plane overhead.

"Are you OK?" Aria asked him.

"Yeah, it's just scary how much money these guys have," he said, referring to the people who had invested in the advertising method.

"What do you mean?" she asked.

"Those advertisements cost like six thousand bucks; twelve thousand if you want them to write something in jet streams or whatever across the sky."

Aria laughed. "What are you, a marketing major now?" Omkar smiled but didn't answer.

Instead of leading them up to the sign, the trail led them to a gate separating Griffith Park from an upper-class neighborhood. "Let's just go back," Aria said, not wanting to hike any further than they already had. Omkar looked around them in search of the perfect place to stop and take a photo. On a hill to their right, he spotted an overlook and coaxed Aria into following him there to a place where the Hollywood sign would be directly behind them. He left Aria standing there and interrupted a jogger who was just about to start his run. The man seemed inconvenienced to be asked to take a picture of them when they could have taken a selfie. Aria watched Omkar whisper to him and hand him his phone before running up to stand beside her. When she posed for the picture, Aria willed the muscles of her face into a tension that she imagined would make her look good in the photo.

"OK, OK, now turn around and look at the sign so he can take one of us looking at it," Omkar said.

All too aware of the annoyance of the man taking the picture, Aria turned around begrudgingly.

"Now point at it," he said. Barking orders about how to adjust her body for the picture was just his way of buying time. Eventually, Aria grew fed up with the task of trying to adjust herself perfectly for his liking and turned back around.

Instead of standing behind her as she had expected, Omkar was down on one knee. Aria covered her mouth with her hands to hide the look of shock that was clearly written across her face. Still conscious of the stranger who had been talked into taking pictures of the whole thing, Aria stood in front of Omkar, frozen, as he began to speak. "Aria, I have loved you since the first moment I saw you. I may be crazy but I don't care. So many girls, they try to be whatever a guy wants. But you captured my heart just by being you … The sweetest, craziest, most compassionate and wild and sensitive person I have ever known. I thought that I had a good life before I found you. But now I wouldn't even want to live a life without you. A girl can't change a man because she loves him, but a man who loves a woman changes himself. With you I can feel myself becoming the man I have always wanted to be, and it's because I love you. Please would you make me the happiest man on this earth and marry me?"

Aria lowered her hands from her face and nodded yes, thinking that Omkar would stand up to hug her. Instead, with tears of happiness in his eyes, Omkar reached into his right pocket and pulled out the gold ring that his mother had given him. He held it up for her to see.

"This ring belonged to my grandmother. In my culture, many families keep their wealth in gold. It is a tradition in my family to give some gold to a bride when she is married into the family. My mother has given me this to give to you. I want you to know that you have a family who will always love you and a family where you will always belong."

The tears that Aria had tried to deny began to well up and weave their way down the side of her face. Omkar took the ring finger of her left hand and slid the ring onto her finger. Taking her hands in his, he stood, then cupped her face to kiss her. She encircled his neck with her arms to hug him and when he hugged her back, he lifted her feet off the ground.

Omkar jogged down to collect his phone from the man, who had in fact been filming the entire proposal with it. The sweetness of the circumstances had washed away his air of irritation. He shouted "Congratulations!" to them both before continuing on his way. Omkar put the phone in his pocket and came back to where Aria was standing, examining the ring on her hand.

"There was no party, was there?" she asked. Omkar shook his head. Aria giggled and hugged him once more. When she did, he picked her up and spun her twice around before putting her back down again. Instead of walking back down the mountain, they found a spot to sit and fathom the monumental step in life that they had just agreed to take together. It was a spot overlooking the immensity of the city.

Aria leaned back into Omkar, letting his arms brace her ecstasy. In that moment, she could feel that light had broken where no sun shines. Where no water had run, the tide of love had broken through the bulwark. In the busy breadth of the city, Aria could just make out the whereabouts of the little car lot. She wondered whether Robert had opened the tribute that she had left him yet. She thought about Luke and Palin wandering through the amusement of whatever festival they had gone to. She thought about Taylor zipping through the city in his bright yellow convertible. She thought about the life she had lived before coming to the city that extended out before her farther than the eye could see. A chapter of her life was closing. Aria could feel its last page turning in the tightness of the ring that now adorned her finger.

Like Aria, no little five-year-old girl or boy sits on the carpet of their kindergarten class during sharing time and says they want to be homeless when they grow up. But the streets had entrusted Aria with a truth. And it was a truth that she would never forget. It was a truth whose whisper reaches all of us in the sweet luxury of a smile, in the grave-grabbing shade of grief. It tells you to look deeper … to look deeper still. To look beyond the space between people and see that you are that smile, you are that grief. You are that man who crawls into his cardboard box for the night. You are that man who owns the high-rise above him. And you are the earth that holds the dichotomy of them both. It is not he who walks the soiled streets of the city, repenting. It is not he, who clings to his proud titles of accomplishment, boasting, that finds his place in the family of things and himself with it. Instead, what Aria now knew was that it was he, who was brave enough to see himself … in everyone around him.